# TAMING THE STORM

# SAMANTHA TOWLE

# OTHER CONTEMPORARY NOVELS BY SAMANTHA TOWLE

Trouble

## The Storm Series

THE MIGHTY STORM

WETHERING THE STORM

# PARANORMAL ROMANCES BY SAMANTHA TOWLE

The Bringer

## The Alexandra Jones Series

FIRST BITTEN

ORIGINAL SIN

*For Mally Towle.*
*Heaven's got a plan for you.*
*Forever in our hearts.*

# CONTENTS

# PROLOGUE
## Lyla

## Ten Months Ago—Backstage, Madison Square Garden, New York City

"Dex! Chad! Cale! Sonny! Where the hell are you?" I call out as I wander down the empty hallway, my voice echoing back at me.

I've been wandering around—*actually, where in the hell am I?* I'm somewhere backstage. It's like a maze back here. I think I might be a bit lost.

Shrugging to myself, I lift the half-empty champagne bottle I snagged earlier to my lips and take a drink.

I also might be a tad drunk.

But I'm celebrating.

My band, Vintage, just opened for The Mighty Storm in Madison Square Garden! That's where I am now, lost in this place. My band won a radio contest, and the prize was to be The Mighty Storm's opening act. This was a huge thing for us! I'm not ashamed to admit that I nearly peed my pants the moment I found out we won the competition.

So, now, I'm celebrating—alone. I can't seem to locate a single one of my band members or my boyfriend. In the excitement and crowd of people, I managed to lose them when we went offstage. I mean, seriously, I'd think my boyfriend or brother would have at least waited for me.

I bet Chad is getting shitfaced with Sonny and Cale, and Dex is probably hooking up and getting his rocks off as I speak.

I cup my hands around my mouth. "Dex, I know you're probably on third base with a hot piece of ass, but come on! We just opened for The Mighty Storm! The. Mighty. Effing. Storm!" I punctuate the words, still unable to believe it.

I take another swig of champagne, stumbling in my heels. I steady myself on the wall with my hand before I resume walking.

"Dex, I want to celebrate with my big brother! Can't you just leave your sexcapades until later…please?"

Dex is lead guitarist in our band, and he's a total whore. When I say whore, I mean, he likes to whore around with men.

I love my brother more than anyone else in the world. I'm lucky to have him. He takes care of me, and I do the same for him. We're a team, the best team.

Turning a corner, I spy a door off to my right. It looks like it could be a janitor's closet.

Dex has a thing for having sex in closets. Hall, coat, janitor's— any closet really will do. He's not fussy.

"I bet you're in here!" I sing. "Well, zip up your pants, bro, 'cause I'm coming in!" The champagne bottle clangs against the door as I grab the handle. "Oops." I giggle.

I yank open the door, but the closet is empty. Just mops and buckets. No Dex. On a sigh, I close the door.

I'm never going to find anyone at this rate. I haven't seen another person in quite a while. This is starting to get eerie, like bad-horror-movie eerie. It's all very Freddy Krueger back here. Just endless hallways.

Resigned to my potential death by a fictional serial killer, I carry on down the hall, and I take a left at the end, hoping for some sign of human life. I clamp a hand over my mouth, stifling a giggle, when I see a couple of people going at it a little farther on. The lighting is bad, so I can't see much, not that I want to, but from the sounds of things, it seems like they're having a really good time.

*Lucky bastards.*

I'm about to turn and leave the sexy-time couple to it when one of them speaks.

"That's it, baby. Take it all. You know you love my big fucking cock."

My heart slams into my rib cage. The floor drops out from beneath me.

*Chad.*

*No. It can't be.*

I'm moving toward them before I realize it. Then, he turns his head and—

*Chad.*

*God, no.*

I'm going to throw up.

2

I freeze to the spot the instant his eyes meet mine. I watch in abstract horror as the shock of my presence reverberates over his face. We stay locked in a suspension of time where neither of us does or says anything.

Then, it breaks, and Chad kicks into movement. He pushes away from the person he was screwing, yanks his pants up, and tries to fasten them before he advances toward me.

And that's when I see exactly whom my boyfriend was screwing. The person turns, and our gazes meet.

I feel like I've been punched in the face. Hard.

I can't breathe.

I stand there, my world shattering around me for the second time in my life. I'm helpless to do anything as I stare into the contrite eyes of my brother.

# TOM

## Two Weeks Ago—Hospital Waiting Room, Cedars-Sinai Medical Center, LA

Seeing Jake cry is not something I ever thought I would witness—let alone, be the one to hold him while he cried.

He never broke apart in front of me when Jonny died, and I didn't with him either. None of us did.

I know why this has broken him. It's Tru, the woman he's loved his whole life. The fact it's broken him as badly as it has is scaring the absolute shit out of me.

Jake isn't as strong as he likes to make out he is. I get that. In the past, he relied on coke to get him through bad times. I could never berate him for it because we all have our ways of coping. I had—*have* mine, and he had his.

But he's clean now. Tru is his everything. And if she goes, then I'm worried what will—

"What if she dies?"

The sound of Jake's broken voice turns my head to him.

I look him in the eye before I attempt to say anything. And that's when I see it—*the* look.

*Fuck no.*

I've seen that look only once before—moments before I lost everything that mattered to me.

It's there in Jake's eyes. A look of fear and pain and desperation and confusion are all banded together, creating a darkness so crippling that the person feeling it can't see anything beyond it. The pain is so bad that the person gives himself over to it. And that's when a person will do things that he wouldn't normally do.

Irrational, desperate, terrible life-altering things.

That's the look that Jake has in his eyes right now.

Fear kicks me hard in the gut. I haven't felt a fear like this since *that* night.

I don't look away from him. I stare hard into his eyes because I need him to *hear* me right now. "Tru's a fighter, Jake. She kicks my ass daily. She's going nowhere."

"But what if…"

*No, Jake. Listen. Hear me.*

I shake my head, not breaking eye contact for one second. I can't lose him right now. "Don't what-if. Don't do that to yourself."

His eyes fill with tears, seeping from the blackness that's owning him right now.

"I don't know what to do"—his voice breaks—"what to think, what to say." He buries his face in his hands.

Staring at him as his body shakes from grief, I wish on everything to take this away for him, to fix this.

The day we lost Jonny, it was bad…horrendous. Nothing can ever prepare a person for losing someone that you *need* above all others. Tru is that person for Jake.

Some people have the strength in them to carry on when they lose that one person they love most above all others. I did. I found my way to carry on.

Some don't. And those are the people who have that despairing, dark look in their eyes that Jake has right now.

I lost someone I loved to that darkness. I won't lose Jake the same way.

I take a deep breath and say, "Don't think of the bad, Jake. Think of the good. Think of the moment you get to hold your boy in your arms. Think of the moment you get to put that ring on Tru's finger when she finally sees stupid and marries your sorry ass. Think of all the amazing fucking things the three of you are gonna do together. And while you're thinking of all that great stuff, I'll pray to the big man upstairs. I'll promise to make some serious lifestyle changes in exchange for you to have all that, to have what you were always meant to have."

I can't remember the last time I was in a church, not that the hospital chapel is actually a church-church. I take a seat on the pew up front. The place is empty. *Thank fuck.* I don't want an audience while I'm here.

I lean forward, resting my forearms on my thighs, and clasp my hands together.

"Okay," I start. "I don't pray, like, ever, which you know. I'm not exactly what you would call religious, another thing you know, but I made a promise, and I have to see that promise through—hence, why I'm here, talking to you." I take a deep breath. "There's a girl in this hospital—Tru Bennett. You need to save her. Aside from the fact that she's amazing, by saving her, you'll be saving someone else. If Tru dies, Jake won't survive. I saw it in his eyes earlier…the same look as my…"

Emotions I haven't felt in years claw to the surface. I scrub my hands over my face.

"Look, I know how this stuff works. I ask for something, and I give in return, right? You might realize what a bastard I am. I'm not great. I'm pretty fucking horrible to be honest. I treat people like shit—mainly women. I use them like inanimate objects made for me to stick my dick in. I haven't killed anyone…but I wouldn't put it past me to do that at some point in the future. I have a shit temper. I'm one motherfucking bastard of a man. Case in point, I can't even manage not to curse while I'm talking to you.

"One less bastard on this planet would work for you, right? Cross one more off your shitlist. So, I'm saying, if you save Tru's life, I'll change mine. Completely. I'll stop the fast living. No more fucking random women in inappropriate places, like when I screwed that nurse in the medical supplies closet after I visited with the sick kids. There'll be no more married women. No threesomes or foursomes or orgies. I'll even stop going to strip joints. I won't look at women in a sexual way. Fuck, I'll live the life of a goddamn monk if you save Tru. I swear, I will only have sex with a woman if she really means something to me."

*Did I actually just say that—out loud?*

*Christ.*

I break out in a cold sweat at the thought. I wipe my brow and take a deep breath.

"I'm promising all this because I know Jake won't survive losing Tru. I saw it in his eyes. He looked exactly the same as…well, I'm sure you know who I mean."

Exhaling, I lean back in the pew.

"Jake loses Tru…we lose him…*I* can't lose him. Jake and Den are all I've got left in the world. And you've got enough good people up there as it is. You've taken enough from us. You don't need her. She's needed here more…so I'm making this promise. You save Tru's life, and I'll completely change the way I live mine." I lift my eyes to the ceiling. "What do you say?"

## Present Day—Studio, TMS Records, LA

"Your vocal is off."

*Um, what?*

The voice in my ears halts my singing. I tilt my head to the side, looking around the huge microphone perched in front of my face to see through the glass.

I stare at the face of the voice—Zane Fox, Vice President of TMS Records, the label my band is signed to.

Total hottie, if I were into that kind of thing, which I'm not.

I don't like men. No, I'm not a lesbian.

I'm asexual. Celibate. Have been for the past ten months.

My history with men isn't good.

All of the important men in my life, barring a few, have let me down—hugely. When it comes to relationships with men—well, let's just say I'm a colossal failure.

Boyfriend One cheated on me with the only close female friend I ever had.

Boyfriend Two stole money from me.

Boyfriend Three was an aspiring singer, whom I found out was only dating me because he knew who my father was. I overheard him telling his friends. It was a sucker punch because I hate my father.

Boyfriend Four dumped me when I refused to have a threesome with him and his best friend. I kid you not.

Boyfriend Five "borrowed" my car. I still haven't seen him—or my car—to this day.

Boyfriend Six—my longest relationship and with a guy I stupidly thought I might love—screwed my brother on the biggest night of my life. After I caught them in the act, I later found out, he'd actually been screwing my brother for the last month of the eight months we were together.

That one was the killer, the final nail in my sex coffin.

After that, I realized that I only ever seem to be attracted to men with issues. I'm sure any good psychologist would say that I'm drawn to this kind of man because of my father and the problems I have with him, being that he's a completely crap dad.

Basically, he was the sperm donor who helped create me.

So, I stay clear of men. Seriously, the closest I get to a man nowadays is sharing a drink with my best friend, Cale.

In my past, I was always a relationship kind of girl—albeit, an unsuccessful one. Casual sex was something I never could do. I tie too many emotions to sex to be able to sleep with a guy and not see him again.

Taking relationships off the menu for me also removed the dessert menu, meaning no more sex for Lyla.

I've been totally okay with it—well, about ninety-five percent of the time.

Okay, if I'm being totally honest, it's more like seventy-five and climbing with the help of ASBOF.

ASBOF—Asexual Battery-Operated Friend. The ultimate G-spot–finding, mind-blowing O-giving, can-do-everything-a-man-can-do, except cuddle and break my heart, vibrator.

ASBOF is my electronic way to a much-needed orgasm.

I use the term *asexual* for my vibrator, so I don't think of it in a male sense in any way. I don't want to think of men in a sexual way at all—well, except when trying to reach the O with ASBOF. Of course I need some mental stimulation, so yes, on some occasions, I do visualize a faceless man, or maybe the hot guy who serves my coffee at Starbucks. But I promptly scrub the guy from my mind as soon as me and the O are done.

Anyway, back to the now…and the fact that I've been staring at Zane for a ridiculous amount of time, like he's got three alien heads on his shoulders.

"I'm sorry. What did you say?" I'm hoping my hearing is off, and I misheard him.

Zane leans forward and speaks into the microphone again, enunciating each word as he says them, "I said, your vocal was off."

I'm guessing he's annoyed at having to repeat himself.

And, no, I didn't mishear him.

My back stiffens.

My vocal was not off. *No freaking way.* It was so not off that it's on the other side of the Not-Off Bridge.

I know my songs. I know *this* song inside out. There's no way I was off.

Face pricking, I stare down at the Keds on my feet, trying to control my rush of anger.

I don't do criticism well. It's not my friend. And to hear this criticism from Zane stings badly because I respect his opinion.

I'm passionate about my work. I love my job. I love singing. I live for it. My band, this album—they're everything to me. My whole world.

I spent years and years singing in shitty bars and clubs, chasing the dream. Finally, I hooked that dream and then spent months and months working on the album—seven days a week, day and night, barely sleeping. I was so desperate to perfect it that I thought I might have a nervous breakdown.

Now, to hear I'm flunking—from Zane of all people—is not good. He hasn't had a problem with my vocals on any of the other tracks. And today of all days, I could do without hearing this.

I feel like I just got an F on my paper from my favorite teacher, and like a child, I want to have a colossal temper tantrum about it.

Not mature, but I don't care.

*Deep breaths, Lyla.*

This is Zane Fox. He won't take kindly to a creative temper tantrum from a small-time singer who just signed with his label.

Taking a calming breath, I force nicety into my voice. "Okay, so maybe my pitch was a teeny, tiny bit off"—*I don't mean that at all*—"but—"

"You weren't a *tiny* bit off," he cuts in. "You were *way* off, so fucking off that it isn't even funny. Nothing about that was working. Seriously, you sounded like the cleaner when she's singing with her headphones on."

*What the hell? Okay, just exactly what the hell has crawled up in his ass and died today?*

I open my mouth to speak, but he beats me to it.

Thankfully, his voice is a little less acidic. "Your usual kick-ass vocal just isn't here today, Lyla. The tone that makes your voice so distinctive, so unique, seems to have disappeared. I'm wondering, what the hell? So, tell me now, is there anything I need to know before we carry on?"

11

He's giving me an expectant look.

"Um…anything you need to know, as in?"

"As in, I don't know, and that's why I'm asking you."

"Nothing's wrong."

"You're on edge."

"I'm not on edge."

*Okay, I might be on edge.*

I took a phone call from my Aunt Steph right before I stepped into the studio, and it's knocked me sideways. She called to let me know that Dex signed with a new band. And that band is based in LA. He moved here a few days ago.

To say I feel on edge is putting it mildly.

Dex being in New York and me here in LA was working just fine for me. Thousands of miles apart with no chance I could run into him helped keep the gut-wrenching, heart-shredding pain I've felt since I caught him with Chad at bay.

But now knowing that Dex is here in LA has brought that all back in full force.

I'm glad Aunt Steph told me. I mean, if I ran into him, unprepared, that would be a killer. But I just wish he wasn't here.

I held it together while Aunt Steph told me. She doesn't know the reason behind Dex and I not speaking.

Dex hasn't told her, and I can't bring myself to do it. She respects our wishes and doesn't push, but I know it hurts her that Dex and I don't communicate anymore, which is not for his lack of trying.

I know she thinks if she knew what the problem was, then she could fix us. But she can't.

There is no fixing things between Dex and me. It was broken the moment he started screwing my boyfriend.

I feel the familiar burn in my chest. Bringing a hand up, I rub at the burn.

"You are on edge, Lyla," Zane says, unconvinced. "If it's personal and you don't want to share, fine. I get it. But we're on precious studio time right now, so you need to leave your personal life at the door before you step in here." He points to the exit. "And you find a way to channel those pent-up emotions into the song, and you sing it as good as I know you're capable of."

He's right. Business and personal should never mix.

I'm tougher than this.

12

Sure, I have a Texas-sized lump in my throat, and I'm aching with the pins and needles of pain, knowing Dex is so close-by.

But I'm strong. I don't even cry anymore. Haven't for ten months.

I think my tear ducts dried up when I cried a river over Dex and Chad.

I lock my gaze with Zane, and with determination in my voice, I say, "You're right. I'll get it perfect on the next run."

He stares at me for a long moment and then something softens in his gaze. "Do you need to take a quick break before we continue?"

His kindness throws me off my strength kilter for a second.

I lift my chin and suck it up. "No, I'm good now."

"Okay." He claps his hands together. "Let's get this track down!" Zane moves away from the microphone and pats Gray, our sound engineer, on the shoulder.

I give a quick look to Cale, Sonny, and Van, who are sitting in the studio with Zane. They put on the music for the track we laid down yesterday. For this song, Zane wanted the music and vocals recorded separately—hence, why I'm in here, singing, on my own.

Cale is our bass player, and I've known him forever. Cale, Dex, and I grew up together. The three of us put Vintage together. Cale is my best friend, the only guy I trust, and I know he has my back because he's proven it to me on more than one occasion.

Sonny is our drummer. He joined the band when we first started. We put up fliers for auditions, and he was the only one who turned up. Thankfully for us, he rocked. He's a demon on the drums. I've never heard anything like him.

Van hasn't been with us long. He joined on as lead guitar when Dex left—well, when I say left...

*"Dex stays. I go." I stiffen my back with my eyes lifted but not on Dex. I can't bring myself to look directly at him. If I do, I'm afraid my resolve will slip. The loss of him in my life will break through, and I will crumble.*

*Dex is the sun, and I can't look directly into his burning gaze.*

*Cale gets up from his seat and walks over to me. He stands beside me and takes hold of my hand. I have to bite back the tears I can feel burning up my throat. A few seconds later, Sonny takes stance beside me, dropping his arm around my shoulder.*

*Dex gets to his feet. "Take care of her, boys. And Ly..."*

*I know his eyes are on me. I can feel his gaze burning a hole in me.*

*"I know this stands for shit, and I can't even begin to tell you how sorry I am."*

*I hear his voice break, and I bite my lip.*

*"Love you, Ly. Always have, always will. And I'll always be your big brother—whether you want me or not."*

I haven't seen Dex since.

Cale catches my eye, and he mouths, *You okay?*

*Fine,* I mouth back before giving him my best smile.

His eyes narrow on me. He's unconvinced. I look away.

Cale knows me better than anyone, and he knows when I'm not okay. I'm just not looking forward to telling him that Dex is here in LA. He won't take it well.

I'm just glad that we're getting out of here in a week to go on tour.

Gray's voice comes into my ear this time. "When you're ready, Lyla, we'll start."

I readjust my headphones, take a deep breath, and shake out my hands. "I'm ready."

I step up to the mic, my lips hovering over the warm cushion. Shutting my eyes, I do what Zane said. I draw up all my emotions, the ones that are bothering the crap out of me today, and I channel them into my song.

Singing is the only thing that makes sense to me. It's my safe place. Nothing and no one can hurt me when I'm in that moment, singing the heart out of a song.

The music I'm all too familiar with comes into my ears, the delicious sound vibrating through my body, taking over my mind.

Parting my dry lips, I lick them and then ease out the first line of the song. I sing until my voice is climbing, hitting its high, and then I belt out the words until I'm wrung dry on the very last line.

Song done, I open my eyes.

Zane can't have any complaints with that. It was flawless.

I pull the headphones off and step around the mic, expecting to see a full booth, but the only person I find in there is Gray.

*Where is everyone?*

I press the intercom button. "Where is everyone?"

Gray leans into the mic. "Conference room. Zane said you're to go there the second you're done."

My stomach tanks.

*Did he hate it?* Jesus, I hate the nerves that come with trying to please studio executives.

"Did he say why?"

"Nope. He took a call and sounded all pissed off. Then, he told the guys to go with him to the conference room, and you were to follow straight after you finished."

Feeling confused, I say, "Okay."

"You did great by the way," Gray says. "Perfect. I can lay the track with that, no problem. Come back later, and I'll have it layered, so you can have a listen."

"Thanks, Gray. Catch you later." I let myself out of the sound booth before crossing the studio and going out the door.

I walk the short distance down the hall to the conference room. Three heads lift when I open the door. The look on their faces isn't great, so I'm guessing whatever it is, they already know.

Zane is standing by the window. His face is devoid of emotion, like always, and his arms are folded across his chest.

His tense stance has me instantly worried.

"Everything okay?" I try to keep the nerves out of my voice. I pull out the chair next to Sonny and take a seat.

"Dina broke her leg this morning while skiing." Zane straightens up and strides toward the table where we're all seated. "I mean, seriously, who the fuck skis nowadays?" he mutters as he yanks a chair out and sits down.

I would actually laugh at his comment if the bottom hadn't just fallen out of my world.

Dina is our manager. She was going to come on tour with us.

I have dreamed about this tour happening ever since I picked up my first guitar.

I know TMS Records policy—no tour manager, no tour.

They don't let their acts go out with support, which makes total sense.

A new band on the road with no support is not a good idea with the amount of sharks in this industry.

I swallow down the house-sized brick in my throat. Dumb question, but I have to ask, "So, Dina won't be coming on tour with us?"

Zane drums his fingers on the table. "No. She ruptured her anterior cruciate ligament. She'll be having surgery in the next few days."

"And we can't go on tour without a road manager," Cale says, looking at me.

He knows the house rules as well as I do. This is as important to him as it is to me. Important to us all.

I swallow down. "Okay, so what's going to happen then?" I try to keep my voice steady, but it wavers slightly.

*Don't postpone the tour. Please don't postpone the tour.*

"The tour will still happen. Jake is currently trying to find a replacement manager to go on tour with you."

Jake Wethers, owner of TMS Records and lead singer of the biggest band in the world, The Mighty Storm.

With relief, I exhale the breath I was holding.

But I come up short again when Van asks, "Yeah, but will you be able to get someone on such short notice?"

*Shit.* I didn't even think of that. We are supposed to leave on tour in a week.

*One week to find a good tour manager.* I don't feel good about those chances. Most tour managers, especially the good ones, will already be booked up.

Zane's eyes dart to Van, narrowing. "We'll get someone." His tone is harsh. He stands. "I'll be in touch soon." Then, he strides out of the room.

## A Few Seconds Later—Studio, TMS Records, LA

"Shit! This is not fucking good," Sonny says the second the door slams shut behind Zane.

"It's gonna be fine. Don't worry." I pat Sonny's hand, hoping that I sound more convinced than I feel.

"But how the hell is he gonna get a manager? Fucking impossible, if you ask me," Sonny fires out.

"He'll get us someone," Cale says, sounding sure.

Sonny shakes his head. "I don't know, man."

"Cale and Ly are right." Van stands. "He'll get us another manager."

Sonny throws him a confused look. "What? You've changed your tune. A few minutes ago, you were the one asking him the same goddamn question."

Van shrugs. "Zane might be a jackoff, but he said he'll get someone, and we have to trust him."

Looking at Van and then Cale, I wish I could feel as sure as they do, but I don't. I feel the same worry as Sonny. I'm just not vocalizing it. I'm doing what I do best, hiding my feelings and avoiding the problem.

"Screw waiting around to hear the news though. I'm gonna hit up some bars." Van raps his knuckles on the table. "You guys coming?"

"I'm in." Sonny gets to his feet. "Could do with a beer after that, and it's been days since I had any pussy."

"Days?" I lean forward. "What about the girl I made breakfast for this morning? You know, the one you hopped out on before she woke up."

"Ah, yeah, I forgot about her."

Does he actually have the memory of a goldfish?

"Sorry, Ly." He gives me his best smile with his puppy dog eyes, looking contrite, as he runs a hand over his shaved head.

It's hard to stay mad at Sonny.

And making breakfast for the guys' hookups, especially Sonny's, is not an unusual experience for me.

If Sonny brings someone back to the apartment, he has a tendency to duck out before they wake up. It's his specialty. Then, I feel bad, and I end up cooking breakfast for the girl.

In many ways, my boys are too good-looking for their—and my—own good. But their looks do work awesome in alluring the female fans. The women just lap the guys up, and the guys let them.

Bunch of muts, but I love them like family.

Oh, *Mut* is my term for man slut.

Sonny is the worst. He's just inch upon inch of muscular dark skin. He's a total gym nut. Women don't stand a chance. They love him, and he lets them. Repeatedly.

Cale is the stupid kind of beautiful—as in, it makes women go stupid over him. He's not as much of a player as Sonny, but Cale gets around. Perks of the job, he calls it.

When I was younger many, many moons ago and Cale was just Dex's best friend—before Cale became my best friend—I had a colossal crush on him. It was hard not to with his beautiful face and dark brown hair that fell into his chocolate brown eyes. And he has the biggest heart of anyone I've ever known.

But my crush quickly passed, and we've been best friends ever since.

And Van has the gorgeous brooding rock star down pat. Women flock to him like birds to bread. He's less vocal about it, but he's racked up more notches on his bedpost than Sonny. I know because I've made all the women breakfast. Van reminds me a lot of Jake Wethers—all tattooed, dark hair, striking blue eyes. I'm just hoping that Van has the same magic touch in the music world as Jake does.

"Yeah, I'm sure you're completely sorry." I give Sonny an unconvinced look.

"Ly, you know I'm sorry." He grins, flashing me his perfect pearly whites. "Cross my heart."

"Do you even have one?" I joke.

This is how it goes with Sonny and me. We banter around the same stuff.

"Wounded." He slaps a hand to his chest. "I'll show you what a big heart I have when I get up at the butt crack of dawn tomorrow and make my awesome pancakes for you."

Sonny does make the most amazing pancakes.

I rest my chin on my hand. "So, does that mean you won't be bringing tonight's hookup back to our apartment?"

He flashes me a grin. "Well, I can't make any promises, except I do promise to make those pancakes for you, whether the hookup is there or not."

I shake my head, laughing.

"So, you two coming or not?" Van asks Cale and me, already halfway out the door.

"Sure." I lift my butt from my seat.

Cale points a finger at me and says, "Stay put."

I pause midair, my brow raised at him. "Um…what?"

"We need to talk," is all he says. Then, he looks at Van, who seems amused at our exchange. "Text me where you are, and we'll meet you there."

The minute the door closes behind Sonny and Van, I'm on Cale. "Um, what the hell was that?"

"That was me knowing something is up with my best friend. You were fine before we left for the studio. Then, you took a call, and your mood went to shit. Who called, Ly? Was it him? I know he still calls you all the time—"

*How does he know that?* I haven't told Cale that he calls me every day because I know it would piss him off.

"Hang on." I lift a hand, stopping him. "He doesn't call *every* day. And even when he does, I don't answer."

"Don't bullshit me. He calls you every goddamn day. I know because you have that depressing ringtone set for him."

Justin Timberlake's "Cry Me a River" is his ringtone because, well, I want him to cry me a river.

"I know you, Ly. You're bound to cave soon and answer his calls…because you still care about him."

My eyes snap to his. "I don't care about him, not anymore. I'm not that stupid, blind weak girl I used to be."

He moves two chairs closer, so he's sitting in front of me. He takes my hands. "You were never stupid, blind, or weak. You're one of the strongest people I know, but you have a good heart, a kind heart. I know what he meant to you."

I grit my teeth. "It wasn't him who called."

"Who was it then?"

I pull my hands free and cross my arms over my chest. "Does privacy count for nothing these days?"

I'm being a bitch, and Cale is the last person I should be a bitch to, but all my pent-up anger from before is desperate to spill out.

"Not when it takes the smile off your face that I've spent the last ten months trying to get back on there."

That stings. I look away from him. "If you must know, it was Aunt Steph. She was calling to tell me that…Dex has joined a new band. He's in LA. Moved here a few days back."

I hear Cale's sharp intake of breath.

"He's here? In LA?"

"Yep." Meeting his eyes, I nod.

His jaw is working angrily. I hate that he's angry because of this, angry for me.

It's my turn to take hold of his hand. Squeezing, I say, "Cale, I'm fine."

"Yeah, sure you are." He pulls his hand from mine as he leans back in his chair. His face all red with anger, he yells, "Motherfucker! He knows you're here, Ly. He knows, and he should've stayed the hell away, like I warned him to."

"It's not a big deal." *It is so a big deal.* "And we're going on tour in a week." *Hopefully.* "I probably won't even see him between now and then."

"He'd better stay away. I swear to God, if he comes near you, I'll kick his ass, like I should've done the moment he broke your heart."

Cale is overprotective of me. He's always had that big-brother syndrome when it came to me. It increased tenfold when Dex betrayed me. And I know Cale is hurting over it, too. Dex was his oldest friend, his best friend. Cale misses him. He'll never admit it to me, but I know he does.

"Cale…don't get mad, but I was thinking maybe you should make contact with Dex."

"What?" He rears back like I just slapped him.

"Just hear me out."

"Sure, go on." He gestures an angry hand at me. "Enlighten me with your wisdom."

"Don't be a bitch."

That raises a small smile from him.

"Cale, Dex was your best friend before all of this, and I know you miss him. It wasn't you he betrayed, and when I made you choose between him and me…with the band…I should have never done that."

His brown eyes flash with anger. He sits up, leaning forward with his elbows on his knees, his face close to mine. "Let's get one thing straight. You never made me choose anything. The minute Dex betrayed you, he betrayed me, the band, all of us. *He* made us choose. And you thinking I should get in touch with him…Jesus Christ." He shakes his head. "I don't even know Dex anymore. I'm not sure I ever did, and call me insane, but I could never call a guy who would betray his own sister, the way Dex did to you, a friend. So, are we done here?"

Swallowing past my emotions, I nod.

Cale takes my face in his hands. "Good. I got your back, Ly, always. I won't let anyone hurt you ever again. And I know you think you don't have a big brother anymore, but you do, right here."

I place my hands over his. "Thanks, Cale."

"Anytime, Ly." He kisses my forehead and releases me.

Getting to his feet, he says, "So, are we going to this bar or what?"

Shaking my head, I laugh at him. "Absolutely. Lead the way, big bro."

## A Few Days Later—Vintage's Apartment, LA

"Tom Carter?"

"Yes. Tom Carter."

"You mean, Tom Carter, bass player for The Mighty Storm. That Tom Carter?"

"Yes, Lyla, that Tom Carter." Dina's starting to sound a bit frustrated with me.

Which I understand because I sound like a broken record right now. It's just that my head keeps rejecting what she's telling me, refusing to stick.

"Tom Carter…but I don't understand."

"What's there to understand? Tom is taking my place as your tour manager."

It seems Zane decided not to give us the news as I'm hearing it from Dina.

*But Tom Carter. Total mut. Hits on me every time I see him.*

*He is the epitome of mut.*

"So, Tom Carter is going to be our manager. He'll be coming on tour with us?"

Dina laughs, but I hear exasperation in it. "For the last time, Lyla, yes! Tom is now your manager, and he will be touring with you for the next six weeks."

*Crappity crappola.*

*Tom Carter.*

*God help me.*

I didn't even know Tom worked for TMS Records. Of course, he's one-fourth of The Mighty Storm, but I thought that's where his association ended. TMS Records is Jake's business. Tom is just the bass-playing mut, who will stick his dick in anything that has a pulse and a vagina. Actually, I don't think he'd care if it had a pulse.

*Meow. Saucer of milk needed at Lyla's table.*

"Call me stupid, but I don't understand why Tom is going to be our manager. He's not a manager. He's a musician."

Dina lets a breath out on the other side of the line. "And Jake Wethers is a singer in a band. He is also the owner of the kick-ass label I work for, the same one your band is signed to." She changes the tone in her voice to business. "I know what you're thinking, Lyla, but this is Jake's call, and he rarely makes the wrong call. He trusts Tom, so *we* trust Tom. I won't question Jake on his decision. He's got enough to deal with at the moment. And Zane backs him on this."

She's right. Now, I feel like a total bitch for whining about this.

Jake's fiancée, Tru, along with her bodyguard and best friend were in a serious car accident a few weeks ago. Even worse, Tru was pregnant at the time of the accident. Their baby boy was born early by C-section. Thankfully, he was fine. But Tru was in a coma for a week.

She's okay now and on the mend, and their baby, JJ, is doing really well. But Jake has had a terrible time, and I'm not about to go bother him about my worries over Tom being our manager.

I'll just have to suck it up.

"I'm sorry," I utter. "I didn't mean to sound ungrateful and whiny."

"You didn't sound like either, Lyla. I get your concerns. I do. They crossed my mind when Zane told me, but Jake wouldn't make any decision that could jeopardize this tour for you. He rates you guys really highly. He wants the best for you, like I do."

That warms me right up. "You're right. Six weeks with Tom as our manager will be…fine. A piece of cake." I'm trying to sound confident, but I don't feel it.

"You've got this, Lyla. And I don't think Tom will be…well, um, Tom. Not while he's working with you guys. There's a lot riding on this tour. Tom's a lot of things, but he wouldn't let Jake down."

"No, he wouldn't," I agree.

Well, I'm not sure that I actually agree. I don't know Tom *that* well, but on each occasion that I've met him, he's hit on me every single time. Each time, I turned him down. He didn't seem to like that so much. I got the impression that women don't turn Tom down.

Well, this woman did.

I might recognize that Tom is hot, very hot, but I'm not about to change my views over a really hot guy.

Especially not Tom, the biggest mut the world has seen.

My virginia is closed for business. *Virginia* is my nickname for my vajayjay.

"So, you've got this?" Dina asks.

"I've got this." I smile for no one's benefit but my own. "I'll let the boys know. Sonny will freak. Tom's his idol."

Dina laughs. "Yeah? Well, let's hope Sonny never reaches the stats that Tom has."

That makes me laugh. "I don't know, Dina. Sonny is already well on his way."

The door to the apartment opens, and the boys all pile in, pizza and beer in hand.

"The boys just got home. Talk to you soon?"

"Absolutely. I'll check in with you and see how things are going."

After hanging up, I slide my cell into my pocket.

I wait until the guys are all sitting on the sofa around me before I speak. "That was Dina on the phone." This brings all eyes to me.

I take the bottle of beer that Sonny is holding out to me.

"So, what's happening?" Cale asks.

The anxious tone in his voice is not lost on me. It's been a stressful few days.

I pop the cap on my beer. "Jake got us a replacement manager."

"And...who is it?" Sonny pushes.

I take a quick drink and then hold the bottle in my lap. "Tom Carter."

Sonny's eyes widen. "Tom Carter...as in Tom Carter of The Mighty Storm. That Tom Carter?"

This feels very reminiscent of my conversation with Dina not a few minutes earlier—except mine was a kind of horror at the realization that Tom would be coming on tour with us where Sonny is at a barely containable excitement.

"Yep, the very one." I press the bottle to my lips again. Tipping my head back, I take a bigger drink this time.

"Holy shit!" Van yells. "Tom Carter! On tour with us! Man, it's gonna be wild! Chicks, parties...chicks! It's gonna be so fucking wild! The man is a fucking legend!"

Sonny looks shell-shocked. Then, he springs to life. "Damn straight, he's a legend! He's a pussy legend! We are touring with the best there is! Just think of the stuff he can teach us." He gets this dreamy look in his eyes.

Honestly, he's starting to freak me out.

"What do you think, Cale?" Van slaps him on the back.

Cale grins. "I think it's pretty fucking awesome."

"Amen to that!" Sonny leans forward, clinking his beer bottle with Van's. He high-fives Cale at the same time.

I'm just staring at them, wide-eyed and sick to the stomach.

This is exactly what I didn't want, but I knew it would happen the instant I told them who was going on tour with us. I'm not boring. I honestly have no issue with the guys having fun. They have tons of fun and sleep with plenty of women.

But Tom Carter's version of fun will be in a whole other league to my boys.

He's going to ruin them and the tour.

It's going to be more about Tom and the boys getting laid than the music. Tom's focus will solely be on groupies instead of making sure the shows on the tour run smoothly.

I know his rep. He's a player, not a hard worker.

We need a manager who has his eye on us at all times, not one whose eyes are all over the next chick he's going to bang.

*This is going to be a disaster.*

I'm going to have to take on the role of manager, making sure the shows run smoothly, and somehow try to keep my boys in line while under Tom's influence. If I let Tom run the show, by the end of this tour, Vintage will be dead in the water, and I'm going to be left with three clones of Tom Carter.

This reminds me of that *Friends* episode where Chandler and Joey start dressing and behaving like Monica's boyfriend, Richard, because they think he's really cool, and they want to be just like him. Both even grow a mustache like Richard's.

Well, this is what I'm envisaging right now—three Tom Carter clones, formally known as Cale, Sonny, and Van. Instead of cigars and mustaches, it'll be women and more women until I can't see my boys through the layers of women they're buried under. Vintage will die before we've begun, and I'll be back to singing in shitty bars for the rest of my life.

I start chugging back on my beer, quickly emptying it, and I reach for another. I listen to the verbal diarrhea coming out of the guys' mouths about what crazy shit they can get up to while on tour with the god of women that is Tom Carter.

I've just popped the cap on my beer when I feel the sofa depress beside me.

"You don't seem overly happy that Tom Carter is our new manager," Cale says in a quiet voice.

I turn my face to him and try to force a smile. "I am. I just—ugh," I sigh, rubbing my hand over my face.

"You're worried about his rep, right?"

"Yep. His rep." And his tendency to try to get into my pants—well, mine and the rest of the population's pants—whenever he sees me.

Cale puts his arm around my shoulder, pulling me to his side. "Ly, it'll be fine. Nothing will change. And don't worry about those two." He points to Sonny and Van while they are currently arguing over who will score the most pussy on tour—after Tom, of course. "Between the two of us, we'll be able to keep those groupie addicts on the right path."

"And what about you?" I raise my eyebrow.

He grins. "I can control myself around women, Ly. Give me some credit."

"Even with the influence of Tom?"

"Even with the influence of Tom. Anyway, if I couldn't control myself, you, Lyla Summers, are the best cockblock around. You've been cockblocking me since high school without even meaning to."

"Hey!" I elbow him in the ribs. "I am not a cockblock!"

"You're a cockblock!" Sonny and Van chime in.

"Piss off!" I chuckle.

"Good to hear that laugh again," Cale says.

"Which laugh?"

"Your real one."

I laugh all the time, but those are fakes. He's right. That was the first time in a long time that I've laughed for real. It quickly fades. My eyes dip to the floor.

"Did I upset you?" Cale squeezes my shoulder.

I look up, meeting his warm gaze. "No." I shake my head. "I'm just not looking forward to the tour as much as I was. Tom will probably make groupie night mandatory or something."

"Doesn't sound so bad to me." Cale grins.

"What doesn't sound so bad?" Van asks.

"Nothing," I answer quickly, shooting Cale a look.

He starts to laugh.

I shove him on the shoulder. "You're gross, you know that?"

"Not as gross as Sonny."

"Who's not as gross as me?" Sonny asks.

"Van," Cale deflects.

A moment later, I feel Cale's finger under my chin. He brings my face toward him. "Ly, don't worry about Tom. It's gonna be fine, better than fine. It's gonna be awesome."

"Awesome. Sure." I roll my eyes.

Seriously, what is going to be awesome about touring with the mut of rock, who has hit on me every time I see him?

Nothing—that's what.

# Lyla 4

## A Few Days Later—Tour Bus, LA

"Can you believe we're here, Ly?" Cale slings his arm around my shoulders.

I shake my head, taking in my surroundings.

I'm more excited now that we're here than I have been since I heard who our new manager was. But I'm over that. It'll be fine. Because we're here!

Today is the day we set off on tour. And tomorrow night, we'll be playing Seattle, and I cannot wait!

I'm standing in the galley of the tour bus, and the place is amazing. Beyond amazing.

Laid out before me is a living area, complete with a leather seating area and a TV fixed on the wall. I spy a DVD player and a PlayStation. *That should keep the boys entertained.* There's a table attached to the wall with seating around it. The kitchen has a wall-fitted unit with a built-in range and oven, a small refrigerator, and a microwave.

I follow Cale down the hall to where Sonny and Van are, and I see the bathroom on the right. Shower, no bath. I'm going to miss my baths for the next six weeks.

"Four bunks here," Van says when we reach them. "And a bedroom for when I want to get laid, which will be every night." He grins.

"Bedroom is Ly's," Cale asserts.

Two pairs of unamused eyes stare at him.

"What the hell?" Sonny whines. "I thought that room was going to be our pussy palace."

*Pussy palace? How does he come up with this shit?*

"Look, I have no issue with sleeping in a bunk. I'm used to the stinky smell of you all," I say.

Honestly, I don't care where I sleep just as long as I'm here, and this is happening.

"I smell like *man*, and you love me for it." Sonny wraps his arm around my neck, pulling to him, squashing my face into his rock-hard pecs.

"Love might be pushing it," I retort, pushing away from him. "More like tolerate."

"You so love me." He grins.

"I love you like I love athlete's foot." I smirk.

"Children, sorry to interrupt, but are we gonna make a decision on the bed situation?" Van asks.

"Ly should have the bedroom," Cale reiterates.

"Like I said, I really don't care where I sleep." Then, I meet Cale's firm stare. "But I'd love to have the bedroom," I backtrack

"You should take the bed, Ly," Van says from behind me.

I turn, looking at him, and I smile.

He smiles back. Van really does have the best smile. His whole face lights up with it.

"We'll just find somewhere else to fuck, if not in our bunks," Van adds.

*Such a way with words. What was I saying about his nice smile?*

"Well, seeing as though you're both saying it, now, I'm gonna have to," Sonny complains. "Ly, you should take the fucking bed."

"Thanks, Sonny." I pat his hard chest. "You're a real gem. How about this? I have the bedroom, and when one of you scores, you can have the room for as long as you need it, but you have to change the sheets."

"And this is why I love you." Sonny presses a kiss on the top of my head.

"Deal." Van offers me his knuckles, so I fist bump him.

"You're a softie" Cale says in my ear as I watch Sonny and Van checking out the bedroom.

I shrug. Then, I feel my cell vibrate against my butt. I pull it out. *Unknown number.* I hesitate, worried. It might be a call I don't want to take, but then it could be someone calling about the tour. It wouldn't be Dina or Zane because I already spoke to them earlier. I haven't spoken to Tom yet. Everything has been arranged through Zane or Dina, so I guess it could be him. I'm not even sure when I'll see Tom, not that it matters. But he'll probably fly in tomorrow. People like Tom don't travel on buses.

"Just gonna take this." I wave my vibrating cell at Cale.

Decision made, I connect the call as I start walking back through the bus. "Hello?"

"Lyla, it's Jake."

That stops me in my tracks.

Of course I've spoken to and met Jake before plenty of times, but he's never called my cell.

"Hi." *Shit.* My voice has gone squeaky. I clear my throat. "Is everything okay?"

"You tell me."

My stomach drops.

"Rally Brochstein—he's your father." It's not a question. Jake knows.

*Shit. Shit. Shit.*

My hand starts to sweat around my phone.

I quickly make my way off the bus and practically run down the side to the back, putting distance between me and the people loading up the tour buses.

You see, there's something about my father that I haven't been totally upfront about with Jake or Zane or anyone at TMS Records. I tend to keep who my father is and who my mother was private. People treat me differently when they find out who my parents are. Especially my father. He's kind of a big deal in the music business.

Okay, he's a *huge* deal.

And he and Jake don't get along.

Rally Brochstein, owner of Rally Records. He's discovered some of the biggest talents the world has ever seen.

The Mighty Storm is one of them.

Yes, I'm talking about *the* Rally Records, the label which first signed The Mighty Storm, TMS. The label that TMS walked away from.

I guess you can see where this is going.

And if Jake knows about Rally, then Rally definitely knows I'm signed with TMS Records.

This isn't good.

I don't have what you could call a relationship with Rally, but that doesn't stop him from trying to interfere in my life, especially when he feels it is crossing over into his.

And *this*? My band signing with TMS Records. He'll definitely feel that this is stepping into his territory.

I clear my throat. "Yes, Rally is my father…in the biological sense of the word."

I'm now standing out in open space and looking over at the tour bus, hoping with all hope that it will still be moving with the guys and me on it.

"Were you ever going to share this piece of information with me?" His voice is so even that I can't get a read on where this is going.

I'm just praying it's not the end before the beginning.

Taking a deep breath, I say, "No…well, yes…no. I don't know." I scrub my hand over my face.

I'm not a deceitful person, but looking at this now, it seems an awful lot like deceit.

I start to feel a little sick.

"I think I would have at some point, but I just wanted you to see us for what we could do, so you could make an informed choice before you knew. I know how you feel about Rally. I feel the same. Yes, he's my father, but that term is used loosely. I don't have a relationship with him. He's a dumbass."

Jake laughs. I take that as a good sign.

"I've heard Rally called a lot of things but never a dumbass. It actually suits him."

*Silence.*

Then, he exhales. "I know Rally, Lyla, too well. I know how he works. I also know a little something about wanting to hide your past. Thing is, when you hide stuff, especially in this business, it has a tendency to come out and bite you in the ass."

My memory reminds me of the news story that came out about Jake's dad last year. From what the press said, Jake's dad hurt him and his mom pretty bad, and his dad went to prison for whatever he did to them.

"And I don't like surprises, Lyla."

I cringe at the turn in his tone of voice.

"I don't like receiving a phone call from Rally Brochstein when I'm just about to eat breakfast with my family, especially when I'm going into that conversation blind."

I swallow down the bitter taste in my mouth. "I should have told you."

"Yeah, you should have."

I know Rally and what he's capable of. His reputation in the music business is notorious.

Jake Wethers is one of the few people who has ever gone up against my father and walked away clean.

Rally is a shark, and he takes no prisoners. Nothing and no one gets in his way. That's how he became the youngest ever CEO of AME—American Music Entertainment—which he ran for fifteen years and then left on questionable terms for an undisclosed sum.

That was when he started Rally Records, and it got big, fast.

Just not fast enough for TMS.

TMS was the first act to sign with them. After that, I don't know much, besides what the press detailed, which was that TMS outgrew Rally Records. Apparently, Jake and Rally had a difficult relationship, which I can understand because my father is not an easy man to get along with.

Jake and Rally's relationship disintegrated, and the band walked away mid-contract, buying themselves out.

Immediately after, Jake and the late Jonny Creed—TMS's lead guitarist who died a few years ago in an automobile accident—set up TMS Records, putting themselves in direct competition with Rally Records.

That didn't sit well with Rally.

And me signing with TMS Records won't sit well with him either.

But I don't care about that. All I care about is that I might have screwed this up because I wasn't honest with Jake from the start.

"I know I might seem like a wayward daughter doing this to piss off her father, but believe me, I don't even care about Rally enough to bother. I signed with TMS Records because you care about your acts."

"That's good to know."

"And I kept it from you because I was worried you'd judge me based on him."

Jake says nothing more.

I'm biting on my nails, dying in the stretch of silence. Finally, I ask, "How was Rally when you spoke to him?" I'm trying to gauge as to where this is going because, so far, I have no clue.

"He was a total dumbass."

I let out a laugh, but that's quickly cut off by his next sentence.

"Rally wants you off my label, Lyla."

And there it is.

*Bye, bye, tour bus. It was nice while it lasted.*

*Have I said how much I hate my father?*

The guys are going to be gutted.

I know Jake is a hard ass, and he hates Rally, possibly as much as I do, but this is hassle he could do without. He doesn't owe me anything, and keeping us on his label will be nothing but trouble for him. Rally won't drop it until he gets what he wants.

"I'm sorry," I say, "about Rally calling and giving you a hard time."

"Lyla, it's not your fault you got a shithole for a dad. You said you didn't tell me about Rally because you wanted to prove yourself, to let me see what you're capable of, so I could make an informed choice. I've seen, and I've made my choice. I told Rally he could go fuck himself. Vintage is my act, and you're staying put."

My hand goes to my chest as the breath I was holding whooshes out.

I could kiss Jake Wethers right now.

And he's not done either. "I don't care if it's the King of fucking England. No one tells me how to run my business. Now, under normal circumstance, I'd say to you that he's your old man, so it's on you to pull him into line and tell him to back the fuck off, but this is Rally Brochstein we're talking about. I wouldn't put you in that position. You say your relationship with him is non-existent. Was that his choice or yours?"

"Growing up, his. Now, mine."

"Okay. I'll deal with any shit that Rally might pull. You just concentrate on the tour. But I need you to tell me now if there is anything else I need to know. Next time, I won't be so forgiving."

Taking a deep breath, I say, "My mother was Joni Summers."

"That I know," Jake replies. "I knew Rally had a kid with Joni Summers. You come from good stock, Lyla, and I'm talking about your mom when I say that."

That raises a smile.

"Must be where you get your pipes from," he adds.

"Thank you," I say genuinely. My mom was the best.

I hear a female voice in the background.

Then, Jake says to me, "I have to go. Good luck with the tour. Relay that message to the rest of the band. Don't worry about Rally. Nothing is going to change your position with TMS Records, no matter what he says or does."

"Thank you, Jake, for understanding and for sticking with us."

"Don't thank me. Just make this album and tour score big. Earn me back all the thousands of dollars that it has cost me," he says with a humorous tone.

Nodding, I smile. "That I can definitely do."

## Sixty Seconds After—Tour Bus, LA

I'm just pushing my cell back into the pocket of my denim cutoffs, pondering my conversation with Jake, when I hear a commotion coming from the bus.

Sounds of cheering and loud laughter.

I look across at the bus, but I'm too far away. Even if I were close, I wouldn't be able to see anything due to the heavily tinted windows.

All thoughts of my conversation with Jake left behind, my feet carry me quickly back to the bus. I jog up the stairs, turn into the galley, and halt in my tracks at the sight before me, my breath leaving me in a rush.

Tom Carter.

Well, it's the back of him anyway. I know it's him because he's impossible not to recognize. His huge size eats up the small space of the bus. His muscular arms are sleeved in tattoos. Gone is his trademark shaved head, and it's now covered in silky brown hair.

*What is he doing here?*

Cale spies me over Tom's shoulder, his dark eyes all lit up. "Ly, look who's here!" he says in an overexcited voice.

I have the sudden urge to walk over there and slap Cale upside the head.

Tom looks over his shoulder at me. His intense jade green eyes hit mine, sending an involuntary heat to travel through my body.

He turns until he's facing me.

His gaze drifts slowly down my body and then climbs back up.

My stomach clenches. Virginia sparks to life.

*Oh God.*

I hate the way my body reacts to Tom Carter. Every single time I see him, my virginia lights up like gasoline on a spark. I might dislike him, but my body doesn't. In fact, my body likes Tom—a lot.

Thankfully, my brain doesn't. To my utter relief, my brain is in the driver's seat when it comes to him.

Tom is an arrogant, sex-crazed mut, whom I want nothing to do with.

Only…Tom just happens to be a hot, arrogant, sex-crazed mut.

I really hate that.

He's now also sporting overgrown stubble that's shaping up to become a beard, and it makes him look even hotter.

Unkempt but hot.

Add that hot, unkempt look with a plain black fitted T-shirt over those thick biceps with jeans hanging low on his hips, showing a sliver of his stomach, and finish it off with black Doc Martens, and Tom Carter makes for one very lickable package.

*Lord, help me.*

I meet Tom's eyes, and he's smirking.

Because I'm staring.

*Fabulous.*

His eyes flicker down to my chest. I watch as his eyebrows lift, and the smirk deepens, forming a dimple in his cheek that I've never noticed before.

He looks cute in a hot, sexy way.

*Hot, sexy cute?*

*What the hell, Lyla?*

Men are not cute, especially not men like Tom Carter. Men like him are dangerous to women like me.

And look at him, just openly staring at my chest. *Total pervert.*

Yes, I'm negating the fact that I just gave him the once-over because it's rude to stare at a woman's boobs. Sure, I was gifted in the boob department, but that doesn't give him the right to openly ogle them.

I cross my arms over my girls and lift my chin.

His eyes come back to mine, and that smirk is still on his face. "Lyla," he drawls in that deep voice of his, "it's been a while."

*Not long enough.*

"It has." I nod. "Thank you for agreeing to be our tour manager."

*That's it, Ly. Keep it pleasant and business-like.*

"No problem." He shrugs those broad shoulders of his. "I'm looking forward to being back on the road."

*Being back on the road? He means that in a figurative sense right?*

He's still staring at me. It's kind of getting uncomfortable, but I can't break the stare. I feel like we're in a staring match, and whoever blinks first will be the loser.

*No way am I losing to him.*

Sonny breaks the silence. "We have great news, Ly." He has that same excited tone in his voice that Cale just had.

I tilt my chin in Sonny's direction, but I don't take my eyes away from Tom's. *I will not lose this game.* "Oh, yeah? What is it?"

A quiet grin appears on Tom's lips.

"Tom is staying here on our bus for the whole tour!" Sonny's voice explodes in my ears.

Then, silence hits as the debris from his dirty ear bomb scatters slowly to the floor, my brain desperately trying to come to terms with what I just heard.

*Tom is staying here?*

Closing my eyes on a blink, I shake my head, trying to clear out his words. "I'm sorry. What?"

Sonny frowns at me like I'm slow. "I said, Tom is staying on the bus with us. How awesome is that?" He's smiling.

Van and Cale are smiling.

Tom is still staring at me. Only this time, his look is curious.

I blink away with my hands on my hips, trying to figure this out in my head.

*Tom is going to be living here on our bus for the duration of the tour?*

*No, that can't be right.*

Then, my eyes land on an oversized gym bag sitting on the kitchen table.

*Oh God.*

*He's staying here.*

*No!*

He can't because…well, for so many reasons that I don't even know where to begin.

This is going to be a complete disaster.

It can't be real. It's just a bad dream. I'm going to wake up, and it's all just going to be a stupid dream. I did think this tour bus was way too nice to be ours. I was expecting a total shithole for our first tour bus, not this awesome setup.

I close my eyes on a long blink and then look back to them.

I'm thinking I might look a little stunned because Cale searches out my eyes, his stare fixed on me.

"Isn't this great news, Ly?"

Subliminal Cale message, *Speak now, Ly, because this silence is getting really weird. And say something nice.*

I do try to say something nice. Really, I do. I quickly think up lots of nice things to say—well, mainly the word *yes*.

But that word doesn't follow through to my vocal cords, and my head is shaking. Before I can stop myself, these words are out, "Honestly, I can't think of anything worse."

*Oh God.*

I'm pretty sure a tumbleweed just blew through the galley of the bus.

"Lyla!" There's a chastising tone in Sonny's voice that I've never heard from him before.

It makes my face sting. I feel like a bitch.

I am a bitch.

I can't bring myself to look at Tom or anyone.

Then, I hear Tom's deep voice say, "Lyla…a word."

I glance at him just in time to see him striding past me, his long legs eating up the floor space, as he heads for the exit of the bus.

Avoiding the eyes of the guys, I swivel on my heel and follow Tom in his angry path.

When his feet hit gravel, he doesn't stop. He just keeps on walking. So, I follow, my gut churning the whole time.

This day is really starting off badly. First, Jake's call, and now, my inability to keep my mouth shut in front of Tom.

Tom might be a mut, but in the last five minutes, he's done nothing wrong to me. I shouldn't have said what I did.

Tom stops about fifty feet from the bus and turns to me. I halt in my stride, nearly tripping in doing so.

His body is tense. He folds his arms over his chest, staring down at me. I try not to look at the straining muscles of his biceps. It's surprisingly hard.

I look up at his face. He seems even taller out here.

I decide to speak first, and I quickly say, "I'm really sorry for what I said back there." I run a nervous hand through my blonde hair.

He lets out a sigh and scratches his beard. "Look, Lyla, I get it. I know why you don't want me staying on your bus—because of our history."

"We don't have history."

"We so have history," he enforces with a raised brow.

"Um…no, we don't. History would involve something happening between us. And *nothing* has ever happened," I say, punctuating the words to drive the point home.

"Yeah, well, it would have if you hadn't been so fucking—" He cuts himself off.

My arms fold over my chest, my eyes narrowing. "If I hadn't been so fucking, what?"

There's a moment of heated pause.

Then, he shakes his head. "Nothing. We're getting off the point."

I decide to let it go. I have an idea of what he was going to say, and if he did, that would have set off an explosion of epic proportions.

That's definitely not needed right now.

My hands go to my hips. "Fine. So, let's get to the point."

"I'm trying to say, what happened in the past happened, and I can't change it. I'd say I'm sorry for hitting on you, but I'm not. Back then, I didn't know we'd be working together, especially not this close. If I had, I wouldn't have made a move. Believe it or not, I don't mix business with pleasure."

"Pleasure's only with groupies, right?"

He gives me a chastising look.

"Sorry." I bite my tongue.

He sighs. "Lyla, I'm not here to try to get you in the sack. I'm here to work. You don't need to feel uncomfortable around me."

"I don't feel uncomfortable around you." I straighten my spine, needing to appear taller in this moment.

He smirks down at me. "Yeah, you do."

"No, I don't."

"So, why the bitch act?"

I raise a brow at the comment, but he's got me there on the bitch act. I was a bitch to him. And I'm about to be again.

"You want the truth?"

Unfurling his arms, his lips press into a tight line. "Sure. Hit me with it."

"Well, basically, I don't think you're the right person to be our tour manager."

His expression doesn't change. "Not the right person to be your tour manager," he echoes.

"Yes. You're not serious enough."

"Not serious enough."

*Why does he keep repeating everything I say? Does he have a mental problem?*

He scratches his cheek and steps up in my space in one swift move.

A little startled and a lot fired-up at his nearness, I blink up at him.

He brings his head down, his mouth close to my ear. "One thing you need to learn about me, Lyla, is that I'm really, really serious about the things I want."

A shiver runs through me, heading straight for my virginia. The smell of his clean, crisp aftershave is befuddling my brain along with my bra and panties.

Then, I kick some female sense into myself.

Tom straightens up, and he is now looking down at me, his eyes burning into mine. He's still standing way too close.

Tilting my head back, I let out a condescending laugh. "You? Serious? I didn't know Tom 'The Man-Whore' Carter could be serious."

His face hardens.

*Whoops. Too far maybe?*

Like I care.

He steps back. I exhale.

"Jesus Christ, woman. I hit on you ages ago. Get the hell over it. I've hit on hundreds of women, and I've fucked and dropped every single one of them—"

"God, you are disgusting."

"Thanks." He smirks. "And because I'm *disgusting*—as you put it—to the women I fuck, that gives them good reason to give me a frosty reception if they ever have to see me again. Considering we haven't *fucked* and I haven't been *disgusting* to you, I don't expect the shitty attitude I'm getting. So, why don't you get over it? Just try to think of me as your new manager, not as the hot guy who hit on you an eon ago. And I'll try not to think of you as the ball-busting lesbian—"

"I'm not a lesbian!" I splutter. There's not anything wrong with being a lesbian. I'm just not one.

"You're not?" He actually looks genuinely confused.

*Oh my God!* He thinks I'm a lesbian because I turned him down all those times. *The guy is an egomaniac!*

"Jesus, you think I'm a lesbian because I wouldn't sleep with you?"

"Well, yeah. What other reason could there be?"

I laugh loudly. I can't help it. This is a real belly-aching laugh. I have to bend over and rest my hands against my thighs just to try to catch my breath.

When I straighten up, a less-than-amused Tom is scowling down at me.

I wipe the tears from my eyes. "God, you're an egotistical asshole. You ever consider that I wouldn't sleep with you because you're not my type?"

He scoffs. "Not possible, darlin'. I'm *everyone's* type."

*Like I said, asshole.*

I place my hands on my hips. "Sorry, but arrogant muts don't do it for me."

He stares at me, stunned. "Did you just call me a…*mut?*"

"Sounded like it."

"So, you're calling me a dog?"

I stare daggers at him. "No, asshat. *Mut* actually stands for man slut." I make sure to punctuate the words to drive my point home.

A smile breaks Tom's face. Then, he throws his head back and roars out a laugh. It's a deep, manly sound.

And it hits me in all the right places.

I have to bite my lip to stop from laughing.

His eyes, filled with humor, meet mine. "You're really fucking something, you know?"

"I'm awesome." I shrug. "But not a lesbian." *Why am I hammering that home?*

He nods his head, grinning. "Yeah, I'm getting that." He scratches his cheek. "But now, I'm trying to figure out *how* you managed to resist me…and *why.*" He tilts his head to the side with a challenging look in his eyes.

"You don't need to figure it out. I just don't like you."

"Like I said, not possible.

"Are you for real?"

His lips curl up. "I'm so real that it's unreal, baby."

I laugh again. "Now, who's something else?"

He gives me a boyish smile, shrugging. It's charming and endears me to him a little.

There's a moment between us. It's the kind of moment when the air is clearing, and everything is settling.

"So, we're good here?" Tom asks, gesturing between us.

Relaxing, I smile. "We're good."

"Cool. Let's make a deal. No more fighting or shitty comments—"

"Or sexual comments," I add.

"Or sexual comments," he agrees, albeit a little reluctantly. "We'll be professional at all times. Deal?" He holds his large hand out to me.

"Dealio." I grin up at him as I slide my hand into his.

The shock of electricity I feel at his touch nearly knocks me on my ass.

He feels it, too. I know he does from the slack in his jaw and surprise in his eyes.

His grip tightens around my hand. Then, his eyes flicker to my mouth.

I lick my lips, feeling suddenly parched. I can feel him moving toward me.

*Or is that me moving toward him?*

Then, it hits me. I think he's about to kiss me.

*Shit.*

I snatch my hand from his. "We should get back." I step back.

"Yeah, we should." He's staring over my head.

I turn and start walking back to the bus.

*What the hell was that?*

I've never felt anything like that before from touching a man. Maybe this is what no sex is doing to my body. It goes into a mad frenzy at the first sign of the Y chromosome.

I've just reached the bus when I hear Tom say from behind me, "Firecracker, I meant to tell you that I fucking love the T-shirt."

My eyes snap down to my Fraggle Rock T-shirt. It's old, a little short in the hem, and snug across my bust, but I love it. I love cartoons. I collect cartoon T-shirts. I might be in a rock band, but I never said I was cool. I dressed for comfort today. I never expected to see Tom, not that it matters how I dress around him. I don't care what he thinks about me, not one iota.

*And Firecracker? Seriously?*

I turn around. "Don't call me that."

He smiles. "What? Firecracker?"

"Yeah. I've just added another rule to our deal—no pet names. Pet names are a deal-breaker."

He clicks his tongue against the roof of his mouth in reprimand. "No can do, *Firecracker.* Because, really, there are no deal-breakers here. You're stuck with me whether you like it or not." He winks and then jogs past me, going up the stairs and onto the bus.

*Ever have that feeling you've been played?*

Yep, I totally feel played right now, but I have no clue as to what the game is.

Confused, and frankly a little pissed off, I stomp my way back up the steps just as Henry, one of our drivers, gets into the driver's seat.

"Everyone on board?" Henry asks me.

"Yeah," I answer.

Henry starts up the engine. The bus rumbles to life beneath my feet as the doors hiss and close behind me.

"Y'all set for this?" Henry asks with a smile.

I look over to where Tom is standing, talking with the guys.

My stomach twists in two entirely confusing, different knots.

"As I'll ever be," I sigh.

## Late Afternoon—Tour Bus, LA

It's late afternoon now, and I've been successfully avoiding Tom since we got on the road. I call that a great feat, considering we're sharing a limited space.

I know we cleared this air, but I still don't feel totally comfortable around him. Part of that is my own body's reaction to Tom, not that he needs to know that. His ego is big enough without me contributing to it.

So far, in my avoid-Tom scheme, I've sat up front with Henry, chatting with him while he drives. I've learned that he's got two grown-up twins, a boy and a girl, who both just started college. He's a keen fly-fisher. He's been married for twenty-five years, and he talks about his wife, who is a kindergarten teacher, with obvious affection.

Good to know there are some decent men out there.

After my chat with Henry, I go to take a shower. The guys are already on the PlayStation. Tom is on his cell, sitting at the kitchen table and having a quiet conversation. He doesn't even look up as I pass. He's probably having a sex chat with one of his many women.

I don't want to use up all the hot water, so I don't stay in the shower for too long, but I linger in the bathroom to kill time.

Then, I head to the bedroom and get dressed in my favorite ripped jeans and a T-shirt. I sit at the desk, my now makeshift dressing table, and sans makeup, I fix my hair into a messy bun on the top of my head.

I hear a knock at the door and then the sound of Cale's voice.

"You decent?"

"No, I'm butt naked."

I hear him laugh.

"You'd better be kidding 'cause I'm coming in."

"Yes, I'm kidding," I call out.

Cale comes in and closes the door behind him. He jumps on the bed and sprawls out flat on his back.

I finish tying up my hair and turn in my chair to face him. "Comfy?" I ask.

"Very." He grins, stretching his arms above his head.

I've just dipped my finger into my face cream when Cale asks, "So, why are you hiding out in here?"

I look in the mirror at him. "I'm not hiding out."

"Yes, you are."

"Fine." I sigh. "I'm hiding out." I spread the cream over my fingertips and start to apply it to my face.

"I'm guessing you're hiding from Tom. So, are you going to tell me what's up? I know you haven't been happy about him coming on tour with us. And you lack a filter, Ly, but you were rude to him before—"

"I wasn't rude." I see his unconvinced expression. "Okay, I was rude."

"So, what don't I know?" he asks with that Cale tone, meaning he won't let this go until I tell him.

I twist in my seat and bring my knees up with my feet resting on the edge of the stool. I hug my knees to my chest, resting my chin on them. "Ages ago, Tom hit on me." I let out a sigh. "He's hit on me a couple of times."

"What?" Cale practically shouts, sitting upright. "When?"

"Shh…" I admonish, eyes flitting to the closed door.

These walls are like paper, and I don't want Tom to hear any of this.

"Keep your voice down. It doesn't matter when he hit on me. Actually, he's hit on me twice. The first time he tried it, I turned him down. He was fine about it"—I tug on my lip—"but then I saw him a few months later, and he hit on me again."

I can see anger rising in Cale's face, prompting me to say, "He never crossed the line. He's never touched me or anything. It's just that I haven't seen Tom since the last time he hit on me, and I didn't know how things would stand…if he'd try again." I grimace. "So, my guard was up—hence, bitch mode."

"Understandable. And has he gotten the message? Because if he hasn't—" Cale is on full overprotective mode.

"Calm down, angry. We talked." *Yelled.* "He apologized and asked if we could move past it and be professional. I said yes."

"Okay…good." Cale relaxes a little, resting back onto his elbows. "But if he does try anything—"

"He won't. But if he does, you'll be the first to know."

There is no way I would tell Cale if Tom made a move on me again. Aside from being able to take care of myself, Tom is a lot bigger than Cale. It's not that Cale isn't muscular. He is, but Tom's biceps are quite literally twice the size of Cale's. Tom has always been a big guy, but he looks even bigger now, like he's been putting in some serious gym time.

I see a smile creep on Cale's face.

"So, you turned down Tom Carter?"

"I did." I smirk.

He lets out an admiring laugh. "That's my girl. I bet that was a massive hit to his ego. No guy likes to be turned down, and I'm guessing it's never happened to Tom, so it would have dented his ego for sure."

"I'm sure I didn't dent his ego. He'll have been turned down by a women before."

I prod Cale in the thigh with my toes. He grabs my foot and yanks it, making me laugh.

"I highly doubt it. Most women will just lie down and spread their legs for him."

"Too much info, thanks. And I'm not most women." I look up at him, giving my best cocky grin.

"I know you're not. That's the problem." He gets to his feet, concern etched on his face. "You're gorgeous, talented, and smart. You're a challenge for a guy like Tom, and you flat-out turn him down—"

"Twice," I remind him. I don't know why I did that.

"See? This is what I mean. He already saw you as a challenge because you knocked him back the first time, so he tried again." He runs a hand through his hair, messing it up. "He wouldn't have liked the second knock-back. It was probably worse than the first. Guys like Tom are not used to rejection. It makes you a challenge, and there's nothing a guy likes more."

"Cale, he's not chasing me. He's given up. He gave up. It was ages ago when he last hit on me, and he hasn't tried to chase me down since then." I get to my feet. "It's done. Over. Anyway, Tom has got way too many other women running after him to bother himself with little ole me. But you're sweet for worrying."

I put my arms around his waist, hugging him.

He affectionately kisses the top of my head. "It's my job to worry about you."

"Taken on that task, have you?" I lean back to look at him, releasing him from my embrace.

He chucks my chin. "Since I was twelve years old."

"Oh, I forgot to tell you. That phone call earlier—it was Jake. He knows that Rally is my dad. Rally called him."

Cale's brow furrows as he leans back against the wall. "How did that go?"

"The tour bus is moving, isn't it?" I smile.

He returns my smile. "It was bound to come out, Ly. And when we're famous—"

"When?" I grin.

"Damn right, when. The minute our music hits the airwaves, we're gonna be big, baby!"

I laugh at his enthusiasm and belief in our band.

"You hungry?" He opens the door.

I follow him through. "Is that translation for, you all are hungry, and you want me to make dinner?"

He turns, walking backward. "You know we can't cook for shit, Ly. So, it's either that, or we starve, waiting for Henry to make his first stop." He pouts.

"Ugh." I roll my eyes and give him a playful shove. "Fine. I'll cook."

"You want some help?" He smirks.

He knows I won't want his help. Cale is a nightmare in the kitchen. He makes more of a mess than imaginable, and he gets in my way. In this kitchen, there's not enough space for us both.

"Go play games." I wave my hand in the direction of Sonny and Van, who are playing some racing game.

*No sign of Tom.* Maybe he's up front with Henry.

Cale sits with the guys. He tells them I'm going to make dinner. They all shout noises of love for me.

Shaking my head, smiling, I hear a door open behind me, and I see a freshly showered Tom emerging from the bathroom, wearing nothing but a towel.

My mouth actually starts to water. I kid you not. My eyes take on a mind of their own as they openly stare at him. Skin still wet, rivulets of water trickle down his tattooed chest. Of course, I knew he had tattoos. Both of his arms are sleeved, but he also has them on his chest and stomach, too. *TMS* is written in large script on his left pec.

*And what an amazing pec it is. There isn't an ounce of fat on him.*

More script is under his pec, just above that amazing six-pack of his—*Yesterday is a memory. Tomorrow may never be.*

I feel a flash of emotion from those words—that is, until I reach the top of his towel. My attention is taken again. I can see some script peeking out, but I can't make out what it says.

I'm brought back to the now at the sound of Tom clearing his throat.

My eyes dart to his. He's smirking.

I was totally checking him out, and he knows that I was checking him out.

*Crappity crappola.*

My guard is back up, and I ignore the heat I feel in my cheeks. In a firm tone, I say, "I'd appreciate it if you'd wear a little more clothing while walking around here."

His expression stays neutral. "I forgot to take clean clothes in with me. My bad. Won't happen again." He turns away from me, but I hear him mutter, "Not her type, my ass."

*Ignore it. He wanted you to hear it. That's why he said it.*

*Just ignore it.*

*Damn it! I can't ignore it!*

"You're not my type!" I yell out.

*Oh God. Why can't I just keep my mouth shut?*

I don't dare to look to see if the guys heard me.

Tom turns with a slim smile on his face. "I'm sorry. What?"

His gaze flickers briefly over my shoulder, telling me everything I need to know. The guys heard me.

*Shit.*

I straighten my back, steeling myself. "I heard what you said."

He tilts his head to the side, an innocent look on his face. "And what did I say?"

*Game-playing bastard.*

"You know what you said."

"No, I don't." He shrugs. "Please enlighten me?"

"Ugh!" I growl, annoyed that he's making me repeat his snide words. "You said, 'Not her type, my ass.'"

"You sure I said that?" He rests a shoulder against the wall.

My hands go to my hips. "A hundred percent."

"But why would I say that?"

"Because I was staring at your bare chest."

*Effing shitting bastard.*

He played me.

My face flames. "You're such a mut!"

He laughs. "I'm a mut? Jesus, what are you? Twelve? And don't throw insults at me. I wasn't the one perving on my hot body."

"I was not perving!" I cry with indignation.

"So, you admit I'm hot."

"I, what? No, I don't admit anything!"

He's laughing at me now.

*Why aren't any of the guys coming to my rescue here? Cale?*

I look over my shoulder to see them watching us with rapt attention. Well, Van and Sonny are. Cale just looks curious. I give him a loaded look and then swing my gaze back to Tom.

"One, I don't think you're hot." *Total lie.* "And two, I was merely admiring your tattoos. I like tattoos. I've been thinking about getting one, so when I see someone with them, I like to have a look and see if they might be something I would like inked on my body."

*Worst excuse ever.*

Tom's eyes flick to mine, his stare hot and heavy. There's this moment—a stifling, blood-pumping moment—between us.

Then, it's gone.

His eyes harden. His hand goes to the back of his neck. He looks to the ceiling and blows out a breath.

I'm expecting some smart-ass comment from him, so I'm surprised when he looks back to me and says, "There's nothing inked on my body that you'd want. Trust me."

I watch his retreating back as he heads to his bunk to get his clothes. My eyes hone in on the huge tattoo there. It's a large wooden cross, spanning his entire back, with a blade at the end, like it's cutting into his skin. It has the words, *Only The Strong Survive*, woven through it.

It's beautiful—in a morbid way.

Then, my eyes focus on the text directly below the cross. *Thomas III*, is inked there, and in much smaller text below that is, *Rest in the peace that life could no longer give you.*

Tom lost someone important—just like I did.
I guess we have something in common after all.

# The Next Day—Backstage at a Club, Seattle

*Thomas III.*

I've come up with so many scenarios as to whom Thomas III could be. It has to be someone in his family for sure. Tom, Thomas III—I'd be stupid not to figure that one out.

I thought maybe it was his father, but for some reason, my thoughts keep circling back to a child.

*Rest in the peace that life could no longer give you.*

I've never heard anything about Tom Carter having a son, but I also know it is possible to keep things quiet from the press for the right amount of money.

Rally taught me that.

I'm not ashamed to admit that after dinner last night—which Tom joined us for, but he was noticeably quiet—I spent the rest of my night in the bedroom Googling him. First search was, *Tom Carter's child.* Nothing came up, so then I tried, *Tom Carter III.* I got nothing relevant, only pictures of Tom. A lot were of him with his band members, but there were also a lot of him with women, lots of women.

I started to feel a bit ill while looking at the pictures of his skankhood, so I gave up soon after and went to sleep.

My mind has been on Tom since last night—well, more his tattoo. The mystery is still bugging the hell out of me. I don't care about him. I'm just incredibly nosy. It's an illness of mine. It's something I'm working on.

"Lyla Summers?"

I lift my gaze from the piece of paper in front of me, the one I've been doodling Tom's scripture on.

I came backstage to our dressing room to work on some new song lyrics while the guys do sound tests onstage where we'll be playing in a few hours. It's fair to say that I've not been very productive with my time.

Looming over me and smiling widely is a model-thin, beautiful woman, wearing what can only be described as painted on jeans with a low-cut tank revealing a lot of her bust. She has long dark brown hair, flawlessly straight, framing her face that has heavily applied makeup.

I'm far from ugly. I'm often told I look exactly like my mother, and I know she was beautiful. But this woman before me is making me feel like a little kid. That's partially due to the fact that I'm dressed like one, wearing my trusty Keds, torn jeans, and a T-shirt that has a picture of Homer Simpson wearing only his underpants with the slogan, *The Last Perfect Man*, on it. It's not a slouchy, oversized T-shirt. I always get them fitted, but still, it's a Simpsons T-shirt.

*God, I'm so lame.*

"Um…yes, I'm Lyla," I answer with trepidation, wondering who she is.

"Well, you are just stunning. The photo Zane gave me doesn't do you justice at all. I'm Shannon, your stylist." She holds a manicured hand out to me.

I lift my hand, cringing at the chewed ends and chipped varnish, and shake hers. Releasing my hand, she sits down in the seat before me, dropping a large bag hanging from her slender shoulder onto the table.

"I didn't realize I had a stylist," I reply.

She lets out a laugh and smacks the gum she's chewing. "Honey, of course you have a stylist. All performers do. With this being your first tour, we're on a budget, so it'll just be Ashlee and me. Ashlee is my assistant."

I feel dumb. I should know this stuff. I'm not exactly new to this world.

"Okay," I reply.

Then, she just stares at me, eyeing me up and down. I shift in my seat, feeling beyond uncomfortable. I've never been appraised like this before.

"You have great skin, doll, and your eyes…"

She leans in close to my face. She's that close I can smell her minty breath.

"They are so…unusual. You have any Asian heritage, hon?" Her eyes run over my blonde hair and pale skin.

I shake my head. "Not that I know of."

My mother was Caucasian, and so is Rally. I don't know much of his ancestry, so I suppose there could be some Asian heritage. But aside from his eyes, he looks Caucasian to me.

Unfortunately, I have Rally's eyes, even down to the crystal-clear blue color of them. I hate my eyes. I wish I had my mother's eyes, big and doe-like. My eyes aren't small, but they are narrow and slant downward, giving them a feline look. It's not unusual for me to receive comments on my eyes. I've been told many times that my eyes are the first thing that people notice about me. Apparently, they're intriguing.

Personally, I think they look empty and cold.

Kind of like my heart.

"We'll use some shimmering silver and black liner on your lids with those ocean blue eyes. Shit, honey, they will look stunning! Not that they don't already. You're gonna be beating those boys, and girls, off with a stick!" She laughs.

It's a hearty, warm laugh that kind of endears her to me.

"Not that I imagine you have any problems in the sex department, looking like you do. Are you straight? I've always had a great read on people, and you look straight to me. I'm bisexual." She presses her hand to her chest. "I've always liked a bit of variety in my life." She winks and laughs again.

*Okay…*

Definitely an information overload.

I can't believe that I have known this woman for all of about sixty seconds, and I'm already well acquainted with her sexual preferences. I might spend nearly all my time with three oversexed men, but I'm not particularly open to talking or hearing about sex, especially with a virtual stranger, and even more so since I'm no longer having it.

"How do you feel about layers?" Shannon asks.

"Um…what?"

"Layers. In your hair. The bangs definitely work for you, but I think some layers in the back and around your face will look amazing."

On her feet now, she moves to stand behind me, and her hands are fluffing my hair, pulling it this way and that.

*My God, this woman is a whirlwind.* I'm getting whiplash from just listening to her.

"Yeah, maybe. Whatever you think."

"Those new lyrics you're working on?"

"What?" My eyes hit the table, and I nearly die when I see the piece of paper with Tom's scripture still sitting there.

I place my hand over the paper. "Uh…no, it's nothing."

Apparently, I'm not covering the paper that well.

Shannon leans in over my shoulder and says, "God, that sounds so familiar. *Rest in the peace that—*"

I scrap the paper up with my hand and shove it into my pocket. My face is burning.

"Lyla, you're—"

At the sound of Tom's voice, my head whips around, and I see him standing in the doorway. Then, without warning, Shannon starts shrieking like a fucking banshee, scaring the shit out of me.

"Oh my fucking God!" Shannon's hands tighten around my hair as she pulls it, causing me to wince. "Tom Carter!"

She drops my hair and runs across the room before launching herself at him. And when I say *launching*, I mean, her long legs wrap around his waist, and her arms link around his neck. Then, she plants her lips straight on his, kissing him.

I look away. I can feel my face burning with irritation.

*Why am I so irritated that she's kissing him. It's not like I want to kiss him.*

*Okay…well, maybe my lips would like to kiss Tom's, but my brain definitely says no.*

I force myself to look back at them, to get over whatever the hell it is I'm feeling, but the sight of her long legs still wrapped around Tom's waist with her lips melded to his scratches over my skin like pins and needles of jealousy.

Tom breaks the kiss, and his eyes flicker past her and meet mine.

I look away—again.

I can feel myself frowning at the sight of her lip gloss shimmering on his lips. I rub my forehead, easing out the frown lines.

"Shannon Archer," he says. "Been a long time."

*He knows her. Of course he knows her—and very well by the looks of things.*

"Too long!" she says in a singsong voice.

I can see her lowering her perfect legs to the floor, but I notice she doesn't let go of him while her hands grip his waist.

"Jake said you were here as tour manager, but I thought he was just shitting me. I mean, this is you we're talking about, and you know what Jake is like, always teasing me. But here you are. Tom Carter, a tour manager. Well, screw me sideways. Then again, you've already screwed me sideways and back ways, right, baby?" She winks.

I want to vomit. I actually want to vomit.

He's had sex with her.

Of course he's had sex with her. Half the female population has had sex with him.

Tom's eyes flicker past her to meet mine—again.

*What's he looking at me for?*

I dip my gaze, pretending to be suddenly enthralled by the words on my notepad.

"Look at you though," she says, her voice sounding softer. "Your hair has all grown out."

My curious eyes have to take a quick look.

Shannon is running her fingers through his hair in an intimate and familiar way. It causes my stomach to clench.

"And you've grown a beard." Smiling, she trails her fingernails over his facial hair. "You look all grown-up."

He rubs a hand over his jaw. "I grew up a long time ago."

"Sure you did, but I like it."

He gives her a smile. "You're looking good, Shan."

"Don't I always?" She wiggles her hips. "So, do you like the new girls?" She steps back and sticks out her chest. "I only went up a cup size. I'm a D now. Didn't want to go too big, you know? I can't stand those in-your-face fake boobs. These feel real though. Can't tell they're implants at all. Have a feel."

Tom's eyes flash over to me. I look away before he can really catch my gaze.

*Seriously, why does he keep looking at me?*

"Yep, they feel real all right."

So, he felt her up. *Awesome.*

"Told ya. I'm really happy with them. My surgeon was amazing. They were a present to myself for hitting the wrong side of thirty. God, I can't believe I'm thirty-five!" She groans. "Where has the time gone?"

*Thirty-five?* God, I thought she was around my age, twenty-two. I'd have given her twenty-five max. Hell, I hope I look as good as she does when I'm her age.

"Yeah, you're getting old now." Tom laughs.

"Hey! You're not that far behind me. What are you now? Twenty-nine?"

"Yep. I'm a baby compared to you."

"Fuck off," she gibes good-naturedly. "You never complained about my age when you had your dick in me. And here I was, thinking you liked older women."

*Oh God.* I roll my eyes, stifling a laugh at the absurdity of what I'm listening to.

Tom lets out a dirty-sounding chuckle. "You know me, Shan. I've always liked any kind of woman—as long as she's hot and game for anything."

"Yeah, that I do know for sure." She giggles.

I shift in my seat, putting my back to them. I stick two fingers into my mouth and fake gag.

"Lyla?"

My head whips around at Tom's stern tone. My eyes meeting with his, I see he's frowning at me. Shannon is beside him with her hand on his arm, her face neutral.

*Did he just see me fake gag?* I had my back to them, so he couldn't have—

*Oh, shit.*

I remember there's a mirror up on the wall. I turn back to look at it.

My eyes connect with Tom's in the mirror, and he raises his eyebrows in suggestion as a knowing grin hits his lips.

He saw what I did.

*Fucking fuck.*

My cheeks are on fire.

I turn in my seat to face him. "What do you want?" My voice comes out sharper than I intended, making me sound like a bitch.

Tom's expression hardens at my tone. "You're needed onstage to do sound checks."

*Oh. Okay.*

*One question—why did he come and get me himself? Why didn't he send a runner?*

Relieved he didn't call out my childish behavior, I say, "Let me get my stuff." I start gathering my cell, notepad, pen, and bottle of water before shoving them into my bag.

"So, what are your plans for tonight after the show?" Shannon asks Tom. "I was thinking we should hook up. It's been a few years since we last fucked."

My back stiffens.

*Seriously? Fucking seriously?*

I'm standing right here!

Shannon is nice enough, and I might learn to like her, but I can't believe she's trying to arrange a sex date with Tom while I'm standing right here.

*What the hell am I—chopped liver?*

I slam my bag down on the table, the metal buckles clanging loudly. I don't care if I come across as rude. I'm not here to stand around like a fucking lamppost while these two arrange a banging session.

My eyes lift to that damn mirror again, and Tom's eyes are already on me, his gaze burning into mine. In this moment, it's almost like he's trying to read me.

Uncomfortable from his stare and their screwing conversation, my eyes hit the floor. I pick up my bag and sling it on my shoulder. I'm more than ready to leave this room and these two sex maniacs.

"Sorry, Shan, no can do," Tom utters.

*What?*

That lifts my gaze just in time to see a flicker of confusion cross over Shannon's face.

"Okay…well, how about tomorrow?"

Tom shakes his head.

*Did he just…turn her down? Did Tom Carter just refuse sex from a woman?*

*My God, am I seeing stars?*

"Oh, you're seeing someone." She nods with certainty.

*Is he?*

That possibility doesn't sit right with me.

Shannon doesn't seem upset or embarrassed by his blow off. If it were me, I would be mortified. But then again, I'd never proposition a man for sex like she just did.

"Well, will wonders never cease?" She laughs. "Tom Carter has settled down!" She claps her hands together.

Tom doesn't respond to her in any way. Actually, all he's doing is staring straight at me.

*Why is he looking at me like that?*

*And why does his eye keep twitching?*

*What the hell is wrong with him?*

Shannon turns and follows his eyes to me. Her eyebrow lifts. She looks back at Tom and then to me again. She grins.

*Why is she grinning? Am I missing something here?*

"You're seeing Lyla!" she exclaims. "Jesus, Tom! Why didn't you say before?"

## One Second Later—Backstage at a Club, Seattle

My body jerks in shock like I've been shot.

*What?*

*What the hell?*

"No!" I yell. "He's not seeing me! I mean, he sees me here, of course, but he's not *seeing me, seeing me*. We're not sleeping together. Jesus Christ!" I drag my hand through my hair. "Tom and I are not together! The end!" I jab a finger in Tom's direction. "Tell her."

He says nothing. He's completely blank. There's nothing but a sly smile on his smug face that I'm more than ready to wipe off.

*What the hell is he playing at?*

Shannon looks between us again. "Okay…" she drawls out, a bemused look on her face. "I get it." She winks at me and lowers her voice as she says, "Don't you worry, Lyla. I'm awesome at keeping secrets."

*Secrets! What secrets? There are no secrets to keep!*

*Jesus, I feel like I've just stepped into a parallel universe.*

"Um…there's no secret to keep because nothing is going on between Tom and me." My voice is rising an octave higher with each word I speak.

I throw an expectant look at Tom, desperate for him to say something, to tell her the truth. But he's just standing there, smirking and not saying shit. So, basically, he's as much use to me as a chocolate fire suit.

"Ugh!" I throw my hands up in the air, more angry than anything.

I realize that if I stay here a moment longer, I'm going to pummel Tom Carter to death.

"I have no clue what the hell is going on here! Especially with you!" I point at Tom. "I don't have time for this bizarre crap, so I'll leave you to your craziness. I'm going to go onstage and do my job. Nice to meet you, Shannon. Tom, I'll hopefully see you…*never*!"

I stomp past them, and I'm out the door in a flash, my face burning like a furnace.

*What the hell was that about? Why did Tom let Shannon think we were together?*

*Fucking Tom Carter!*

*Maybe he's gone crazy.* He has seemed different from the guy I met before. And he has gone all hobo with the hair and beard.

*Men! See? This is why I stay clear of them. They're all crazy bastards.*

"So, we're not together then?" Tom's lush deep voice comes from behind me.

Shivers prickle the hairs on the nape of my neck at the baritone of his voice.

I ignore the sensation and spin around, my anger unleashed to rain hell all over him.

"What the hell are you talking about? Have you lost your goddamn mind?" I'm yelling at him, and he totally deserves it. "Why did you let Shannon think that you and I are together?"

His brow furrows. Being this close to him, I notice a little cute line that has appeared from his frown.

*Cute? Jesus, Lyla. Get your head back in the game.*

"I didn't make Shannon think anything," he replies evenly.

"Um…yes, you did. She assumed you were seeing someone, and you looked directly at me! I mean, what the hell, Tom? We don't even like each other."

His lips curl. "Well, that's not entirely true." His eyes give my body a lazy perusal.

I hate that my body lights up like the Fourth of fucking July under his heated gaze.

"I *definitely* like your tight, little body, that flat stomach just begging me to lick it, and your rack—*fuck*, Firecracker," he says, his voice gruff, and so completely hot.

I can practically feel his words on my body, like he's touching me with each one.

He steps closer. He's a breath away from me, and now, I'm finding that I can't seem to catch my own.

"And your face…gorgeous, really gorgeous." His minty hot breath blows over my face. "I can honestly say, the only thing I don't like about you…is your no-filter, ball-busting mouth!"

"Ugh!" I shove him hard in the chest. "Screw you!"

"Please do. It would make my fucking year to see you riding my cock," he says with a masculine groan, smirking at me.

"Ah! You're a nightmare! Don't you ever stop?"

"When it comes to you, Firecracker, I'll never stop. *Never.*"

Flustered and turned-on and angry and confused, I press my thighs together trying to keep my virginia in check, and I wrap my arms across my chest. All the while, I'm firing daggers from my eyes straight into Tom's.

He stares right back. His chest is heaving up and down.

Then, my anger suddenly deflates, and I'm just left feeling flat. *Way to kick off the first show of the tour.*

I rub my nose. "It's only been one day, Tom, and we're already yelling at each other. It's not good—at all. And what you just pulled back there...*Jesus*, that was way out of line." Disappointment drags my voice down.

Tom lifts his eyes to mine. In this moment, I see a shade of real in them that I don't think I've ever seen in him before.

"Okay," he exhales. "You're right. I'm sorry."

I can't imagine that Tom Carter apologizes to many people, if any, so I take the fact that he just apologized to me as he really means it.

"I crossed the line. I didn't exactly dissuade Shannon of her assumption that you and I were sleeping together. In my defense though, technically, I didn't actually say anything."

I unfurl my arms, stretching them out in his direction. "But that's worse!"

"How so?"

"I don't know!" I say, flustered. "It just is!" I shove my hands through my hair. "I don't get you, Tom. Why would you even want Shannon to think that you and I are seeing each other?"

He shifts his stance and shoves his hands into his pockets. He actually looks uncomfortable.

*Interesting.*

"Because I don't want to have sex with Shannon. If you didn't gather, she doesn't take no for an answer, but she's a good girl, and I've known her for a long time. I didn't want to hurt her feelings, and I knew the only way she would back off was if she thought I was seeing someone."

*Ah...*

I actually soften to him.

I know. I could slap myself, too.

"But you could have said you were seeing someone else. It didn't have to be me."

He gives me a confused look. "But you were the only other person in the room."

I let out a laugh. "Tom, for you to be seeing a woman doesn't mean that she has to be in the room at the time. If you made up a name, I'm pretty sure that would have been good enough for Shannon."

He shrugs, his lips pressed into a grin. "Kinda didn't occur to me."

I roll my eyes. "Yeah, well, just make sure it does next time, okay?" I lean against the wall, eyeing him. "Do you do that often?"

Mirroring me, he rests his back against the opposite wall. "Do I do what often?"

"Create imaginary girlfriends to dodge having sex with women? You could just tell them no, you know."

"I've never dodged having sex with a woman who has laid it out for me—before today."

I don't like the way his admission makes me feel.

"So, why dodge this time? Why not just have sex with her? I thought that was your *thing*."

He pushes off the wall and comes close to me again. "Sex is my thing. It just…" He pushes a hand through his hair. "Things just change is all."

I stare up into his eyes. My mouth is suddenly dry, and my brain is fogged up with the clean scent of his cologne.

"I'll make sure Shannon knows that we're not seeing each other."

His words lift me out of my fog.

"Good." I straighten my back and step away from him. "And make sure you do it soon. I don't want Shannon telling other people that you and I are together."

He follows me forward, closing the gap between us again. "Why is the thought of being with me so bad?"

It's my turn to lift an eyebrow. "Really? I thought that would be plainly obvious. One"—I tick off on my finger—"this is my first tour, and you're my tour manager. I don't want to get a reputation in the industry as someone who tries to sleep her way to the top. Two, you're my *tour manager*! And three, I hate beards!"

I don't actually know why I said that last bit because I don't really hate beards. I do kind of like the way Tom looks with his.

His expression is wounded as he runs a hand over the growth covering his chin. The sound of his coarse hair scratching against his rough fingers brings a shiver to my body.

"Come on, Firecracker, don't hate on the beard. I'm going for the roadie look. Don't you think it's working for me?"

"No. You look like a hobo."

He throws back his head and roars out a laugh.

The sound hits me like rapid fire. I feel it in every one of my censored hot spots.

I bite my lip to stop the giggle that wants to escape. "Your hair is okay though. I like it longer."

"Whoa there, Firecracker. Was that a *compliment?*"

"No." My eyes catch his smiling ones.

"So, if I get rid of the beard but keep the hair, would you pretend to be my girlfriend to save me from the Shannons of this tour?"

"Um…" I rub my forehead in thought. "No."

"Damn." He chuckles.

I start walking again, and Tom follows.

When we reach the stage door, I turn to him. I'm keen to push the question again, so I can try to get a real answer this time. "Why would you want me to pretend to be your girlfriend to put women off anyway? I thought banging lots of women was your favorite pastime."

"Like I said, things change." He shrugs as he averts his eyes, looking down the hallway. "I thought I was the last perfect man."

"What?"

His face comes back to mine, and he nods down at my shirt.

"Oh, right." I let out a laugh, smoothing my hand over the picture of Homer. "Nope, not a chance. Homer wins out every time over any man. He's the ideal." I flash a cheeky grin.

"Big guts and big butts are your ideal—duly noted. Makes sense to me now why you kept turning me down. Thank fuck that's cleared up. My ego is now fully restored."

I roll my eyes. "You're such a guy."

"I fucking hope so, Firecracker. With the size of my junk, I'd worry if I wasn't."

"Oh my God!" I laugh. "You just can't help yourself."

He gives a boyish grin followed by a chuckle and a shrug of his shoulders. I feel that chuckle like a whispered breath over my skin. *Lord, help me.*

"You know, Lyla," he says, his voice lowered, "Henry looks a bit like Homer Simpson. I bet if you stripped him down to his tighty whities, you'd have your ideal man right there."

I sputter out a laugh, which turns into me choking on my own spit.

*Classy, Lyla. Real classy.*

"Easy there, tiger." Tom leans over and pats my back while I hack out a cough. "With it being the first show of the tour and all, we need your vocals in good shape for tonight."

I rub at my chest, trying to right myself, while taking deep breaths.

"You okay?" His hand comes to rest on my shoulder.

He's not even touching my skin directly, but the gentle grip of his fingertips sears through the cotton of my T-shirt and burns into my skin, branding me.

My heart starts to hammer in my chest.

His hand on me feels right…too right.

The air is suddenly thick with something—

*No.*

I drop my shoulder, quickly pulling from his touch.

"So, what is it with you and cartoon T-shirts anyway?" Tom asks, talking past that moment "That's the third one I've seen you wear in two days."

*He's keeping count?*

I wore my blue My Little Pony *Friendship Is Magic* T-shirt teamed with my blue pajama shorts for bed last night.

Yes, Tom saw me in my pajamas. He was climbing in his bunk as I was exiting the bathroom.

"I love cartoons." I shrug, leaving out the fact that I collect cartoon T-shirts because of my mom.

It started when Mom had to go to Paris for a show. I couldn't go with her, and she felt guilty, so she went to Disneyland and brought me home a bucket load of toys and clothes to make up for it. Out of everything she got me, the thing I loved most was a Little Mermaid T-shirt. I had a serious love for Prince Eric. I wore that T-shirt all the time, even for bed. Apparently, I drove her nuts with it. So, to get me wearing something different, the next trip she took, she bought me a new cartoon shirt with Beauty and the Beast. Of course, I loved it. I wore it in rotation with my Little Mermaid shirt.

After that, it became our thing. Every time she took a trip, I would get a new cartoon T-shirt.

Mom is out of town permanently now, so in her homage, I buy myself a new shirt whenever I travel. I'm going to have to carve out time to buy a new shirt in every town we hit on tour—well, at least one in each state.

I hear the soothing sound of guitars firing up through the door behind me. My bandmates are gearing up for tonight. Then, Sonny start banging on the drums, drumming a beat I'm all too familiar with. It spreads warmth throughout me.

Smiling, I say, "I should get onstage." I reach for the door handle.

"Lyla?"

I turn back.

"I am sorry…about before. It won't happen again."

"Good." I give him a curt nod and yank open the door, hurrying onto the stage to join my boys, leaving Tom where he stands.

# The Next Day—Tour Bus, en route to Boise

I awake with the feeling of last night's show still buzzing in my veins.

For the first show and considering the level of nerves we were all feeling, it went amazingly. Afterward, we had a few drinks backstage with some of the other bands.

Tom was noticeably absent.

Tom had been there when we came offstage, but he'd disappeared soon after. I didn't even get a chance to speak to him, not that I needed to speak to him. I guess it just would have been nice to hear what he thought of our first show.

But when we had come offstage, he had been talking to a woman, a stunning brunette. And the way her body had been leaning into his, it'd seemed pretty certain what her intentions were with him, and he hadn't seemed to be pushing her off.

His gaze had hit mine and then slid down my body. His eyes had widened and flared when he took in my breasts that were fitted into the black corset top, which was actually easier to breathe in than it looked. I could see his gaze soaking up my skin-tight black jeans, the ones that had been shredded with a pair of scissors by Shannon. She'd cut into them, giving the impression of rips, starting at the tops of my thighs and going down to my ankles. Then, his lips curved into the sexiest smile I'd ever seen at the silver stilettos on my feet.

Heat had spread throughout my body at his blatant perusal.

My thick hair had been set in loose waves down my back, and my makeup was smoky while my lips were glossy.

I'd known I looked hot, and I would be lying if I didn't say I'd liked the fact that Tom was affected by the way I looked.

Then, the brunette bombshell had pressed her body into his. She'd whispered something in his ear, and that had been when I looked away, telling Cale I was heading to the bathroom.

By the time I'd returned, Tom had been gone, and so had the brunette.

I'd known Tom left to do…*whatever* with her.

And I'd ignored the sick feeling I got at the thought of the *whatever.*

So, I drank with my boys, not wanting to go back to the bus and possibly walk in on Tom and the brunette.

I made sure to have fun, and I watched with mild amusement as Shannon and her assistant, Ashlee, flirted their way around my boys.

Ashlee is a pretty blonde who wears her skirts too short and her tops way too low. Understated is not a word Ashlee appears to know.

I'd met her before the show while she and Shannon had gotten us ready. Shannon had focused on me—my hair, makeup, and clothes—while Ashlee had prepared Van, Sonny, and Cale. They hadn't needed much help.

They all have that annoying man thing. No matter what they wear, they look hot—whereas I, as most women, have to work to look good.

I'm not bad with clothes. I just don't really bother to dress up. I'm happiest in a pair of jeans and a T-shirt. Sure, I know how to dress for shows. I've been dressing myself for those for a long time now. But Shannon's ideas of clothes are different than mine, and I've got to say, I actually like her idea of clothes—the ones she puts on me anyway. She seems to know what will work perfectly on me.

After the time I've spent with Shannon, I'm actually starting to really like her. She's funny when she's not hitting on guys in front of me—well, mainly Tom. Thankfully, she didn't mention him or what had happened earlier. I'm guessing he straightened things out with her.

At our after-show drinks, Ashlee was all over Cale. But I knew he wasn't interested.

I know Cale's type, and she isn't it. Cale always goes for brunettes or redheads. I've never seen him with a blonde.

When Ashlee figured out that he wasn't interested, she turned her attention to Van, who was more than happy to entertain her.

I'm pretty sure he entertained her in the restroom for a short while.

Shannon and Sonny spent a long time talking to each other. I got the distinct impression that she was interested in him. And I know Sonny. A hot woman shows interest in him, and he's on her like white on rice. Shannon is considerably older than Sonny, him only being twenty-four, but I know that wouldn't bother him. From the way I'd seen Shannon acting with Tom—cue upchuck moment—and with knowing how Sonny is, I was surprised that he and Shannon didn't hook up. As far as I know, they didn't because Sonny left with me, Cale, and Van—after Van was done with Ashlee—and we all went back to the bus together.

When we arrived, the bus was set in darkness. Tom was already in his bunk, sleeping, with his curtain drawn. He was probably tired from doing *whatever* with the brunette.

I scrubbed the makeup from my face and pulled on a pajama tank and shorts before getting into bed. I was out before my head hit the pillow.

Rubbing the sleep from my eyes, I reach over and get my cell from the bedside cabinet. I check the time—ten o'clock.

Hungry, thirsty, and in dire need of the bathroom, I climb out of bed and steady myself from the motion of the moving bus.

Cracking open my door, I hear someone moving about in the kitchen, so I slip straight into the bathroom.

It's all steamy in here. Someone's been awake for a while and already had a shower. Knowing my boys, they wouldn't be up early, so it had to be Tom.

My stomach does a stupid little flip at the idea of him showering in here.

Wiping the image of Tom wet in the shower, from my mind, I pee, brush my teeth, and tie my hair up into a messy knot.

Exiting the bathroom, I see that the curtain to Tom's bunk is open.

My stomach fizzes from just knowing he's out here—which is crazy.

*What am I? Twelve?*

Pushing my attraction for Tom out of my mind, I brace myself to see him.

Ignoring my attraction for him lasts about three seconds until I see him sitting at the table, and my hormones go into overdrive from the sight of him. With still damp hair, he's wearing an ancient-looking Clash *Rock the Casbah* T-shirt and ripped blue jeans.

There's a cup of coffee in front of him and an empty cereal bowl, a box of Froot Loops, and a carton of milk off to the side. He has a newspaper in his hands.

But one thing is noticeably gone—his beard. He's clean-shaven.

*Did he do that because of me? Because of what I said about hating his beard?*

*Don't be so conceited, Lyla.*

Taking a deep breath, I push my shoulders back and walk toward him.

His eyes lift from the paper to me. His gaze almost burns a hole in my panties.

"Mornin', Firecracker," he drawls. His voice sounds all deep and throaty.

*Smoking hot.*

I ignore the Firecracker nickname. I figure there's no point in arguing it because he'd get a rise out of it.

I smile and force a neutral tone into my voice as I say, "Good morning."

Deciding to join Tom in eating kid cereal, I head straight to the cupboard. I reach up onto my tiptoes and get a bowl, and then I grab a spoon from the drawer. I take a seat across from him, pour myself some Froot Loops, and drown them in milk.

When I glance across at Tom, I see his eyes are on my chest, and his greens are on fire. Jade is almost burning blue.

It's then I realize I'm not wearing a bra.

*Shit.*

And this is the exact moment that my nipples decide to stand to attention under Tom's heated gaze.

*Fuckity fucking shit.*

Okay, so I've got one of two choices. One, I can get embarrassed, run to my room and put on a bra, but I know if I do that, it will only give him future ammo to tease me. Or two, I can act cool.

Cool it is.

Raising my arms above my head, I pretend to stretch, which of course pushes my girls out and in his direction.

I have to stifle a giggle at the look on his face. His eyes are as wide as saucers.

Then, he drags his tongue across his lower lip.

74

Fire licks between my thighs.

Gulping, I lower my arms. I put my sweetest-sounding voice on as I say, "Um, Tom?"

His eyes slowly lift to mine. The look is still there, and I have to stop from squirming under his lusty stare.

"Unless the human body changed overnight, eyes are up here." I point two fingers at my eyes.

His face cracks into a grin, and a throaty laugh sounds from him. He lowers the paper to the table. "Sorry. You just have a great fucking rack. It's hard not to stare." He grazes his lower lip with his teeth.

A blaze of heat strokes up the back of my neck, threatening to circle and set my face ablaze.

"Well, try to do your best. Respect goes both ways."

He lifts his shoulders. "Maybe you could wear a bra. That might help. Actually, no, it wouldn't."

"God, you're such a pig!" I exclaim. "Seriously, would you like it if I just sat and stared at the huge bulge in your pants all day?"

*Did I actually just say that? And did I really call his bulge huge? Oh God.*

A full smirk spreads across his gorgeous face. "Firecracker, are you asking me if I would like it if you sat and looked at my cock all day?" He grins, his eyes questioning me. "Are you sure you want me to answer that question? Because you know it would be a resounding—"

I throw my hand up, stopping him. "Stop! Seriously, I don't want to know." I'm laughing as I say this, and Tom rewards me with a boyish laugh.

Smiling, I dip my spoon into my cereal and load it up.

Tom is watching me, but the fun in his face is gone now, replaced with something a little more serious. His fingers start to tap against the table.

I swallow down my cereal and milk. "Everything okay?" I gesture to him with my spoon.

"I spoke to Jake last night. He told me about Rally, that he's your dad."

The cereal I just swallowed hits my stomach like rocks.

I put the spoon down in the bowl. "Oh, right. Okay…and do you have any issues with that?"

He tilts his head to the side, looking confused. "Why would I have issues with it?"

"Because my father is an asshole, and he's caused you and your friends a lot of problems over the years."

"Trust me, we've endured worse than what Rally has thrown at us."

"So, you don't dislike me now by association?"

He gives me a wicked smile. "Ah, so you do care whether I like you or not?"

Not wanting to answer *that* question, I give a noncommittal shrug of my shoulders. I pick my spoon back up and start eating again.

Tom links his fingers together and leans toward me. I can't help but look at his hands. Strong, masculine hands. Hands that I have no doubt he knows how to use very well. They look rough from years of playing bass. I can only imagine how good they would feel against my skin.

"Jake explained your situation," Tom says, bringing my attention back to him, "and how things are for you with Rally. But even if you got along with him, it wouldn't change how I view you."

"Thanks." I smile. "And I really mean that."

He nods and rests back in his seat.

"So, you know my father is the bastard of the music industry. I'm guessing you know that my mother was—"

"The darling of it. Your mom was beautiful, Lyla. Really talented. From the pictures I've seen of her, you look exactly like her, which is good. You could look like Rally, and that would be a total fucking waste." He grins.

I laugh.

Then, he says, "I'm sorry you lost her."

And my mood drops, right along with the spoon into the bowl in front of me. "Yeah, so am I."

"Tell me about her."

A ripple of uncertainty moves through me. He knows about my mother. Everyone does. She was tabloid fodder for the press for most of her short life. Every breath she took was documented.

Tom asking to hear about her warms places in me that have been cold for a long time.

"I'm sure you know most of it from the papers."

76

"Yeah, I know what the press said about your mom. But I don't know how she really was, who she was to you."

I stare at him, stunned from the depth in his words. And that's what has my lips parting and my voice speaking. "My mother was a child star. First, TV, and then she moved onto singing. She quickly became one of the biggest country singers we've ever had."

"She had an amazing voice, Lyla. You sound a lot like her when you sing."

His compliment spears me in the heart.

"So, you know she was beautiful and talented...but she was also kind and sweet and so smart. Real business savvy, you know? Then, she met Rally at some fundraiser. He wanted her, and you know what he's like when he wants something. Anyway, Mom signed with AME when she was nineteen. She was at that in-between stage of coming out of her clean-cut child-star image and growing into the woman she was becoming. Rally was instrumental in making that happen. They got married a year after she signed with AME, and I was born the year after that. We were happy for a time." I ease out a breath. "Then, Rally got bored, like he always does. When something stops being a challenge, he goes out and finds a new one, which was Tanya Olsen. Have you heard of her?"

Tom shakes his head.

"She's not around now. I think she performs on cruise ships these days. She was another one who Rally screwed over. Anyway, Tanya was nineteen years old, an up-and-coming pop singer. He signed her to AME, but obviously, Rally's interest in her didn't stop at the music." I roll my eyes. "He wasn't discreet about the affair. Everyone, including my mother, knew about it, and when it finally hit the tabloids, it was the excuse he needed to leave us."

"How old were you when he left?"

"Four."

"And how old were you when your mom passed?"

"Eight."

"She died from an overdose, right?"

My defensive eyes snap up to his. "She didn't kill herself."

"Hey"—he leans forward, resting his arms on the table—"I never said she did."

"Sorry," I huff. My elbows hit the table, and I drop my head into my hands. A surprising tear escapes. I discreetly wipe it away on my sleeve. "It's just that everyone says she killed herself, and I know she didn't." My eyes lift to his. "She would never have left me like that, not on purpose."

There's a look on his face—kindness but something more...concern.

"You want to talk about it?" he asks softly.

I shake my head. "I don't talk about...what happened—ever." The only person I ever really talked about it with was Dex.

"Well, maybe it's time you did." He stands. "I'll make us some coffee, and then you can talk."

I watch Tom, confused. He says nothing. The only sounds are the kettle boiling and my thudding heart.

Tom places a mug of steaming coffee in front of me, and sits back down, holding his own mug between his hands.

I push away the half-eaten bowl of cereal, my appetite gone. I wrap my hands around the mug, pulling it closer.

"So, you were eight when she died."

"Yeah. My nanny and I went away on a school trip for a few days. When we returned home, I found my mother's body on her bed. She'd taken a cocktail of pills and vodka. She'd been dead for a whole day. She was there all alone."

A stupid tear escapes, but I quickly catch it.

"She was only twenty-nine years old when she died." My teary eyes meet his. "Seven years older than I am now."

"Too young. But then, they say the great always die young."

I can see on his face that he's thinking of Jonny Creed.

"You miss Jonny."

His gaze hits mine—hard. "Every damn day. So, after your mom passed, you went to live with Rally?"

"No. I went to live with my Aunt Steph, my mom's sister, and her husband, my Uncle Paul. They already had a kid, Dex, my cousin, who became my brother overnight." I take a deep breath. "Rally didn't want me."

The angry look on Tom's face makes the hurt from Rally's rejection surface. I try to shrug it off like it doesn't matter.

"It wasn't a surprise," I say, trying to sound unaffected. "I barely saw Rally after he'd left us and married Tanya."

"He's been married a few times now, right?"

"We hit wife number seven last year. Olga, the Swedish supermodel, who is two years younger than me." I roll my eyes.

Tom chuckles a deep sound.

I take a sip of my coffee. "That's just what Rally does. He gets smart, talented, beautiful women—well, maybe calling Olga smart is pushing it."

I give a cheeky smile, and Tom laughs again.

"And he destroys them. He did it to my mother. To the world, I know it looked like she was okay, but she wasn't. Sure, she carried on touring and recording, but she was broken." My eyes lower to the table. "I used to hear her crying at night when she thought I was sleeping."

Tom reaches over and squeezes my free hand.

Liking his touch too much, I pull my hand free under the pretense of needing it to lift my coffee cup to my mouth.

"She was medicating to get through the days. I didn't know. I should have seen it."

"How exactly? You were a kid. Trust me, as a grown-ass man, I watched Jake fall to pieces in front of me, and I didn't realize it was happening until it was almost too late. Some people are just really good at concealing stuff."

I look at Tom, surprised. Surprised that we're having this conversation. Surprised that there is this side to Tom.

But most of all, I'm surprised because I'm telling him these things. I'm opening up to him. Now that I've started, I don't seem to want to stop.

"But Jake's okay now," I say.

"Yeah, but no thanks to me." He runs a hand through his hair.

"Don't sell yourself short. You're a good guy, Tom."

"You'd better be careful, Firecracker. I'm gonna get to liking these compliments, and I'll start to demand them all the time."

"You're a mut." I grin.

"Better." He winks.

"I'm not a good guy—well, I wasn't, but I'm working toward becoming one."

I look at his sincere face, a little shocked at his blatant honesty.

"You're not a bad guy. A bad guy is one who has his four-year-old daughter deliver divorce papers to her mother."

Tom's features tighten, anger firing up his eyes. "He did what?" His tone is seething.

I conceal my pain by sipping my coffee, wondering why the hell I just told him that. But now, I know I have to tell him the rest.

"The first time Rally came to collect me after he'd left…well, my mom…she kind of lost it when she saw him. She was begging him to come back." I cringe at the memory, hating that Rally reduced my mother to that.

"Of course, Mom was upset, so I started crying. Rally picked me up and carried me out of there before dumping me in his car. I couldn't stop crying, so he took me for ice cream. The entire hour we were in that ice cream parlor, he spent talking on his cell. Then, he said he had business to attend to and had to take me home. He pulled up in front of my house and didn't get out. He handed me a brown envelope and told me to give it to my mother. It turned out the envelope contained the divorce papers, and he'd gotten me to serve them to her."

I remember walking up to the door, and my mother was waiting on the other side. Rally had already driven away before I'd even gotten the door open. Handing her the envelope and how her hand was shaking as she took it from me. I can still hear the desolate tone in her voice as she told me to go to my room. Instead of going to my room, I hid on the landing, watching, as she tore open the envelope and pulled out the papers inside. Feeling tears in my eyes, seeing as she steadied herself against the wall.

To this day, I can still clearly see the look of crushing devastation on my mother's face.

"Fuck, Lyla. I knew I hated that guy for a good reason."

"Yeah. That was the last time Rally picked me up for a visit. My childhood relationship with Rally consisted of calls with his PA and presents and cards all done by his PA. That worked just fine for me since I pretty much hated him after that." I meet Tom's eyes. "He didn't attend my mother's funeral, you know. Didn't call to see if his eight-year-old daughter was okay after losing her mother."

"Some people don't deserve to have kids. I always say, family is the one you make."

I smile. "My Aunt Steph and Uncle Paul are great." I avoid mentioning Dex again. That's a whole other can of worms in my pathetic life story, which I'm not ready to open with Tom. "I'm lucky to have them."

"How do they feel about you coming into the music business?"

"They're really supportive."

Then, unease sweeps through me. *I've told Tom things that only a handful of people know. People I trust.*

After worrying my lip with my teeth, I say to him, "Tom, all these things I've told you about Rally and my mom, it's not stuff that many people know. Only people I trust."

*So, why did I tell him?*

He smiles. It's warm and genuine. "As far as the rest of the world is concerned, this conversation never happened. But to me, it happened. You ever need to talk again, you come to me."

He leans back against the seat with one leg crossed over his other thigh and his arm around the backrest, his strong, masculine fingers tapping against the wood. "I didn't get a chance to say it last night, but you fucking rocked the place."

*He's changing the subject.* I appreciate it.

I smile, curling my fingers around the cooling coffee mug. "Thanks. That means a lot."

Then, I remember why he wasn't there to tell me that last night, and the smile disappears from my face.

Sharing my life history with him and him being so sweet had me forgetting for a moment just who I was talking to.

He takes a sip of his coffee. "You have fun last night after the show?"

*Yeah, but not as much fun as you had, I'm sure.*

Nodding, I say, "Yeah, it was all right."

"Did you get back late?"

"Yep. You were sleeping."

Nodding, he rubs his hand over his smooth chin. "I was wiped."

*From banging the brunette.*

*Stop it, Lyla.*

Then, an unwanted image flashes through my mind.

*Ugh. Image of Tom with the brunette be gone!*

"You shaved," I say, trying to direct my thoughts elsewhere.

I glance down at my coffee, and when I look back up, his eyes are intense on me. I have to stop the shiver I feel.

He rubs his hand over his chin again. "Yeah, it wasn't working for me. Women seemed even more attracted to me with the beard. Go figure." He grins.

"Like the one from last night?"

*And there it is.*

*Why can't I keep my mouth shut about anything ever? Even more so when it's something I don't want to know.*

It's like I have a self-inflicted torture button in my brain.

Tom tilts his head, giving me questioning look. "The one from last night?"

I bring the mug to my lips and take a drink before speaking. "Yep, the brunette groupie you were talking to after the show. The one you left with."

He rubs his forehead in thought, his eyes meeting mine. I see something there in them, but I can't quite decipher it. I don't get a chance to though because whatever it is disappears, and it's like a light comes on in his eyes.

"Oh," he says, nodding. "You mean, the one with long dark hair, legs that went on forever, and the biggest pair of fake tits I've ever—"

"Yes, that one," I cut him off just as he's sizing a pair of breasts with his hands in front of his own chest.

He stands and moves away from the table. "Yeah, I didn't leave with her."

"You didn't?" It's hard for me to keep the surprise out of my voice.

"No, I didn't. I left alone, came back here, and crashed out." He turns back to face me. "You sound surprised."

"No, I'm not. Well, kind of."

"But more so, you look…relieved." He places his large hands on the table, leaning in close to me. "Are you?"

His nearness has my brain scrambled. "What?"

He leans in a little closer. "Relieved."

"Of course I'm not relieved." I force indifference onto my face.

But he knows I'm relieved because I am. It's written all over my imperfectly indifferent face.

"I guess that's a good thing then." His voice sounds husky. "If you were relieved at the thought of me not being with another woman, then that would mean you care…about me. And if you cared, that would mean you want—"

"I don't care," I say quickly. "And I certainly don't want anything." I lift my chin, trying to give off more of that indifference but failing miserably.

All I really manage to do is put my face closer to his. Well, technically, my mouth is closer, like within kissing distance.

I can feel his hot breath all over me, and the scent is minty mixed with coffee. It's like an aphrodisiac.

We're just staring at one another. Tom's breaths are deep and fast. Mine are even faster. My panties are wet, and he hasn't even touched me. I'm so wet that it'll be embarrassing when I have to stand.

His eyes dip to my lips. I squirm at the sight of his teeth dragging over his lower lip.

He's going to kiss me.

And I'm pretty sure that I'm going to let him.

The bathroom door bangs shuts.

Tom and I jerk away from each other like we've been shot.

Seconds later, Cale comes wandering into the kitchen. "Fucking Sonny. Beat me to the bathroom, and I'm dying to piss."

My eyes are still fixed on Tom. He's standing by the bench he was just sitting in with his hand gripping the back of it, his eyes on Cale.

"Too much info as usual," I say, dragging my eyes from Tom to Cale. "And please don't piss in the sink," I add, knowing that has happened on more than one occasion in the past.

"Spoilsport." He chuckles. "Mornin'," he says as he moves past Tom to the kitchen cupboard.

Tom gives him one of those manly chin nods.

Cale comes back, bowl and spoon in hand. "Scoot over," he says.

I shuffle over, making room, and take my now empty coffee mug with me.

"You sleep okay?" Cale asks me, knowing that I always struggle to sleep well on the first night in a new bed.

"The alcohol I drank last night helped." I grin at him.

"Getting into the rock-star lifestyle already?" he teases.

I give him the middle finger.

Chuckling, he slings his arm around my neck and pulls me to him before planting a kiss on the top of my head. Laughing, I push him away.

I grab the box of cereal and pour some into his bowl. "Eat your breakfast, and stop hassling me."

Shaking his head, smiling, Cale reaches over to get the milk.

That's when my eyes meet with Tom's.

He's silently watching Cale and me. Arms folded tight across his chest, his face is perfectly blank, but in his eyes, I see a flare of anger.

He seems to realize that I'm staring at him, and he loosens his arms and gaze.

"We'll be stopping to refuel soon, so if you need anything, get it then because we won't be stopping again until we reach Boise." Then, Tom walks away.

I watch him move down the galley to the driver's area, and he slams the door shut, the same door we always keep open.

*Is Tom angry because Cale interrupted was about to happen between us? Or is it because of the affectionate way Cale was with me?*

*Cale is always that affectionate with me, so it's not unusual.*

*Because if he is pissed over Cale, then that would mean—*

*No.*

I'm not thinking about what any of this means, and I'm definitely not thinking of the fact that I came pretty close to kissing Tom.

Or that I just gave him my life story.

The only ones who know my shit are Dex and Cale, and even Cale doesn't know all of it.

But now Tom knows, and I don't know what to do with that. I don't know what's happening between us.

One thing I do know is that I trust Tom with my past. And to me that means a lot. A real lot.

## Later That Day—A Club, Boise

"Are you fucking Cale?"

I turn, wide-eyed, ignoring the heat of Tom pressed against my side. His breath hot as he speaks into my ear over the loud music.

We're in a club in Boise, and we just finished playing our set fifteen minutes ago. We decided to stay, have a drink, and listen to the rest of the bands play before we have to get back on the road.

I'm at the bar, waiting to order drinks for me and the guys. Cale, Van, and Sonny are already out fishing, and Tom, so it seems, has a seriously inappropriate question for me.

"What?" I say slowly.

His jade green eyes are burning down on me.

I expect him to retract, or maybe I made a mistake and didn't hear him correctly.

He keeps his gaze fixed on mine as he leans in, putting his face close. He tucks my hair behind my ear, his fingers lingering there.

"I said, are you fucking Cale?"

I push away from him. "Are you being serious right now?"

"Deadly."

I stare at him, completely taken aback.

I've hardly seen him all day, and when I did, he was a moody bastard.

Now, the first words he speaks directly to me all night is to ask if I'm having sex with Cale.

Ignoring him, I turn back to the bar just as the bartender approaches. "Three beers and a vodka and tonic, thanks."

The bartender's eyes shift to Tom. I wonder if he knows who Tom is.

"Add a double Jack to that order." Tom hands the bartender his credit card.

"I don't need you to buy me a drink." I scowl at him.

"I thought maybe you'd answer my question if I did."

"Why does it matter to you if I am sleeping with Cale?"

Saying nothing, he stares at me.

I start to fold under his intensity.

"It's none of your business."

"I need to know what the members of my band are doing."

"Even their bedroom activities?"

He steps close to me. "Even that. Knowledge is power."

"Well, Sonny should make you plenty powerful then."

He barks out a laugh. Then, moves in closer, his hand going to my exposed lower back. "Answer the question, Lyla."

His fingers press into my skin. Heat infuses me.

I'm pissed at his question, knowing the reason he gave for asking is complete bullshit, but I'm getting more than turned-on by his touch.

It's seriously confusing wanting to punch a guy and fuck his brains out at the same time.

"Have you asked the guys this same question?"

He gives me a slow smile. "Not yet."

"You know, I don't recall Dina asking us this question when she was managing us."

"Yeah, well, Dina's not thorough. *I* am."

Something tells me Tom is very thorough in all he does.

The drinks appear on the bar. Grabbing mine, I toss it back. I wince from the burn, my lips tingling. I place the glass down on the bar and look up at Tom.

"Not that it's your business, but no, I'm not fucking Cale. He's my best friend. End of." I turn from him and start to walk away. *Destination—hide in the restroom.*

"So, you're not screwing Cale. Are you fucking anyone else?" he calls from behind me.

Mortified, I spin around, my face flaming, and I stare at him in shock. I feel like all eyes in the bar are on me when most people probably didn't hear Tom over the loud music. But that doesn't stop me from feeling even more pissed off.

I give him a death stare and start to walk away again.

"Answer the question, Firecracker."

I look back at him over my shoulder. "Here's an answer for you." I lift my fist in the air and shoot my middle finger up at him.

I hear his rumbling laughter from behind me.

*Asshole!*

I stomp across the club to Cale, who is sitting on a bar stool at a table with a redhead situated between his thighs.

"Your beer is at the bar with Tom," I toss the words at him in my angry stomp-by.

Cale catches my arm, stopping me. He moves the redhead aside and slides off the stool before coming to stand in front of me. "What's up?"

"Nothing."

He examines my face in that way he does.

I know I look annoyed. I'm frowning, so I relax my features. "Really, nothing's wrong. I'm just going to the restroom. Get back to your"—I look over his shoulder at the redhead, who is now throwing daggers at me—"fun." I bring my eyes back to his.

"Am I missing something here?" he asks.

*Yes! Tom is being an ass, and he's asking inappropriate questions.*

*And I'm attracted to him and turned-on pretty much twenty-four/seven because I have to live on the same bus as him. For a woman who is on a sex ban, that's like sticking a dieter in the middle of a chocolate factory!*

But of course, I say none of that because I don't want Cale to get all pissy with Tom and end up getting his ass kicked over me.

So, I paste on my breezy smile. "You're not missing anything. Get back to your redhead. I'll be back soon." I turn my eyes away from him.

He tugs on my arm, forcing me to look back to him. "No one is more important to me than you, Ly. You know that, right?"

"I know." I smile, for real this time. "And the same goes for you. But if you don't attend to your redhead, you'll be flying solo tonight."

"I never fly solo, not when I've got my girl right here." He cups my cheek and presses a kiss to my forehead. "Restroom, and come straight back to me."

"Yes, boss." I salute.

The stalls are empty when I go in, which allows me the opportunity to give myself a good mirror talking-to.

*No more letting Tom Carter get to me. And no more sexy feelings while I'm around him.*

*I'm getting back to kick ass, Lyla, who doesn't let a man get to her.*

*So, screw you Tom Carter.*

Feeling pumped I wash up and head back out into the club.

Glancing around, I see a few women surrounding Tom. Sonny is with him, enjoying the attention that Tom always brings.

One of the women hands Tom a pen. Then, she shimmies up close to him, shoving aside the other women, and she pulls her top down, revealing her chest to him. Tom grins and starts to write on her chest.

I roll my eyes.

*Getting your tits signed by a celebrity. Classy.*

"Breast-signing is so last season," a male voice says from behind me.

Laughing, I turn to see Robbi Kraft, lead singer of The Turnstiles. I'm a fan of their music, but I haven't officially met anyone from the band.

Robbi is very good-looking. The dangerous kind of good-looking. Dirty-blond hair. Inky blue eyes. Eyebrow pierced. Tattoos covering his arms and one on the side of his neck.

"Yeah, I hear it's all about ass-signings nowadays." I smirk.

Robbi laughs. He has a great laugh. It's not deep and manly like Tom's. It's a happy, contagious sound.

I watch Robbi's eyes work their way down my body before they land back on my face.

"Robbi." He holds a hand out to me.

"I know who you are." I smile shyly as I slide my hand into his. "Lyla—"

"Summers," he finishes for me. "I know who you are."

Blushing, I take my hand back.

"You sounded great before," Robbi says. "I really like your music."

"Thanks." I smile, pleased by his compliment. "I'm really looking forward to hearing you guys perform tonight. I've been following you since your Vegas days."

The Turnstiles started off by recording their live shows in Vegas and uploading them to YouTube. They quickly got a big following. On the heels of that came a record deal with none other than Rally Records.

I'm surprised Rally didn't try to put the kibosh on Vintage performing here at the same time as one of his bands.

*Or maybe he did, and I just don't know about it.*

Robbi pushes a hand into his blond hair and gives me a cocky grin. "A fan."

"Maybe." I shrug, biting my lip.

Butterflies have taken flight in my stomach. *What's that all about?*

Robbi's eyes move down to my empty hands. "You don't have a drink. I can't have a beautiful fan of ours watching the show without a drink. Let me buy you one?"

I don't get a chance to answer.

A guy with greasy long hair taps Robbi on the shoulder. "You're needed backstage. Seth and Dougie are going at it again."

Seth and Dougie are his band members. It's well known that members of The Turnstiles have a volatile relationship.

I couldn't imagine what that would be like, fighting with your band members all the time. I would hate it.

I'm lucky to have Cale, Sonny, and Van.

Robbi heaves out a sigh. "I'm coming," he says to greasy-hair guy. Robbi looks back to me. "I'm sorry. Gotta go – band stuff."

"It's okay." I offer him a smile. "Hope you get it sorted before you go onstage. I'd hate to miss out on hearing you play live tonight."

"Don't worry. I'm a pro at sorting those two out." He starts to leave but then turns back. "You never answered my question about whether you wanted that drink or not?"

Holding out my empty hands, I smile softly. "Guess you'll never know."

Putting his hand in his pocket, he pulls something out and takes a step toward me. "You ever feel like giving me the answer, call me." He presses a card into my hand. With a charming smile, he's gone, disappearing into the crowd.

I'm left with those damn butterflies and a tingly warm feeling in my chest.

I don't even get a chance to move when I hear Tom's voice in my ear. "So, are you gonna call him?"

The scent of him washes over me, and my earlier pep talk flies out the window.

"Seriously"—I round on him—"what is it with you tonight? Questioning if I'm sleeping with Cale and the rest of the male population. And now, Robbi?"

Tom studies my face for a moment. I can feel my body heating under his gaze.

He gives a wry smile. "I never asked if you were sleeping with Robbi. I asked if you were going to call him."

"Whatever," I bite out, my hands going to my hips. "Why the sudden interest in my love life?"

"Maybe I just care about your well-being."

I scoff at that notion.

His eyes narrow. "I'm just looking out for you. Robbi Kraft is a player."

"So are you!" I throw my hands up.

He leans into my face. His dark gaze penetrates me, and his heat is all over me, licking at my skin. He's confusing the hell out of me. And I don't like it one bit.

"That might be," he says, his voice rugged and low. "But I'm not trying to get into your panties."

I step back, shaking my cluttered mind. "Not anymore you're aren't, but you were not so long ago."

Then, it hits me, and I wonder if that's part of the problem. *Did I actually like it when Tom was hitting on me before? Does it bother me now that he's not?*

Suddenly, I feel like crying. My throat thickens, and my eyes water. My emotions are all over the place, and it's because of him. I pin my eyes to the floor, trying to regain control of my feelings.

Seeming to sense my rising emotions, he steps back, giving me space. In a kinder voice, he says, "I'm just looking out for you. Right now, on this tour, you're my responsibility. As your manager, I'm telling you, a girl like you does not want to call a guy like him."

My eyes snap to his. "A girl like me? What the hell is that supposed to mean?"

He runs his hand through his hair, tugging at the strands. He looks like he's struggling for words. "You're a good girl. Robbi's a bad guy. You're moving up, and he would drag you right back down. I know girls like you, Firecracker. And I know even more about guys like Robbi. He's not somewhere you want to go."

"You don't know me," I scoff.

He does know me, more than I care to admit. And that's because I can't seem to stop spilling my sad guts to him.

His eyes darken. "Yeah, I do."

I feel off balance. So, I do what I do best. I react to feelings I can't control.

I let out a hollow laugh. "You keep telling yourself that." I crumble up Robbi's card in my hand and toss it at Tom's chest. "You don't know shit about me. If you did, you would know that I had no intention of calling Robbi. I'm off men. Being screwed over by one will do that."

I turn to leave, but Tom pulls me back to him. With one hand on my arm, his other cups the side of my face.

"Who screwed you over?"

The concern on Tom's face sends my insides reeling. It's all too much to take at once.

I shake my head. "It doesn't matter."

"Sure seems like it matters. And I need to know whose ass I have to kick."

My eyes meet his. "Wouldn't that be considered fighting over a woman? Not something I thought you'd be down for."

Something in his eyes shifts. "We're friends. I don't like it if someone hurts my friends. I wouldn't see it as fighting over a woman...more like fighting *for* one."

*He thinks I'm worth fighting for.*

*Words, Lyla. They're just words.*

*Men are real good at words. Actions are where they fail.*

Needing a moment away from Tom, away from the ease of his touch and words, I move and sit down on the recently vacated sofa nearby.

Tom takes the empty space beside me, filling it up and putting himself close to me. He catches the attention of a passing waiter and orders us some drinks.

I don't start talking until I have my vodka and tonic in my hand.

Running my index finger up the side of the glass collecting condensation droplets, I let out a sigh. "My ex-boyfriend, Chad...is bisexual. Something he failed to tell me when we got together."

Tom stares at me. "Okay...so you went out with someone named Chad, who likes cock *and* pussy...and you didn't like that he used to bang dudes?"

"No. The problem was that it wasn't *used to*. He continued to bang dudes while we were together—well, not dudes. Just *one specific* dude."

*My brother.*

"He cheated on you," he murmurs in understanding.

91

He just doesn't get the whole picture.

I nod in answer, and then I take a large drink of my vodka, relishing the burn in my throat as I swallow.

"Well, I gotta say, you're starting to make a lot more sense to me now."

My eyes lift to his.

"And as for Chad, the cheating fuckhole of an ex—well, he's clearly an idiot. I mean, he had you...and *these*"—he gestures to my girls—"*the* best rack I have ever seen in my life. And I've seen a lot of tits—racks in my life. Chad had the best ever in his hands every day, literally, and he traded them for cock?"

"Um...thanks, I think."

"You're welcome," he deadpans. "Seriously, I don't get the whole dude-screwing-another-dude thing. Sure, I love to fuck ass but a woman's ass. You—I mean, women in general," he corrects, "are just pure sex. So soft and warm, and you have those"—he gestures to my girls again—"which are amazing. God was on the right track the day he designed women. Give me a tight, warm pussy any day, and I'm a happy man."

"Um...way too much info, Tom. Really. And isn't that the problem? You've been a happy man for a long time now. What will you do if you run out of women? You might have to turn to men."

He looks momentarily horrified at that thought. Then, relaxing, he settles back into the sofa, his arm going around behind me. "That'll never happen."

"You go through women at the speed of light. Even though you're seemingly having a hiatus or rest or whatever, you being you will restart, and it's possible that you could screw the entire female population of the U.S. by the end of this decade—excluding me, of course."

"Of course." He smirks, bringing his whiskey glass to his lips, and he takes a drink.

I ignore his pointed look. "So, what will you do then? Start recycling?"

He clanks his glass down on the table. "Nope. I'm not an environmentally friendly kind of guy. And just so you know, I might have gone through a lot of women in my time, but when I fuck—I fuck long and slow...real fucking *slow*."

An image of Tom and me having sex flashes through my mind.

My heart speeds up. I can feel my body heating at the thought of Tom and sex and me.

Him and me…fucking.

I know my chest is flushed. I don't have to look down to see. I know it is because Tom's eyes are on it, staring, right now.

Stupid, traitorous, underused, and currently oversexed body.

Tom's eyes lift, meeting mine, with knowledge.

Looking away, I force my spine straight as I hold the glass to my chest, trying to cool myself down. "And I need to know your screwing speed, why?"

He leans in close, real close this time, leaving our mouths centimeters apart.

I gulp down.

His whiskey-scented hot breath blows through my parted lips and fires down signals to my long-unused girl parts, sending them into a frenzy.

*Shit.*

Squeezing my thighs together, I bite down on my lower lip to regain control.

*I will not lose my shit over Tom.*

His eyes flicker down to my mouth. "You're not ready to hear the answer to that question."

"And what if I ever am—"

*What the hell am I saying?*

I'll never be ready for Tom "Screw Anything" Carter. Ever.

"I mean, if I am, at some point in the imaginary, not-real-ever future?"

I see surprise flicker over his face, but he quickly covers it with a grin.

"Well, on that *imaginary* day, you would let me know, and then I'd tell you. But until then, just use that *imagination* of yours."

He stands, running a hand through that outgrown sexy hair of his. "And, Lyla, let it run wild." With a wink, he's gone, sauntering through the bar, leaving me and underused girl parts on fire.

## A Few Days Later—Tour Bus, Somewhere Mid-America

My imagination did run wild, too freaking wild.

I spent the next few days thinking about Tom. It was way more time than a person should spend thinking of someone she's living with.

I also took a lot of cold showers, and during restless nights, I would try to expel the ache he left in me with my hand. I couldn't even use ASBOF because I was afraid the guys would hear the vibrations through these paper-thin walls. So, it was, *Hello, Hand*, for me.

But what's made things even harder for me is seeing a different side to the Tom Carter I thought I knew.

He's—dare I say it?—sweet. He's still pervy, but he's kind.

I like him—the Tom who resides inside the womanizing, hardened, bad-boy exterior.

Like tonight, I'm watching him play video games with the guys.

He is fun, like he always is, but he is also relaxed. No pretense, no guard up, no being the Tom Carter. He is just Tom.

Seeing him like this softens me to him even more than I already was.

After a night of the guys playing video games while I watch in between reading on my Kindle and making food for them— nothing out of the ordinary—we all decide to turn in early, and catch up on much needed rest since we didn't have a show tonight.

As it has been every night, after I climb into bed, I lie awake, staring at the ceiling, while I think of Tom and sex.

And sex with Tom.

Restless, I decide to get up and make myself a hot chocolate instead of trying to masturbate the ache away since that is clearly not working.

I'm hoping some cocoa will help me sleep.

If not, I'm hitting sleeping tablets next.

Quietly, I crack open my door, and I immediately hear the soft sounds of a guitar playing.

Seems I'm not the only one who can't sleep.

I tiptoe out into the hall, and when I pass the bunks, I find Tom's curtain is the only one open. My stomach flutters at the knowledge that he's out there, playing the guitar.

I stop just before the entryway to the living room area and watch from my vantage point. Tom is sitting on the sofa, one leg bent up, with Van's acoustic guitar in his hands. He's strumming the chords and softly singing the words to Justin Timberlake's "Cry Me a River."

I feel ignorant of the fact that I didn't even know he played anything outside of the bass—let alone, that he could sing.

He sounds…amazing.

And he looks…beautiful.

*Oh God.*

The way he sings. Eyes pressed close. Feeling the lyrics. Like on some level, he understands the pain of betrayal.

I stay where I am, watching, not wanting to encroach and break the song.

Partway through a line, one that really hits home for me, Tom's eyes flick open. His gaze hits straight onto mine.

I wonder how long he's known that I've been standing here.

His eyes on mine while he's singing, it feels like he's singing to me. Something coils around my chest, squeezing my heart tightly.

I expect him to stop singing, but he doesn't. He just holds my eyes and continues. So, I decide to join in. I take the seat before him, and I sing the lyrics that are etched into my mind.

I tortured myself with this song for months after I caught Dex and Chad together.

"I didn't know you could sing," I say as he strums the last chord. I prop my feet up onto the little coffee table between us.

He puts the guitar down beside him on the sofa. "I'm a man of many talents."

I bet he is. I think of the way his fingers were moving over the strings. Plus, he has had a lot of practice with his hands—

I scratch the thought of Tom and other women from my mind.

"I love that song." I might torture myself with it, but it is a beautiful tune.

"I know."

I give him a look of confusion. "How do you know?"

He puts his leg down. The sight of his bare feet does strange things to me, heating parts of me that have not seen any action for quite a while.

"Well, for starters, it's set as your ringtone, and you sing it a lot."

"I do?" *He noticed that?*

Nodding, he rubs his thumb along his lower lip. It's a ridiculously sexy movement.

"Yeah."

"It drives you nuts?" I smile, knowing it drives Cale mad.

He tilts his head to the side. A cheeky grin appears on his lips. "A lot of things you do drive me nuts, Firecracker. But listening to you sing isn't one of them."

A flush starts at my chest and ends at my virginia. I cross my legs, linking them at the ankles.

"You should perform it onstage sometime," he says.

*What?*

"You think?" Unconvinced, I lift a brow.

"I definitely think."

I fold my arms. "Okay, I'll sing it live, if you play the melody for me."

He lets out a laugh. "Not a chance."

"You got a little stage fright there, Carter?"

"Nice try. I'm not afraid of shit, and you know it. This one is all yours. Your show, your tour. You don't need me onstage with you. But this song, you singing it…the fans will love it. I'll teach Van the melody, and he can accompany you. That's all you're getting from me."

"Spoilsport." I stick my tongue out at him and get to my feet.

"I wouldn't stick your tongue out at me unless you intend to use it in the right way."

Pausing, I turn back to him. "You're disgusting."

"Just the way you like me." He stands, towering over me.

I feel very much like a *girl* in this moment.

My hands go to my hips. His eyes follow the movement.

"I never said I liked you."

"You never said you didn't."

"Dick."

"Dick? Yes, I have one." He leans in close. "And it's fucking *huge*."

I push a hand against his chest. Sparks ignite at the connection.

"Like I said…disgusting." I grin, so he knows I'm messing with him.

He tosses out a laugh. "As in…it's disgusting just how big my cock is."

A giggle escapes me. I could slap myself.

Turning, I say over my shoulder, "I've never seen it, so I can't comment."

"Easily rectified."

I spin around just as his hands are going to his jeans.

"Stop it!" I hold my hand up.

"Stop what?"

"Getting your…*thing* out."

"My cock?"

I nod.

"Say it, Firecracker."

"Say what?" I bite my lip. "Cock?"

His eyes flash with intensity and lust. My stomach tightens. Another flash of heat ignites between my legs.

He steps closer. "Say it again."

I should feel embarrassed, but I don't. This is the effect he has on me.

"Cock." I'm surprised by how breathy my voice sounds.

He touches his thumb to my lower lip. I hold my breath.

"Do you know that your mouth makes a perfect O when you say cock?"

Dumbstruck, I shake my head.

His eyes are on my lips.

And I can't move.

He's going to kiss me. It's actually going to happen.

There's no one awake to walk in and interrupt this time.

*Do I want him to kiss me?*

*Yes!*

*No.*

If he makes a move, I'll push him off.

I think.

He slides his fingers along my jaw, cupping it. His skin is rough against mine.

"Lyla…" he breathes my name.

I melt into a puddle on the floor.

Then, "Zzz-zzzz-zzzzz-hnggggggh-ppbhww-zzzzzzzz."

Tom's hand drops from my face.

We both look in the direction of the bunks and then back to each other as we burst into laughter, our kissing spell instantly broken.

I clap my hand over my mouth. "Sonny," I say, the word muffled under my palm.

Tom removes my hand from my mouth, but he doesn't let go, holding my hand between us.

"No kidding. The dude has the bunk across from mine, and only curtains are separating us, remember?"

It's hard for me to concentrate on anything but my hand in his, as he ever so lightly runs his thumb over the soft skin on the top of my hand.

"Of course. You must be missing sleep."

"Goes with the tour bus territory. I had to put up with Denny's snoring for years. Earbuds were my friend for a long time."

I'm smiling, but my heart is currently doing a thump-thump-thumpity-thump dance in my chest.

"Well, if you ever want a break from Sonny the Dragon Snorer, you can always take the bed."

"You offering to give me a side?" He tilts his head, grinning.

And that full body flush I always get under his scrutiny is back in force.

"If you want to get me in bed, Firecracker, you only have to tell me." His fingers tighten around my hand, gently squeezing.

I roll my eyes. "Ha! You wish. I'm offering you the bed, minus me. I'll take your bunk."

"And where would the fun be in that? Seems stupid for you to go in my bunk when we could both get a good night's sleep in the same bed."

I can't imagine getting a second of sleep with him lying beside me.

Knowing how much my body would like that, my brain quickly advises me that it would be the worst idea ever.

I tug my hand free and give him a gentle poke in that hard chest of his. "Nice try, Carter."

"What?" He holds up his hands in innocence, but his face shows me anything but.

"I'm not having sex with you."

His eyes widen. "Who said anything about sex? Jeez, Lyla, I was just talking about sleeping. You have a really dirty mind, you know."

I open my mouth to come back with a retort, but all that comes out is a scoffing sound. Heat creeps up my neck, and I turn my back on him. I walk through to the kitchen, and I reach up on my toes, opening the cupboard. "I'm making hot chocolate. You want some?"

"No, thanks."

I busy myself with getting a mug and the hot chocolate. I fill the kettle with water, plug it in and turn it on.

It's so quiet in here that I'm positive Tom has snuck off to bed, but when I turn, he's still here, shoulder leaning against the wall of the archway, as he watches me.

Half-smiling, I lean my back against the counter, curling my fingers around the edge. "You hanging around for a bit?"

He gives me a slow nod and then his eyes fix onto mine. "Are you over him?"

My body stiffens. "Am I over whom?"

"The ex—*Chad*," Tom says with a surprising level of venom.

And hearing Chad's name serves as a reminder of that night. The betrayal.

My hands slide from the counter and come around to my chest, pressing down on the ache I feel.

"Yeah, I'm over him. I have been for a while."

Tom's expression remains stoic. "But he's the reason you always sing 'Cry Me a River,' right?"

Shaken to the core, I realize that he's thought about this, thought about me. I shake my head gently. "What makes you think I sing that song because of him?"

He gives me a confounding look. "Because we're musicians, Ly. Music bleeds into everything we do. We tie all feelings—pain, happiness, anger, sorrow—to music…lyrics. I know he hurt you…*bad*. And that song isn't exactly light and roses, and you sing it all the time."

When I don't immediately respond, he says, "I have a song for every person I've lost."

I want to ask him about the tattoo on his back, but I chicken out.

Instead, I softly say the one person I know he's lost, "Jonny Creed."

Tom's face tightens, pain lancing through his eyes. He nods, and his voice is quiet as he says, "'Hear You Me.'"

"Jimmy Eat World?"

"His folks played it at his funeral. I've listened to it every day since."

In this moment, I hate that he's felt pain and still feels it now. It makes me want to go over to him and wrap my arms around him, hold him tight.

But, of course, I do nothing.

"'Cry Me a River' isn't Chad's song," I admit.

Tom gives a curious tilt of his head.

"I never told you who Chad cheated on me with." I take a deep breath, the pain in my chest bursting. "My brother."

Anger flashes through those green eyes. His expression is still stoic. He braces his arms above him. His hands are gripping the archway, lifting his T-shirt and giving me a glimpse of those fabulous abs of his.

See? Even now, at this moment, while rehashing painful past memories, the sight of him distracts me.

"Dex, my brother. Technically, he's my cousin, my Aunt Steph and Uncle Paul's son, but he was my brother where it counted." I press my hand to my chest. "After I caught them mid-act, Dex admitted that he and Chad had been having an affair for a month. Dex, aside from being my brother and best friend, was also lead guitarist in Vintage. We originally formed the band with Cale. After it happened"—I gestured, unable to say the words, *I made my best friends choose between him and me*—"he, um...left the band. We replaced him with Van. I haven't spoken to Dex since." My hands move to grip the counter edge again.

Tom hasn't said anything. He's just staring at me, his jade eyes piercing me, while he's working his jaw angrily.

I'm not sure as to where his anger is coming from. I can't believe he would be this angry for me. There definitely has to be some other reason.

Awkward in our silence and confused by his reaction, I start talking again, "The night I caught them together was the night we opened for you at Madison Square Garden. Afterward. While you were performing onstage."

Tom gives a slight nod, acknowledging but still saying nothing.

"Chad had come along to support us during our big night. After we went offstage, I lost the guys in the excitement, so I was wandering around, trying to find one of them. I got a bit lost, turned a corner, and stumbled upon a couple of guys going at it. I mean, they were actually having sex, and I saw it." From out of nowhere, my eyes fill with tears, my lip trembling.

"Jesus, Lyla."

The next thing I know, Tom is pulling me hard to his chest, and his arms are around me, holding me.

*Tom is hugging me.*

Surprised by his act of compassion, I freeze for a moment before relaxing into him. I slide my arms around his waist until I'm pressing my palms on his back, ignoring how very right this feels.

"I'm sorry that happened to you." He runs his hand up my back, his fingers playing over the exposed skin from my tank.

From just those slight touches of his skin on mine, my body is calling for so much more of him. I can only imagine what it would feel like to have his hands all over my body, his lips on mine…him inside me.

I swallow down. "Dex calls me every day. I don't answer. I have 'Cry Me a River' set for him to remind me of how much he hurt me, so I don't weaken and answer, which is why the song is always in my head."

"That's not healthy, Firecracker." His hand gently strokes my hair.

"I know," I say quietly. "But it's all I got right now."

I hear and feel a murmur of understanding rumble through his chest.

"And you don't answer his calls because you don't know how to forgive him."

"No," I whisper into his shirt.

His mouth is close to my hair, his breath blowing through the strands.

"Forgiveness is the hardest thing in the world to give. It can take some people a long time to get there. And some never get there at all."

My heart ratchets up a beat. I lift my head from his chest, looking up at him.

"Just don't beat yourself up on the trek to it." He's smiling at me softly. He tips my chin up with his fingers. "You know, the more I learn about you, Firecracker, the more you make sense to me."

I don't even ask what he means by that. I'm not ready to dig any deeper into this moment than what's already happening.

"So, aside from the music torture, you're doing okay?" His beautiful eyes are boring into mine.

Tenderness rises in me. I stare right back into his sincere eyes and then at his mouth. The mouth I'm so desperate to reach up and kiss.

I move my eyes past him. "I'm doing okay."

His fingers move from my chin to tuck my hair behind my ear. "Well, if you find you ever get stuck…you know, getting there, I'm here."

Looking back to him, I smile. "How do you manage to make everything sound dirty?"

He laughs lightly. "I don't, Firecracker. Like we established before, you just have a dirty mind."

Shaking my head, I chuckle as I press my palm flush against his chest. I can feel his heart pounding beneath my hand.

"Thank you," I say with sincerity.

"Nothing to thank me for." He releases me, stepping away. "I'm gonna hit the sack now—*alone*." He emphasizes the last word. "So, don't try to follow me to bed."

"Good night, Tom." I force a smile, feeling bereft without his touch, and squashing the feeling of disappointment that he's going to bed.

I turn back to making my hot chocolate.

"Ly?" Tom says.

"Yeah." I look at him over my shoulder.

"Not all men are cheating idiots. Rally, Dex, Chad—all muts."

"Muts," I agree with nod.

"Your guy is out there. One who won't be a mut. There's a guy who deserves an awesome girl like you."

My heart starts thumpity-thumping again.

And I can't help but hear that ridiculous, over-romanticized voice in the back of my mind that's telling me if I ever saw stupid and trusted a guy in that way again...then I would want it to be Tom.

# A Few Days Later—Sketchy-Looking Bar at a Truck Stop, Somewhere Between Kansas and Missouri

We're seven days into the tour. We've already done six shows.

I'd say I'm exhausted, and I am, but I'm loving every minute of it!

We're currently somewhere between Kansas and Missouri in a bar called—

Actually, I have no clue what the name of the bar is.

Before heading to Jefferson City to play a show tomorrow night, we have a rare night off.

And we're at a truck stop.

When on the road, glamour doesn't come into it.

I did just want to chill and have a quiet night on the bus, but the guys talked me into coming out for dinner with everyone.

So, here I am, finishing off my fries after eating half of a very questionable burger.

The food might be a bit sketchy here, but the beer on tap rocks! I'm two pints in and ready for another. I'm ready for that other beer because I've had to endure watching Ashlee paw over Tom during the entire dinner. Granted, he's kept his hands to himself, but it hasn't stopped him from flirting right back with her.

And he's barely spoken to me—let alone, looked at me.

Hard to take when I've had his attention all week.

Yes, I know exactly how I sound, which is why I'm seriously considering banging my head against this table any second now.

"You all right, honey?" Shannon pulls up a chair beside me at the end of the table.

"I'm great." I give her a megawatt smile to emphasize the fact that I really am.

Even though I'm kind of not.

I'm feeling all these confusing things about Tom. The more time I spend with him, the more I like him.

But I don't want to like him. I can't like him.

And it really pisses me off when I have to see other women all over him.

I know it's irrational, and it's my shit to deal with, but that doesn't make it hurt any less, especially when it's happening right in front of me.

I've really gotten to like Shannon after spending more time with her. Ashlee, not so much. If she's not hitting on my boys or Tom, she's busy looking in the mirror.

Shannon smiles at me and pats my hand. "Honey, when a girl tells me she's all right and I get to see all her teeth in that smile, then I know she's far from all right." She looks down the table at Tom and then back to me.

"It's Tom, right?" she asks, lowering her voice.

Realizing that I'm worrying my lower lip with my teeth, I immediately stop it, freeing my lip. "I'm fine. Maybe just a bit tired, but that's it."

She smiles and shakes her head. "He's not interested in Ashlee. If he wanted her, he would have done her by now, probably in the restroom. I know Tom. Spent a long time on the road with him and the boys way back when. If Tom wants something, he just takes it. No foreplay—in the figurative sense." She takes a drink of her beer, reminding me that I'm in dire need of another.

"I know you said nothing is going on between you and Tom. Tom also heavily highlighted that fact to me. Sure, there might not be anything physical going on between the two of you, but currently, the level of sexual tension between you and Tom is enough to light the whole city of LA for a year."

I stare at her. "Don't be crazy." I sweep her statement away with my hand.

"Deny it all you want, but I see what I see. And what I see is some serious eye-fucking going on between you two. Either Tom is a changed man—he has seemed different lately—or you're holding off on him, which I can't figure out. Any red-blooded woman would be dragging that man back to her bed and not letting him out for days. And I speak from experience there."

I can't help it. I wince at the reminder of the fact that Shannon and Tom have history—of the sexual kind.

"See!" She points a red talon at my face. "There it is. It bothers the crap out of you whenever I mention me screwing Tom years ago. Girl, you have the serious hots for him. And he clearly has them for you. So, do something about it before someone else turns his head, and you're left wishing you had." She picks her beer up as she stands and sashays back over to her table.

*If only it were that easy...*

I pick up my glass to have a drink, and then I remember it's empty. *Fuck.* I decide to hit the restroom first before getting another drink.

On my way back to the bar, a few women pass me, and I hear them gushing excitedly about Tom Carter being in the bar. I guess he's been spotted.

I feel a sudden sense of privilege in this moment. I sleep under the same moving roof as Tom. I've seen the dude freshly showered and wearing only a towel. I get to talk with him all the time. He's become a real friend to me over this past week.

I guess these women would think I'm lucky.

Maybe I am, and I just don't appreciate it.

Or maybe this is just the beer talking.

Smiling to myself, I step back into the bar area, and that's when I see Tom standing at the bar. And there's a pretty bottle-blonde woman with hair down to her tiny waist, legs like bar stools, and big boobs that look real. And Tom is looking at them with full appreciation.

*She's his ideal.*

I feel a war of emotions all at once. Witless—and yes, jealous—I decide against going to the bar, and I grit my teeth as I head back to our table.

*Why the hell am I bothered that Tom's talking to the blonde?*

*For the same reason I was bothered by him flirting with Ashlee.*

I glance at Ashlee, and she looks seriously pissed at losing Tom to some random bar chick.

*She's jealous just like I am.*

God, it would be funny if it wasn't so depressing.

"I got you another drink," Cale says, handing me a fresh beer.

"Thanks." I smile at him gratefully as I sit down.

"Ly," Sonny catches my attention. "We were just saying, it looks like Tom will be getting some tonight. I thought he'd be doing Ashlee, but I'm thinking it's gonna be this chick at the bar. About time, if you ask me. He's been low-key since we got on the road. It's time Tom got in the game. Looks like you're giving up the bedroom tonight." Sonny nudges my arm, grinning.

I'm instantly irritated. Mix that with jealously and you've one very sour Lyla.

*Over my dead body. Tom is not screwing her in my bed tonight—or ever.*

Giving a noncommittal shrug, I turn away and gulp down a mouthful of beer.

"Another five minutes," Van says, "and Tom will be out of here and banging her. Lucky bastard. She's hot as hell."

"Five minutes?" Sonny laughs. "More like two."

I'm blaming the beer for the next words out of my mouth. "I bet you fifty dollars that Tom doesn't have sex with that blonde tonight."

*What am I doing? Stop, Lyla. Stop now.*

But I can't stop because I've said it, and now, Sonny is glaring at me with his gambling face on.

If there's one thing that Sonny can't resist, aside from women, it is a bet.

"One hundred dollars," Sonny drawls. "Because I'm that fucking sure he will."

"Done." I stick my hand out.

Sonny shakes it. "You're gonna be changing your bedsheets in the morning," he incites. "And I'm gonna be a hundred bucks up."

He's goading me.

Did I mention I have a competitive streak?

Ignoring him, I twist in my seat, praying to God that Tom has not left the bar with the blonde already. I look for him while I figure out how I'm going to win this bet.

He's still here, and he's not kissing her. Good sign.

But she's all over him, and he's not pushing her off.

Tom glances across the bar at me. I quickly look away.

I wait a few seconds and then look back.

The blonde is whispering in his ear. He laughs. Then, his hand comes to rest intimately on her hip.

I start to feel a bit sick.

He can't have sex with her because…because…

I can't lose this bet. If I lose, I'll never hear the end of it from Sonny.

Chaka Khan's "Ain't Nobody" starts to play in the bar. The blonde seems to get overly excited by the song.

She slips her leg in between Tom's, straddling his thigh. She starts to gyrate against his leg—well, *gyrate* is putting it cleanly. She's dry-fucking his leg.

*Shit.*

He'll have her bent over the bar, and be doing her in seconds at this rate.

My eyes squeeze painfully shut on the thought. My fingers curl into my palms, nails biting into my skin.

And that's the reason for what I do next. I'm blaming Chaka Khan for initiating dry-leg-fucking, and I'm sticking with it.

Nothing to do with the fact that I'm sick with jealousy.

Nope, nothing to do with it at all.

I stand, picking up my beer, and head straight for Tom and his blonde groupie. I'm so beyond ready to put an end to their little show that it's not even funny.

Tom's eyes flicker up at my approach. There's a note of wariness in his look. Then, he smiles—no, he grins, which pisses me off to no end.

*Bastard.*

My blood starts to boil.

"I just can't fucking believe this!" I cry at Tom.

The blonde jerks away from him at the sound of my wailing.

"I can't believe that you're doing this to me—*again!*" I thrust my hand out at him.

Shock slackens his features.

"You promised you loved me!" I say in a whiny voice, making strangled noises like I'm about to start bawling. I even wipe my nose on my sleeve for effect.

"You promised this wouldn't happen again! After the last time, when I caught crabs from you, I had to go to the doctor and have all that smelly medicine spread all over my vagina! I trusted you when you said it wouldn't happen again! But here we are—*again*—with another groupie!"

I throw my arms up just for good measure. A bit of beer sloshes from the glass onto my wrist.

"You're a lying, cheating son of a bitch, Tom Carter! We're so fucking over that it's not even funny! One hundred percent *over!*"

Tom opens his mouth to speak, but I don't give him a chance.

I chuck my beer in his face.

The blonde jumps back, avoiding the splash.

It's then I realize the whole bar is silent. Chaka Khan has stopped singing, and all eyes are on me.

*Shit. Fuckity fuck.*

I think I might have gotten a little carried away.

Tom drags a hand down his face, clearing the beer away.

Reaching over, I place my now empty glass on the nearest table. "Okay…well, I think it's time for me to go."

I give an uneasy smile to the bartender who is staring at me from behind the bar.

Avoiding Tom's eyes, I turn on my heel and quickly make my way back to the guys. Eyes down, I don't look up until I reach our table.

The guys are looking at me like I've grown three heads, but I catch the knowing smirk on Shannon's face.

"Um…what the hell was that?" Sonny practically growls at me.

"That was me winning our bet." I give him a smug smile as I lift my hand to my mouth. I lick the sticky beer droplets from my wrist. "Cough up. I believe you owe me one hundred dollars."

"Holy shit!" Van laughs. "She totally stung you, man."

Grinning at me with admiration, Van lifts his hand to me, so of course, I have to high-five him.

Sonny gives us both a dirty look, and then he reaches into his pocket. After pulling out my winnings, he dumps two fifties onto my outstretched hand.

"Nice doing business with you. I'll see you boys back on the bus."

Then, I'm out of there lickety-split, ignoring the look Cale is giving me. The one that's saying, *We'll be having words later.*

When I hit the nighttime air, I stop, my heart pounding like a bitch in my chest.

*Oh my God! I can't believe I just did that!*

A strangled laugh escapes me.

I start walking again, but the farther from the bar I get, the realization of what I just did in starts to sink in.

I just made a public scene and threw beer in Tom's face.

People will now think he and I are together.

And Tom is famous. Really famous. Stunts like the one I just pulled are newsworthy.

*No, it'll be fine.* I can't imagine anyone in there being the type to call up the tabloids.

I'm halfway across the parking lot, heading for the bus, when Tom's voice rumbles out like thunder from behind me.

"What the *fuck* was that?"

I turn slowly. The fierce look on his face makes me almost buckle under the pressure.

I steel my confidence, keeping my expression neutral. I place my hands on my hips. "You're welcome," I say, giving some attitude.

His eyes narrow. "I'm welcome?" He takes a few steps toward me, his long legs eating up the space between us.

I fight the urge to back up.

"Welcome for what exactly? You screaming at me like a banshee in a public bar or for the beer you threw in my face?" He slashes a hand down his beer-soaked T-shirt, which is clinging to his hard chest and thick biceps and—

*Focus, Lyla.*

"Um…for saving you," I say calmly. I feel anything but calm. My insides are rattled, and my thoughts are swirling like a storm.

"Saving me? From what?"

I give him a duh look. "From the blonde who wouldn't leave you alone."

His face goes from angry to confused and straight back to angry.

"You're telling me that all that in there was because you thought I needed saving from the hot blonde who was minutes away from sucking my dick?" He takes another seething step closer. "Have you forgotten who I am? I'm not the fucking pope, Lyla! I'm Tom Carter, and it's well known that I *really* like hot blondes, especially ones who are more than willing to get down on their knees and suck my cock!" Another step. "And just because you haven't seen that from me this past week doesn't make it any less true."

His words pierce my chest like a knife. I shrink back.

"Okay, I'm sorry. I didn't know you wanted her." *Jesus, those words hurt.* "I thought I was helping. I just…well, it seemed like you didn't want women all over you, considering what happened with Shannon on the first day, and I bet Sonny—"

*Shit.*

Those jades of his narrow to slits. "You bet Sonny what?"

I swallow down. "Nothing. I bet nothing."

I turn to leave, more than ready to chickenshit my way out of this and hightail it back to the bus, but Tom catches my upper arm, pulling me back to him.

"Finish the rest of that sentence."

"Fine." I blow out a breath, removing my arm from his hand.

I push my hair back off my face and lift my chin. "Sonny was giving me a hard time, saying that you were going to sleep with that blonde and I'd have to give up my bed so that you could use it to do...*whatever* with her." I wave my hand, trying not to choke on the words.

"So, I bet Sonny that you wouldn't have sex with her because I actually thought you, um...wouldn't."

He lifts a brow, which does nothing for my confidence.

"Well, it was just...from things you've said to me and the whole Shannon thing and, um...just the way you've been in general...so, yeah." I straighten my back and look him in the eye. "And because of those things, I thought my money was safe...but then you started looking like you were actually going to do something with her and, um"—the words are sticking in my throat—"I, um...didn't want to lose the bet." I look away.

*Liar.*

*I didn't want you to have sex with her because the thought of it makes me feel sick.*

Blinking, I look up at him.

The look on his face. He's pissed off, sure, but he looks...hurt. I can see it there in the depths of his eyes.

And I feel like the bitch I am.

It's too hard to look at him and say what I'm about to say, so I stare over his shoulder to the glowing lights of the bar behind him. "Look it was a real shitty thing to do...and I'm sorry, all right?"

His face is blank, but his eyes are saying a hell of a lot right now. None of it is good.

"How much?" His tone is brittle.

"What?" I look at him.

His eyes cut to mine. "How much fucking money did you bet Sonny?"

I swallow what feels like gravel. "Does it matter?"

"How. Much?"

"A hundred dollars." I'm trembling on the inside.

Tom's eyes widen, and he lets out an incredulous laugh. "A hundred dollars. That's all I'm worth?" He thrusts his hands through his hair before linking them behind his neck. "Jesus Christ!" His gaze rips through me. "Nice, Lyla. Real fucking nice."

"Look, I said I'm sorry." I frown.

He drops his arms and folds them over his chest. "Did Sonny pay up?"

I know I'm stepping into something I really don't want, but I have no other choice. "Yes."

In one swift move, he pulls off his beer-soaked T-shirt, exposing that smooth expanse of total awesomeness. He shoves the shirt in the back pocket of his jeans, and then he's moving. In a few steps, he's on me, right up close. His chest is in my face. He's everywhere, consuming me. I can't breathe. I have to practically nail my feet to the ground to keep me from moving.

I tilt my head back to look up at him just as he leans down into my face.

He smells of beer. But mostly Tom. Everything that makes my toes curl.

"Okay, this is how it's gonna go. You're gonna go back to that bar. You're gonna hand Sonny two hundred dollars—his own hundred back and the hundred for the bet you lost."

My brows draw together. "I didn't lose—"

"No, but you're going to in about five minutes. Lucky for me, the blonde wasn't put off by your little show in there. She's coming here, and I'm taking her up onto the bus and into *your* bedroom where I'm gonna spend all night fucking her brains out while you sit outside, one hundred dollars lighter, listening to the kind of sex a frigid bitch like you could only dream of having."

If he'd shot me, I don't think it would have hurt as much.

Tears sting my eyes. "Fuck you!" I yell, shoving him away. I turn and start to run toward the bus.

I just want to get away from him and to rid myself of this goddamn pain in my chest.

I almost make it to the bus, but Tom catches me and shoves me hard up against the side of the bus. My breath leaves me in a whoosh.

"That's what you want, isn't it?" He presses his body onto mine.

My body starts to tremble.

"Me to fuck you. You were jealous, Firecracker. Admit it. That's why you pulled your little stunt back there."

I let out a laugh, but it sounds hollow, even to my own ears. "Jealous? You wish! I wouldn't want you if you were the last man on Earth!" I'm saying this, but it's clearly not true.

And he knows it.

If he can't tell from the trembling of my body or my quick breaths or the fact that my eyes are glued to his lips, then all he would need to do is put his hand on my panties, and the damp evidence would be there for his confirmation.

"Yeah, well, the feeling is one hundred fucking percent mutual, sweetheart."

He's saying this, but I can tell from his quick breaths, the dilation of his pupils, and the fact that he's dragging his teeth over his lower lip that he's lying. And even if there weren't all those signs, then his huge erection, which is currently pressed into my belly, would have told me all I needed to know.

"I think you're a disgusting man slut," I hiss, smoothing my hand up his bare chest.

His body shudders under my touch.

*God, he feels so damn good.*

Tom's hand runs up my arm, skimming the edge of my breast. His fingers slide into my hair, and he pulls it down, tilting my face up to his. "And like I said, I think you're a frigid bitch."

I glare into his eyes. "I fucking hate you," I seethe. But my voice sounds really breathless. Sexy breathless. I don't sound like me at all.

He moves his mouth closer to mine. "Yeah, and that feeling is *more* than mutual."

We're locked together. Chests heaving. Neurons of sexual chemistry firing between us like bullets.

And I know all it's going to take is one more move from either of us and we'll be kissing.

*Is that what I want?*

I lick my lower lip.

The last thing I register is Tom growling out, "Fuck!"

Then, his mouth is on mine, hard and fast.

On a groan, I open up for him. His hot tongue plunges straight into my mouth, and he starts kissing me like a man starved. My hands go straight to his hair, and I attack his mouth with the same ferocity.

Tom's large hands go to my ass, and he lifts me. I wrap my legs around his waist, linking them at the ankles.

In this position, his erection is now nicely pressed up against the seam of my jeans, sending my whole body into a frenzy.

I moan. I can't help it.

Seeming to like my response, Tom moves his hips back, and then he thrusts upward.

"Oh God," I whimper. My eyes rolling, my head drops back against the bus with a thud.

Letting out a groan-fuelled chuckle, Tom starts on my neck, kissing and sucking his way back to my mouth. The whole time, he is torturously rubbing that amazing erection of his against my hot spot.

When his mouth reaches mine, he hesitates. Eyes on my face, he slowly moves his hand under my shirt.

Letting him know that I'm okay with the direction where this is heading, I run my tongue along his lower lip, and then I suck it into my mouth.

Tom's hand cups my breast through my bra. His rough fingers trace over my hard nipple through the lace.

"Jesus, Lyla." Staring down at my breasts, he lets out a groan. "Your tits feel even better than they look. So fucking good. I can't wait to have them in my mouth." His tongue trails his lower lip as he gives my breast a squeeze.

A lightning bolt of lust shoots straight to my core.

Bringing his mouth back to mine, he runs his tongue along the seam of my lips and then takes me into a deep lush kiss.

I turn to putty in his hands as he takes control of the kiss.

Takes control of me.

My fingers tighten in his hair. He groans in my mouth.

*Weak spot.*

I smile to myself.

Then, I hear the sound of loud voices. Cale, Sonny, and Van are heading straight in our direction.

Tom's mouth disconnects from mine.

"Shit," I gasp.

I stare into his eyes, unsure what to do. I don't want the guys to see Tom and me together like this. And I'm thanking God right now that the bus parked next to ours is shielding us.

"We need to move," I urge.

Nodding, Tom lowers me to my feet. Grabbing my hand, he pulls me toward the back of the bus, getting us out of view. We stand here with a foot of space between us, just staring at one another, as the guys all pile onto the bus.

When the sound of them has settled, Tom says quietly, "You go on first. I'll follow in a minute."

He glances down, and my eyes follow, seeing that he's still very hard.

*How is that even possible?*

"Um…where was I?" I ask him.

He gives me a sexy grin. "Just a few feet down there with your legs wrapped around my waist, moaning into my mouth, while I dry-humped you against the bus."

"I didn't mean that!" I slap his stomach, hitting rock. "I meant, where do I tell the guys I've been?"

He shrugs. "Just tell them you were making out with a hot stranger in the parking lot."

I jab him in the arm this time.

"Ow!" he whisper-shouts, rubbing his shoulder.

*Like I could hurt him.*

I roll my eyes.

Tom glances over his shoulder at the lit store behind us. "Just tell them you went to the store."

"Good plan." I nod.

"What about me? Where was I?" he asks.

I give him a saucy grin. "Tell them you were making out with a hot chick in the parking lot."

His hands come up to the sides of my head, caging me in against the bus. "Talking of hot…" His mouth starts to descend toward mine.

"No." I press my hands against his chest, stopping him.

The one thing the guys turning up gave me was clarity, reminding me of what I don't want to do.

My body was in the driver's seat for a while. Now, my brain is back and functioning.

"No?"

"No." I duck out from under his arms. "This was a mistake."

He looks over his shoulder at me. "A mistake? Are you fucking kidding?"

Biting my lip, I shake my head. "It shouldn't have happened. And it won't happen again."

Turning, he steps into my space. "It should have happened a long time ago. And it for sure will happen again."

"No, it won't."

His slow smile causes my belly to whoosh.

"We'll see." He walks away from me, heading in the direction of the front of the bus.

*That's it?*

I expected him to fight me on it more.

Then worry grips tight hold of me. What if he's going to collect what he's not getting from me from the blonde groupie, who's due to show up here any moment.

"Where are you going?" I despise how needy my voice sounds.

He turns to me, continuing to walk backward. "Shower. I stink of beer." He gives me a look. "Then, to bed."

*With her.*

I grit my teeth. "With your blonde skank?"

I really need to filter this crap coming from my mouth.

He grins, and it spreads right across his handsome face. "Nope. Haven't got a clue where she is."

"But you said..." I frown.

He gives a slow shrug of his shoulders. "Never intended to sleep with her. I was just"—Tom rubs his head thoughtfully and then smirks—"putting on a show."

*Mother. Effer.*

He played me.

All that in there—he was just doing it to drive my jealousy to the front.

"You-you're a...mother-effing *mut*!" I hiss.

"Yeah, and you're the sexiest fucking thing I've ever seen in my life. Sleep well, Firecracker." He winks and then climbs up onto the bus, disappearing from my view.

I fall back against the bus.

Touching a finger to my lips, I realize that I'm actually smiling.

Then, a giggle escapes me.

I've just been dry-humped against the side of a tour bus by Tom Carter.

And I wanted it.

I want him. Really bad.

Well, there goes my chastity. That belt has been snapped in two and fed to the cock wolves.

And me? Well, I'm in big trouble. Not only did I want Tom before, but now, I want him even more after that kiss.

## The Next Day—Tour Bus, St. Louis

Avoidance is my friend.

When I climbed back onto the bus a few minutes after Tom, he was laughing and joking with the guys, acting like nothing had happened between us only moments before.

Of course, that was good. It was exactly what I wanted.

But the sexual tension between us was still there, smoldering with intent. It was to the point that I thought it was going to actually drive me insane.

I tried my best to act natural, but it was difficult. Every time Tom spoke, I would remember the feel of his lips on mine.

Cale knew something was off with me, and his questioning eyes weren't helping my overall state. It was hard to keep myself in check when he pulled me aside and quietly asked what my stunt in the bar was all about.

He knew that was out of the ordinary for me.

I played it off. He wasn't convinced, but thankfully, he didn't argue me on it. Van and Sonny were oblivious. Sonny was still grumpy because he'd lost our bet.

It was long after that when I went to bed.

I woke up early, feeling restless, but I stayed in bed, not wanting to get up and risk finding myself alone with Tom. So, I waited until I heard the noise levels rise as the boys all crawled out of their bunks, and then I made an appearance.

I could feel Tom's eyes on me when I came out to have breakfast, but I steadfastly ignored his gaze.

From now on, my plan is to avoid being alone with Tom under any circumstances.

It's going okay so far.

Tom is currently in my bedroom on a conference call with Jake and Zane.

The guys and I are going over a song we've decided to add to the set. It's a song I wrote a long time ago. I could never get the sound to work, but Van has come up with an amazing riff for it, which gives it the perfect tone. We've decided to try it out on the crowd tonight and see how it goes down.

I feel Tom enter the living area before I see him. That has been happening more and more lately, like I'm connected to him in some way.

He has his cell in his hand. "Got a minute, guys? I've got Jake and Zane still on the line. A few things are moving forward, and we want to bring you up to speed."

I put my music sheets on the coffee table, but I keep my pen in my hand.

Tom places his cell in the middle of the table. He stays standing. "Jake, Zane, you're good to go."

"Hey, how's it going?" Jake asks.

"Really great," I answer for us.

"Cool. Okay, so we've made some decisions on how we're going to move forward with you guys. Actually, this is Zane's baby, so I'll let him tell you."

"Hey, guys," Zane speaks.

"Hi," we all say in unison.

"So, like Jake said, we've been working on things here. The album is cut, so Jake, Tom, and I have been discussing which song should be released first. Of course, you guys had input before you left for the tour, and I know you all felt that 'Nonsense' would be better as your first release. But after tests and looking at the market lately, we think that 'Better Than You' would be the perfect song to release first."

There's a silence, and then Zane says, "What do you think?"

I think on it for a moment and then look around the table.

We're all looking at one another, waiting to see what the others think.

"What do you think, Ly?" Cale asks, the first one to break the silence.

It is a great song with commercial appeal, and I can see why they want to put it out first.

"It's a great song," I echo my thoughts. "I'm happy with that if you're happy with that."

"What about you guys?" Cale asks Sonny and Van.

"I'm easy," Sonny says. "Just happy to be cutting a record and touring."

"What he said." Van smiles.

"So, we're good?" Cale checks with me.

For some reason, I feel the need to look at Tom, almost like I need his reassurance on this.

My eyes slide to his. His are already on mine.

For the first time since last night, I actually speak directly to him. "You think it's the right song?"

I see a flicker of surprise in his eyes, and then his expression softens.

"Yeah, I do." He smiles. "The track will bring the right kind of attention to you. The kind of attention we want."

I look back to Cale, who is glancing between Tom and me with a furrow of confusion in his brow.

"Then, yeah, we're good," I finally answer Cale's question.

"Okay, so that's settled," Jake says.

"Zane's team will hit up the radio stations across the country. We'll concentrate mostly here in LA, but we'll also hit all the areas where you're playing now. We're going for big coverage and fast. Then, we'll see how it goes from there."

"Sounds great," Cale leans forward to say.

"So, I think we're done here," Zane speaks. "Unless there's anything else anyone needs to talk about?"

"Nothing else from me," Jake says. "Wait. What?"

Jake's voice is muffled as he starts talking to someone in the background.

I hear the words, "What the fuck?"

Then, "Jesus fucking Christ."

"Jake, all okay?" Zane says.

"Tom, take me off speaker. Now. Zane, I'll call you after I've talked with Tom."

Frowning, Tom scoops up his cell and takes it off speaker before pressing his phone to his ear.

I watch as he walks into my bedroom and closes the door behind him. I get an uneasy feeling in my gut.

"Wonder what that was about?" Van asks the table.

I shrug. "Beats me. Probably TMS stuff." Even as I say it, it doesn't feel right.

It's feels like—

*Oh no.*

*Holy fucking no.*

121

I quickly pull out my cell phone from my pocket and type into the search engine, *Tom Carter. Lyla Summers.*

Then, I press enter.

And I watch in horror, my stomach sinking, as my screen fills with headlines and pictures of Tom and me.

### THE MIGHTY STORM'S TOM CARTER CAUGHT CHEATING BY THE GIRLFRIEND WE DIDN'T KNOW HE HAD!

### WATCH THE EXCLUSIVE VIDEO FOOTAGE OF TOM'S GIRLFRIEND CATCHING HIM WITH ANOTHER WOMAN. JUST MAKE SURE TO STAND BACK TO AVOID THE SPLASH!

### TOM CARTER, WE THOUGHT YOU WERE SMARTER!

### BAD BOY OF ROCK, TOM CARTER, CAUGHT CHEATING! FULL CONFRONTATION CAUGHT ON VIDEO! WATCH HERE!

### CARTER CAUGHT CHEATING!

*Ladies' man of rock and The Mighty Storm's bassist, Tom Carter was caught cheating by his girlfriend in a bar last night. According to onlookers, Tom was flirting up a storm with a leggy blonde. Before leaving with her, his girlfriend came storming over. We have confirmed his girlfriend is Lyla Summers, lead singer of up and coming band, Vintage.*

*A patron at the bar said, "She was wailing at him, calling him a liar and a cheat. Then, she threw her drink all over him and left. Tom went chasing after her."*

*If only he would come chasing after us!*

*Right now, we should thank the storm gods because someone caught the full action on video.*

*For the full stormy show, watch below.*

*Oh, holy crapping mother of God.*

## Sixty Seconds Later—Lyla's Bedroom, Tour Bus, St. Louis

"Are you fucking Lyla?" Jake's hard voice comes at me the instant I press the phone to my ear.

Unwilling to have this conversation in front of an audience, I wait until I've shut the bedroom door before responding.

"No, I'm not fucking Lyla," I grind out.

"Are you saying what you think I wanna hear or the truth?"

I clench my jaw, shoulders stiffening. One thing I don't ever do is lie. And I don't like being accused of it by anyone, especially someone who knows me as well as Jake does.

"It's the truth. Have I ever lied to you before? No, and you fucking know it. You might not like the truths I've told you in the past, but they were just that—the truth. So, if anything, that should one hundred percent tell you that I don't fucking lie. Have I kissed Lyla? Yes, last night, as a matter of fact. But fucked her? No." *Sadly.*

"Jesus, Thomasina. Calm the fuck down. Are you PMSing right now?"

"Ha!" I laugh. "Not fucking likely. I'm not the one who's grown a vagina, remember?"

"Screw you." He laughs.

The tension I felt with Jake is gone, but there's still some remaining, and it has everything to do with a certain little blonde out there.

"So, I'm guessing you haven't been on the Internet this morning?" Jake asks.

"No. Do I need to?"

"Yeah. There's a video doing the rounds on all the gossip sites, showing you and Lyla in a bar last night. You know, the bar where you were with some blonde chick, and Lyla was yelling at you before she proceeded to chuck a drink all over you—which was perfectly timed, might I add. Tru just showed me the video."

*There's a video of that?*
*Of course, there's a video of it.*
"Shit," I exhale.
"What happened, man?"
I press the heel of my hand against my eye, rubbing it. "It was something and nothing. Lyla just had this bet with Sonny that I wouldn't score with the blonde I was talking to. She doesn't like to lose, so she made sure she didn't."
Jake lets out a laugh. "Jesus, she's a live wire that one."
"Yeah. No fucking kidding."
"So, did you kiss her before or after the beer drowning?"
"After. I chased her out of the bar. We argued. Minutes later, I had my mouth on hers. Her ass was in my hands, and her legs were wrapped around me while I dry-humped her against the side of the bus."
Jake laughs. "And you didn't have sex with her?"
He's surprised, which isn't surprising because usually nothing stops me from having sex.
"We were interrupted."
"And when has that bothered you before?"
"I didn't stop for my benefit, assface. Lyla's not that kind of girl."
And for some unfathomable reason, I didn't want the first time I had sex with her to be against the side of this bus.
Not that I'd admit that to Jake. I'd never hear the end of it.
"Well, as interesting as it is to hear about you dry-humping the lead singer of my act, let me remind you that she is just that—the lead singer of my act. The act you're managing."
I rub a hand over my hair. "I know. I fucked up."
"I wouldn't say you fucked up. Lyla made an unwise move in the bar. But, man, come on, I know how it is on the road."
"Yeah, but things are different. I'm trying to be different."
Jake lowers his voice. "I know. But you don't have to be."
"Yeah, I do."
There's an unwritten silence between us.
I break it. "We need to do damage control on the video."
"Yeah, we do. Leave it to me. I'll get Stuart and Zane on it."
Stuart is Jake's PA, and a fucking expert at cleaning up our messes. "I don't know how much I can do since it's already out there, but we'll do something."

"I just don't want anything to harm Lyla's rep."

"No press is bad press," Jake says.

"Yeah, I just don't think it's the right time for things with her to go public. If she's linked to me, they might start digging and find out who her mom and dad are."

"Yeah, you're right," he agrees.

I think we're about to wrap up the conversation when he says, "So...you like her."

"Lyla?"

"Yeah, Lyla."

"You know I do. I was trying to get in her panties earlier this year, remember?"

"I remember. And I also remember that she shot you down—*twice*. But I'm not talking about fucking here, Tom. I mean, do you like her? 'Cause it seems she likes you now."

I shrug. I don't care that Jake has just said that Lyla likes me. Why would I? I'm a guy, and guys don't care about shit like that.

I just want to fuck her, multiple times, because she's hot, and she has the best pair of tits I've ever seen.

"Yeah, I mean, she's cool. She's...I don't know. I guess she's different than other chicks."

"Did you just admit that you actually like a woman, not just because you want to bang her?"

*Shit.*

"No." I grimace.

"Yeah, you fucking did. And just so you know, I'm recording this call, so I have the evidence."

"Fuck off. What are you? Twelve?" Still, I can't help but smile.

He laughs. "So, should I prepare myself for more headlines then?"

That's Jake's way of asking if I'm going to pursue her.

I scratch my cheek. "I don't know. I mean, I'm her manager. We're living on a bus together."

"So, that means you're gonna bang her. Okay, well, so you know, I have no issues with you doing her."

"Gee, thanks, Dad."

He laughs. "Just don't screw it up. I don't want my most promising act to up and leave the label because of you."

"Thanks for the confidence." I scowl.

"Don't get your panties in a twist. You know what I mean. And don't go getting yourself hurt either."

I let out a sharp laugh. "Did you actually just say that to me? You're not talking to Denny right now, you know."

"Fuck yeah." He chuckles. "I forgot who I was talking to for a moment."

There's another weird silence between us.

Then, he says, "Tom, did we just have a fucking heart-to-heart?"

I rub a hand over the stubble on my chin. "Dunno, man. Maybe...yeah."

"Wanna talk about guy stuff? Pretend like it never happened."

"So, the Mets really fucking suck at the moment."

We stay on the phone for a few more minutes, talking baseball and cleansing our guy souls. Then, we finish up. I have to talk to Lyla. She needs to know about that video online—if she doesn't already.

I pull open the door and step into the hall.

I can see Lyla sitting close to Cale. Their heads are bent close together as they're talking.

I feel a strange tightening in my chest.

Then, Cale puts his arm around her shoulders and pulls her to him.

My blood starts to boil. My hands are balling into fists at my side.

And I have a vision of striding over there, ripping his arm off of her, and then pummeling him until I drive the message home.

It's weird and irrational.

I know she said there's nothing sexual between them, and I know she wouldn't lie to me. But every time I turn around, he's got his hands on her. Now, I'm starting to think that maybe he wants her, and she just can't see it.

And what annoys me the most is the fact that it annoys me.

I really want to tear his goddamn hands off when I see him touching her.

The only thing stopping me is the fact that Jake will have a problem if I tear off Vintage's bass player's hands. That, and I don't want to scare the shit out of Lyla.

Of course I have a temper. I've gotten into fuckloads of fights over the years but never over a woman—well, not over one who I actually cared about. But, yeah, I've gotten into a few brawls over me borrowing another guy's woman for the night, without his consent.

I've just never cared about seeing another man's hands on a woman I've fucked—let alone, one I've only kissed once. I've gotten off plenty of times from watching a woman I've just screwed getting screwed by some other guy while I move on to the next.

But the thought of another man touching Lyla makes me want to punch a hole in the nearest wall.

I feel territorial over her. Even though I have no right, I feel like she's mine. And I don't want anyone but me touching her.

"Lyla, got a minute?" I grind out. I don't mean to sound so pissy, but there's nothing I can do about it now.

Her head jerks, and her gaze hits mine. I don't even bother to look at Cale.

I just relish in watching her stand, forcing his hand to fall away from her. I enjoy watching her walk toward me.

My eyes never leave her once, not even to blink.

She's not looking at me though. Her eyes are lowered.

*Fuck.*

She's been avoiding me since last night, and I took it in stride, giving her space to come around to things…to us.

Before, when she asked my opinion on something important to her, I thought we were taking a step forward.

But now, it appears we've gone two steps back.

And when I tell her about the video—well, I have a feeling that's going to take us back even further.

As she nears, I step back, letting her pass by me and into the bedroom. The smell of her perfume has my head spinning and my cock hardening. She goes over and stands by the desk, putting the bed between us.

I raise an eyebrow and close the door. The click of the latch is loud in our silence. I turn back to her, wondering how to start.

Then, she blurts out, "I'm sorry!" She covers her face with her hands.

The sight of her upset feels like I've just been punched in the chest.

Striding around the bed, I cover the distance between us quickly. I slide my hands into her hair, forcing her face up to mine.

She slowly drops her hands from her face. I don't like what I see staring back at me from her eyes.

She looks sad and worried. It makes the punch in the chest feel like child's play, compared to the bulldozer I just took, seeing her like this.

I'm guessing she knows about the video.

Well, I'm hoping she knows, so that her apology isn't over something else. Something I don't even want to think about. *Cale.*

"You've seen the video."

Shaking her head, she blinks up at me. "I haven't watched it, but I saw the headlines." Her eyes lower. "I'm so, so sorry, Tom. I should have thought about it before I pulled my stunt last night. I know how famous you are, and believe it or not, even with who my parents are, I'm just not used to the fame. I was shielded from it, especially after my mom died. I sometimes forget—"

"Shh…it's okay." I press a soft kiss to her forehead.

"No, it's not." She moves her head gently from side to side. "I've embarrassed you."

I let out a soft laugh.

*That's what she's worried about. Not herself. But me.*

"Trust me, you haven't embarrassed me. Nothing embarrasses me. And even if I could be embarrassed, you"—I draw a line down her cheek with my finger, and I really like the shudder I feel in her from my touch—"could never embarrass me."

She blinks those blues up at me. A feeling flashes through my chest.

"Is Jake angry?" she asks.

I notice she's not moving away from me, so I take advantage and move closer, cupping her cheek in my hand.

"No, he's not angry. He's doing damage control now."

"For you?"

"No, Ly, for you. He's making sure that your connection to me won't have the press digging things up on you."

Her eyes lower again. She bites her lip.

I feel my cock jerk at the sight.

"I never thought of that," she whispers.

"Don't worry. I made mistakes, colossal fucking mistakes, in the beginning when TMS started getting recognition. Jake did as well. We know what it's like. But it gets easier with time. It becomes the norm."

She nods, eyes still lowered.

I don't like it. I don't like it when she's not looking at me.

"Hey." I tap her chin with my finger.

She brings her eyes to mine.

"It's not a big deal. No one will care tomorrow. Okay?"

"Okay," she breathes, a gorgeous smile edging those kissable full lips of hers.

Her eyes move over my face before settling on my mouth. *She wants me to kiss her.*

"Ly...I'm gonna kiss you again."

Her head moves infinitesimally. I take that as a yes. I don't want to waste a second and give her a chance to change her mind. Moving in quickly, I capture her lips with mine. I slowly run my tongue along her lower lip, and then I seal my mouth over hers.

I kiss her with as much force as I can without hurting her. I want her to know how much I want her.

Her body goes limp in my hands.

I wrap my arms around her, encasing her. I lick the sweet-tasting inside of her mouth. She moans the sexiest fucking sound, and then she swirls her tongue around mine. Her hands go around my back, clutching me, and she digs her nails in. I can feel the pressure on my skin through my shirt.

I'm as hard as stone, and my cock is pressed up against her toned stomach.

The stomach that I'm going to get down on my knees and lick while I unbutton her jeans. Then, I'm gonna take her in my mouth and finally get to taste that sweet pussy of hers.

"I want you," I breathe into her mouth.

"Oh God," she whispers, her body trembling. She opens her eyes, staring straight into mine.

Her gaze is hazy and lust-filled, and in this moment, I really believe that I have her, that I'm going to get what I've been desperate for from the instant I laid eyes on her.

I slide my hand down her side and across her stomach, heading for the button and zipper on her jeans, when the loud sound of the bathroom door shutting jerks that look from her eyes and her body from mine.

Stumbling back from me, that hot chest of hers heaving, she shakes her head. "No. I can't do this with *you*."

I hate the way she says *you*. It's like she would do this with any other guy but me.

She makes a move to go past me, but I stop her, catching her wrist.

"What do you mean, you can't do this with *me*? There someone else you want screwing you?"

"You're disgusting," she hisses. "Don't you ever stop?"

"No, I don't. Not when it comes to you." I lean down into her face. "You know what I think? I think you want me bad, Lyla. And it scares the shit out of the frigid bitch you became after what your brother and that dick of an ex did to you."

It's low, and I know it. But I can't seem to help it around her. She brings out the bastard in me at times.

I see her eyes glaze with hurt, and it bothers me. I hate that I care enough for it to affect me.

And the worst thing is the silence that follows.

She doesn't give a retort. She just calmly pulls her arm from my hand and starts to walk away.

Panic claws at my chest.

I don't know what to do with it because I've never felt it before. Not in this way. Not over a woman.

"That's it, Lyla. Run away. Do what you do best."

She stops and turns to me. The hurt is gone, and her expression is blank.

I don't know which is worse. Seeing her hurt, or seeing that she doesn't care.

"I'm not running. I'm making the smart choice—and that's getting away from you."

*Jesus, that fucking hurt.*

My hand rubs across my chest as I shake my head slowly. "No, you're running because you're scared."

"I'm not scared of anything—least of all, you."

I let a smile slide onto my lips even though smiling is the last thing I feel like doing right now. "Yeah, you are. But there's nothing to be scared of. I'm gonna show you that. You can keep running, but I will catch you and soon. I'm not giving up, Lyla."

Her eyes adjust, and the cold in them chills me to the bone.

"But you should give up, Tom. You really should."

Then, she's out the door.

And I'm left here with a raging hard-on, the worst case of blue balls, and a pain in my chest that I can't explain.

## A Few Hours Later—Diner, St. Louis

We've come to a diner to have an early dinner before tonight's show. The rest of the crew is setting up at the venue, so it's just me, Cale, Sonny, Van, and Shannon. I have no clue where Ashlee is, and I don't care to ask. I'm just glad I don't have to watch her fawning all over Tom again.

Oh, yeah, and the man himself is with us.

He hasn't tried to speak to me again since this morning. He's barely looked at me.

It bothers me way more than I care to admit to myself right now.

Maybe he's changed his mind about not giving up. And I'm not even going to go into how much that thought affects me.

He was pissed after I pulled away from our kiss. But then, I can't blame him. I must have come across like a total tease.

I'm not.

I'm just confused and scared.

He was right about that part.

Tom lights up parts of me that I want to stay dark.

I can't seem to control myself around him. All he has to do is put his hands on me, and all my senses along with my inhibitions just fly right on out.

I was just glad for the interruption—again. But I can't keep relying on interruptions to save me.

I have to find a way to be strong around Tom. I have to stop teasing him. It's not fair.

What Tom thinks of me matters. I don't want him to dislike me. Before all the kissing, we got to a good place where we were friends. I want to get back to that place even though the kissing is awesome.

Jesus, I'm so confused.

Rubbing my head, I huff out a sigh.

Van looks at me. "You all right?" he asks around a mouthful of food.

Nodding, I say, "Yep. All good here." I give him a dazzling smile.

Then, I look down at my plate. I cut a piece of pancake off with my fork. I stab the fork into it, letting the syrup drip to the plate. I lean forward and deposit the piece of pancake into my mouth. I decided to have breakfast for dinner. My appetite is off, but I needed something, and I thought pancakes would go down easy.

I chew slowly, trying to focus on the sweetness of the syrup, but I'm too distracted by the sound of Tom's voice. He's sitting one seat over and across from me, next to Van, and he's talking to Cale about guitars.

I never knew how hard it could be, trying *not* to look at someone. But with Tom, it is. I have to physically restrain myself from looking at him. My eyes seem drawn to him, like bees to honey.

Blinking hard, I set my face forward and stare ahead, fixing my gaze on the picture on the wall behind Van's head. It's a boring painting of a field and trees with some cows and sheep in it, but I force myself to intricately examine every part of that painting.

I've just reached the third sheep when I feel my phone vibrating against my butt. Sliding a hand into my pocket, I pull it out and find Tom's name lighting up the screen.

Heart in my throat, I look at him. He's not looking at me. His eyes are on Cale, listening to him talk.

Looking back down to my phone, I open the text.

*I can still taste you.*

Holy shit! Where did that come from?

Guess he meant what he said earlier about not giving up.

Whamming against my rib cage, my heart lurches in two different directions—one straight toward Tom, the other running out this diner.

I stare at him and place my phone down on the table, letting him know that I'm ignoring him.

He smirks. Then, he picks up his phone again.

Mine vibrates a few seconds later.

I sigh and ignore it for about two minutes. Then, curiosity wins, and I pick it up.

*I bet your pussy tastes as sweet as that mouth of yours. I can't wait to find out.*

*Jesus.* My thighs clench, my core tightens, my body tilts in Tom's direction.

Steadying myself against the table, I take a calming deep breath and type out what my head is telling me, not listening to my traitorous body.

*Stop it.*

I hit Send and set my phone on my thigh.

I hear the buzzing of Tom's cell vibrating against the table. Out of the corner of my eye, I watch as he picks up his cell and reads my text.

His gaze is impassive.

Then, he looks up, but I quickly direct my eyes back on the painting.

A few moments later, my phone vibrates.

*Ugh!*

I lift my angry eyes to his.

He's staring right at me with a determined look, which makes my stomach flip.

Looking down at my cell, I leave it where it sits on my thigh and open the text.

*I told you, I'm not stopping until I have you. And maybe I won't even stop then.*

*This is harassment. I could sue you for stalking.*

I hear him chuckle softly. Then…

*It would be worth every fucking cent.*

I almost growl in frustration.

*Tom, get this through your head. We are never happening.
Ever. Last night was a mistake. And this morning was an
even bigger mistake.*

I stare at him, trying to enforce my point. He picks up his
phone and reads the message. I see his eyebrow lift, and then his
fingers move over the screen.

A few seconds later, my phone vibrates against my thigh.

*The only mistake was me letting you walk out of that
bedroom. It will happen again, Lyla. Again and again.
And again.*

*No. No and no. And no!*

The waitress comes over and refills our coffees, distracting the
table, so I take the chance and catch Tom's attention.

Shaking my head lightly, I mouth the word, *No,* to him,
wanting to drive my point home.

I need him to leave me alone.

I can't get involved with Tom. Being with someone like him
would get me hurt.

And I can't get hurt again.

He frowns, giving me a hard look. *Yes,* he mouths back.

My mind and body are working separately. I want him so bad.

My body is craving his words, loving that he's not yet given up
on me.

But my mind is terrified, telling me to run far, far away.

The waitress leaves, and conversation picks back up at the
table.

I think that's it. I'm home free.

I'm wrong.

My cell buzzes against my thigh. The need to read it is
overwhelming. I open up the message.

*I know you want me, so there's no way I'm backing off.*

*I really don't want you.*

*Don't fucking lie. I can smell your arousal from here. And
it's making me hard, Ly. Rock. Fucking. Hard.*

Holy crap.

*Tom, please...*

I'm pleading now because I don't know what else to do. If he comes anywhere near me, pushes me further, I will cave to him again. And the next time, we'll do more than kiss.

*I can't wait for you to wrap that begging mouth of yours around my cock.*

Oh God.

My sweating palm tightens around my cell. My body flushes from the top of my head down to my toes. Every part of me is turned on by his dirty words. My arousal is drenching me.

I flick my eyes to Tom, and his are on mine, still determined.

I press my thighs together, trying to relieve the ache he's created from a few words in a text message.

I think for a moment, my fingers hovering over my phone screen.

*I want...*

I pause, struggling with what to say. Then, I accidently hit Send.

*Shit.*

My stomach turns at the open-ended message I just sent him.

A second later Bruno Mars's "Gorilla" starts to play loudly. It takes me a second to realize that it's coming from Tom's phone, signaling the text I sent.

I freeze.

*He just turned on his ringtone?*

*Why?*

*To get my attention.*

Well, if it that's the reason, then he's got it. And not just because of what the song is about, but also because of the exact part he has set as his message tone.

I think you know which part I mean—*motherfucker.*

I look at him. He's staring back at me with lust and defiance in his eyes.

I move my gaze away.

The guys don't even seem fazed by the lyrics belting out from Tom's phone. Cale has even started singing along with it.

Tom waits, letting the ringtone finish, before he picks up his cell and reads my text.

Cale says, "I fucking love that song."

I mumble in agreement.

"That song is genius. It's gotten me laid so many times. I now worship at the altar of Bruno Mars," Sonny says around a mouthful of burger.

"Nice," I say.

I now can't take my eyes off of Tom, knowing what he's reading.

Tom's eyes flash to mine. They're filled with question, confusion, but mostly hunger.

"Ly, you not eating those?"

I drag my eyes from Tom to see Van holding a fork over my plate, pointing at my pancakes.

"No, you can have them." I push my plate toward him.

My phone vibrates.

*What do you want, baby? Tell me, and I'll give it to you.*

I hover over the screen, torn between my body's truth and my mind's right-thing-to-do.

I decide to go with my mind.

*I want you to leave me the fuck alone.*

I place my phone down, waiting for the retort.

But it never comes.

I wait for what seems like ages but nothing.

And when I look at Tom, he's not looking at me. He's talking to Shannon, and his cell is nowhere to be seen.

Panic scratches just beneath the surface, but I shove it away. *This is good. This is what I wanted.*

Then, my cell starts to ring, frightening the crap out of me.

It's a cell number I don't recognize.

I hesitate for a moment and then answer, "Hello?"

"Lyla, it's Robbi, Robbi Kraft."

My stomach does a little somersault. "Oh, Robbi, hi."

I glance at Tom to see if he heard me. He did.

I don't know how I expect him to react from knowing that Robbi is on the phone—anger maybe.

But that's not what I get.

There's nothing at all.

No reaction.

His face is perfectly blank.

Shannon says something to him, and he looks back at her.

Feeling oddly empty but a little tingly that Robbi is calling, I get up from my seat and move away from the table. I walk over toward the exit, so I can take the call privately.

The first thing out of my mouth though is, "Um…how did you get my number?"

I hear him take in a breath.

He sounds nervous as he says, "Okay, so I know this might sound a little stalkerish, but I promise, it's not. Okay, maybe it is a little bit. But you never called, and I have a friend…in the police. He got your number for me."

"I'm pretty sure that's illegal," I say around smile.

"I'm pretty sure you're right, but if I say that I haven't been able to stop thinking about you since Idaho, would that help?"

"I don't know. That's a pretty serious crime you've committed."

"Okay, how about you agree to have dinner with me? If you still feel the same about my criminal, stalker ways, I'll personally turn myself into the cops."

"You mean your cop friend who broke the law with you?"

He chuckles. "The very one."

I tap my finger against my chin. "I'm not sure if going to dinner with a criminal and stalker would be a good idea."

He lets out a tsking noise. "Yeah, I think you might be right. Shit. I've screwed this up at the first hurdle."

I giggle. "You haven't totally screwed it up."

"I haven't?"

I like the hope I hear in his voice.

"How about next time we see each other, you buy me that drink you didn't get a chance to buy me last time?"

I hear paper rustling.

Then, he says, "Five days. Pittsburgh. We're both playing there. It's a date."

"I never said it was a date, Robbi," I say, adding levity to my voice so not to sound bitchy.

"Okay, no date. Just a drink between two friends. Just promise me one thing…"

"I don't generally make promises."

"Can you make an exception this time for me?"

He sounds so charming, and I can't help but say, "Okay, shoot."

"Promise me that you won't let anyone buy you a drink between now and Pittsburgh."

"Hey, a girl's gotta drink!" I laugh. "How about I promise not to let anyone who isn't a friend buy me a drink between now and Pittsburgh?"

I can almost feel his smile down the line.

"Perfect. So, I'll see you in five days, Lyla."

"You'll see me in five days."

A smile on my face, I hang up the phone and push it into my back pocket. I start to walk back toward our table. As I lift my gaze, I meet Tom's eyes.

And he's looking at me in a way I've never seen before.

Like he's looking through me. Distant. Almost as if he isn't really seeing me anymore.

And I'd be lying if I said it doesn't hurt.

# Five Days Later—Onstage at a Club, Pittsburgh

Okay. So, Tom is not avoiding me. He's not ignoring me.
He's being nice to me.
Which is good, right? It's what I wanted.
Well, it should be good...but it's not.
Because he's been too *nice*. Too mother-effing nice.
Cordial. Well mannered.
Basically, not the Tom I know.
There's been no joking. No flirting. No sex texts. No attempts at getting me alone.
Nothing.
For five freaking days.
Nothing!
And it's driving me crazy. He's driving me crazy. Slowly.
Every time I walk into a room and he's in there alone, he gives me a polite smile before he gets up and walks out. Like I have the plague or something.
At first, I wondered if it was a game he was playing, trying to wear me down until I crack and give in to him.
But after day three, I realized it wasn't a game. He really has given up on me.
I know this because on day three of Nice Tom, I saw him flirting with Ashlee, and he wasn't doing it because he thought I was there. He wasn't trying to bring my feelings to the surface with jealousy.
He had no idea I was there, and he was, flirting with her.
Seeing him with her—his hand resting on her shoulder, his fingers playing with her hair—hurt like a bitch.
But I told myself that it was okay. I wanted him to leave me alone.
He's doing what I asked.
So, it's good.
Except, it doesn't feel good. I don't want this anymore.

I want it to go back to the way it was.

I want Tom back.

The only thing keeping me sane during these past five days is the attention I've been getting from Robbi Kraft.

After his stalker call, I received a sweet text from him the next day. I texted back. We've been texting a few times a day since then.

He's sweet.

He doesn't give me hot fire in my belly like Tom does.

But fire is dangerous. Fire gets you burned.

I don't really see this thing with Robbi going anywhere. I'm still not in the market for anyone. I'm just enjoying Robbi's attention.

Tom might have temporarily broken the straps on my chastity belt, but I padlocked that fucker back up, and I'm not ready to take it off for anyone else.

It's just nice to have something to take my mind off Tom.

I am looking forward to getting to know Robbi a little better, though. The geeky fan in me is excited to talk music with him.

Tonight, we're in Pittsburgh, and Pittsburgh is my non-date drink with Robbi.

I'm onstage, singing my anger out before finishing up our set.

I haven't seen Robbi yet. The Turnstiles played earlier, and then another band went on between our sets, so I'm guessing I'll see him when I go offstage.

Pressing my lips to the mic, I sing the last line of "Better Than You."

A few days ago, Tom decided that it should be our closing song. The single has been doing really well on the airwaves, and the number of downloads are looking great. He said if it keeps going this way, we stand to chart well, which is awesome.

I just wish I felt awesome.

When Sonny's sticks hit the drums for the last time tonight, I yell into the mic, "Thank you, Pittsburgh! You've been amazing!"

With a wave of my hand, I exit the stage, easing the strap of my guitar over my head. The moment I'm offstage, I hand my guitar to Jon, one of our roadies, with a, "Thanks."

I come down the steps and see Tom waiting for us, like he always does. He looks deliciously hot in low-slung jeans and a vintage *David Bowie, Live Santa Monica '72* T-shirt.

Unfortunately, Ashlee is here and standing close beside him.

She's wearing a tight, short red dress that displays all her assets. She looks good.

But I don't feel inferior tonight because I know I look really good. Shannon gave me the full works earlier since I told her I would be meeting Robbi for a drink tonight, and she took that to mean this is a date. No matter how many times I told her it isn't, she wasn't listening, so she went to town on me. Which I'm glad for now.

My lips are red, nails painted to match, and I'm wearing a kick-ass dress. It's short and black with full sleeves, but the best part about this dress is the cut to the navel. This is a no-bra, boobs-taped-in-place, shit-hot dress. And to round it off, I'm wearing a pair of high-heeled black suede ankle boots.

I look good—no, I look hot, and my girls look amazing.

Head up, I stick my best assets out, the assets I know Tom is fixated on, and I strut my way over to them.

"Hey." I smile.

Ashlee looks me up and down. "Shannon asked me to give you your purse." She holds it out to me.

*So much for pleasantries.* "Thanks," I say, taking it from her.

She gives me a fake smile.

Tom aside, I really dislike this girl.

"Great set as always," Tom says, eyes on my face. "Your vocals were on fire tonight." Then, he smiles his polite smile at me. He doesn't even look at my boobs.

Well, he might as well have just kicked me in my virginia.

I have to contain the scream of frustration crawling up my throat. Even more so when I see the smug look on Ashlee's face.

Pissed off and feeling stupid for trying to get his attention with my breasts, I give him a sharp nod. "Cool. Well, I'll be at the bar if anyone wants me."

I spin on my stiletto heels, not even bothering to wait for Cale, Sonny, and Van, and I stomp away.

I'm vexed, and I'm pretty sure it's showing in every step I take.

Not that Tom will notice. He'll be too busy looking at Ashlee's fake tits.

*Meow.*

Reaching the bar, I slam my credit card down and drop my purse next to it. "Shot of tequila, and keep them coming."

The cute bartender raises an eyebrow at me and smiles. He takes my card and puts it by the cash register. Then, he puts a shot glass on the bar and pours the tequila.

"I thought you weren't letting anyone buy you a drink, except for me?" Robbi's smooth voice comes in my ear.

I turn to him.

*Jesus, he looks hotter than I remember.* At the sight of Robbi, some of the Tom tension in my body starts to head for the door marked *Exit.*

I smile at Robbi, my eyes making a quick journey over his body. *I might be on a man hiatus, but I'm not blind.* Robbi is lean and toned, but he isn't ripped like Tom.

I really like the way his torn black jeans hang on his trim hips. The fitted black T-shirt he's wearing has a skull surrounded by flames on it with *Hellraiser* written underneath. It shows off his defined chest and arms perfectly.

I hope Robbi is a hellraiser. That's exactly what I'm in the mood for tonight—raising some hell.

I pick the shot up and throw it back, relishing the burn from the alcohol.

I turn back to Robbi and look at him from under my lashes, giving him a coy smile. "I bought this one myself."

His eyes darken on me, and I like the way it makes me feel.

"A girl like you shouldn't be buying herself drinks," he says, leaning a little closer to me.

"Smooth."

He throws his head back and laughs that contagious sound of his.

I imagine that sound has women dropping their panties left, right, and center.

"So, can I finally buy you that drink?" He gives me a panty-dropping grin.

"You can." I smile.

Leaning over the bar, he lifts a hand, catching the bartender's attention.

"Another shot?" Robbi asks me.

I shake my head. Probably not a good idea for me to do shots and get shitfaced. "A beer, please."

"Two beers," he says to the bartender.

I turn and lean against the bar, looking around. I see Van chatting with some girl and Sonny with his tongue down another girl's throat. Cale is not in sight.

I scan the crowd for Tom, and I see him across the room. My stomach ties into a thousand knots, and I feel like I'm going to throw up. He's sitting on the edge of a stool, his long legs spread out, and standing between his legs is Ashlee. She has her hand on his chest, saying something into his ear.

His eyes meet mine across the room, and the burn I feel is painful.

Finding it odd that Cale isn't around and not wanting to watch Tom with Ashlee, I get my cell from my purse, and I check to see if Cale has texted his whereabouts.

Sure enough he has.

> *Taking that chick from earlier back to the hotel. Tom said he'll make sure you get back safely. I would have come over before I left, but I saw you talking to Robbi. I didn't want to interrupt. ;) Love ya. x*

We're staying at a hotel tonight since we have two shows at two different clubs in Pittsburgh. One was tonight's show, and the next is tomorrow night. So, Tom decided we could do with a night off from sleeping on the bus, and this was the ideal time while we're not in transit.

I quickly tap out a reply.

> *Have fun. And you wouldn't have interrupted. I'm just having a drink with Robbi, that's all. I'll see you at breakfast. Love ya right back. x*

Robbi holds a beer bottle in front of me. Taking it, I lock the screen on my cell and put it back in my purse.

"Thanks." I smile.

"So…" he says.

He seems nervous. It's cute.

I turn my body toward his. "So?"

He runs a hand through his hair and shifts on his feet. "Okay, I'm just gonna put this out there. I really like you."

"Okay…" I bite my lip, a little unsure how to respond. I wasn't expecting this.

"And you make me really nervous."

I let out a laugh. "I make you nervous? I highly doubt that."

"Seriously." He moves a little closer to me. "I never get nervous around women, but you…I do."

I put the bottle to my lips and take a small sip. "I'm not sure if me making you nervous is a good or bad thing."

Lifting a hand to my face, he tucks my hair behind my ear. "Good. Really good. You're seriously gorgeous, Lyla. It's a little unnerving."

"Unnerving?" I frown.

"Yeah. You could have any guy you want in this room."

His fingers run down my jaw, and he leans in even closer. His bottle clanks against mine.

"And that unnerves me because I want you to want me, and I want it more than I've ever cared for before."

He's looking at me like Tom looks at me.

Only, his stare isn't having the same effect on me as Tom's does. There's only a warmth in my stomach, not the blazing heat I get from Tom.

Demi Lovato's "Heart Attack" starts to play loudly through the speakers.

With Tom in my mind and being aware of the fact that he is just across the room, I move back a little, leaving Robbi's hand stranded midair.

He quickly retracts it, putting it around his bottle before holding it to his chest. A look of distress flickers across his face. "Have I moved too fast and scared you off?"

"No." I shake my head. "It's not that." My eyes drift, and that's when I see…Tom kissing Ashlee.

I feel like I've been slapped, punched, and kicked for good measure.

The music dulls to a painful throb in my head.

Everything has stopped. Time. My heart. Life. The earth spinning.

*Jesus. This hurts.*

Everything ceases to move, except for what is happening across from me right now.

He's kissing her.

He's actually kissing her.

And his hands are on her arms, holding her.

And he's…kissing her.

*Jesus.*

I'm going to throw up.

Tears are burning my eyes, and a pain is scratching its way up my throat.

I know I have no right to feel this way. I pushed him away.

But that fact doesn't make the pain any less.

"Lyla?" Robbi's voice pulls me back.

My eyes meet his. I'm fairly sure he can see something in them.

Then, he says, "Tom…" He turns his head in the direction of where Tom and Ashlee are. "Are you two—"

"No."

"I saw the video online, and you looked—"

"We looked nothing. The video was nothing. Just a bet."

"Okay." He smiles. "I'm glad to hear it." He moves close again. "Really glad."

I stare at Robbi. He's sweet and good-looking, and he smells nice. Clean. Soap and aftershave. Like a man should smell.

Not as amazing as Tom smells, but that's a good thing.

I don't need anything resembling Tom right now. I need the exact opposite of him. Something to make the knowledge that he's kissing Ashlee hurt less.

That's why I lean into Robbi and tilt my face up to his, offering him my mouth, letting him know exactly what I want.

He smiles softly, his hands lifting to cup my face.

I close my eyes as he moves in.

The moment Robbi's lips touch mine, I feel a sharp stab of guilt.

Ridiculous, right?

I feel guilty for kissing Robbi while Tom has his tongue stuck down Ashlee's throat.

Ignoring the guilt, I push myself into the kiss, putting my hand around the back of Robbi's neck, and I open up my mouth to him.

He seems to like that. I feel him smile against my lips, and then his tongue slips into my mouth.

It's…nice. His kiss is slow, gentle. Nothing like Tom's kisses. Robbi's lips are surprisingly soft for a guy. Not like Tom's lips, which are firm and delicious.

*Stop thinking about Tom.*

Robbi's fingers thread through my hair, and he deepens the kiss.

*This is a mistake.*

*No. This is good. Perfect. Robbi is great.*

I shut my brain off and keep kissing him.

Then, out of nowhere, a prickly sensation creeps up my spine, and my Spidey sense has me suddenly stopping the kiss. I press a hand to Robbi's chest, pushing him back.

He stares at me, breathing heavily. His lips are swollen with my red lipstick smeared across them.

"Wow," he breathes.

I see a figure behind him, and suddenly, he's wrenched away from me. Where Robbi was now stands a seriously pissed off Tom.

"What the fuck are you doing?" Tom growls at me.

"Excuse me?" I blink.

His face darkens. "I said, what the fuck are you doing?"

I narrow my eyes at him, my hands going to my hips. "What does it look like I'm doing?"

He scowls. "Making a fool out of yourself—that's what this looks like."

*Well…that hurts.*

Tears sting my eyes. My anger hits, full force.

"Fuck you!" I spit at him.

"Am I missing something here?" Robbi's voice comes from behind Tom.

Tom's head swivels around to Robbi. The look Tom gives Robbi would take down any man—quite possibly a polar bear, for that matter. Tom looks *that* scary.

"Yeah, your teeth, if you don't walk the fuck away."

Robbi looks past Tom to me, his eyes questioning.

Tom turns fully to face Robbi. "Don't look at her. Look at me." His voice is as hard as stone. "Whatever you thought might happen with Lyla isn't happening. Ever. Do you read me?"

Robbi scowls and takes a step toward Tom. "And if I don't read you? Then, what?"

Tom lets out a humorless laugh. He moves so close to Robbi that I would definitely call it an invasion of space.

It causes my heart to ramp up speed.

Tom leans down into Robbi's face and says with intention, "You *really* should learn to close your dressing room door, Kraft. You don't, and someone passing by could hear all kinds of things."

I see something flash over Robbi's face. Something I don't like.

Tom straightens up. "Lyla is a no-go area for you. So, I'll say it again. Do. You. Fucking. Read. Me?"

Robbi backs away. "Loud and clear." He looks at me over Tom's shoulder, giving me an apologetic face. Then, he turns and disappears into the crowd.

Tom turns to me and grabs my arm. "We're leaving."

I wrench it free. "I'm not going anywhere with you, you freaking Neanderthal!" After smoothing a hand over my hair, I grab my purse. "Anyway, I'm pretty sure your girlfriend over there is waiting for you to finish what you started, so you'd better get back to it." I jerk my head in the direction of a stunned-looking Ashlee, who is still standing where he left her.

His jaw tightens. "Ashlee's not my girlfriend, and you know it." Something flickers through his eyes. "That's why you kissed Robbi, isn't it? Because you saw Ashlee and me—"

I hold a hand up, cutting him off. "Don't get ahead of yourself there, Casanova. I kissed Robbi because I wanted to. Because he's hot and a really *great* kisser. A better kisser than you in fact."

I might as well have just stuck my tongue out at him and said, *Na-na-nana-na.*

*God, I'm pathetic.*

Tom's eyes narrow to slits. "Don't be ridiculous. You're acting like a child right now."

"Me?" I yell, slapping a hand to my chest. "I'm not the one who just kicked a kid out of the sandbox 'cause I thought he was playing with my toys."

His face tightens, his eyes darkening to mega scary. "He was playing with *my* toy."

I hide the shiver I feel at his words. Instead, I scowl up at him. "My God, you are an egotistical bastard!"

"Yeah, and you're a crazy bitch. We're leaving. Now."

"Are you deaf? I said, *I'm not going anywhere with you!*"

I'm pretty sure the whole club is staring at us right now. But I don't give a shit.

The next thing I hear is this caveman growly sound coming from Tom. Then, I'm being lifted off the ground before being thrown over his shoulder.

"Argh!" I cry out. "What the hell are you doing?"

"What does it look like I'm doing?" he says, throwing my earlier words back at me. "You won't come quietly, so I'm carrying your bitchy ass out of here."

"Put me down, you lunatic!" I hit his back with my purse. Then, I very quickly become aware of how short my dress is. I give the hem a sharp tug, making sure my ass is covered.

"No," he grinds out.

"Psycho!"

"Drama queen."

"Argh!" I scream again. "I hate you!"

"Yeah, so I keep hearing. Now, shut the hell up because you're making a scene." He slaps my ass.

My mouth drops open.

*Arrogant asshole!* I cannot believe he just told me to shut up and then slapped my ass.

I ignore the fact that in some other scenario—a bedroom one—that would have actually been really hot. I snap out between my gritted teeth, "You're a fucking mut." Then, for good measure, I hit his back with my purse again.

"Yeah, I keep hearing that, too." He chuckles.

The vibration of it hits me in all my tingly places.

In this moment, I'm glad that it's my ass in his face, so he can't see the smile forcing its way onto my lips.

Tom jogs down the club steps before heading for the exit, carrying me like I weigh nothing at all.

If it wasn't so embarrassing, it would be majorly hot.

I know people are staring at us, so I keep my head down and my eyes closed, praying he puts me down soon.

He whistles for a cab. I see one pull up. Tom opens the door and then dumps me on the backseat.

My ass hits the seat, my breath whooshing out with an oomph.

Tom climbs in next to me. "Fairmont," he tells the driver.

The cab pulls out into traffic.

I shift in my seat to face Tom.

It's a long moment before he turns his head to look at me. "What?"

"What!" Giving him an incredulous look, I jerk a hand between us. "Are you gonna explain to me what the hell that was all about?"

Grabbing my hand, he holds it up, presses his palm flat against mine, and then links our fingers.

My heart stutters.

A ghost of a smile touches his lips, making him more handsome, if that were possible. "I know you like public shows, Firecracker, but this isn't the place. We'll talk about it when we get to the hotel."

Then, he looks ahead. Sitting here, I'm stunned by everything that has just taken place. But mostly, I'm just speechless from the feel of his hand holding mine.

Knowing I don't want to give him a reason to let go, I don't say a word the entire ride back to the hotel.

# Lyla 17

## Fifteen Minutes Later—Fairmont Hotel, Pittsburgh

Keeping a firm hold of my hand, Tom leads me through the plush lobby of the Fairmont and straight into a waiting elevator. He presses the button for the twenty-third floor—his floor, I'm guessing. My room is on the fifteenth floor.

Feeling defiant, I lean over and punch the button marked fifteen.

The next thing I know, his hard body is pressing into mine, backing me up. I have no other choice but to go where he wants, and I end up against the wall of the elevator.

I try to steel myself against the mouthwatering scent of him and the erection I can feel pressed into my stomach. But my body is in control, and my body loves Tom Carter.

Desire explodes in my belly and trembles its way through me.

Tom's hands come up to either side of my head, caging me in.

His lips hover over mine. His eyes darken, becoming pools of lust.

*Holy fuck.*

"You get off on your floor, and you and me are gonna have an even bigger problem than we already have." He licks his lips.

I'm distracted by the sight. It only serves to increase the pressure I feel between my thighs.

"We need to talk, and going by our track record, it might get... *loud.*" His eyes flash another meaning, sending a shiver to race through my body. "Your room is next to Cale's, but mine is the only one up there, so no one will hear us."

He moves away from me with that damn smirk on his face. He leans back against the wall across from me, and he folds his arms over his chest, showing off those amazing biceps of his.

"Besides, I have something for you in my room."

Lifting my eyebrow, I flick my eyes to the very visible erection in his jeans.

Tom lets out a sexy laugh. "Not that—well, not right off the bat."

Ignoring the lusty tingles I'm feeling, I flip him off.

He laughs again, louder this time. I look to my feet to hide the smile forcing its way onto my lips.

I hate the way he can get to me like this.

It's not long before the elevator comes to a stop at my floor. I watch the doors open, considering my options.

Tom is stubborn, and I want to get some things off my chest with him, so I swallow my pride and let the doors close. I'm expecting a smart retort from him, but nothing comes.

When I look at him, he's smiling softly at me.

It causes my heart to squeeze.

Soon enough, the doors are opening on the twenty-third floor. I follow Tom down the hall. He stops outside a door marked *Presidential Suite.*

Of course he's staying in the best suite at the hotel.

He slides the key card in and opens the door. "After you."

I'm surprised at his gentlemanly way, but I don't let it show. I walk past him and into his suite. It's gorgeous, and the views of the city are breathtaking.

"You want something to drink?" he asks.

Stealing the view from my eyes, I drop my purse onto the coffee table and turn to find Tom already at the minibar. Knowing how extortionately priced minibar drinks are and how mad I am with Tom right now, I decide to order the priciest thing in there.

I move in beside him, leaving a safe gap between us. I lean down and peer into the fridge. I run my eyes over the price list. *Great.* The most expensive thing is a miniature bottle of Thomas Segal whiskey.

I don't like whiskey, but I still say, "I'll have the Segal and a carton of pistachios."

*I'll force the effing drink down and cover the taste with the nuts.*

*Yes, I'm that petty.*

Tom's body stiffens beside me. "No. I'll buy you anything you want out of here but not that."

"The nuts?" I frown.

"No. Segal. I won't buy you that."

I tilt my head around, so I can see his face. "Seriously? After the shit you pulled tonight, you're denying me a drink?"

"I'm not denying you anything. I just won't buy you that." His voice is stony.

"What the hell is wrong with you?" I yell. Apparently, I'm still in the mood to fight with him. My claws are out and raring to go.

"Lyla," he says my name like a plea, his fingers holding the bridge of his nose. "Just drop it, *please*. I'll buy you anything you want but not that." His voice sounds different and weird.

He looks at me. His eyes are pleading. He looks sad. All the anger in me dissipates.

I don't get why buying me *that* drink makes him sad.

Curiosity aside, I don't push, but decide to drop it. "Actually, I could do with a clear head. I'll just have a Diet Coke."

His body relaxes. I walk away from him, but I hear him sigh softly, leaving me even more confused as to just exactly what that was.

I sit down on the sofa and gaze out at the twinkling lights of the city around us.

Tom brings over two cans of Coke and a container of pistachios for me. He puts them on the table and takes the seat beside me.

I lean forward, pop open my can, and take a drink. My throat is a little dry from all the yelling at Tom tonight. In this moment, it occurs to me that I've never yelled at someone as much as I do with Tom. No one has ever gotten under my skin like he does—sexually or angrily. And I don't really quite know what it means.

Putting the can down, I twist in my seat to look at him. "So, are you gonna explain the caveman behavior?"

He turns to face me, bringing his leg up onto the sofa, which presses it nicely up against my thigh. Every particle in my body hones in on the one part of me that his body is touching.

"I'm not sorry."

That brings my attention right back to him.

"I'd do the same thing again, if presented with the same situation. The guy's an idiot."

I rake a hand through my hair. "You barely know him."

"I know enough."

"I liked him, but you've gone and ruined that now."

I don't know why I don't tell him that I was only interested in Robbi as a friend.

155

Okay, I do. It's because I'd have to explain why I kissed Robbi. And that would mean telling Tom that I did it as a knee jerk, because I was jealous that he was kissing Ashlee.

His eyes narrow. "I thought you were off men. So, why aren't you off him? Why kiss him?"

*Shit.* How do I answer this?

"I…" My mouth goes dry. "I wasn't *on* him," I say slowly. I pick imaginary lint off my dress, so I can avoid his heavy stare. "I don't know why I kissed him."

*Liar, liar, pants on fire.*

Tom grabs my hand in his and runs the pad of his thumb across the palm of my hand. "You wanted to make me jealous."

"No!" I snatch my hand back.

He leans forward, getting in my space. "Why can't you just tell the fucking truth? Why can't you just admit that you want me and go with it?"

*Because I'm a coward.*

I stare at him, seeing the frustration etched like lines in his face. But then, in the depths of his eyes, I see a flicker of pain.

*Am I hurting him?* I don't want to hurt him.

Lip trembling, I say, "Fine. You want the truth. It's because you scare me. This"—I gesture between us—"whatever it is, feels intense." My voice quiets. "And intense scares the shit out of me."

Something crosses his brow, and surprisingly, he gets to his feet and puts his back to me.

It leaves me feeling wide open and vulnerable.

"You want to know why I scared Robbi off?" His voice is low. He turns to look at me.

"Of course I do."

"Two reasons. When I tell you the first one, know that I don't want to hurt you in any way. The last thing I would ever want to do is hurt you."

My stomach starts to free-fall.

"But you need to know the truth, so you stay away from that asshole." He rubs his forehead.

I sit up a little straighter, my stomach forming little balls of tension. I'm worried about what he's going to say.

"The contract for The Turnstiles is up for renewal, and Rally isn't going to renew it."

I give him a confused look. "Why isn't Rally renewing their contract? The Turnstiles are doing really well."

Tom shakes his head. "Not as well as Rally wants them to be doing. You know what an asshole he is and how savage he can be with his decisions. Anything is dispensable if it's not working for him."

*Even his daughter.*

I know he's thinking the same thing. I see it in his eyes.

"When I knew Robbi was making a move on you, I made it my business to find out his. Turns out their tour is a desperate act. They fronted the cash for the tour themselves. Luckily, I happened to walk past Robbi's dressing room earlier, and I heard him talking to someone on the phone." He takes a deep breath. "Lyla, when I tell you this, I'm saying it from a good place, and you have to know that Robbi is a fame-hungry asshole who will do anything to get where he wants to be."

I start to feel a bit sick. I stiffen my spine and harden up. "Just spit it out. Whatever it is, I'm sure I can take it."

He runs a hand through his hair and looks at me with careful eyes. "Robbi knows you're Rally's daughter. He was looking for an in with you to help his career. I heard him telling whoever he was on the phone with that he was gonna smooth his way into your life and get you to fall hard for him, so that you'd talk Daddy into keeping the band on his label."

I swallow down rocks. Humiliation floods through me. I get to my feet and shake my head. Needing to protect myself, I say, "You must have heard wrong. Outside of my circle, hardly anyone knows that Rally's my father. I've made sure of that. Robbi couldn't have known."

Tom gives me a sad look. "He knew, Ly. I'm sorry."

My humiliation quickly turns to anger. I lift my chin and square my shoulders. "I don't need your goddamn pity. Obviously, Robbi didn't do his homework properly because Rally couldn't give a shit about me. It's not like he'd ever listen to me." I let out a dry laugh. "I wouldn't be able to influence jack shit over what happens to Robbi's crappy band."

Tom says nothing. He just stares steadily at me.

I'm starting to feel like I'm going to break apart. The whole night is crashing down on me.

I hate how men have the ability to hurt me so damn easily.

I hate how weak I am.

Most of all, I hate how I keep inviting them in to do so.

I was so stupid to let Robbi in. God, I let him kiss me, and the whole time, I was just a means to an end for him.

But Tom saved me.

My heart reaches for him. Then, I quickly remember his tongue fest with Ashlee.

Hurt needles me. I need to get the hell out of here. This is all too much.

"Well, if that's all, I'll be leaving."

"I'm not done." Tom's rough voice keeps me where I am.

Moving quickly, he closes the gap between us.

Suddenly, everything narrows to this moment. To him and me.

Desire exploding between us like a dirty bomb.

There's nothing but blazing heat and sexual tension. The likes of nothing I've ever felt before.

It's total sensory overload.

He's perfect and gorgeous. Desire coils in my belly. My hands itch to touch him.

"I said, there were two reasons I dragged Robbi off of you. The second, if I'm being truthful, is the main reason." He takes a ragged breath. "I couldn't bear to see you with him."

"You kissed Ashlee."

He shakes his head slowly. "No, she kissed me. And I didn't so much as let her kiss me. I just didn't want to hurt her feelings. I gently pushed her away. Told her I was into someone else. But you didn't wait to see that part."

"Oh, I'm sorry I didn't wait around to watch you suck face with Ashlee!"

His brows draw together. His jade eyes darken with anger. "Enough, Lyla." His voice is so hard, and the words are said with so much force that it brings my whole body to attention.

Just those two words, and I'm done for. I love the way his commanding voice makes me feel.

Hot. Really fucking hot.

Heat is licking up and down my body. And I'm so wet that it's embarrassing.

"The only woman I want right now is *you*," he says, his voice hoarse. "I can't stop thinking about you. What it will feel like to be inside you. God, Ly, I can't stop imagining how sweet your pussy will taste on my tongue."

*Holy shit.*

Tom does the dirty talk well. Really well.

I'm currently a puddle on the floor.

His hand comes up and grabs my chin, forcing my eyes to his. *My God, his eyes are on fire.*

Dark eyes roam my face, stopping on my mouth. A flicker of anger moves through them. "You let him kiss you." The pad of his thumb presses against the center of my lips.

I swallow down.

Tom moves his thumb roughly over my lips as he removes the remaining lipstick, erasing any trace of Robbi's kiss.

My body starts to tremble. The intensity of the moment owns me.

He owns me.

His eyes flash up to mine. The look in them has my nipples tightening and my panties dissolving.

My body is hitting levels of desire I didn't even know existed until this moment. Until him.

"You're mine," he growls, making a sound filled with the sweetest agony. Then, he's kissing me, hot and hard. "No one gets to touch you but me," he breathes hotly into my mouth. "You got that?"

The intensity of him, the feel of him kissing me, has fried all my brain cells. I couldn't argue if I wanted to.

And I don't.

I've given up fighting this thing between Tom and me. I'm handing all control of my body over to him. For tonight only, I'm letting Tom have all of me to do with as he wishes.

And tomorrow, after we've screwed each other out of our systems, things will go back to the way it was.

"I got it," I breathe.

# Five Minutes Later—Fairmont Hotel, Pittsburgh

"Tom, I need you to fuck me...*now*," Lyla moans.

I'm running my tongue up her throat, heading back for that sexy but frustrating mouth of hers, and my cock almost bursts out of my pants.

*Jesus Christ.*

I almost can't believe this is happening. I keep waiting for her to pull away and run out on me again, but she hasn't. And now, she's asking me to fuck her.

*Christ, I want to fuck her.*

*More than I've ever wanted to fuck a woman before, but—*

"You don't want to do this with me."

*What?*

Okay, I know I sound like a pussy, but she's hurting from the stunt that idiot, Robbi, pulled. No matter how much I want to bang her, I do actually care about her, and I can't have sex with her while she's hurting. It wouldn't be right.

The last thing I want is for her to regret fucking me.

Trying to keep my control, I dig my fingers into her waist. But all that does is make me harder as I feel the soft flesh of her skin beneath the fabric of this fuck-hot dress she's wearing.

"Firecracker, I need the truth here. Are you doing this because Robbi hurt you? Or because you really want me?"

She eyes me with insouciance. "I'm not hurt, Tom. I'm horny."

I let out a sigh. "I just can't keep doing this push-and-pull shit with you, Ly."

Her eyes soften. She rests her hand on my chest. My heart is beating like a motherfucker beneath her palm.

"Is that what I do? Push and pull with you?"

My eyes narrow. "You know you do."

Her fingers grip my shirt as her eyes lower. "Have I...hurt you?"

I let out a short laugh. "No, you haven't hurt me. You just confuse the hell out of me, so I want to make sure you're doing this for the right reason—not because you're feeling hurt and pissed off over some little dipshit who wasn't smart enough to see you for your real worth."

I know she usually reacts badly when she's angry. I got that loud and clear when she kissed Robbi because she thought I was into Ashlee.

"I don't want you to regret having sex with me."

*Why am I still talking?*

Now, I actually sound like I'm trying to talk her out of this.

I have her right where I've literally dreamed about having her for months. I'm minutes away from being inside her, and my lips won't stop fucking flapping.

I seriously need to learn to shut the fuck up.

She inches up, hovering her mouth over mine. Her lips whisper, "I'll regret it if I don't. I regret walking out on you when we were in the bedroom the other day. I don't want any more regrets, Tom. I know you want me. I can feel that you do." She reaches her hand down, wrapping her delicate fingers around my denim-covered cock.

My eyes roll back into my head. I can't seem to catch a steady breath. My lungs are full of her. She's everywhere…around me, on me, in me.

I've never felt this way with a woman before. I really need to get a grip and regain some control.

She grazes her teeth over my bottom lip. I feel it *everywhere*.

"I want this…I want *you*. More than I've ever wanted any man before. I want you to fuck me, Tom…*please*."

The feel of her and the sound of her sexy voice begging me to fuck her snaps my control.

I plunge my fingers deep in her hair and crash my mouth on hers.

I'm a man possessed. Uncoordinated and out of control. My tongue is fucking her mouth. There's no restraint, no patience. I can't get enough of her. Weeks of pent-up frustration from wanting *her* for so damn long explodes out of me and is channeled into this one kiss.

If I carry on like this, it'll be over in minutes.

*It can't be over in minutes.*

My fingers find the hem of that sexy dress, and I pull it over her hips.

Grabbing her ass in my hands, I lift her off the floor, our mouths still fused together.

Her legs go around my waist, and her hands pull at my hair while she moans in my mouth.

*I know the feeling, baby.*

It's like I'm climbing out of my skin and into hers. I can't get enough…be close enough to her.

This is insane. I've never felt like this about a woman before.

I'm always in control. I take my time. Women beg me to give it to them.

But this…it feels like I'm the one begging her. I might not be saying the words, but my body sure as hell is.

Regaining a margin of control, I start moving toward the bedroom, toeing off my shoes as I go. I lay her down on the bed, positioning myself between her thighs. We still haven't broke from kissing. Well, maybe *kissing* is too good of a word for what we're doing. We're basically mouth-fucking.

Finally stopping for a breath, I break the kiss. No matter how much I want to keep on kissing her, I want to see her naked more.

I stare down at her. The only light coming in is from the living room, but I can still see that her eyes are glazed over with lust.

"I want you," she whispers, breathless, as her wide eyes blink up at me.

*She's finally mine.*

The knowledge makes me want to beat my chest and thank the gods.

"You have me," I say. "You've had me for a long time."

I shift up onto my knees. Sitting over her, I reach for her dress. She sits up, allowing me to remove it. I have to tug a bit around her tits as the dress seems to be stuck, and as I do, I hear this weird ripping sound.

*Shit, did I tear her dress?*

*Whatever.* If I have to, I'll buy her a new one. I'll buy her a million dresses if it means I finally get to be inside her.

I drop her dress to the floor, and when I look back, I see— well, not what I was expecting to see.

Lyla's looking down at her tits as she picks something off of them.

My head tilts to the side. "Um…what the fuck are you doing?"

Her eyes lift to mine, and a blush rises in her cheeks. "Tit tape." She scrunches her nose as she holds up a piece of sticky tape between her thumb and index finger.

She looks so fucking adorable right now.

"Had to keep my girls in place somehow." She shrugs, letting out a sweet-sounding laugh.

I chuckle, shaking my head, watching her, as she peels off another piece of tit tape. I hope to hell it's the last piece because I don't know how much longer I can keep my hands to myself.

She balls up the pieces of tape and flicks it onto the floor.

"Done." She gives me a sexy smile as she pushes her chest out to me. "They're all yours."

I laugh again. Then, I look down at her tits, and all laughter fades from my mouth.

Perfection. Absolute perfection. Just like I thought they would be. Big. Real. Perky. With taut pink nipples waiting for me to pay them the attention they deserve.

I reach out and cup her tits in my hands.

They feel as good as they look. Perfect fit for my hands, like they were made just for me. Heavy and so very real. After way too long of handling fake tits that seem to be the norm in LA, I cannot wait to wrap my mouth around those beauties of hers.

I lick my lips at the thought.

She arches into my touch. "Like what you see?"

I lift my eyes to find hers looking all lusty and sexy as hell.

She is perfection.

Grinning, I say, "Without a doubt." I lick my lips again, feeling suddenly parched. "You seriously have the best tits I have ever seen in my life. A-fuckin'-mazing. I could stare at them all day and not get bored once."

She lets out a throaty laugh, causing them to jiggle in my hands.

She rests back onto her elbows and lifts her chin. "Get naked. Now." Her eyes are watching me with determination.

I don't usually take well to commands from women. The bedroom is my domain. Sex *always* runs at my pace. But I don't want to do anything that might ruin this or set off her crazy mouth, so I'll keep quiet this time. I have her where I've wanted her for a long time, and she's currently pliable, so I'll indulge her and do as she asks.

Still, I am a little reluctant to let go of these beauties now that I finally have them in my hands.

Giving them one last squeeze, I smirk. "With pleasure, darlin'."

I tug my shirt off, letting it join her dress on the floor. When I see the look in her eyes as she stares at me, I get a feeling I've never had before.

She's not looking at me the same way other women do when they know they're about to be fucked by me.

When a woman has sex with me, she's having sex with my band, my name, giving herself notoriety. She can say she was fucked by Tom Carter from TMS.

Not that I don't use women in equal measure.

But Lyla's not looking at me like that.

The only thing in her eyes is…me.

She's looking at me like I matter—to her. Like this is real.

Then, she meets my eyes, and something happens. I'm not sure what exactly, but whatever it is, it tightens its hands around my chest, making my lungs burn and my heart pound like a bitch.

Then, she smiles, and her eyes move down my chest, heading south. I almost exhale in relief.

I watch as her gaze hits my cock, which is straining against my jeans, desperate to get out and into her.

Her eyes widen.

I grin.

This I can work with.

Grabbing my cock, I draw the denim even tighter against him, giving her some idea of the size that is about to impale her.

There's a nervous flicker in her eyes. She bites her lip. Then, she lifts her gaze to mine. I have to stifle a laugh as I watch her force determination into her stare.

"Naked," she reiterates.

Once again indulging her, I get to my feet.

Standing on the bed, a foot on either side of her hips, I unbutton my jeans and shove them down past my hips, letting my cock spring free.

In surprise, her mouth forms a perfect O, showing me her blow-job mouth, which I'll be putting to use real soon.

She's either shocked by the fact that I've been commando all night, or she's amazed by the actual size of my cock.

I'm not what you would call…small.

"Like what you see?" I smirk.

Wide eyes stare back at me. I watch her blink herself back to reality, and I hold back the laughter I feel.

Lifting her eyebrow, she drags her tongue along her lower lip. "Yeah, I like what I see—a lot."

*Jesus.* That almost brings me to my knees.

My dick pulses, throbbing against my stomach.

I look down at her pussy. "Lose the panties, Firecracker. *Now.*"

She practically jumps to attention at the command in my voice. I like that she does. It'll work well for future fuckings. Moving her legs from between mine, she pulls off those sexy boots. I enjoy the sound of them hitting the floor.

My eyes are fixed on her hands, watching rapt, as she slides her panties off.

*Perfect. Just fucking perfect.*

She's blonde there, too. Trimmed to exquisiteness. A sexy landing strip.

A cat flap just awaiting my entrance.

*Thank you, God.*

I let my eyes roam.

My cock hardens further at the unadulterated sight of her.

Long blonde hair spilling across slender shoulders. Stunning eyes. Soft, creamy skin. Perfect tits.

Then, a wave of anger hits me. She's wanted me all this time, but she has been denying me, keeping her amazing body from me.

"Don't ever say no to me again."

She tilts her head to the side, an unsure smile on her lips. "Okay…"

I choose to ignore the lack of surety in her voice.

Mirroring her, I cock my head to the side. "You really should be naked all the time, you know."

She throws her head back and laughs. The sound makes my cock ache.

"You're seriously fucking hot, Firecracker."

She crooks a finger at me. I get down to my knees and crawl up her body. Unable to stay away a second longer, I crush my mouth to hers.

She moans a sound of absolute pleasure. I feel it under my skin, like a drug slipping into my veins.

Her lips part on a soft moan. I slide my tongue inside her mouth. Holding her head in my hands, I take control of the kiss, deepening it. I'm taking my time, enjoying the feel of her sexy tongue slide against mine.

Then, she wraps her hand around my cock. He jerks at her touch. And so does my control before it snaps.

Our mouths are going at it, hard and fast.

*Shit, if I keep this up, it'll be over before it begins.*

Leaving her mouth, I kiss across her jaw to her neck, and I slide down her body until I reach those gorgeous tits of hers.

Tongue on her nipple, I lave it, licking and sucking, getting off on the sweet taste of her.

Lyla arches up, pushing into my mouth, offering herself to me.

Wanting to play a little, I move away.

"Tom, *please...*" she moans, her hands grabbing my hair as she tries to guide me to where she wants.

I love how much she wants it...wants me.

I blow lightly over her wet nipple, and then I take one of her perfect tits into my mouth. I lick and suck and bite until her nipple is distended, and she's writhing wild under me.

Her pussy is wet and rubbing against my thigh, reaching for what I'm going to give her three times over before the night is over.

I lift my body slightly and slip my hand between her legs.

She jerks at my touch.

"Jesus, Ly," I groan. "You're soaked."

I knew she was wet, but this is beyond hot. She's practically dripping down her thighs for me.

I slide my finger through her folds and find nirvana when I push into her pussy. "Fuck," I hiss, feeling her insanely tight pussy clamping down on my finger.

She hasn't been fucked in a while. I've been inside enough women to know.

No wonder she's so cranky all the time. She's one hot ball of frustration.

I plan on relieving that tension very soon. She'll have a smile like the Joker by the time I'm finished with her.

I lean up and gently kiss her lips. "How long has it been since you were last fucked?" I murmur as I continue to glide my finger in and out of her.

Her body stiffens. I know she's about to pull away.

I capture her gaze. "Don't run. It's just a question. No hidden agenda. I just want to know how many orgasms you're owed…because I'm ready to pay up."

*Quick thinking there, Carter.*

She blinks back at me, eyes wide and unsure.

"How long, baby?" I run my tongue over her bottom lip before nipping it with my teeth.

Her body softens in my hands.

She exhales a light breath. "It's not a really long time…ten months. I haven't been with anyone since…"

*Since that motherfucker broke her heart.*

And seriously, ten months is a fucking long time to go without sex. I'm going without, and it's killing me. But that's mostly because of her.

I press another kiss to her lips while doing quick math in my head. "You're owed six hundred orgasms," I murmur into her mouth.

Pulling back, she stares at me like I'm crazy. "How do you figure that?"

"Ten months dry, averaging each month at thirty days. That's two a day—"

"Two?"

"Bare minimum when you're with me, baby." I wink.

She laughs, and her tits jiggle, drawing my attention back to them. Moving down, I cup them with my hands, and I press a kiss between them.

"So, that's thirty times two. Sixty orgasms times ten months equals six hundred."

"You can count quickly."

"I'm not just a stunningly handsome face."

She slides her fingers into my hair. "I'm starting to realize that."

Feeling pressure on my chest again, I ignore it and begin licking a path between her tits.

"Six hundred," she purrs. "That's a lot of orgasms."

"I could clear that in a month," I murmur over her skin.

"That's quite a challenge."

"Easy street for me."

"Tom, you do realize that I've been coming all by myself during the last ten months, right?"

Dropping my head to her chest, I groan. "Jesus, I wish I'd been there to see that—or at the very least, helped." I lift my head. "Please tell me you were imagining me when you were getting yourself off?"

She lifts a sexy eyebrow and nips her lip with her teeth. "Maybe...once or twice."

"Jesus fucking Christ," I moan, dropping my head back to her chest.

The sound and feel of her laughter brings a smile to my lips.

My head comes back up on a thought. "In the world of orgasms, you do know that self-helps don't count, right?"

She shakes her head, her eyes glinting. "I did not know that."

She bites that damn lip again, making me want to bite it and more. I take hold of her lip between my thumb and finger, tugging it free. Her eyes darken.

"Six hundred orgasms, Firecracker. Just think of it..."

There's this moment between us. Something happens, something I've never felt before. I'm not quite sure what it is.

She lets out a laugh. "All nice in theory, but we both know this is only going to happen once. It's a shame because I would totally be up for six hundred orgasms."

Her words stick in my throat.

*Once.*

I can't just fuck her and walk away. Aside from breaking my promise to the big man upstairs, the thought of *once* with her doesn't sound like nearly enough.

*I need to keep her...for a while at least.*

Leaving all thoughts and talk behind, I crawl my way down her body. Pushing her thighs apart, I settle between them and lift one leg, hooking it over my shoulder. Lowering my mouth to her pussy, I lift my eyes and find her staring at me.

"Stay exactly like this. I want you to watch the whole time I'm licking you until you come around my mouth. You close your eyes, and you don't get to come. Understand?"

Her tongue slides over her lower lip, and she nods her head.

I love how pliant she is under my hands. *Seems sex is what makes Lyla agreeable.*

"Good girl."

Pressing my nose and mouth up against her pussy, I inhale. *God, she smells so fucking good.*

In this moment, I wish that I'd kept that tongue ring I used to have. I got rid of it because it was driving me nuts, but I know the feel of it would have driven her wild.

*Guess I'll just have to work some extra magic with my tongue alone.*

Tilting my head back slightly, I let my tongue out, and I lick up her pussy until I reach her clit.

Her hips jerk, and she cries out loudly the instant I make contact with her clit.

I love her reaction. And it spurs me on more.

I repeat the motion a few more times until she's writhing, pushing against my mouth.

Then, I just lose it. I lose myself in her.

Licking and sucking hard, I plunge my tongue inside her pussy, getting off on the feel of her hands pulling at my hair. I'm literally dry-humping the mattress in time with the movement of her hips as she rocks against my mouth.

Her voice breathy, she curses and cries out my name.

She's vocal, and it's seriously hot.

Her eyes have stayed on me the whole time, just like I told her…right up until that tight hold of hers snaps. Then, she's exploding in my mouth…screaming out my name.

The absolute satisfaction I feel at her reaction to me is like nothing I've felt before.

I feel heady.

Full of her yet not full enough.

I feel like a fucking king.

Off that bed, I grab my jeans from the floor, getting a condom from my wallet.

She watches me put it on, her eyes greedy on my cock, so I make sure to let her enjoy the show.

When I'm sheathed, I'm back between her legs and ready to hit that home run.

"I need you inside me," she whispers, breathless.

I take both her hands and move them up over her head, pinning them to the bed.

I lower my mouth to hers, lips just touching. "I'm gonna fuck you so hard that you're not gonna know where you start and I end."

Then, I lick a path along her lips while teasing my cock at her slick entrance. "Ask me to fuck you."

Her eyes meet mine. "Fuck me, Tom."

"Say please."

"*Please*, Tom!" she cries out. "Just fuck me! Now!"

In one swift move, I slam inside her. I'm pretty sure I lose consciousness for a few seconds. It's been way too long since I've been inside a woman, and Lyla feels like nothing I've ever felt before.

Tight. So tight and hot and perfect.

My ears are ringing, my blood pumping and my heart pounding. I'm about to burst out of my skin.

And I'm so close to coming that it's not even funny.

I slide a hand down her thigh. "Wrap your legs around me."

She puts her legs around me, no questions asked.

I love how controllable she is in bed. *Maybe I'll just keep her locked up in here all the time.*

Now, there's a thought.

"Tom…please," she moans.

I move out of her slowly and then slam straight back in.

"Oh God." Her eyes close, and she arches her back, pushing her tits into my chest.

I lower my head and suck her nipple into my mouth, hard.

"Holy shit!" she cries, breathless. "Harder, Tom! Fuck me harder!"

And I'm undone.

I start fucking her like there's no tomorrow. Driving her up the bed with each hard thrust. The sound of my skin slapping against hers is pushing me closer to the edge.

I can feel her tightening around my cock. She's ready to come, which is fucking relief because I'm about two seconds behind her.

I reach a hand between us and rub my thumb over her clit.

"Two orgasms, Ly," I murmur over her mouth before I capture another kiss. "Give it to me. *Now*."

"Oh God…Tom…Tom…"

I press my thumb against her clit, then, she's screaming my name and God's and a whole bunch of curses as her body bucks skyward.

I fucking love how vocal she is. It's seriously sexy.

I'm swift as I move up onto my knees. I grab hold of her hips, yanking her to me, and then I start to slam my way home. I pump in and out—once, twice—while my sack slaps her hot ass, and then...

"Lyla! Fuck!"

I come harder than I ever have come before.

I fall on top of her, my body twitching with aftershocks.

Still inside her, I rest up on my elbows, easing my weight away from her. Her eyes are glazed, and she's wearing a cute, goofy smile.

"That was amazing," she breathes. She lifts her hand to my face and runs her fingers over my cheek.

"Of course it was." I give her a cocky grin.

She giggles. The sound has my cock standing back to attention. Even he can't seem to get enough of her.

I'm staring at her. She's staring at me.

Then, I see the shift in her expression.

"I should go," she says.

*What the fuck?*

# TOM 19

## One Second After—Fairmont Hotel, Pittsburgh

"What?" I frown, my eyes wide.

I'm still inside her, and she's talking about leaving. That's usually my line. *Have I missed something here?*

She gives me a wary look. "I should, um…leave and go to my room."

These are the words I always want to hear from a woman, but never do. If I ever did, I would have been singing. But hearing Lyla say them…

Yeah, not so great.

I actually feel a little…*used.*

*What the fuck? Have I grown a vagina? Have I turned into Jake or Denny?*

*Jesus Christ.* She's turning me into a man I barely recognize.

I slip my semihard cock out of her and remove the condom before tossing it into the trash can by the bed.

I look back to her. She's not looking at me. Her eyes are staring out the window.

There's something niggling inside me, like an ache in my chest. Then, I realize that ache is there because I don't want her to leave. Not yet anyway.

I don't want her to leave because…well, because I haven't had my fill of her yet. I'm not done fucking her.

*Yeah, that's why my chest is aching like a bitch.*

"Not happening," I say firmly. "I'm not finished with you yet."

Her eyes come back to me with a hard look in them. "And what if I'm finished with you?"

I put my hand between her thighs and slip my finger between her folds. Still soaking. "Doesn't feel like you're done with me."

She smacks my hand away.

I chuckle.

"You really are disgusting."

"Yeah, and you fucking love it."

She tries to give me an angry look, but a smile edges her lips. Then, out of nowhere, she lets out a sad sigh and rubs her hands over her face before leaving them there.

I pull her hands away from her face. "Talk to me."

She lets out another sigh. Focusing her eyes on mine, she gives me a lost look. "I thought we'd be done now. That this"—she waves a hand between us—"drive-me-crazy sexual tension would be gone if we had sex this one time. Then, we could go back to normal, you know, being friends like we were. But…" She bites down on her lip. "Now, we've had sex, and well…" Her eyes lower. "It doesn't feel like we're done."

This weird sense of relief spreads through me.

"That's because we're not. We haven't even begun. Once was never an option. It was never going to be enough to satisfy what's between us."

I see a flash of fear cross her face.

"I can't have a relationship, not with you or anyone." She turns her head from me.

"Hey." I catch her chin, bringing her back. "I'm not saying we should have a relationship, Ly. Come on, this is me you're talking to. You know that I've never had a relationship in my life, and I'm not about to start now."

Her face relaxes, and she nods lightly. "Okay, so what are you saying?"

"That we should keep fucking. Outside of that, we'll continue to be friends."

She screws up that gorgeous face of hers. "You want us to be fuck buddies?"

"Yeah."

"I don't know," she says, unconvinced.

"Well, what do you suggest?" I run my fingers down her side, enjoying the feel of her squirming under my touch. Stopping at her hip, I grip it. "I sure as hell can't come up with anything else. Trust me, if I could, I would have by now. Plus, everyone already thinks we're fucking, so—"

"That's not a reason for us to continue doing so." She frowns.

I'm starting to get pissed off. She's seriously hard work, and it's fucking exhausting.

"I never said it was. But like you pointed out, we have a hard time staying away from one another. After what happened tonight, it's pretty damn clear that you don't want me to be with anyone else, and I sure as hell don't want you fucking anyone but me. You're also seriously down on orgasms due to that stupid-ass sex ban you put on yourself, and I can more than make up for them. I'm a machine when it comes to sex. I literally *never* tire, and as you've just discovered, I'm awesome at it. Also, I haven't fucked anyone but you in a really long time, so I'm down on blowing my load inside a woman."

*Okay, where the hell did all that just come from?*

I'm starting to think that this woman will be my undoing.

She gives me a look of distaste. "Jesus, Tom, blowing your load? You think using words like that will bring me over to the dark side?"

Rubbing my head, I let out a frustrated laugh. "Okay, I could have said that last part differently. How about, I haven't had an expulsion of semen while inside a woman in a very long time?"

That breaks her angry resolve. A small smile quickly works its way onto her lips. "A little better." She laughs. "If not a bit creepy sounding."

Relaxing, I smile and tuck her hair behind her ear.

I like to see Lyla happy. I like it even more when she's happy because of me.

"How long?" She traces a finger over my eyebrow.

"How long, what?"

"Since you last had sex?"

I check my watch. "Um…about sixty seconds."

"Knock it off!" She gives me a playful shove.

I laugh at her daintiness.

"I meant, before me," she clarifies.

I close my eyes in thought.

*Who was the last woman I fucked before Lyla?*

Oh yeah, the blonde waitress from that bar. Can't remember the name—or hers. She took me back to her apartment after she finished her shift. We started fucking on the sofa. Then, her roommate came home mid-fuck and joined us. So, my last fuck was actually a threesome. I ended up doing the roommate up the ass. She was a bit weird. Insisted on sucking my cock with the condom still on after it had been up her ass. But, hey, whatever floats her boat. I got off, and that was all I cared about.

And it was all I cared about for a really long time—until Lyla.

"Ages," I answer. "About five weeks ago."

She starts to laugh. "Five weeks isn't long!"

"Hey!" I poke her waist.

She lets out a squeal and wiggles, slapping my hand away.

*Hmm...she's ticklish.* I might just have to use that to my advantage and soon.

"Five weeks is a really long time, Firecracker." *Especially when I'm used to fucking daily, usually multiple times with multiple women.*

Not that I'm going to say that to her.

I'm not stupid. I want to keep fucking Lyla, and reminding her of how I used to be is not the way to make that happen.

"And it felt even longer while living under the same roof as you. Teasing me with your hot body and your amazing tits hidden under those tight little cartoon T-shirts while you strut your sexy ass around the bus."

"I do not strut, and I definitely don't tease." She sticks her tongue out.

I go to pinch it, but I miss. Instead, I tug on her lower lip. "You tease me, and you know it. I had a serious hard-on for days after the dry-hump against the bus. I couldn't get him to stay down."

"Sorry." She giggles.

The sound is like wet lips sliding down my cock.

"Living on that tour bus with you has been pure torture. I haven't dated my hand so much since I was a teenager. I've had the worst case of blue balls ever."

I pout, going for full effect. I'm trying to win on guilt here.

Hey, I never claimed to be a good guy.

She wraps her fingers around the one I have on her lip, and she kisses the tip. "Poor baby. Have I been driving you crazy?"

"That's putting it mildly," I grumble.

"So, I guess then you're owed..." She closes her eyes in thought. Opening them, she says, "Seventy expulsions of semen." She finishes that with a sexy smile.

*Seventy?*

I do quick math in my head.

She's averaging me having two fucks a day. Not like I'll be telling her the truth and reminding her of the man I was, so I just go with it. "Well, it's sixty-nine now, thanks to you, gorgeous. Sixty-nine—my favorite number." I give her a cheeky smile.

She shakes her head, laughing.

"But to keep the average up, we'll have to fuck twice a day, every day." I rest my elbow next to her head, putting my head in my hand. I stare down at her.

She blows out a breath. Pushing a hand into her hair, she stares past me at the ceiling. "No one could know we're sleeping together."

*And she's mine.*

I climb on top of her, positioning myself back between her thighs. "No one will know."

Her eyes meet mine. "I don't want people to think I'm trying to screw my way to success."

"People wouldn't think that." I brush her bangs off her forehead.

"No, they'd probably think I lost my mind."

I ignore the sting her words cause. Brushing over them, I say, "Yeah, well, I like it when you lose your mind over me." I press a kiss to her neck.

"How are we going to do this—have sex without anyone finding out while we're living together on the tour bus? I don't know if it's possible."

I bring my face back to her, putting the tip of my nose against hers. "It's more than possible. I can be *very* inventive when necessary." I nudge my hard cock against her thigh.

"Oh, I'm sure you can be." She lifts an eyebrow. "And you don't think it'll be awkward—us living and sleeping together?"

I cup her cheek with my hand. "Things are only as complicated as you make them, darlin'."

I watch, rapt, as she processes my words.

"No complications. No ties. Just sex."

"Just sex," I murmur before pressing a kiss to her lips.

I can feel her body softening beneath me, giving in to me.

She puts her hands in my hair, running her fingers through the strands. "And when the tour ends, so does our arrangement."

*Will I be done with her by then?*

Yeah, I think I will be.

And I'm still keeping my promise. Only sleeping with one woman. No screwing around.

Perfect.

"When the tour ends, so do we." I tilt my head back, enjoying the feel of her gentle fingers running across my scalp.

"Okay…I'm in," her breathy voice whispers.

Then, her hands leave my hair. I open my eyes, missing the feel of her, only to find her hand stuck in front of my face. She's holding it out to me like she wants me to shake it.

"Er…what the fuck do you want me to do with that?"

She gives me a sardonic look. "Er…shake it."

I raise an eyebrow. "Do we need to spit on them first, you know, to seal the deal properly?"

"Just shake my hand, assface."

"Firecracker, when I shake on something with a woman, it *always* involves tongues." I take hold of her hand and run the tip of my tongue very slowly up her palm. Reaching her middle finger, I lick my way up and then suck it into my mouth.

She shudders.

Smiling, I make my way down her sexy little body. I hook her leg over my shoulder and press my tongue straight onto her pussy.

She gasps, her hands going for my hair.

I suck her clit into my mouth and push a finger inside her. Then, I go to work until she's writhing beneath me, unashamedly fucking my mouth.

She couldn't be any hotter if she tried.

Then, she's coming off the bed, crying out a bunch of expletives, as she orgasms into my mouth.

And I lap up everything she gives me.

I wipe my mouth on the back of my hand and climb up her trembling body. I press a kiss to her lips. "There—it's a deal."

I push myself up, jumping to my feet. "I'm just gonna grab a bottle of water and fuel up. You need anything?"

She gives a small shake of her head a stunned look on her face.

Chuckling, I say, "Two secs, darlin', and I'll be right back to give you that fucking we both need."

I grab a water from the fridge and quickly down it before getting another to take back with me.

When I get back to the bedroom, she's still lying where I left her, blonde hair splayed across the pillow, looking liking a goddess.

"Hey," she says, resting up on her elbows, pushing those gorgeous tits of hers up into my view. "In the elevator, you said you had something for me. Did you actually have something for me? Or was I right, and it was actually just a euphemism for sex?"

"No, pessimist." I lean against the doorjamb. "I actually have something for you."

Her face lights up. I like the way it makes me feel.

Putting the bottle of water down on the dresser, I head to my overnight bag and pull out the plastic carrier containing what I bought for her earlier.

This is a first for me. I've never got something for a woman I want to fuck or am actively fucking.

I feel a quick stab of nerves that she won't like what I bought her. Then, I slap that pussy thought right out of my head.

"It's not much," I say, handing the bag to her. "But I saw it at the gas station when we stopped this morning, and it had you written all over it."

I watch her face as she reaches into the bag and pulls out the yellow Angry Birds T-shirt.

"Angry Birds," she reads. "A is for angry." She lets out a giggle.

Then, without warning, a broken-sounding sob follows.

She slaps a hand over her mouth, surprise and tears filling her eyes.

The breath is knocked out of me.

*Shit.*

"Christ, Lyla, I didn't mean to upset you." I reach for her, pulling her to me.

"You haven't. I love the shirt…I do. It's just…the cartoon T-shirt thing was something my mom and I shared. She'd always buy me a new shirt while she was on the road. I carried on the tradition after she died, and no one else has ever bought one for me but her." She rubs away a tear that has fallen.

The sight of her crying makes me feel like I've been sucker-punched. I've never been affected by a woman's tears before. But seeing Lyla cry bothers me—a lot.

"I meant to buy a shirt from each city we visited, but there hasn't been time to get to the store since we're always so busy when we stop. Then, before I know it, we're back on the road. We're nearly two weeks into the tour, and I haven't bought single T-shirt."

I cup her face. "We'll start now." I rub my thumb over her damp cheek. "I'll make sure we carve out time in each city to get to a store and buy you a new shirt."

Hopeful, beautiful blue eyes blink back at me.

I have this sudden feeling of falling.

"You think we could? It wouldn't cause any time issues?"

I brush my sudden vertigo aside. "I schedule this tour. People work to my timing. They do what I say. And I say, we're getting you a T-shirt in every town we stop in."

"Thank you." She takes hold of my hand, turning her face into it, and presses a kiss to my palm.

It's warm and caring. And loving.

*No.*

I feel like my balls have just been put into a vise. My heart starts to hammer out of its cage.

I move away from her touch and climb off the bed, using the excuse of getting my water bottle from the dresser. I keep my back to her while drinking from the bottle until I feel my heart rate return to normal.

When I turn, her arms are up in the air, and the Angry Birds tee is descending, almost about to cover up those perfect tits of hers.

"What do you think you're doing?"

She stops, the shirt teetering way too close to coverage for my liking. She gives me a look of confusion. "Putting on the cute shirt you bought me."

Shaking my head, I stride over and pull the shirt back off. I toss it to the nearby chair. "New rule—no clothes when you and I are together."

"That could get a little awkward on the bus, and you know, in public."

"All right, smart-ass. You and I in a bedroom, clothes stay at the door."

"I don't like to sleep naked."

Leaning over her, my hand quickly moves up her inner thigh, and without stopping, I push two fingers inside her. "Well, get used to it."

She tightens around my fingers, her head falling back onto the pillow.

"I need you inside me," she breathes.

"Say please."

Her eyes bore into mine. "Please," she growls, her jaw clenched.

In seconds, I'm sheathed and fucking her again.

She's sleeping now. Worn out from the four orgasms I gave her.

And she's wearing the damn T-shirt.

I caved after she got all cute on me. I'm not happy about it. I don't see the reason for covering up her gorgeous body. But she wanted to wear it, and I gave in.

Definitely something I need to work on. Giving in is not something I'm used to doing.

She pulled that shirt on, lay down in my arms, her head on my chest, and was out in minutes.

She's not used to all the sex. Well, she'll have to learn and fast, because my sex drive is really high. We're going to be screwing like this the whole time we're on tour.

I stare down at her. She looks even more beautiful in sleep.

Then, I look at the T-shirt and smile. I don't why, but I get a ridiculously happy feeling from knowing she's wearing the shirt I bought her.

But, that smile disappears quickly when my mind reminds me that shit is still here, sitting out there in the goddamn minibar.

I specifically requested no Segal in the minibar, like I do at every hotel I stay in. Stupid fuckers here obviously don't give a shit about their guests' requests. Yeah, well, tomorrow, they're going to get a taste of pissed off Tom Carter.

Knowing I won't sleep with that shit in here, I ease my arm out from underneath Lyla, and quietly slip out of bed and go through to the living room.

I open the door to the minibar and grab all the bottles of Segal. I can't even stand to have that shit in my hands, so I quickly dump them in the wastebasket. Walking over to the door, I open it and leave the wastebasket out in the hall for the cleaners to take away.

The minute I shut the door, all the tension I was feeling leaves my body.

I go back to the bedroom and climb into bed. Lyla has turned over in her sleep, so I move up behind her and wrap my arm over her waist, feeling strangely soothed by the warmth of her body.

I've never slept with a chick like this before. Usually, we fuck, and then I go home.

I thought it would be weird, sleeping here with her, but it's not. I really like it.

"Where did you go?" she asks in a sleepy voice.

*She's awake.* I press a kiss to her neck. "Just to get a drink," I lie.

"Are you going back to sleep?" She yawns.

I smile against her skin. Then, I lift her shirt and smooth my hand down her side and over her ass.

"No, I was thinking I might give you another orgasm, if you're not too tired that is."

I slip my hand between her legs. She parts them for me. I run my finger between her lips, finding her wet and so very ready for me.

*God, she's so fucking hot.*

She shrugs, trying to feign nonchalance. "I'm not tired anymore. Sure, I guess I could go for another orgasm. I mean, you do give them so very well."

Grinning, I reach over and grab a condom from the bedside table. Only two left. Looks like I'll have to stock up on these babies. Not that I'm complaining.

I have that condom on in seconds. Gripping her thigh with my hand, I lift her leg higher and push inside her.

"Christ, Lyla. You're so tight, so fucking hot."

"Oh God," she moans.

I start fucking her, sliding my cock in and out of her slick hole. Having sex with Lyla is like finding my nirvana.

And I suddenly realize that this is all I want. To keep doing this with her. I can't imagine ever stopping.

*No.*

I will stop. The tour will end, and so will this thing I have with her.

Instantly, I'm hit with a barrage of feelings.

A part of me—the part that is with her right now, inside her, feeling her all around me—is exhilarated and light in a way that I never have before.

But the other part of me, the part that knows I have to let this go—let her go—well, that part feels very fucking dark indeed.

## The Next Morning—Tom's Suite, Fairmont Hotel, Pittsburgh

I awake with a heavy arm resting over my stomach, hairy long legs tangled up in mine, and that sated feeling a woman can only get from having amazing sex.

*Oh my God. I had sex with Tom.*

Lots and lots of mind-blowing hot sex and some serious out-of-body orgasms.

So, I guess, bang goes my sex ban…with an actual bang.

Having a total girl moment, I slap my hand over my mouth to stifle a giggle.

Tom and I had sex four times. I've never had so much sex in such a short amount of time. Our last sex session was only three hours ago.

And I say *session* because sex with Tom is not a wham-bam-thank-you-ma'am affair. No, siree. He's the kind of guy who believes in oral and more oral, and sex and more sex, until I think I might die from orgasming too much.

*I wonder if you can die from too many orgasms.*

If you can, then…what a way to go. I'd definitely want to die from a Tom Carter orgasm.

*The things that man can do with his tongue and fingers…magic.*

Turning my head, I look at him sleeping beside me.

Hair falling softly across his forehead, long dark lashes fanning his cheekbones, lips slightly apart with his warm breath brushing my own.

He looks so much younger in slumber. Softer. Not the badass I know he is.

The man is a machine in bed. I didn't know a guy could go so much and so hard and come so many times in one night.

Tom proved to me that it's possible.

The guys I've slept with have all been one-timers and then lights out.

But not Tom. He just goes and goes, like the Energizer Bunny. Except, Tom is no bunny.

He's pure primal male. The man is a beast. A very hot beast.

I should feel totally exhausted, but I don't. My body feels worn but in the best kind of way.

I feel alive.

I haven't felt alive in a really long time. And now, I do…because of him.

*Because of him.*

*Oh God.*

*Shit! No!*

I can't have these sort of feelings for anyone, especially not Tom. Definitely not Tom.

I can't *feel* anything but horny because of him.

*What am I thinking?* Saying I feel alive because of Tom is not good. It's so far from good that it crossed the finish line to bad, and it's heading for fucking insanity.

Feeling anything for him, attaching emotions to the sex we just had, is a slippery slope to a path I don't want to end up on.

Panic grips me. I feel suffocated. I can't breathe.

I have to get out of here.

Carefully, I lift his arm and slide out of bed.

I tiptoe around the bed, collecting my dress, panties, and boots on the way.

Heart pounding, I dress quickly in the living room and smooth my just-fucked hair down with my hand.

Turning back, I look through the open doorway and see the Angry Birds T-shirt on the dresser by the bed. I feel a pang in my chest. I can't believe he bought me such a sweet gift.

Not wanting to leave it behind, I tiptoe back into the bedroom and pick it up. Holding it to my chest, I inhale and smell Tom on it. I can smell him all over me.

It makes me want to stay, yet I want to run away all at the same time.

I stare down at Tom, confusion raging in my head and heart. The feelings in my heart are way too heavy and happening way too quickly.

I need distance. Maybe I'm confused because we slept together after sex. It's not very fuck buddyish.

*Yeah, it's the sleeping together. That's the reason. I'm sure of it.*

I do feel like crap, leaving before he wakes, but this is Tom. It won't matter to him whether I'm here or not when he wakes up. He'll probably be relieved at not having the awkward morning-after moment with me.

Holding the T-shirt, I grab my purse from the coffee table where I left it last night, and I slip out the door quietly.

I make my way to the elevator and press the button. It quickly arrives. I step inside and press the button for my floor, watching as the doors close, ending the night I just had with Tom.

As I exit the elevator, I pray that no one is around. Doing the walk of shame is bad enough without people bearing witness to it. The worst would be if one of the guys caught me. There would be no explaining that away. It would be catastrophic.

I quickly walk to my door and manage to make it inside without seeing another soul. I fall onto my bed with a sigh of relief.

Freshly showered and dressed, I'm seated in the hotel restaurant, having breakfast. Bacon, eggs, pancakes, and toast—I'm having a fatty-food-and-carb fest. I need to bring my energy levels up after last night's sex marathon.

Cale comes wandering in just as the waitress has finished refilling my coffee cup.

"Mornin', gorgeous." He leans over and kisses my forehead before taking the seat across from me.

"Mornin'." I beam at him.

He gives me a curious look and signals for the waitress to come over.

"God, it was so good to sleep in a proper bed last night."

I try to direct my thoughts away from beds and Tom.

"Yeah, it was. But I didn't think you'd be getting much sleep last night." I give him a sly grin.

Then, I'm hit with a memory of Tom thrusting inside me. My whole body shivers in remembrance.

"She didn't stay over." He smirks. "Stayed for a few hours. We did the good stuff, and then she went on her merry way, so I could get my beauty sleep. Anyway, you look overly happy this morning, not that I'm complaining. I'm just wondering what sparked the happiness." He looks to the waitress to place his order. "I'll have the same as my girl here. Thanks."

She gives him the sex eye like most women do, but he turns back to me, not even giving her the time of day. She looks a little downcast as she wanders away. I want to tell her that blondes aren't Cale's thing, but obviously, that would seem a little weird if I did.

"So, is that smile because of Robbi Kraft?"

At the mention of Robbi's name, my lips turn down. Cale notices, so I have to tell him what happened last night. I just leave out the whole sex-with-Tom part and the fact that he and I are now fuck buddies.

"That motherfucker," Cale seethes. "I'm gonna kick his ass when I get my hands on him."

"Whose ass are we kicking?" Sonny asks. He and Van have just rocked up.

"Robbi 'Cuntface' Kraft." Cale then proceeds to fill them in. By this time, I'm feeling pretty small.

"Guys, please, can we just leave it alone? I know you're looking out for me, but to be honest, it's just really embarrassing, and I want to forget it."

Cale reaches over and squeezes my hand. "I just don't like seeing you hurt. You hurt, I hurt. And it makes me want to hurt the motherfucker who did it."

"I second that," Van says.

"Third. You're our girl, Ly," Sonny adds. "Nobody messes with you. They mess with you, they mess with us all. We're a team."

My insides warm.

Then, my irrational guilt reminds me that my team is missing one member, and I remember why. Suddenly, I don't feel so great anymore.

Swallowing past my conflicting emotions, I say, "Thanks, guys. But, honestly, Tom took care of it last night, and now, I just want to forget about it."

"Forget about what?"

My eyes flick up to find Tom standing over our table.

*Um…definitely not the hot sex you and I had or the multiple orgasms you gave me only hours ago.*

"Robbi Kraft," I cough out.

Tom's face darkens at the mention of Robbi's name. I grab my coffee and take a sip.

"Ly told us what he did," Van says.

Tom takes the empty seat beside me.

"Yeah, thanks for looking out for Ly and taking care of Robbi 'Cuntface' Kraft," Cale says to Tom.

"No problem." He gives a one-shoulder shrug as he drapes his other arm over the back of my chair.

*Why does he have his arm around my chair? He doesn't do that normally. If he starts acting out of the ordinary, people might realize something is going on between us.*

"And thanks for bringing her back here safely," Cale adds.

My whole body tenses.

*He did more than just that.*

I can practically feel the smirk on Tom's face from beside me.

A heat is burning up my neck, heading for my face.

"It was my pleasure," Tom says, his voice smooth.

His fingertips touch the back of my arm. His callous fingers gently tickle my smooth skin.

And just like that, my body is immediately tuned to his.

I'm aware of him. Every movement he makes. The hitch in his breath as he draws a line down my arm with the tip of his finger.

A blazing trail is left in his wake.

*God, I want him again.*

*How is that even possible? I would think my body had its fill last night. Apparently not.*

I'm getting horny and antsy at the feel of Tom's touch, and I'm ready to bolt out of here.

He suddenly removes his hand from around my chair, leaving me feeling oddly bereft.

He waves the waitress over.

When she sees Tom, I see the way her eyes light up like the Fourth of July.

I find myself watching him closely for his reaction to her because she is exactly his type.

"Coffee, black," he says to the waitress. Then, he turns to me.

*Wow.*

He barely looked at her, and now, he's looking at me.

He leans in close. "You left," he says quietly into my ear. He doesn't sound happy.

A shiver runs through me.

I quick a glance at the guys. They're talking among themselves.

I meet Tom's eyes. "You were sleeping," I whisper. "I didn't want to wake you."

His eyes narrow. "Next time, wake me. I woke up with a raging hard-on, and no *you* to relieve it."

Feeling daring, I give him a saucy look. Then, I give the table another check to make sure no one's watching. I reach my hand under the table and palm his cock through his jeans.

His stomach muscles tense against my arm.

I meet his stare, biting my lip. "Shame. Guess you'll just have to wait until tonight," I whisper, removing my hand.

He catches my wrist, pulling me back. His voice sounds lethal as he says, "I'm not fucking waiting."

I stifle a moan as lust coils low in my belly, bolting straight to my sex.

Tom lets go of my wrist and stands. "Bus will be up front in thirty minutes, guys, so be ready to leave. Lyla, come with me."

I blink up at him, stunned. "Um…what? Come with you? Why?"

I'm pretty sure I know why. I just don't want everyone else to know why.

His jade eyes harden, darkening. "Because I need to let Jake know about Robbi, and it would be best if you are there when I make the call."

"Okay…" Slowly, I get to my shaky feet. "Guess I'll see you all on the bus." I wave to the guys and follow Tom out of the restaurant.

The instant we're out of view, he grabs my hand, yanking me to his side. "This is a one-time warning, Firecracker. Next time you grab my cock in public, make sure you're willing to do something about it right fucking then and there."

My eyes widen while I search for a retort, but I'm moving again before I get the chance as Tom starts dragging me through reception. He stops abruptly at the reception desk, and I crash into his back.

Looking past Tom, I see a thirty-something, guy wearing a badge that reads, *Todd Archer, Assistant Manager*, standing behind the desk.

Tom's eyes go to his name badge before looking at his face. "Todd, do you know who I am?"

The guy looks at him. "Yes, sir." He nods. "I do. You're Tom Carter."

"Good. So, you won't be surprised when I ask, do the elevators have active cameras in them?"

*What the hell? Is he asking…?*

*Holy shit…he is.*

My whole body freezes, but a fire starts between my legs.

The guy slowly shakes his head, eyes going between Tom and me. "No, sir, our elevators don't have cameras."

Tom reaches into his pocket and pulls out some bills. He puts what looks to be three one-hundred-dollar bills on the counter. "Thanks for your time, Todd."

Then, I'm on the move again, being pulled toward the elevators. I'm trembling because of what just happened, but also with anticipation of what's about to happen.

"What the hell was that?" I hiss when we come to a stop outside the elevators.

Tom presses the button before staring down at me, his jade eyes blazing hot. "What the hell do you think that was? You got me worked up, and now, I'm gonna fuck you in one of these elevators."

My jaw hits the floor. A door pings open.

He gives me a gentle shove. "Get in the fucking elevator, Firecracker."

I stumble in, hot with embarrassment, but turned-on beyond rationale.

Tom follows in behind me, then, presses the button for his floor.

We wait for the doors to close, and with each ticking second, the sexual tension between us becomes a living, breathing entity.

It's fire crackling hot.

My whole body is wired and jittery. I can't even remember wanting a man as much as I want Tom in this moment.

The second those doors come together, we're on each other.

Tom has one hand in my hair, the other grabbing my ass, as his tongue plunders my mouth.

I'm not exactly on the side of finesse as I try to climb his body, like a monkey in a tree.

Tom lifts me off the floor, using the hand on my ass, and then he slams me up against the metal wall. His hand is now on my breast, squeezing with just the right pressure, as his tongue licks in my mouth.

His cock is rock-hard and pressed up against my stomach, but I don't want it there. I want it against my clit.

I'm wiggling, trying to shift it to the right spot, when Tom suddenly stops kissing me and drops me to my feet.

On seriously wobbly legs with my breaths heaving out of me, I watch as he presses the Stop button, bringing the elevator to a grinding halt.

Then, he starts to back up. Stopping, he leans against the metal wall across from me.

I have a flash of memory from last night when he did the very same thing, except things were a little different between us then.

He is clearly turned-on. I can see that. I just can't figure out why he stopped what was just getting started.

"Strip. *Now.*"

*Ah…okay.*

Hearing the command in his voice, I start to remove my clothes without hesitation. I go a little slower to tease him, but I don't go too slowly as I'm very aware of the fact that our time is limited.

I toe my sneakers off and step out from my jeans. Then, I pull my T-shirt over my head and drop it to the floor, leaving me in just my bra and panties. I thank God I had the foresight to put on good underwear.

Lacy pink panties and bra. Very girlie.

By the look in Tom's eyes, he seems to approve.

"Pink's a good color on you," he says, his voice hoarse.

I give him a coy smile. "So, now that you have me here in only my underwear, what are you going to do with me?"

From out of nowhere, his eyes harden, and he straightens up. "First off, you're gonna get down on your knees and suck my cock. Then, when I've had my fill of fucking your mouth, I'm gonna fuck your pussy…*hard.*"

*Um…what the fuck? Where the hell did that come from?*

Feeling a little knocked off-balance, my hands go to my hips. "Are you being serious right now?"

192

He stares me down. "Sugar, I'm always serious when it comes to blow jobs."

I don't like the way he calls me sugar. It feels patronizing and impersonal.

A sudden chill descends down my arms. I rub my hands over them. "Don't call me sugar. And really, you couldn't ask me nicely to suck your cock?"

He frowns. "I don't ask nicely, *Lyla*, because I don't need to. Most women are more than willing to get down on their knees and suck my cock without a fucking word."

*Jesus, that stings.*

Hiding the hurt I feel at his callous words, I bite out, "Yeah, well, I'm not most women. You want *me* to suck your cock, then you learn to ask nicely."

His eyes narrow dangerously. "Yeah, well, you want me to talk nice to you, then don't sneak out of my bed before I wake up. You do that, and then maybe I'll feel like being *nice* to you."

And there it is—the reason for his assholery.

Meeting his hard stare, I think I see a flicker of hurt in his eyes. *Did I hurt his feelings by leaving this morning?*

I honestly thought it wouldn't bother him. But, apparently, it does.

I feel a strange tightening across my chest, so I press the heel of my hand on the ache to relieve it. "Tom, I'm sorry if I hurt you by leaving this morning—"

He lets out a harsh laugh. "You didn't hurt me. No one can hurt me. I'm just pissed off because I wanted to fuck, and you weren't there. As I made this deal to have sex with *only* you for the rest of this tour, it wasn't like I could go get myself some other pussy to bang the hell out of."

Tears hit the backs of my eyes, but I force them away along with the obscenities I want to throw at him. Irrespective of what he says, I know he's being an asshole and lashing out because I hurt him.

I ease my voice into a neutral tone and say, "Well, as our agreement stands, we only have each other to screw, and if you want me to suck your cock, then you need to say please."

*Suck on that, asshole!*

He's so used to getting what he wants with women always falling at his feet...or cock as the case might be. Well, if he wants this woman to suck his cock, then he can ask nicely.

If he doesn't, then I'm done.

His frown deepens, giving him that cute little line between his brows. "You want me to beg you to suck my cock?" The distaste at that idea is clear in his voice. His face tightens as his jaw tics. "I don't think so. Begging isn't something I do."

"Fair enough." I shrug and turning, I bend down to retrieve my clothes. I make sure to stick my ass up and in his direction, and I let my boobs hang right in his view, just to annoy him further.

"What the fuck are you doing?"

Still bent over, I look up at him. "Getting dressed. Then, I'm leaving this elevator."

T-shirt in hand, I straighten up.

*One, two—*

He growls, and then he grabs my arm, yanking me to him. My back slams into his hard chest, his large hand comes around me, spanning my stomach. He pulls me hard against his erection, which is now sticking in my back.

"Fine, Lyla." His voice is harsh and throaty. "Get down on your knees, and suck my big fucking cock with that hot fucking mouth of yours...*please.*"

I bite back a smile. Tilting my head back against his chest, I look up into his eyes. "Could do with a little work...but better." I turn in his arms and shove him against the wall of the elevator.

I can feel his heart pounding beneath my palms. His breathing is ragged.

Keeping my hands pressed against his chest, I reach up on my tiptoes and kiss his lips softly. "I'm sorry I left this morning," I whisper, keeping my eyes on his.

Tom brings his hands to my head. Sliding his fingers through my hair, he cradles my head, his eyes softening. "Don't be sorry. Just don't do it again."

"I won't," I say, giving a gentle nod of my head.

Then, he kisses me fiercely.

After he's finished kissing the life out of me—teaching me that Tom Carter doesn't like to be walked out on—I remove his T-shirt and kiss my way along his jaw, to his neck, and then down his chest, peppering kisses downwards until I'm on my knees and level with his cock.

Reaching up, I undo the button on his jeans and pull down the zipper. I shimmy his jeans down over his hips, finding him commando again.

*Doesn't he own a pair of boxer shorts?*

I find myself face-to-face with not only his beautiful big cock, but also a tattoo right at the cut of his hips just above his neatly trimmed hair. Somehow, I didn't see it in the dark during last night's escapades.

And really, only Tom would have a tattoo that says…

RUB THE LAMP

Snorting out a laugh, I stare up at him, my eyes incredulous. "You had *Rub the Lamp* tattooed above your cock."

Shrugging, he eyes me with cocky insouciance. "He's magic. A few good rubs, and he'll make a woman's wishes come true."

I bark out a laugh. "My God, you are beyond ego."

Holding my chin, he tilts my head back, so I'm looking at him. His eyes are blazing with something I don't understand.

"Right now, I am your god. And as for my ego…well, you got four tastes of that last night, and you weren't complaining then."

He's got me there. There's no arguing with that.

Giving him a suggestive look, I run the tip of my index finger up the length of his steely cock. "So, if I rub your lamp, does that mean I get three wishes?"

"Firecracker, you put those gorgeous lips of yours around my lamp, and you can have as many wishes as you want."

I smile seductively. "Just the three will do," I murmur before licking the head of his cock. Opening up, I suck him into my mouth.

"Jesus, Lyla." His voice is hoarse. "Your mouth feels so fucking good."

Relaxing my throat muscles, I take more of him into my mouth, and I'm rewarded with a jet of pre-cum hitting the back of my tongue. He tastes like pure man. He's virile in every way.

I hum with pleasure, letting the sound vibrate through him, before I start to move my mouth.

And when I do, he lets out a sound of absolute male satisfaction.

Hand palming the back of my head, he starts fucking my mouth, uttering, "Yeah. That's it, baby. Suck me hard. Jack me off with your mouth."

So, I do as he asks.

After I'm finished giving Tom his blow-job apology—my mind still echoing with his ragged, heated praise of how good I am, how amazing my mouth feels sucking him, how beautiful I am—he gets down on his knees and gives me a lot more than the three wishes I earned in that camera-free elevator.

## One Week Later—A Festival, Lexington

Another week has passed, and throughout the week, true to his word, Tom has carved out time to take me to stores, so I could buy new T-shirts. Shopping with him has been surprisingly fun. And I'm starting to build quite the tour T-shirt collection.

Also, a day hasn't gone by when Tom and I haven't had sex. And it's not just once. Two, three...four times.

Tom just goes and goes. I'm surprised I can still walk.

Around everyone else, including on the bus with the guys, Tom and I act normal, as if nothing is different. But when no one's around, we spend our alone time together, naked.

On the night after our elevator escapade, once the guys were sleep, Tom spent the night in my bed on the bus, teaching me how to have sex silently. Not easy when you're as vocal as I am. But I sure had fun learning.

Every time I have sex with Tom, it feels like the first time. I'm not sure what it is about him, but he brings out a side of me that I didn't know existed.

Daring and willing.

I will pretty much do anything he asks, no matter the time or place.

He's fucked me in more positions than I knew possible and some I didn't and in places I didn't think I'd ever have sex. He really wasn't kidding when he said he could be inventive.

We've had sex in a coat closet at a club, the fitting room in a store, a restroom in a restaurant, and another one in a club we played. He had me up against a tree behind the back of a rest stop. But the strangest place was...in the luggage compartment of the tour bus.

Seriously, don't ask. I have no clue how that even happened.

That man could talk my panties off while sitting at dinner with my family.

I can't say no to him, and I don't want to.

I like the way he makes me feel, and it scares me exactly how much I like it. But what scares me the most is when Tom comes to my bed late at night when the bus is sleeping, and we have slow, deep…and what feels to be meaningful sex.

If I didn't know better—at those times in the dark of the night, our bodies tangled up together—I could almost believe we're making love.

But I can't think that way because to do so will only get me hurt.

Tonight, we're in Lexington, Kentucky, and we're playing at an outdoor festival. The festival has been going since we arrived mid-afternoon, and we're scheduled to play at seven for a thirty-minute set.

It looks to be our biggest crowd yet, and I'm excited to get up onstage.

Tom has been in a weird mood since we arrived, and it hasn't gone unnoticed. He's not being himself, and he's been cold and distant with me.

All afternoon, I've wanted to ask him what is wrong, but I haven't been able to get a moment alone with him.

I have no clue where he is now. I haven't seen him since we were in the dressing room, which is actually a trailer that we're sharing with Star Point Five, a vocal band made up of five girls. Each girl is gorgeous in her own right. I think Cale, Van, and Sonny thought they'd died and gone to heaven when they saw who we would be sharing a dressing room with.

And one of the Star Point Five members is a standout. Aurora Simmons is tall and blonde with average-sized—*meow*—boobs. She's a standout because she's Tom's type…and I know he has slept with her in the past.

No, he didn't tell me.

I saw how she looked at him when he stepped into the trailer behind me. She looked him up and down, and her expression held a familiarity that said she knew what he looks like naked. She knows what it's like to…be with him. What confirmed it was how she shrieked and practically knocked me out of the way to get to him. Then, she planted a kiss on his mouth right there in front of me.

It stung like a bitch, but I swallowed past it because he's not mine to lay claim over.

We might be exclusive fuck buddies…but we're just that—fuck buddies. I have no place to bitch-slap her and tell her to get the hell off him even though I really, *really* wanted to.

I knew Tom was uncomfortable with her kissing him because he not so politely extricated himself from her. He left soon after, and then a minute later, I got a text from him that said one word.

*Sorry.*

I didn't reply because I didn't know what to say. So, I put my cell away and let Shannon work her magic on making me look pretty for tonight.

Now, I'm ready, and I'm standing on the side of the stage with Cale and Van, watching Emerson, a very cool heavy rock band. Sonny is off somewhere. I'm guessing he's with some chick.

We're not due onstage for another hour, and I'm starting to think these five-inch heeled boots Shannon talked me into wearing might not be the best idea as my feet are starting to hurt already. Looking down at them, I see that a buckle on the front of a boot has come undone. I bend down to fasten it, and then I hear a mighty *rip!*

*Fuck.*

I instantly slap my hand over my ass, and I feel the massive tear right up the back seam of my denim shorts, which Shannon had to practically stitch me into earlier.

*Shit! I can't believe I ripped the ass in these shorts! Sure, they're tight, but it's not like my butt is the size of Texas!*

Inching onto my tiptoes, I hiss, "Cale," into his ear.

"What?" he says, not taking his eyes off the band.

"I've ripped the ass in these effin' shorts I'm wearing."

He looks at me. "You're kidding, right?"

I can see laughter shining in his eyes.

"No, I'm not effing kidding," I grind out.

He starts to laugh.

"It's not funny," I growl, giving him a shove.

"Sorry," he says, still laughing. "You need me to go and get Shannon for you?"

"No, I'll go back to the trailer and change. Can you give me your jacket, so I can cover up my ass?"

"Sure." He takes his jacket off and gives it to me.

In one quick move, I have that jacket on, and I'm pulling it down, making sure it covers my butt.

"I'll be back soon," I say to Cale. Then, I take off, heading for the dressing room.

*I'll just take these off and put something else on from the rack of clothes that Shannon brought with her. And I'll make sure it's something that will definitely not rip if I bend my ass over.*

A few minutes later, I breathe out a sigh of relief when I see the trailer. Picking up my pace as best as I can in these heels, I climb the few steps, open the door, and step inside the safety of the trailer.

And my heart dies in my chest.

*No.*

*Not again.*

Tom looks at me, stunned, from his position in the dressing-table chair with a panty-wearing Aurora Simmons straddling him.

Silence hits the trailer with a dull thud.

Tom pushes Aurora off of him, and he's out of that chair and advancing on me. "Lyla, this isn't how it looks."

*Pulling up his pants, Dex moves quickly toward me. "Ly, this isn't how it looks."*

My lower lip trembles.

Tom stops before me. "Lyla."

All the pain and fury I've kept pent-up for the last eleven months explodes out of me. My hand is moving before I realize it, and I slap Tom, hard, across the face. The sound of the slap echoes in the deafening silence.

"Fuck you!" I spit. Hand stinging like a bitch, I spin on my heel and run out of there.

"Lyla!" Tom calls after me.

Nothing is stopping me from getting away from him, not even these damn heels, and I keep running until I find myself in a portioned-off section backstage.

Seeing no people around, I stop and back up against the wall. I bend over, putting my hands on my thighs, as I try to catch my breath.

And deal with the agonizing pain in my chest.

*Jesus, this hurts.*

*Bad.*

I can't even determine if this hurts more than the last time.

*God, listen to me…the last time.*

*How many times does this have to happen before I learn?*

*Motherfucking Tom Carter. How could I have been so stupid to trust a mut like him to be faithful?*

*I really must be the dumbest bitch in the world.*

My eyes are full of tears, but I won't blink. I won't cry one goddamn tear over that bastard.

I catch a sob in my throat, and a sneaky tear slides down my cheek.

"There you are!" Tom's voice comes at me loud and hard.

I jerk up like I've been shot. "Don't you come another step closer!" I put my hand out between us, a weak attempt at keeping him away. I know Tom, and nothing will stop him when he wants near me.

He moves quickly, eating up the space between us. "I'm not going anywhere until you hear what I have to say."

"Thanks, but I don't want to hear another word out of your lying mouth!"

Then, he's before me, and his hands are around my upper arms.

"Get the fuck off me!" I cry, trying to get his deceitful hands off me. I can't bear him touching me. "If you wanted to have sex with someone else, you could have at least had the courtesy to let me know, so I could get the fuck out of dodge. Or was that it? You wanted to keep having sex with me and her…and who else, Tom?" I'm yelling. I'm near hysterical right now.

It's a good thing loud music is playing. Otherwise, we'd be attracting a crowd with all our yelling.

"Jesus, Lyla!" He thrusts his hands through his hair. He stares back at me with fear in his eyes. "I don't want to have sex with Aurora or anyone else."

"Bullshit!"

"Seriously." He grabs me again. "You need to listen to me. I didn't touch her. The only time my hands were anywhere near her was when I pushed her off me. I was there, looking for you. She said that you just left to get a drink, and you were coming back. Said you wouldn't be long and that I should wait. I wasn't sure because I know what she's like—"

"You've slept with her before?"

He lets out a sigh, releasing me, his eyes dim. "Yes."

I ignore the pain that the confirmation forces into my chest. "When?"

His eyes meet mine. "Does it matter?"

"Yes, it matters! More so now because…because I need to know if you've had sex with her while you've been with me. If you've had sex with…anyone…since…me." My voice peters off at his sharp expression.

"There's been no one since you and I started sleeping together. I had sex with Aurora a few years ago. It was unmemorable and not something I would ever want to repeat. Stupidly, I made the decision to wait for you with her in there."

He ducks his head, stepping into my space. "You never replied to my text…after she kissed me in front of you. I just wanted to make sure you were okay, so I went to the trailer to find you. I literally just sat down, and I was checking my cell. The next thing I knew, she was half-naked and on me. Then, you were there." He stares deep into my eyes. "It was that quick, Ly. I didn't get a chance to react."

I look at him, assessing him. *I actually think I believe him.*

"And if you had…the chance to react?"

He moves closer, so close that I have to tilt my head back. The scent of him overwhelms me. I feel my body teeter.

"Then, I would have pushed her off, told her it wasn't happening…because I'm with someone…*you*." His hands cup my face. "I made an error in judgment, waiting there with her, but that was my only crime. I didn't betray you. I wouldn't. I'm a lot of things, but I'm not a cheat." His fingers brush my cheek tenderly. "This arrangement…this commitment I've made to you—to most people, I know that *exclusive fuck buddies* might sound like a laughable commitment, but to me, it's *big*. It matters. *You* matter…to me. I care about you."

*He cares about me.*

I curl my fingers around his wrist, closing my eyes, as I soak up his words. "I care about you, too," I admit softly.

Emotions overwhelming me, a lone tear runs down my cheek, and Tom catches it.

"I would never willingly do anything to hurt you, Ly."

I lift my hand and place it against his red cheek. The cheek I hit.

I've never hit anyone before, not even Dex after catching him with Chad.

*So, why did I react like that from seeing Tom with her?*

"I'm sorry I hit you." I give him a sad smile.

"Don't," he says roughly. "No sorry, no regrets."

Then, he's kissing me. But there's something in this kiss, something different...something more.

Tom wraps his arms around me, holding me tight.

I melt into him.

Lips close to mine, he says, "Would it be inappropriate to say that I *really* need to be inside you right now?"

A smile takes over my lips. "Since when have you cared about being inappropriate?"

"Good point. Come with me."

He leads me by the hand. We stop a little farther on by a large stage panel marked, *Entry Point. Wear Hard Hats Upon Entering. Employees Only.*

Tom lifts up a latch and pulls open the panel, which I now know is a door.

A door which will take us under the stage. The stage that currently has a band performing on it and a few thousand people watching out front.

"Here?" I blink up at him.

"Yep."

"Is it...safe?"

"Are you interested in safe?" His darkened eyes stare deep into mine.

Mouth suddenly dry, I shake my head.

"Then, come with me."

Bending his head, he steps inside.

Excited by the danger...by him, my trembling legs follow him.

The space is limited. Tom can't stand straight. His head is dipped forward. We're surrounded by scaffolding and the thumping of bass and drums and singing.

Tom closes the door, plunging us into total darkness.

I shiver.

Then, I feel Tom press up against me, his warmth infusing me.

His fingers trace a path down my arm. He takes hold of my hand. "You okay? You're shaking."

"I'm fine." I smile even though he can't see it.

*Just shaking in my boots because I'm so turned-on that it's borderline ridiculous. This is what you do to me.*

Tom's hands come up to either side of my neck. Pushing out, he slips Cale's jacket off my shoulders and down my arms until it hits dirt. Then, he removes the off-the-shoulder black top I'm wearing, leaving me in just my bra. His hand goes to my back, and he pulls me in close. His deft fingers creep down toward my ass. Then, I feel him touching my panties through the tear in my shorts.

*Crap, I forgot all about that.*

"Um…Ly, you do realize that you have a massive rip in the ass of your shorts, don't you?" A lone finger is moving up and down the huge hole in my shorts, grazing the crack of my butt through the thin fabric of my panties. "Are you going for easy access with this look? Not that I'm complaining." He slides his hand inside and grips the edge of my panties, moving it aside, so he's just touching skin.

A shiver takes me over as he caresses my ass.

"No. I bent over, and they ripped. That's why I went back to the trailer, and—"

Tom cuts my words off with a kiss. Swift and fast.

"Don't," he breathes.

Then, I feel a change in him, and I know this ride is about to get rough.

Just how I like it.

"Turn around," he says gruffly into my ear.

Doing as he says, I turn slowly on the spot.

He presses up against my back, and his hands run down my arms until he reaches my hands. "Bend over."

I do as he asks.

Tom is still holding my hands. He places them on a metal scaffolding bar in front of me. I can feel the vibration of the music playing above through it. "Hold this, and don't let go." His voice is commanding in my ear. "You let go, you don't get to come."

"Okay," I say, breathless with anticipation. My body is sizzling.

Then, I register the song the band above is playing. It's a cover version of "Thought I'd Died and Gone to Heaven" by Bryan Adams.

From what I can hear, it's a really great cover of the song. The crowd sounds like they're going crazy.

My eyes close on the sounds of the song, the lyrics, the crowd singing along...and then the feel of Tom getting to his knees behind me.

His hands grab my shorts, and he rips them open further.

*Holy. Shit.*

*He's so fucking hot.*

Next goes my panties in one quick snap. He pulls them out, leaving me standing here in just my bra and the shorts, exposing me.

"I wish I could see how you look right now." His voice is a growl.

His finger moves between my folds. My body jerks at his touch, needing this, needing him.

Then, his face comes close to my ass, his hot breath hitting all my nerve endings. "Scream as loud as you want, Ly, 'cause no one will hear you."

He plunges his tongue into my pussy and starts fucking me with it, his finger playing my clit to perfection.

I'm panting, wild under his mouth, and in this moment, I'm solely living off the feel of him driving me to the brink.

Each time I get close, he pulls back.

I'm beyond hot and needy and desperate. "Tom, please..."

"Shh...I got you, darlin'. Ly, have you ever been fucked in the ass?"

Nerves shoot through me, and my body tenses at the thought of Tom going somewhere so private. "No, I haven't, and I don't know if I could." My head shakes in the dark, my hair brushing over my sensitized skin.

"Do you trust me?"

"You know I do...but I don't know if I can do...*that*." The thought of Tom's huge cock in my ass is terrifying.

"I won't use my cock. Your ass is virgin territory, so we need to start off slow. Just my finger, darlin'." He presses a kiss to my ass cheek. "I promise, it won't hurt, and we can stop whenever you want. Just trust me when I say"—his voice thickens with lust—"if you let me fuck your ass with my finger...it will top any orgasm I've ever given you before." Another kiss. "Let me give this to you."

And just like that, I'm his.

So ready to give all of myself to him that it's terrifying…but so very hot.

"Yes," I hear myself saying.

He teases my skin with light flicks of his tongue. "Yes, what? Say it, Lyla. Tell me what you want."

I'm dizzy with lust. Drunk on him. I'd say anything, do anything that he told me to right now, if it would mean having him.

"I want you to fuck my ass with your finger."

He growls and then sinks his teeth into the fleshy skin of my ass cheek, biting me gently. He slips his finger into my pussy. I clench around him. Then, he pulls out, his finger drawing my slickness back to my rear.

I tense up the instant his finger touches my puckered hole.

"Relax…I won't hurt you. Just give yourself over to me. I'll take care of you."

So, I do as he asks. I close my eyes, relax my body, and allow Tom to take care of me.

His finger moves back up, repeating the motion, but this time, his finger goes to my clit. He strokes it, drawing my body up, and then he's gone into my pussy and again moving my slickness to my rear.

My hips start to shift restlessly, my body climbing higher and higher, each time he repeats the movement.

I feel wetter than I ever have before, my slickness coating the most intimate parts of me. Tom stays at my ass and starts to rim my puckered hole with his finger, moving my wetness around and into it.

Craving more, reaching for something I'm not really sure of, I start to push back against him.

At the exact moment I push back, his mouth finds my clit, and his fingertip slips into my ass.

The feel of him *there* is shockingly intense. I let out a cry of pleasure.

"Fuck, you're tight." His words vibrate through me. "Are you okay?"

"Uhum." I can barely form words right now.

He applies a little more pressure and moves his finger in a fraction deeper. Then, again, and he continues moving in a little farther each time.

I'm starting to feel frustrated. I need more. Then, Tom suddenly withdraws his finger to the tip and slides it back inside to the knuckle.

My breath whooshes out of me. Lights flicker behind my eyelids. My body going into total sensory overload.

I'm full of him. And it feels amazing.

I let out a moan, and that seems to be all he needs to spur him on because Tom starts to fuck my ass with his finger, sliding in knuckle deep each time, while his tongue frantically licks at my clit.

I'm coming in seconds.

My hands tighten around the metal bar, a scream tears from my lungs.

I feel like I've just skyrocketed into orbit. I'm weightless. I have no idea how I'm actually still standing.

He wasn't kidding when he said it would top any orgasm he's ever given me so far. That was off the charts.

I'm aware of Tom's finger pulling out of me, the feel of him moving behind me.

The next thing I know, a very naked Tom is pressed up against me. His thick, condom covered cock seated between my ass cheeks.

He leans over my back. He sweeps my hair over my shoulder, and his tongue flicks at my neck. "You are *the* sexiest woman I have ever known. You're fucking amazing, Firecracker."

Taking a wild guess at the number of women Tom has known, I try to take what he said as the compliment he meant it to be.

Leaving my back, he curls his hand around my hair and holds it tight as he stands. His cock moves away. I miss the contact for all of a second. The next thing I know, his hand grips my hip and he slams inside me.

I whimper.

"Christ, you feel so fucking good. Perfect for my cock."

He slides out to the tip, his hand pulling on my hair, and then slams back in me.

My eyes close on a groan.

"Squeeze my dick with your pussy," he tells me in that commanding voice, which means he's not asking.

Clenching my inner muscles, I squeeze his cock as hard as I can. The sound he makes has me nearly coming again.

"Fuck yeah," he hisses. "I wanted to go slow, but I can't. I need to fuck you hard and fast."

And he does.

He slides his cock out and slams it back in. Increasing in speed each time, he hits me with those sure, hard thrusts. He's balls deep, hips slamming against my ass, his heavy sack slapping against my clit while he pulls on my hair.

My heels are dug into the dirt, and I'm holding onto the metal bar for dear life while Tom fucks me good and hard.

I couldn't feel any hotter than I do right now.

He releases my hair, letting it spill across my back. His hand moves to my heavy, sensitive breast. He tugs the cup of my bra down and twists my nipple with just the right pressure.

A scream tears out of me.

"That's it, baby," he growls. "Scream for me."

His other hand finds my clit. All the while, he doesn't lose pace fucking me with controlled thrusts.

"You're gonna come again, Ly. No less than two times, remember?"

"Yes...yes..." I moan, my body climbing again, reaching for that second orgasm.

"That's it, baby. Give it to me. Come for me. I need to feel you coming around my cock."

"Fuck...Tom!" I'm exploding around him, my inner walls tightening, my body and mind spiraling out of control.

"Jesus..." Tom groans. "I'm coming...I'm fucking...*fuck*!" He slams into me and lets out a sound of pure primal pleasure.

I feel a powerful shudder move through him as his cock starts jerking inside me, spilling everything he has into the condom.

We're both breathless. And I'm boneless. If it wasn't for Tom holding me, I'd be on the floor right now.

He leans forward—still inside me, cock semi-erect—and lays his damp hot chest against my back. His arms come around my waist, holding me. He presses a kiss to my shoulder and then one to my neck. "Sexiest woman ever."

I giggle and turn my face to his. He brushes his lips over mine.

"You're not so bad yourself," I murmur.

Feeling the happiest I've felt in a long while, I smile the whole time that Tom helps me dress. I laugh when he bangs his head on one of the metal bars, and then I kiss it better when he makes me feel bad for laughing.

I'm still smiling when he opens the door, letting us out.

Closing the door and latching it, he turns to me, taking both of my hands in his. We're standing here, facing each other, our eyes locked. Then, something passes over Tom's face, and it settles.

It looks a lot like contentment.

It makes my heart beat faster.

Releasing one of my hands, Tom touches my cheek. "Ly…"

He brushes my hair behind my ear. "I've been thinking…for a little while now…that maybe we should—"

"There you are!" Shannon's voice shatters through whatever Tom was about to say.

And the sound of her voice has me jerking away from him, putting clear, safe distance between us.

I see his brow furrow.

Ignoring his frown, I turn to Shannon, wondering if she saw our intimate exchange.

Judging by her expression, I'm going to say no.

*Thank God. I don't want anyone knowing about Tom and me.*

"I've been looking everywhere for you, missy! Cale said that you ripped your shorts and went to change, but I went to the trailer, and you weren't there. And I know you and clothes, Lyla Summers. You're not so fucking great at dressing yourself, and I wanted to make sure you put on something appropriate—" She stops mid-rant, eyeing my shorts. "But I see you're still wearing them."

She looks between Tom and me. Her eyes run over us and then go to the stage door directly behind us.

I see realization flicker in her gaze.

She grins.

My stomach drops.

"Were you two…" Her grin widens. "Did I interrupt something? Or did you already have sex?"

*Shit. People cannot find out about Tom and me. I don't want people thinking…*

*What?*

*What will they think?*

209

*They'll think that I'm another one of Tom's easy lays. Another dumb chick he's been screwing. Some small-time singer who's trying to bang her way to the top.*

"We haven't had sex." I let out a strangled laugh. "As if I'd have sex with Tom! I mean, he's a total mut! I do have standards, you know." The words are out before I can stop them. And I hate myself instantly.

Shannon's eyes slide to Tom. The changing expression in them has me turning to look at to him.

Whatever Shannon saw on his face is gone when my eyes meet with his. I see nothing there. His eyes are clear, his face perfectly blank.

Tom looks from me to Shannon. "Not that it's your business, Shan, but we weren't having sex." His voice is cold, detached.

I've never heard him sound like that before. It sends a chill hurtling through me.

His eyes slide back to me, and that's when I see it—the cold masking the hurt.

I've hurt him.

"Like Lyla said, she has standards. She would never waste her time on a *mut* like me." He looks at his watch. "I've gotta go." Then, he walks away.

I start to panic.

"Mut? What the hell are you two talking about?" Shannon laughs and comes over to me, clearly oblivious to what just happened between Tom and me.

*I should go after him. Tell him I'm sorry.*

*But if I do, then Shannon will know that something is going on between us.*

*What should I do?*

Torn by indecision, I stand here, confused

Then, Tom is gone, disappearing around the corner.

And I let Shannon take the decision away from me when she leads me away in the opposite direction. "We need to get you changed. You're onstage in less than half an hour, and I can't have you on there with your ass hanging out. Otherwise, Zane will have mine for letting you perform while dressed like a hooker. Not that I'd mind Zane having my ass. Damn, that man is fine."

Heart thudding, I zone Shannon out and pull my cell from my pocket.

I open up a new text.

*I'm so sorry. I didn't mean what I said. I just wanted to put Shannon off the scent.*

I search though my contacts, select Tom, and press Send.

I never should have said what I did. Right now, I should be tracking Tom down and begging him to forgive me, not hiding behind my cell like the coward I am.

But even knowing that, I don't do what's right. Instead, I keep walking with Shannon and wait for his response. My heart is in my throat the whole time.

I don't get a text until I'm back in the dressing room— thankfully Aurora is nowhere to be seen—while Shannon wrestles me into a shiny pair of tight black leggings.

*Don't worry. I get it.*

Tears sting my eyes because he doesn't get it. He doesn't get it at all.

And I'm not sure that I do either.

# TOM 22

## A Few Days Later—Suite, Mandalay Bay Hotel, Las Vegas

*Where am I right now?*

I'm in a hotel suite in Vegas, watching Lyla get it on with some preppy dickhead.

*Why haven't I pummeled his face, you ask?*

Trust me, if I could, I would because this is driving me nuts, seeing his hands on her.

It's like acid in my eyes.

I'm getting an idea of how Lyla felt when she saw that half-naked nympho, Aurora Simmons, all over me.

I can't do anything *but* watch because this is business.

Acting.

They're taping a music video.

The single has been hitting the airwaves. Interest is growing. Downloads on iTunes alone have skyrocketed this past week. The band needs a video, so we can get the song on all the music channels.

Lyla and the boys had a show at a club here in Vegas last night.

Zane had decided Vegas would be a good place for the shoot. He acquired a suite at Mandalay to film the video. Of course, the hotel was more than happy to oblige for Jake's label. They even offered the best suite they had available at no charge.

So, Zane and his team met us in Vegas.

Denny's here. He tagged along with Zane. Den could never resist a trip to Vegas. I'm glad he's here. I haven't seen him since I left on this tour. It'll be good to catch up.

This morning, they taped the band shot of the video down in the House of Blues Music Hall. It was a great location for the shot.

Now, we're mid-afternoon and doing the love-interest part of the video. They're filming in the bedroom. I'm sitting out in the living room, watching. I have a clear view of what's happening from here, and I can't fucking wait for it to be over.

They've barely started, and I want to punch the guy.

Andy, the preppy dickhead.

When he arrived, he was all, "*Lyla, it's so fantastic to meet you! Love your music! So looking forward to filming with you!*"

Kisses on the cheeks. Hands all over her.

*Little prick.* I should have ripped his hands off the second he touched her.

I know Lyla feels uncomfortable with all this. Apart from the artsy director, Julio, pointing out that she needs to relax every five minutes, I can see it in her eyes.

And worse, things have been weird between us these last few days, and now, she's got the preppy-boy toy all over her, doing his pretend acting.

The weirdness is because of me. I've pulled back a bit. I was getting too close to her. I figured that out the moment I was about to tell Lyla that I wanted to go public with us.

Looking back, I'm glad that Shannon turned up and Lyla acted the way she did. It was what I needed to knock some sense into me.

*I mean, seriously, what exactly was I wanting to go public about? The fact that I'm fucking her until the tour is over?*

I don't think so. People knowing our business would only complicate things. And I did a good enough job of complicating things in my own head.

I don't need any outside help.

But all is good now. I'm right back in the place I need to be.

The newly grown pussy I was acquiring is gone, and I'm back to all big, manly cock.

When I saw Lyla later that night after I'd acted like "Pussy" Tom, I made sure to fuck her like the man I am and the casual fuck buddy that she is.

I might like Lyla…I might care about her…

But I care about her as a friend and nothing more.

I got that twisted up in my head for a short time. It won't happen again.

"This seems to be going well, don't you think?" Zane takes a seat beside me.

"Yeah, not bad."

"Lyla's nervous, which is understandable with it being her first video shoot, but I think we're gonna get something good out of this."

I look at him. "The actor is a bit of a prick."

Zane stares at me. "You think? He seems all right to me."

"Too preppy. Should have gone for someone more...hardcore. Tatted up. Rocker-looking."

*Me.*

"Julio thought it would be a good look to have a clean-cut guy contrast her image and also to help keep things mainstream."

*Julio's a prick as well.*

I shrug. "Whatever. Guess he'll have to do, not like you can bring in another actor now."

Zane looks back out at the scene before us. "No, guess not," he muses.

"So, we going out after this?" Den slumps into the chair on the other side of me and passes me a can of Coke.

"Yeah," I answer, cracking the can open. Then, I get distracted by something Julio is saying.

"Lyla, honey, put your hands on Andy. We gotta make the audience believe you're in love with him. Andy, take off your shirt. It might work better if we have a bit of skin to work with."

*Um...what the fuck? Why do they need his shirt off?*

I can't help the laugh that escapes, when Andy removes his shirt.

There's not an ounce of man about him. Sure, he might be toned, but he's all waxed chest and fake tan. I'm pretty sure he's wearing guy-liner. He doesn't even have a tattoo, for fuck's sake. *I mean, what kind of man doesn't have a tattoo? The preppy kind—that's who.*

"So, what do you think?" Den's voice filters through my thoughts.

Lyla now has her hands pressed against the prick's chest, and he's kissing her neck.

My hands clench into fists on my thighs. I have to drag my eyes away from the set. "What do I think of what?"

Den gives me a strange look. "I said, do you wanna go gambling before or after we go out clubbing?"

"Don't care." My eyes go straight back to Lyla.

She's unbuttoning the top button on his pants.

*What the hell?*

*Okay, top off—sure, I get that, kind of. But why the pants?*
If she takes off his pants, I'm shutting this fucking circus down. We're not shooting a porno here.

"Tom, you all right, man? You seem a bit distracted."

My eyes flick to Den. "I'm not distracted." I look back to Lyla. Okay, we're good. The little prick's pants are still on. She was just unbuttoning them for a shot that Julio wanted to take.

*Cool. All is goodish again.*

Then, fucking Julio opens his mouth, "Lyla, honey, I think we should have you shirtless for this part. Top off, but keep your bra on. Skin on skin will make this work better."

*Hold the motherfucking phone.*

I'm out of my seat, and before I realize it, I say, "Are you fucking serious? You really need her to take her top off? We're not filming a goddamn porno here."

Silence hits the room.

Julio turns and stares at me. Actually, everyone in here is staring at me. Lyla included.

I avert my eyes from her.

I'm acting like a jealous boyfriend.

I'm not a jealous boyfriend. *No fucking way.*

"Tom." Zane gets out of his seat. "I know you've had a few issues with some of the ideas we had. Why don't we go have a chat while they get this scene down? Then, we can bring your ideas back."

Zane is actually being genuine. But now, I just feel like a complete dick, and I need to get the fuck out of here.

"No, it's fine. I don't have any ideas. Everything you're doing is fine. I've got something I need to be doing"—*drinking*—"so I'll catch you later." I pick up my jacket, and I'm out of there like a shot.

"Wait up!" Den calls from behind me.

I slow my stride, but I don't stop. I can't even bring myself to look at him. I know what he's thinking.

"What the fuck was that?" He laughs, sounding a little out of breath from running to catch up.

"What was what?"

"Um…your little outburst."

"It was nothing." There's bite in my tone, but I don't care. I stride ahead and stab at the button for the elevator.

We don't speak again until we're seated in the hotel bar, and our drinks are ordered.

"So, you're screwing Lyla," Den says, amusement in his voice. It instantly raises my guard. I meet his stare with a glare. "Yes, I'm screwing Lyla. What of it?"

A grin slides onto his face. "I'm taking it you were jealous back there, watching her with that guy. That's why you were acting like a complete fucking weirdo."

"I wasn't jealous," I scoff. "I don't get jealous."

*I was so jealous.*

*What the hell is happening to me?*

"How long have you been banging her?"

I frown at him. "Jake been talking?"

He lets out a laugh. "No, surprisingly, Jake's kept his mouth shut, which tells me he thinks this is as serious as I do."

"Don't be ridiculous. It's not serious. You know I don't do serious."

"So, how long?" he pushes.

I smile in thanks at the waitress who just brought our drinks over. I wait until she's gone before answering, "About three weeks."

"You fuck anyone else in that time?"

"What is this? Twenty fucking questions?"

He picks his drink up, a shit-eating grin on his face. "You're not usually shy about sharing the details of your sex life."

He's right, I'm not. *Motherfucker.* I don't want to say anything about Lyla and me, but I know he'll turn this into a bigger thing if I don't offer up the goods.

"Okay, fine. I'm only fucking Lyla. I haven't fucked anyone else since I put my cock in her hole."

"Holy shit!" He barks out a laugh. "I never thought I'd see the day when you'd be with just one woman. Dude, I'm sorry to break this to you, but you're in a relationship with Lyla."

My heart stops. Dead.

*I'm not.*

*Am I?*

*No.*

*No way. We're just fuck buddies.*

"I'm not in a relationship with her."

"Yeah, and I'm Steve Jobs."

"You do realize he's dead, don't you?"

"Fuck off! And whatever. You're in a relationship with Lyla."

"What are you? Five? I'm not in a relationship with Lyla, dickhead. She's my fuck buddy."

"Fuck buddies usually have sex with other people. That's kinda the point. They have a regular, but they get to fuck others, too."

"I know that, assface, but Lyla's not that kinda girl, and I wanted to fuck her—badly. Seriously, have you seen how hot she is? And her tits are real, Den, motherfucking real. I haven't touched real tits in years. All chicks seem to have that silicone shit nowadays. So, of course I agreed to exclusively fuck her until the tour is over. We bang as much as we want until we arrive back in LA. Then, it's bye-bye, birdie."

*What's that pain in my chest?*

"You're in denial." He shakes his head, chuckling.

I rub at my sternum. "I'm not in denial."

"You are so in denial. You like this girl, Tom. I can tell. I've known you for a long fucking time, and I've never seen you look at a chick the way you were looking at her—let alone, sign yourself up for exclusivity to one. And don't even get me started on the jealously thing."

"I wasn't fucking jealous," I growl. "And you're barking up the wrong tree. All I want from Lyla is her tight pussy and awesome rack."

"Nope." He smirks. "You like her."

"Of course I like her, fucknut. She's a cool chick. She has the best tits I've *ever* seen, and she fucks like a porn star. What's not to like?"

"Nah…you like her, like her."

"You're spending way too much time with Simone. You're actually starting to sound like her. Have you grown pubic hair on that pussy of yours?"

Giving me the middle finger, he says, "I'm guessing Lyla likes you, too, since she's letting you in her bed. She doesn't strike me as the sleep-around type."

"She's not."

That raises another know-it-all grin from him. "So, you like her, and she likes you. Why don't you just see where this thing goes?"

"Because it'll go nowhere." I sit up, rubbing my head at the ache brought on by his bitching. "Can we just drop it now and get to drinking?" I pick up my whiskey.

Den's face turns serious, and he sits forward, elbows on the table. "Tom, being with Lyla, finally letting yourself be in a relationship, wouldn't be a bad thing. It could be a really great thing. You're not your father. Things won't—"

"Seriously," I snap, "shut the fuck up. We're not talking about this." I drive my hand through my hair, feeling on edge, and then I down my drink and signal the waitress back over.

"Okay, keep your fucking panties on." He picks up his own drink and downs it. "All I'm saying is, I think you'll be making a colossal mistake if you walk away from Lyla at the end of this tour. You could have something really great with her if you give it a chance."

## Later That Night—Hotel Room, Mandalay Bay Hotel, Las Vegas

I'm in my pajamas, Beyoncé's "Drunk in Love" playing on the TV, when there's a knock at my door.

Butterflies in my stomach, hoping it's Tom, I climb out of bed and pad my way over to the door.

I pull it open, the butterflies instantly turning into lightning bugs when I see him.

I keep the relief from my face, not sure as to where we stand at the moment. Tom was clearly pissed off earlier at the shoot. That was loud and clear from his outburst and exit.

Cale noticed Tom's behavior, and he questioned me about it at dinner earlier. I downplayed it, saying I had no clue what it was about. I told Cale that Tom was just probably in a bad mood or something.

Tom's behavior at the shoot has been on my mind all night. I've been running around in circles, trying to figure out what it means, what's going on with him.

"Hi," he says, his hands lift to the doorframe above his head, fingers gripping it.

With his movement, his shirt lifts, showing me his delicious six-pack. My belly instantly squeezes with lust.

Opening the door wider, I step back to let him in.

As he brushes past, I catch a whiff of whiskey on his breath.

The smell of whiskey on Tom somehow makes him even hotter.

I've barely gotten the door closed when his body is pressing mine up against it.

"I didn't like seeing that dickhead's hands on you." His voice is a low growl.

The force of his words shudders a breath from me.

I guess that answers my plaguing question. He was jealous.

"I didn't like his hands on me either, but it was just acting, Tom. You of all people know how it is. I've seen your music videos, remember?"

He rests his forehead against mine, breathing heavy. "I just— fuck, I don't get jealous, Firecracker. I'm not *that* guy. But seeing him with you…" His eyes meet mine, burning with an intensity, the likes I've never known. "Today, I am that guy." Then, his mouth comes crashing down on mine.

I wind my fingers into his hair, opening up for him.

I'm desperate for him. I was so scared that he was mad at me, and things have been so different between us since Kentucky, so to have him here, saying this to me, I couldn't be happier.

Yes, it scares me that I'm relying on Tom for my happiness.

But right now, I'm brushing that aside, and just focusing on the now and how I feel when I'm with him.

We're tearing at each other's clothes, like we're in a race to see who can undress the other the quickest.

Tom wins.

He picks me up, kicks off his jeans from around his ankles, and carries me to bed.

He brings us both down to the mattress, supporting his weight with his hand.

"You're mine," he says low. "For this tour, you belong to me."

"Yes," I whisper. "Yours." I cup his face in my hands and bring my lips up to his.

Rough fingers climb my thigh. I lift my leg, hooking it around his hip, my heel digging into his ass.

His fingers find me wet and waiting.

"So fucking wet…always ready for me." He slants his mouth over mine at the exact moment that he pushes a finger inside me.

My back arches up, pushing my breasts into his chest.

He lowers his head, taking my nipple into his mouth, and he teases it with his tongue. "I need inside you so fucking bad." His deep voice rumbles through me. I feel it everywhere.

"What are you waiting for?" I give him a sexy, sassy smile.

Burning jades meet my blues. "Firecracker, you know I'm a greedy man. I need my starters first. Then, I'll dine in your pussy…and for dessert, I'll have you sitting on my face."

*Holy fuck.*

Tom moves off me, reaching for his jeans, he gets his wallet from the pocket.

"Shit," he groans.

"What's wrong?" I sit up.

He drives a hand through his hair. "I'm out of condoms."

*He's out of condoms?*

*How is that possible?*

Tom always has condoms on him. And yes, the knowledge that the guy sack carries condoms around with him is a mental challenge I battle every day.

"I knew I'd run out. I meant to go to the store to get some, but I forgot. I was eager to get back to you."

*He was eager to get back to me.* My heart sprouts wings and flutters out of my chest.

"Well, you know I haven't got any." I blow stray hairs off my face.

Tom sits down beside me. "Are you on the pill?"

"Yes…"

"Okay, so why don't we just go without this time?"

My eyebrows hit my hairline. "Are you drunk?"

"No, I'm not drunk. And even if I were, what's that got to do with it?"

"Well, I just know that sober you wouldn't suggest going bareback."

Leaning close, he hovers his lips over mine. "I've been drinking tonight, sure, but I'm far from drunk. I can hold my liquor, Firecracker. Point is, I'm not a patient man. I don't want to have to wait to be inside you."

"Tom…" I press my hands against his chest, putting some distance between us. Having him this close is starting to cloud my judgment. "I'm not sure. I mean, it's just…you've slept with a lot of women."

He gives me a less than amused look. "And you've slept with other guys, one who used to bang dudes, but I'm not asking for your sexual history sheet."

I suck in a sharp breath, my face prickling with hurt, as I turn away from him. "Jesus, Tom. That was low."

"Fuck." He grabs my chin, forcing my eyes back to his. "I'm sorry, babe, that came out wrong. I just mean…I trust you."

Climbing up on the bed, he positions himself between my legs, pressing me back into the mattress. Arms either side of my head, he stares down at me. "I trust you, and I want you to trust me, too. I'm clean, I promise. I have regular checkups. And I *never* go bareback. I've singlehandedly kept Trojan in business for the last fifteen years. You have nothing to worry about."

*Fifteen years? He started having sex when he was fourteen?*

*How am I surprised by this?* This is Tom Carter we're talking about.

And I was just starting to consider maybe giving in after his whole trust thing. But now, all I have ringing in my ears is, *I've singlehandedly kept Trojan in business for the last fifteen years.*

*Nice reminder of his whoring ways.* I feel sick.

I hold back the rising bile and clip out, "Nothing to worry about? Oh, okay…" I can feel my anger climbing to epic proportions. Only he can get under my skin this way. I try not to think just what that means. "I gotta say, Tom, I feel a whole lot better about your proposal of letting you have sex with me *bare-fucking-back,*" I yell, "when you just reminded me that in the past you've been ridden more times than an elevator in the Empire State Building!"

His eyes narrow. "You knew all along who you were getting into bed with, sweetheart."

"Ugh! Sometimes, I wonder what the hell I'm doing with you." I don't mean that. But I'm angry, and when I'm angry, I'm not rational.

I push against his rock-hard chest and start wiggling, trying to get out from underneath him.

But Tom is a lot bigger and a lot stronger than me. Pinning me with his hips, he grabs my hands and holds them tight against the pillows above my head. I can't budge an inch. And I don't like it one bit.

"You know exactly why you're with me. Because I fuck you like no man ever has before or ever will again."

Not impressed, I scowl up at him. "Let. Me. Go."

"No. Seems you need reminding of a few things. One, I am *always* the one who does the riding, *not* the other way round. The bedroom is *my* domain."

Shifting his hips, he presses the bare length of his hard cock against my clit. I have to bite back a moan. But my body shudders, giving me away. I hate the way my body betrays me when it comes to him.

He smirks. "You got that, or do you need a little more reminding?"

Ignoring my body's screaming needs, I snap out, "Fuck you!"

"We'll be doing that real soon, but for now, just answer the goddamn question. I said, you got that, or do I need to remind you again?" He thrusts against me, harder. It's more precise this time, hitting that perfect spot.

I'm sure that man has a mental blueprint of my vagina because he knows just when and where to touch me at the exact right moment. My eyes roll back in my head, a moan escaping this time. The words leave my lips without thought, "I got it." My voice sounds breathy, girlish, not like me at all.

*Just who am I with him?*

"Good girl."

I see a look of power take over his face before he lowers his head to mine. Our lips are almost touching but frustratingly not. And it scares me just how badly I need his mouth on mine in this moment.

His hot breath mixes in with my own as he rumbles out, "For some ass-backward reason, *you* are the only one I want to ride. Constantly. Over and over. I can't get enough of you, and *you* are the only one I have ever wanted to ride bare-fucking-back. So, that kind of erases the rest, wouldn't you say?" He sucks my bottom lip into his mouth. "I want to *feel* you," he murmurs.

Breath knocked out.

Tom doesn't push for an answer because he doesn't need to. I'm a limp, pliable mess of emotions under his firm hands and mind-fucking words.

"Tom," I whisper, breathless. "Ride me… *now*… bare-fucking-back."

Releasing me, he takes his cock in his hand and rubs it up and down my center, coating himself in my wetness. He stops, positioned at my entrance.

I close my eyes.

"Open your eyes."

I blink them wide to see his blazing down at me. "I want you looking at me the whole time."

Holding his stare, I nod, gently.

Then, he slams inside me.

"Oh God." I'm fighting for breath, the feel of him bare inside me…it's intense.

Him. Me.

Connected in this way.

Strange how the removal of a piece of latex can change things in so many ways.

His eyes have filled with something I don't understand.

"Christ…I've never…you're so fucking tight, Ly. I can't…" He shakes his head.

"I know…" I touch my hand to his face, tracing my fingers over his cheekbone.

His skin is taut. Eyes dark. Jaw clenched.

He's a man on the edge.

His forehead comes to mine, eyes still open and on me, as he slowly pulls out to the tip and then thrusts back in.

A rush of breath leaves his mouth, gusting straight into my own. "Jesus, I don't think I'm gonna last long…not like this. It's too fucking good. You feel amazing, baby."

"Just let go," I whisper. "Give it to me. I want to feel everything you have to give."

His head lifts from mine, and I see from the look on his face that whatever restraint he was holding on to is now gone.

Teeth gritted, he starts to fuck me like a man possessed.

This is pure, primal fucking at its absolute best.

He's pushing me up the bed with each hard thrust. I'm clawing at the sheets to keep traction.

"Tell me you're close," he grinds out. "Because I can't hold off…for much longer."

"I'm close, Tom…yes, just keep…doing…that…"

His pelvis hits my clit, and the orgasm tears through me. My eyes close, unable to stay open from the magnitude of the orgasm, breaking our connection.

"Jesus…this is…I can't…"

I feel his cock jerk inside me.

I open my eyes to see his shut tight, his head thrown back, his chest heaving with the force of his orgasm, as he pumps himself empty inside me.

Seeing him like this, feeling him bare, the feel of him coating my insides—it's too much.

My chest feels tight. I can't catch a breath.

It's like he just punched his fist into my chest and took my heart back out with him.

*Oh no.*

*I'm in too deep. I'm starting to feel things...for him.*

Tom lays his damp chest against mine. He kisses me. "Wow, that was something else."

I force my feelings away and smile at him. "Who knew it could be so good without a condom?" I run my fingers through his hair.

"No, it wasn't just that...it's you. You're amazing."

*Too deep...*

"Well, you're not so bad yourself. Not that you need me to tell you."

"True."

His laughter rumbles through his chest. I feel it deep inside me.

"But it's nice to hear. I don't often get compliments from you."

"True." I smile.

He kisses me once more. Then, he lifts himself up onto his hands. "I'm just gonna go clean up. Back in a sec."

He eases out of me, and I watch him walk to the bathroom.

I hear running water, and he's back moments later with a cloth in his hand. He crawls up the bed and presses the cloth between my legs.

I rest up on my elbows. "What are you doing?"

"Cleaning up after myself." He gives me a cheeky grin. "And I wanted to take care of my girl."

*His girl?*

He cleans me up and takes the cloth back to the bathroom. Then, he climbs back onto the bed, laying on his front.

Rolling onto my side, I start to trace my finger over his tattoo. "Who's Thomas, the third?"

He stiffens under my hands. "My father."

"You lost him?"

He sighs, and then his head turns my way. "Yeah."

I lean down and press my lips to his tattoo. "I'm sorry you lost him. When did he pass?"

"A long time ago." He moves away. Rolling onto his back, he puts his hands behind his head.

"So, that makes you Thomas, the fourth."

"Yep."

Remembering what he said before about having songs for people he's lost, I ask in a soft voice, "What's your dad's song?"

Something painful passes through his eyes, and I instantly regret asking.

"'Ordinary World." His voice sounds odd…stiff.

"Duran Duran."

He nods, once.

"So…do you listen to your dad's song every day, like you do Jonny's?"

He sits up abruptly. "Jesus Christ," he snaps. "What the fuck is this? Grill Tom time?"

Taken aback by the sudden venom in his voice, I start to stammer out, "I'm sorry. I didn't mean—"

"Yes, you did. You know exactly what you're doing. You want to know about me? Fine. No, Lyla, I don't listen to that fucking song every day. I haven't heard that song in sixteen years, and even that's not long enough. So, is that sufficient information for you? Have you gotten enough out of me? Or do you need more?"

Tears hit my eyes, a lump forming in my throat. Confused and hurt, I sit up. Turning my back on him, I start to move away.

I hear him sigh. Then, he catches my wrist. I feel him move up behind me. His long legs come either side of mine. His chest against my back, his arms close around me, holding me, he presses the side of his face to mine.

"I'm sorry. I just…I don't talk about my dad. Ever."

I remember what he said to me about needing to talk about loss. I want to remind him of this, but I'm afraid to push it, worried that I'll push him away if I do.

"It's okay. I understand." I close my hand around his wrist.

We're trapped in this awkward moment, and I don't know what to say, so I say the first thing that comes into my mind. "Do you have a song for me?"

He moves his face from mine. I can feel his eyes on me, so I turn my head to look at him.

He looks puzzled. "I haven't lost you, have I?"

"No." I shake my head gently. "But the tour will end, and—" I stop because I don't know how to finish the sentence, or if I even want to.

Tom's eyes flash with something I don't understand.

228

Then, he says, "'Thought I'd Died and Gone to Heaven.'"

And my heart stills in my chest.

That song was playing the night we had sex under that stage.

"Bryan Adams," I croak out.

He nods, eyes fixed to mine. "Well, either Bryan's version or the one that band was playing the night you let me go where no man had gone before." A sexy smile lights up his face.

I'm speechless. For once in my life, I have no words.

That song...its meaning...

*Is he saying what I think he's saying?*

Because if he's saying what I think he's saying, then—

"So, do you have a song that reminds you of me?" His voice breaks into my thoughts.

I rub my head, trying to gather my wits. "Oh, um...yeah...'Gorilla.'" I force a smile to my face.

He lets out a laugh. "Because I'm a beast in the sack, right?"

"More like, because you tortured me with it when you were on your text message roll in that diner."

He lets out another laugh, taking us both down to the bed.

Tucking me into his side, he starts to stroke my hair.

But I'm still stuck in my head, stuck on that song. I run the lyrics over and over in my mind, wondering if Tom just said that because it reminds him of that amazing moment under that stage...or, if because he also *feels* the meaning of the song.

*If he does, then what does that mean for him and me? And do I want it to mean something?*

*Could it mean something? Could someone as emotionally broken as I am and someone like Tom, who is as emotionally closed off as he is, have something together?*

I close my eyes on the thought.

And when I open them, squinting against the morning light, Tom is gone, and I have my answer.

# Lyla

## Five Days Later—Last Night of the Tour, A Club, San Diego

Tom has been pulling away from me.

After our night in Vegas, he changed toward me.

Barely talking to me during the day, when he did, it was related to work. He stopped actively seeking me out to have sex during the day. Avoiding being alone with me.

Only at night when the guys were sleeping, would Tom come to my bed.

I wanted to ask him what was wrong, but I didn't for fear that I wouldn't like his answer.

Each night, we would have sex for hours. There was no talking. Only our bodies communicating. Sometimes, it felt like Tom was making love to me, but I'm not naïve enough to believe that's what it was.

Then, when we were done having sex, and I was replete and exhausted, I would fall asleep in his arms.

And I would wake to an empty bed.

I've lost him.

I knew it would happen. Just not like it this.

Now, the last show of the tour is finished, and after tonight, Tom and I are done.

I'm telling myself it's the right thing, what should happen. It's what we agreed on. What I wanted.

But my heart is telling me different. It's wanting more. Him.

I desperately want to fight my feelings for Tom, but for once, my heart seems to be winning the war against my head.

My heart can war and want all it does, but Tom isn't in the same place as me.

Sure, little things he's done and said have had me thinking he might have feelings for me.

But I know who Tom is. And these last five days, he's spent reminding me exactly where we stand with each other.

We're in San Diego, only a few hours from home, so the plan is to stay in the club that we just played, celebrating with the rest of the crew. Then, the bus will take us home, and that'll be the end of the tour.

The end of everything.

I haven't seen Tom since we came offstage.

I'm worried that he's left. That I won't even get to have one last night with him. Wishing I knew last night, so I could have made the most of the time. I would have memorized every second.

The DJ is on at the moment, and Fall Out Boy's "Thanks for the Memories" starts to pump out of the speakers.

I'm standing at the bar with Shannon and Ashlee, my hands nursing a bottle of beer, as my body starts to sway to the music.

I feel a hand on my shoulder. A smile comes to my mouth, hoping for Tom, I turn and come face-to-face with Robbi Kraft.

My smile drops.

I managed to successfully avoid Robbi at the one other show we had together, so it's just my dumb fucking luck that I have to see him on my last night.

"Lyla."

I put my bottle down on the bar. Then, I stare at him. If I could strike a man dead with a look, Robbi Kraft would be on the floor, out cold, right now.

"What do you want?" My voice is tight.

"Look…" He scratches his head. "I just want to apologize—"

"Don't waste your breath because I won't accept your apology."

I turn to walk away, but he grabs my arm.

"Just hear me out—"

"No. I'm not interested in anything you have to say. Now, let go of my arm." I yank it free.

"Lyla?"

My body freezes cold.

*No. God, no. Not now.*

I turn slowly. Then, feel like I'm going to die on this very spot as my eyes collide with Dex's.

Everything else around me fades to black.

Dex steps toward me.

I want to move, but I can't get my legs to work.

All I can think is, *He's here. Is Chad here?* And how much I need to get away.

"How-how are you?" Dex pushes his hand through his hair in that nervous way he's done ever since we were kids.

"Why are you here?" My voice barely gets out the words.

My eyes start to scan the crowd, looking for Cale or Sonny...Tom.

*I need Tom.*

I see Robbi walking away, making his way back through the crowd. I can't even be relieved that he's leaving, because I'm too full of panic that Dex is here.

*Tom, where are you?* I call out a silent plea.

Dex takes another step closer.

My legs finally awaken, and I step back.

I see the hurt pass over his face at my physical rejection of him.

*Good. Hurt. I want you to hurt exactly like you hurt me.*

"My band...we're playing here," Dex answers my question. "We're on in an hour."

*How did I not know this?*

Then, I realize that I never knew the name of his band. Aunt Steph never gave me it, and stupidly, I never asked.

"I have to go..."

I'm backing away when he reaches out and grabs my hand.

"Wait...Ly, I need to talk to you."

"Don't touch me!" I yank my hand from his, like he's scalded me. Because he has. He burned my heart a long time ago.

"Please, Ly, I miss you...I miss my sister. I need to talk to you. I need you to know how sorry I am. Make you understand—"

"Understand what? How you fucked my boyfriend behind my back? What do you want from me, Dex? Forgiveness? Because I can't give that to you. I want you to leave me the hell alone. Stop calling. Just get the fuck out of my life." My body is shaking so hard that my teeth are chattering together. I clench my jaw.

"Ly...please..."

He reaches for me again. I dodge him.

"I miss you so much," he pleads.

"Cry me a fucking river," I spit. "You should have thought of that before you fucked Chad." I turn away, tears stinging my eyes.

Dex grabs my arm, spinning me back around. "I'm your family, Ly. You don't get to ignore me like this—"

He never gets to finish that sentence because he's pulled off of me by Tom, who puts himself between Dex and me.

The relief I feel at Tom being here is immense.

"You're the brother?" Tom says with distaste. "Well, you heard Lyla. She doesn't want to talk to you, not now, or ever, so you need to leave." There's an unmistakable threat in his voice.

Dex looks him up down. He knows who Tom is, but that doesn't seem to faze him. "This has got nothing to do with you."

Tom steps up close to Dex. Alarm bells start to go off in my head.

"This has more to do with me than you think." Tom's voice is low, menacing.

Dex's eyes flick to me. "Jesus, Ly, you're sleeping with *him?*" He shakes his head with disappointment. "You're better than him, and you know it."

My body freezes as a war of emotions rage within me.

Dex's disappointment in me hurts, and angers me all at the same time.

*What right does he have to judge me?*

"She is better than me," Tom states. "And she's clearly better than you. What you did—it doesn't get lower. Now, leave." Tom shoves Dex hard in the chest.

Then, it all happens so quickly. Dex comes at Tom, but Tom quickly sidesteps him and punches Dex on the side of his face.

"No!" I cry out.

At the sound of my voice, Tom's eyes swing to me. His distraction gives Dex the advantage and he charges Tom, taking them both to the floor. He punches Tom in the face.

"No," I cry again, tears blurring my vision. I swipe at my eyes.

Tom seems to lose his shit completely. With one hard shove, he has Dex off of him. Then, Tom is on top of Dex, hitting him, hard. Over and over.

I move toward them, needing to put a stop this, but Shannon catches me around the waist, pulling me back.

"You go in there, you're gonna get hurt."

"But we have to stop them," I whimper. "They're gonna kill each other."

"Leave it to the men to sort," she says, pointing her finger.

I follow it and see Cale, Sonny, and Van pushing their way through the crowd of spectators.

"Cale!" I yell.

He catches my eye.

"Stop them, please."

He gives me a sharp nod, and then he starts to barrel through the crowd. Sonny, with his big frame, has no problem getting people to move out of the way.

Dex is on the floor, and Tom is beating the crap out of him. Cale grabs Tom from behind, but he's too far gone and he tries to take a swing at Cale, who somehow manages to dodge it.

It's scaring me to see Tom like this.

Van helps Cale restrain Tom, while Sonny pulls Dex up from the floor.

"Get him out of here," Cale tells Sonny.

My eyes meet Dex's. He wipes blood from his mouth with his hand. Then, I see a lone tear run down his cheek.

"I'm sorry, Ly," he says.

I turn away, retreating into Shannon's arms, and when I look back, Dex is gone.

"You okay?" Shannon asks me.

"Yes…no." I give a sad smile.

"So, I have no clue what the hell that was about, but there's definitely no doubt left in my mind that you and Tom are sleeping together."

I lift my shoulders and give her a weak smile, seeing no point in denying it now. Even though after tonight, Tom and I will be no more.

"Ly, you okay?" A breathless Cale is at my side.

I can see the anger still flaming in his eyes.

"I'm sorry I wasn't here. I was—"

"It's okay. I'm okay." I rub his arm. "How's Tom?" As I speak, I turn and see Tom talking with two of the club's security men, who have finally made an appearance.

"I should go and see if he's okay." Stepping away, I leave Cale with Shannon.

At my approach, Tom's eyes meet mine. He says something to the security guys. Then, he moves away from them, coming to me.

We stop a foot apart. "Are you okay?" I ask.

He looks okay. His cheek is a bit red from where Dex hit him, but apart from that, Tom doesn't appear to have a mark on him.

"Are you?" he asks, turning my question back on me.

"Yeah." I nod. "You hit him…"

He stares at me for a long moment. "I take care of what's mine."

*I'm his?*

My heart thuds against my ribs. I close the distance between us. Tentatively, I lift my hand to his face and gently press it to his cheek.

In his eyes, I see the surprise from me touching him like this in public.

I lower my hand. "This is our last night together."

His eyes darken. "Then, we should make the most of it."

I'm beyond relieved that I'm going to have this one last night with Tom. I know I'll hurt badly for it tomorrow, but for tonight, I don't care. All I care about is being with him.

Tom slips his hand into mine. "Let's get out of here," he says.

"Wait." I tug on his hand. "I need to let Cale know that I'm leaving. He'll worry if I just disappear."

Tom leans down, and presses his lips to mine. I feel his kiss all the way down to my toes.

"You've got one minute," he says over my mouth, before releasing me.

I take a shaky step back. "One minute." I turn on my heel, and walk quickly back to where I left Cale.

He's still standing with Shannon.

"Cale, I'm going to…" *Shit, what do I say?*

"Leave with Tom." He gives me a look. "Come on, Ly, I know you and Tom have been doing the nasty."

*What?*

The shock must be written clear on my face, because Cale says, "Don't look so surprised. You've always been a shit liar."

"Hey." I give him a gentle jab in the arm. "I'm sorry though, that I didn't tell you."

"We'll talk about that tomorrow. You've had enough shit going on tonight from seeing…" He doesn't say Dex's name.

Seeing Dex here tonight has had an effect on Cale, too.

"You okay?" I ask, touching his arm.

He wraps his hand over mine, gripping my fingers. "I'm fine. Go with Tom. And tomorrow, you and I will have a long talk about how you don't keep secrets from your best friend." He smiles.

Letting go of his arm, I wrap mine around him, hugging him. "You're the best friend a girl could ever hope for," I say against his shirt.

He squeezes me tight. "And you're the best girl a guy could ask for."

I lift my head from his chest, looking up at him.

He gives me a rueful smile. "He hurts you, Ly, and—"

"You'll kick his ass. I know the drill." I put on a smile.

Right now, I don't want to tell Cale that Tom and I will be no more by tomorrow, and my heart will pretty much be kicking its own ass. I can confide in Cale when it's over.

Giving him one last squeeze, I say good-bye and walk back to Tom, who's waiting for me where I left him.

He's got a scowl on his face.

"You okay?" I ask.

"Uhum." His eyes find mine, softening on me, the scowl instantly disappears. He puts his arm around my waist. "Let's go."

Tom guides us out a side door of the club, and he opens the door of a waiting black limo, ushering me inside.

The instant we're seated, I curl my body around his big frame, just needing to feel him. His strength. His warmth.

One hand slides around my back before settling on my hip. His other finds my chin. He tilts my face to his. "You doing okay, Firecracker?"

"Yeah…I'm good. Here with you, I'm happy."

He stares at me. Then, his eyes close, and he leans in, pressing a sweet kiss to my lips while grazing his knuckles against my cheek.

The limo starts to move.

Settling my head against his shoulder, I ask, "Where are we going?"

"Home."

"Home?"

"Yeah, my house in LA."

"That's a bit of a drive." I smile, secretly happy at the thought of seeing Tom's house. Happy that he wants to take me there.

"Don't worry." He grins as Usher's "Scream" starts to play in the limo. "I'm sure I can find a way to keep you entertained for the few hours it'll take to get us there."

# *Lyla* 25

## A Few Hours Later—Tom's House, LA

I awake to the feeling of the world falling out beneath me. My body jumps.

"I got you," Tom's deep voice says from above. "You fell asleep in the limo."

Then, I realize that I'm in his arms, and he's carrying me. Sliding my hands around his neck, I nuzzle into his throat, inhaling the scent of his aftershave, loving the feel of his stubble against my skin.

We made out for a while in the limo. Things got a little heated, and I ended up with Tom's head between my legs where he used his mouth and fingers to bring me to orgasm. I returned the favor by getting on my knees and taking him in my mouth. After he spilled himself down my throat, he hauled me onto his big body and held me. I must have fallen asleep in his arms.

"You okay if I put you down for just a minute? Need to get my key."

"Sure."

Tom lowers me to my feet, and I lean against the wall by the door.

He pulls a key from his pocket and unlocks the door before pushing it open.

I wait to follow him in, but the next thing I know, he's picking me back up.

"I'll be okay to walk now." I laugh.

"I like to carry you. You're like a little doll."

"I'm not little. You're just huge."

"In every way, darlin'." He winks.

He kicks the door shut with his foot and proceeds to carry me up a wide staircase. I can't see much as Tom hasn't bothered to turn any lights on, but from the size of this staircase, I'm guessing his house is big.

Quickly reaching the top of the stairs, he takes us to the left and then through a door a little farther down the hallway.

He crosses the spacious room and sets me down on his massive bed. I watch him walk over to the wall, and he presses a button on a panel. Dim lights come on. Then, he moves over to the iPod docking station, which is set up on his dresser. I watch him scroll through the music before he finally selects a song. The music starts to play through the speakers in the room.

"Last Request" by Paolo Nutini.

Tears instantly fill my eyes. I blink them back while swallowing the pain I feel from listening to the lyrics, from what Tom is telling me with this song.

He's saying good-bye.

As I watch him walk toward me, my heart breaks. The soulful voice of Paolo Nutini spurring my pain on. Hurting from how much I want Tom in this moment, knowing it's our last.

The last time I'll get to touch him. Kiss him. Feel him inside me.

Even with the weight of that bearing down on me, I still stand when he reaches me.

I need to make the most of this night.

I slip my hands under his shirt and press my fingertips against his hard stomach, loving the sound of his sharp intake of breath at my touch.

His eyes glitter down lustfully at me.

Gripping the bottom of his shirt, I lift it. Tom raises his arms, allowing me to pull it over his head.

I drop his shirt to the floor, and then put my hands on his chest. Inching up onto my toes, I brush my lips gently over his. As I move back, Tom takes my head in his hands. His eyes burn into mine with such intensity that it takes my breath away.

Then, he seals his mouth over mine, leading me into a knee weakening kiss.

He grabs my ass in both hands, lifting me, as I wrap my legs around his waist.

Tom climbs up onto the bed on his knees, kissing me still, he takes us down to the mattress.

This time is different. Slower. He takes his time undressing me—caressing, and kissing every part of me. Looking at me with reverence. It's almost as if he's memorizing me with his eyes and hands and mouth.

When I'm naked and wanting beneath him, I reach for his jeans and unbuckle his belt.

Tom takes over, sliding it free from his jeans. Belt in hand, he takes both of my hands and moves them up above my head. He looks down at me in question.

I nod, letting him know I'm okay with it, feeling excited beyond measure.

He fits his belt around my wrists with a precision that I choose to ignore.

"Is that okay?" he asks.

"Yes." I'm breathless with anticipation.

He moves his big body between my legs. "Keep your arms up there. Don't move them. You move, I'll make you wait longer to come."

"I understand," I whisper. My body is vibrating with excitement.

He takes my nipple into his mouth and tugs it with his teeth, leaving a sting that he immediately soothes with his tongue. Moving to the other breast, he repeats the action.

He gets to his knees, sitting between my thighs. "You look so beautiful right now," he says in a throaty voice. "Spread your legs."

I part them wider for him.

He runs his finger between my wet folds. "So goddamn beautiful," he murmurs. Moving down the bed, he positions his head between my legs and starts to lick me with enthusiasm.

His fingers go into my pussy, pumping in and out. Then, they start to trail down toward my ass.

"Yes." I lift my hips, letting him know how badly I want him there.

"I wanna fuck your ass so bad." He kisses the inside of my thigh, finger rimming my puckered hole. "I want to be the first man to give that to you."

*Can I do this?*

We've been doing the fingers-up-my-ass since that night under the stage. Tom has increased it to two fingers, but we've never gone so far as to actually have anal sex.

It's our last night. This could be something that's ours…his alone that I gave to him.

I do trust him. I know he would never hurt me.

*Yes, I want this with Tom.*

"Let's do it…" I hear myself saying.

He lifts his head, eyes dark and fixed on my face. "You really mean that?"

"I really mean it. I want this with you."

Dismay suddenly passes over his face. "Fuck," he utters. "I don't have any lube in the house."

I'm surprised by how disappointed I feel. "You don't have anything?"

"No…my home is not a place I have sex in."

My eyes widen. "You've never had sex here before?"

Knowing Tom, I find that hard to believe.

"Don't sound so surprised. In the past, with other women, I either went to their place or the apartment I have in town, which is specifically for—" He cuts himself off, realizing I don't need to hear about his fuck pad. He moves closer to me. "You're my first."

*I want him to be my first.*

Swallowing past my girly emotions that his declaration has set off in me, I say, "Can we do it just using…me?" I nod down to the ridiculous wetness I'm currently providing.

His eyes sweep down my body, settling between my legs. His eyes start to burn again. "We can try." His hands come under me, then, he's flipping me over onto my front. "Get up on your knees. Face on the bed. Arms above your head. Lift that sexy ass of yours for me."

Spurred on by his commands, I do exactly as he asks. I get my hands comfortable so the belt isn't digging into my wrists.

Tom comes up behind me, and his thick finger dips into my entrance. He moves my natural lubricant up to my puckered hole. Carefully, he works his finger in. I feel that slight unease I always do when we first start doing this, but sensation quickly overrides, and I fall into the feeling.

No time has passed before he's working in a second finger, stretching me. All the while, rubbing my clit with his skilled fingers.

I'm panting, heart pounding, my legs trembling. "Tom," I moan. "I need it…you…*now.*" I can barely breathe. My body is on fire, and my head is swimming with desire. I'm desperate to have him.

Without a word, he gets up on his knees, and thrusts his cock deep into my pussy.

"Oh my God." My eyes roll back in my head, while my inner muscles clench around him.

"Fuck!" he bites out. His hand comes to rest on my hip, his fingers gripping me tight.

Then, he starts to fuck me.

After some well-aimed thrusts, he pulls out. I feel the head of his cock move upward, over that delicate piece of skin that separates my most intimate places.

His cock gently nudges at my puckered hole, his hold on my hip tightening, his fingers digging deliciously into my flesh.

The feel of him there has me warring within myself. Fear fighting with desire.

"You sure you want to do this?" he asks, his voice rough.

I realize that I've tensed up. My muscles are locked tight.

*Yes, I want this with him.*

Closing my eyes, I force myself to relax.

I nod, unable to speak, too focused on the feel of him *there*.

"Answer me," he commands.

"Yes!" I cry out. "Just fuck me now!" My voice is needy. I want to power through. I don't want to wait around. I just want him inside me.

He growls, then, I feel him push hard against my tight hole.

The head of his cock slips in. I feel the familiar burn at having something in there, but this is far more intense than his fingers.

Biting hard on my lip, I instantly tense again.

"You need me to stop?" he asks, gruff.

I can hear the barely there control in his voice.

"No, don't stop. Keep going."

"Okay. But I need you to relax." He slides his hand up my spine. "You need to open up and let me in."

I relax my muscles again, allowing Tom to work himself in a little farther.

"Jesus." My voice is caught somewhere between a sob and a moan.

Then, the burn suddenly goes, and all I feel is a maddening desire. The intense need to have Tom Carter buried as deep in my ass as he can go.

"More," I demand.

He pushes in another inch.

A breath hisses from me.

His fingers go to my clit, playing with me, and then he pushes one inside my pussy, fingering me, getting more of my natural lubricant. Removing his finger, I feel him rub it around me and himself.

I'm hot and desperate, wanting this more than I ever thought I would.

He's lubricated us up, but he isn't making a move.

"Tom, please, I need this…you…don't stop now." I'm half-crazy with lust. On the edge of the precipice he's taken me to. I need him to finish this. "Just fuck my fucking ass!"

He thrusts in another couple of inches.

"You still okay?" He sounds breathless.

"Stop talking, and just fucking do me!"

I love that he cares and doesn't want to hurt me, but I'm desperate beneath him. I'm so turned on that I can't see straight. I'm hot all over. I can't remember ever being this turned on before.

Having him in such a private place, dominating my body, owning me—it's beyond anything I could have imagined.

Another thrust. "I'm almost there, baby." His hand comes around, and he starts to rub my clit again. "You ready for the rest?"

My eyes close. "So ready."

He drives the remainder of his big beautiful cock into me.

I'm full of him. Desire coursing through my body, I feel like I might go insane from the sensation alone. I've never needed someone as much as I need Tom right now.

"How do you feel?" he asks, his voice strained.

I twist my head to look back at him. "Amazing." I graze my teeth over my lower lip.

The fire in his eyes burns brighter than I've ever seen before. He pulls halfway out, and thrusts straight back in. The sound that comes from him nearly has me coming.

My head falls forward, my hair curtaining my face.

The pleasure is so intense that it's blinding.

"Ly, I've never felt anything like this…you. I could do this forever with you."

*Forever.*

Then, he starts to fuck my ass with an unrestrained passion.

And I'm lost to him. Heart and soul and body.

I'm Tom Carter's.

I'm coming minutes later and coming hard.

"I'm gonna come, Ly. Now...I'm gonna..." Tom grunts a rough, dirty sound. It's the sexiest fucking thing I've ever heard.

He pulls out, and I feel the hot spurts of his come as it hits my ass and lower back.

When he's done, he falls onto the bed beside me. I let my lower half come down, so I'm lying flat.

He brushes my hair off my face. "You're gonna kill me one of these days." He smiles, and then it falls when he realizes what he's said.

*There'll be no more days after this.*

"Stay there. I'll get something to clean you up with."

I turn my face into bed, hiding my sadness. "Wasn't planning on moving," I say muffled into the duvet.

He chuckles. I hear the sound of running water, and then Tom is back, cleaning me up with a wet cloth.

He's frees my wrists of the belt.

"Come take a shower with me."

Sliding his hand into mine, he gently tugs me off the bed, and I lazily follow him into the en suite bathroom.

With my hip propped against the sink, I watch as he turns on the shower, letting the water heat.

Taking my hand again, he leads me into the shower and under the spray. I tilt my head back, allowing the water to cascade over my face. Pushing my hair back, I clear the water from my face with my hands, and I open my eyes.

Tom is watching at me.

The look in his eyes sets my body trembling under the intensity of his stare.

He moves a step closer, putting us both under the water. We're body-to-body, my breasts crushed up against his chest. He takes my face in his hands, and he kisses me.

His kiss is deep and full with meaning. A kiss that feels like good-bye.

Though my heart is breaking under the weight of it, I can't bring myself to stop, and in this moment, I realize that I will take anything Tom has to give me. Any scrap of him that he throws my way, I'll gladly have.

He kisses me like time has become meaningless as though we have all the time in the world.

I'm brought crashing down to earth when he parts his lips from mine. And I'm reminded that time is relevant and that I have very little left with him.

Mere hours.

I want to make the most of all those hours. Picking up a sponge, I squeeze shower gel onto it, and I begin washing his body. I run the sponge over his clean-cut lines, memorizing every part of his body, until I'm on my knees, staring up at him. He's already hard, his eyes blazing down at me. After smoothing my palm up his thigh and across the cut of his pelvis, I take his cock in my hand. I grab the bottle of shower gel. Squeezing some into my hand, I start to rub it all over his cock, working up a slippery lather.

Tom groans. His fingers graze my jaw. "Suck me."

Hands against his hips, I push him back under the spray, letting the water run down his body, washing the soap from his cock. Then, opening up, I slide his steely length between my lips. I love the rumble of pleasure that comes from him and the way his hand goes to the shower wall to steady himself.

I suck him until he's coming in my mouth, and I greedily swallow every drop he gives me.

Tom pulls me to my feet. His heated praise is still echoing in my mind as he moves me under the spray. Then, he starts to wash my body. Soapy hands linger on my boobs, his eyes not straying from them.

"You really do have the best tits I've ever seen, Firecracker."

I let out a laugh. "You have a serious boob obsession."

He runs his finger down the valley of my breasts. Moving across, he circles a nipple.

A bolt of lust shoots between my thighs.

"No, I just have an obsession with *your* boobs." He presses his finger hard against my nipple. Then, his other hand comes up, and he cups them both.

I arch into his touch.

Soapy thumbs tease my nipples. "Your tits are amazing. Fucking perfection. I've never seen a rack as perfect before, and I never will again."

I think he sees it flash in my eyes—our ending, the pain I feel at the thought—because his hands quickly leaves my boobs, and one finds its way between my legs. He pushes his finger inside me. My head falls back on a moan, which Tom captures with his mouth. He kisses me hard, while fingering me.

Then, his finger is pulling out, and he's moving down my body, his tongue licking the running water from my skin. He lifts my leg, resting it over his shoulder, and he presses his mouth to me.

"Oh God." I brace my hand against the shower wall. Tom's hands grip my ass, supporting me.

I'm coming minutes later, my lips crying out his name.

My body is still shuddering with aftershocks when Tom gets to his feet, and starts to wash my hair.

After turning off the shower, he steps out and wraps a towel around his waist. Then, he comes to me and wraps me in a big, fluffy white towel before leading me back to the bedroom.

Drying my skin and squeezing the excess water from my hair, I watch as Tom drops his towel to the floor, and I'm surprised that he's once again hard.

He pulls back the bed covers.

I climb into bed.

He turns the music and lights off.

Then, he gets into bed, crawling up between my legs.

In the dark, Tom stares down at me, his fingers working through my damp hair.

He lowers his mouth to mine, kissing me softly, and then he's pressing against my entrance.

A soft moan leaves me as he slowly enters me. His kiss quickly turns deep…passionate. His movements become more intense…urgent.

He cradles my head in his hands, his eyes locked with mine, his look worshipping, as he moves inside me.

In this darkness, for this one last time, I let myself believe that Tom is making love to me.

When I'm coming, I close my eyes, so he won't see the tears in them.

Tom comes seconds later. His cock buried deep inside me, his face pressed into my neck, his hot breath burning my skin, while he marks my insides with his come.

Then, without moving out of me, he rolls us over, putting me on top of him. His hand holds my head to his chest, and he presses a kiss to my hair.

We don't speak. No good nights, no good-byes.

And this how I fall asleep—my body wrapped around Tom's, our chests pressed together, while my heart bleeds out of my own and straight into his.

## The Next Morning—Tom's House, LA

I wake up on my back, the warmth of the sun on my face.

Turning my head, squinting against the bright morning light, I find I'm alone in bed.

Sitting up, I slide my legs over the edge of the bed, letting my toes sink into the soft carpet. I see Tom's belt that he used on me last night on the floor, and I register the slight soreness in my ass as a vivid memory of Tom moving inside me comes to surface.

I close my eyes, letting it wash over me.

How he felt. How I felt.

Everything about last night was perfect.

But last night is over. And this is the harsh reality of morning.

My last morning with Tom.

I close my eyes and take a deep breath, forcing my feelings back.

Getting to my feet, I look around and take Tom's room in properly in the daylight, trying to learn a little more about him.

It's a total guy's bedroom. All dark wood and white walls. The bedsheets I spent the night wrapped up in are black. A huge flat screen is up on the wall.

Getting up, I walk over to the window, which basically covers the entire far wall. Looking at the view, I see the Hollywood sign and realize that I'm in the Hills.

*Figures.*

Tom wouldn't exactly be short of cash, thanks to TMS.

I don't see my clothes or panties anywhere, so I go to Tom's walk-in closet and grab a shirt.

Wearing only the shirt, I tread out of the bedroom, looking for the stairs.

Finding them easily, I start to make my way down.

Looking around as I walk, I take in my surroundings since I didn't get the chance to do it last night. I had other things on my mind then…mainly Tom.

In the light of day, his house surprises me. It's all soft furnishings, beautiful paintings hanging on the walls, and plush carpets and hardwood floors, kind of surprising.

Not how I would expect a rock star's house to look—well, not Tom's house anyway.

I imagined his place as a fuck pad with pictures of naked women up on the walls and empty pizza boxes and beer bottles lying everywhere. Considering the Tom of old, I thought he might also have a few actual naked groupies littered around the place for extra decoration and personal usage.

But some serious thought and care has gone into making this house look warm and inviting. Actually, I wouldn't even call it a house because it's more than that. It's a home.

*Tom's home.*

Then, I'm reminded of what he said last night, how I'm the first woman he's brought back here.

A warm, gooey feeling fills my chest.

Pushing the feeling aside, I try not to read too much into the fact that Tom brought me to his home. I remind myself of his apartment that he uses for the sole purpose of screwing women. I bet that place definitely has groupies in it.

Because that's the man Tom is.

The reason he hasn't brought women here is because he doesn't want his one-night stands hassling him at home. He thinks I'm a safe bet. That I won't bother him after this morning.

And he's right. I might have some serious feelings for him, but I also have pride.

Reaching the hall, my feet move over hardwood flooring, and I head toward the sounds and smells of food being fried.

I push open the kitchen door, and the sight awaiting me is…well, it's outstanding, and it takes all thought with it.

Because Tom is standing at his stove—barefoot, shirtless, wearing only a pair of running shorts.

And he's frying bacon.

It's like all my Christmases have come at once.

"Isn't that a little risky?" I lean against the doorframe.

Tom turns, spatula in hand, and raises a questioning eyebrow.

"Hot fat. Very little clothing." I point to his bare chest.

He grins that sexy grin of his. "I'm hardcore, Firecracker. You know that." Then, he winks.

And I puddle to the floor.

He's so dreamy.

*And I'm such a fucking girl.*

I see his eyes on his shirt that I'm wearing.

Feeling a little awkward, I say, "I hope it's okay that I borrowed a shirt. I couldn't find my clothes."

"It's fine. I had your clothes laundered. They're just over there."

I follow his gaze to where my clothes are hanging on the back of a door.

*Wow, that was quick.* It's only nine in the morning. *Exactly what time did he get up?*

"You have a super-fast cleaning service on call?"

He chuckles. "No, my cleaner. She comes in early. I had her wash and dry your clothes."

"What time did you get up?"

"Early. I went for a run while you were still sleeping."

*He runs?*

He never went for a run while we were tour, but then I guess he didn't get a lot of chances. And to keep looking like he does, he must work out.

"You hungry?" he asks, turning back to the bacon.

"Sure, I could eat something."

I watch as Tom serves up bacon onto two waiting plates, and he walks over to the kitchen table with them. I follow behind. A pot of coffee and toast are already there.

I sit down, tucking one leg underneath me. Tom takes the seat opposite of me.

I pick up a piece of bacon and take a bite. It practically melts in my mouth. "You cook some good bacon." I smile.

He returns my smile, but he surprisingly doesn't give me a retort.

It leaves an uncomfortable feeling in my chest.

Over breakfast, we chat about my band's single and our album, upcoming plans for TMS, and everything else but him and me.

Breakfast done, I'm upstairs dressing into my clothes. I've just fastened up my jeans when Tom comes in the bedroom.

"You ready to go?"

"Yeah." I smile. It's weak. I know it, he knows it, but neither of us acknowledges the fact.

"I'll just get changed and then I'll take you home." He disappears into his closet.

"Okay," I say. My mouth feels like it's stuffed with cotton. "I'll wait for you downstairs."

I wander down and hover in the massive hallway. Feeling nosy and wanting more of a glimpse into Tom, I walk over to a door sitting slightly ajar.

Music room.

There's an array of guitars, a drum kit, and a piano.

I take a seat at the piano and start tinkering on the keys.

"You play?"

I jump and turn to find Tom in the doorway, looking gorgeous in a pair of dark blue jeans, a plain black T-shirt, and biker boots.

"No." I shake my head. "I didn't realize you did."

"Piano lessons from the age of five until I was twelve." He sits on the seat beside me. "Some things you just never forget. Who do think taught Jake to play?" He winks.

And there it is—another small snippet of Tom. It makes me hunger for more.

"Will you play something for me?"

He looks at me. I think he's going to say no, so I bat my lashes at him and rest my chin on my shoulder, going for cute.

"Please," I say sweetly.

He lets out a laugh, shaking his head. "Fine. Any requests?"

"No. You choose."

He pauses for a moment, his fingers over the keys. Then, he starts to play. It takes me a good few seconds to realize what song he's playing so beautifully.

"Clocks" by Coldplay.

Then, it just makes me ache with sadness.

When he starts to sing the lyrics softly, I feel like I can't breathe.

I force air into my lungs. My heart is heading toward a slow agonizing death in my chest.

I join him, singing softly along, my shoulder pressed against his.

"You play amazingly," I say as he plays the last note. "Remind me again, why do you only play bass? Not that bass isn't important," I add at his raised brow. "Because it's the most important instrument in band." I smile. "But...you could do, be so much more. You are so much more."

He stares at me, then, looks away, back to the piano. He starts to tinker the keys. "The frontline isn't somewhere I want to be. I like things easy, simple. I get to play, do what I love, get the rewards from it with marginal cost to myself."

Nodding, I understand what he means. To be the front of a band, the face, as I am, then you have to give more...and lose more.

He lifts his hand to my face, gently tucking my hair behind my ear. His gaze on me is soft.

Then, from nowhere, it hardens. "I'll just grab my keys, and then we can go." He gets up and exits the room.

I stand, disappointed.

I'm just passing through the door when he meets me in the hall with a set of keys in his hand.

"Ready?"

I nod and then follow him down the hall, through the kitchen, and out a door in the utility room.

We walk over to his garage. When I say *garage*, I mean, a four-door wide garage.

He takes me in through a door on the side and flips a switch, illuminating the place.

There are three cars here and a motorcycle at the far side.

I don't know much about cars, but they all look expensive.

He has a black Range Rover and a smaller black car that looks like a race car. It has two orange stripes running down the hood and around each headlight. It screams money. The last car is gunmetal gray, and I know it's an Audi from the badge on the front. I have an Audi, a TT Roadster, but mine is nowhere near as expensive as his looks. I bought it when I got my license. My car is bright red, and I love her.

"Exactly how many cars do you need?" I ask, running my hand over the hood of the fancy-looking race car.

"A man can never have too many cars."

Shaking my head, I give him a mocking look. "Okay, I know that's a Range Rover." I point in the direction of the black beast. "And that's an Audi."

"R8," Tom clarifies for me.

"What's this one?" I tap my knuckles lightly on the sports car.

"That goddess you're touching is a Bugatti Veyron."

"Wow."

I might not know a lot about cars, but I know Bugattis are made-to-order cars. Figures with a man like Tom.

"You call your car a goddess?"

"She is a goddess. Look at her." Tom comes over and runs his hand over the roof of the car. "She's pure perfection. A total fucking goddess."

"You're such a guy." Leaving the Bugatti, I start to walk toward the dangerous-looking motorcycle.

"Custom-designed Harley." Tom's voice comes up behind me. His breath tickles my neck. I shiver.

"Custom designed?" I reach out and touch the rustic red body of the bike.

"Means I had a hand in designing her. I told Harley what I wanted. I worked on the designs with them, and this is what we came up with. You like her?"

I turn, finding him closer than I expected. "I do. She looks cool, if not a little dangerous."

"You like dangerous though, right?"

In his eyes, I see all our times together, all the risks I've taken with him.

"Yes," I say, my breath suddenly coming in short.

"Good." He smiles. "'Cause I'm taking you home on her."

I tense up. "I've never been on a motorcycle before."

He tilts his head to the side, a wicked grin teasing his lips. "Guess I get to take another virginity of yours then."

It takes me a moment to realize he's referring to last night's ass sex.

I blush from my head right down to my toes.

Tom touches his fingers to my heated cheek. My breathing hitches. Desire quickly pools in my belly.

It doesn't go unnoticed by him. And I'm not alone in it either. His eyes have darkened with lust.

We're frozen in a moment together, and I wonder...hope...pray that he's going to kiss me.

Then, something clouds his face. His eyes harden just like they did before in the music room.

He removes his hand and steps away from me.

I feel the loss of his touch like ice on my skin.

"I don't have a jacket that will fit you," he says, heading over to a coat hook on the wall, where a bunch of jackets are hung. "You'll have to wear one of mine. That okay?"

"Sure," I say, steeling myself, not letting my disappointment show.

He takes two black leather jackets from the coat hook and brings one over to me.

I slide my arms in, pulling it on, and then zip it up. It's huge and smells of Tom.

His scent is filling my lungs, choking my insides.

I look up to see him zipping up his jacket. He looks illegally hot in it.

Tugging at the big jacket, I grumble, "I bet I look stupid."

He grins. "Nah, you look cute. Anyway, I like to see you in my clothes."

He can say the sweetest things at times. Things that make me think maybe this isn't the end. Maybe there's more for us.

I smile at him. And his eyes harden again, and my hope fades.

He hands me a helmet. "Put this on."

Doing as I'm told, I pull it on over my head. I'm struggling with fastening the strap, so Tom takes over.

"All set." He gives me a gentle smile before pulling my visor down.

He pulls on his own helmet and fastens it with ease. Then, he climbs on the bike.

Kicking off the stand, he keeps his feet flat on the floor and pats the space behind him.

Hand on his arm, I put my foot on the rest and hoist myself on, swinging my leg over. I set my other foot on the rest and place my hands on Tom's waist. He grabs my hands and pulls them around to his front, bringing me right up against him.

My breathing hitches.

He turns on the engine. The vibrations run through my body, highlighting every lusty feeling I'm having right now from being this close to him.

He takes out a tiny remote from his pocket and opens the garage door.

Slowly, he drives us out of the garage, maneuvering around the house. When he hits the gravel driveway, he starts to pick up speed.

My thighs grip him tighter, my fingers digging into his leather jacket.

He removes one hand from the handlebar and gives my thigh a squeeze. "Relax," he says over the roar of the engine "You're safe with me."

Knowing Tom would never let anything happen to me, I let myself relax a little.

He slows as we approach the gate. It opens automatically. Tom drives through.

He gives the road a quick check, and then turning left, he hits tarmac and quickly picks up speed.

I let out a little squeal, squeezing my eyes shut, as I tighten my grip on him again.

I feel his laughter beneath my hands, rumbling through his chest.

After a while, I open my eyes, figuring I should just try to relax and enjoy the ride.

Enjoy just being close to Tom for this last time.

All too soon, we're in Silver Lake and pulling up outside my building where I share an apartment with the guys, courtesy of TMS Records.

Tom kicks out the stand and pulls off his helmet. He hangs it on the handlebar. He runs his hand through his hair, mussing it up.

My heart feels as heavy as bricks.

I hold on to him as I swing my leg over. Feet hitting concrete, I take a minute to steady my wobbly legs. As much as I loved being close to Tom and a huge part of me didn't want to let go, it is nice to be on safe ground again.

Removing the helmet, I shake my hair out. "Thanks for the ride." I hold the helmet out for him to take.

"Keep it," he says, pushing it back to me. "I can't ride home with it. Keep the jacket, too. Not that you'll have any use for them, but they're yours."

He's rejecting me.

He would rather have me keep his things than have to chance seeing me again.

*Just say fine and walk away.*

But I can't seem to stop my big stupid mouth from saying, "I could bring them to the studio for you." And now I sound desperate.

*Fabulous.*

He stares straight ahead. "No, it's fine. Keep them."

He can't even bring himself to look at me. "Okay." I take a small step back. "Thanks...I guess."

*Keep moving, Ly. Say good-bye and get your ass into your building.*

I'm trying—really, I am—but the ache of his rejection is stinging like a mother, and I can't seem to move.

"So, yeah, um...thanks for the ride."

*You said that already. Just leave pride intact. Come on, look at him. He can't even bring himself to look at you. He's itching to leave.*

Then, it hits me. This is it. I leave Tom now, and I don't know when I'll see him again, if ever.

We don't exactly run in the same circles. The only possibility of me seeing Tom would be at the studio, but if he really doesn't want to see me, then it wouldn't be hard for him to avoid me.

*I don't want to lose him.*

The realization strikes me like a blinding, sickening panic.

I can't envisage a day where I don't get to see him or speak to him, and the thought of never being close to him again...never being able to touch him or have him touch me...

*Jesus...*

I rub my hand against my chest, the thought physically hurting me.

I lift my eyes to him, and find his beautiful greens staring back at me.

*Oh God.*

I'm in love with him.

*I'm in love with Tom.*

"Lyla..."

He pushes a hand through his hair and lets out a heavy breath, completely unaware of the fear peddling through my mind and body right now.

"Um...shit, I don't know what to say. I've never done this before."

He gives me a rueful smile, and it tugs on my heart. The one I now apparently want to hand over to him.

"I know in the beginning, we agreed that it, *us*, would end here at the end of the tour, but...well, I didn't get around to fulfilling all those orgasms you're owed...and I was thinking..." He shifts his position, looking uncomfortable.

I'm hanging on his every word, waiting, desperate to see where he's going with this.

He rubs a hand over the stubble on his chin. "What I'm trying to say is, I don't want to lose you from my life completely, and I can't ever imagine us just being friends."

He gives me a soft, sexy smile that seeps into my chest and curls around my heart.

"So, I'd still like to see you…"

*He wants to see me again. He wants me like I want him.*

My heart lights up.

"A few times a week to, you know, hook up. So, what do you think?"

And my heart dims.

*He wants us to keep being fuck buddies.*

*He doesn't want me. He just wants to screw me a couple of times a week.*

My heart drops to my stomach, free-falling, taking the rest of my insides with it.

I feel so stupid. Heat is prickling my face. My throat is thickening while tears are threatening my eyes.

"You want us to continue being fuck buddies?" I can't hide the edge or emotion in my voice.

His eyes meet mine, a wariness in them. "Yes."

"Right." I step back.

"Was that the wrong suggestion?" He scratches his cheek. "Because you don't look so happy with the idea."

*The wrong suggestion? Not happy with the idea? You could say that.*

And I do. "No, I'm not happy with the idea."

"Right…" His fingers lift to his forehead, and he presses them against his skin. A second later, he drops his hand, and his gaze hits mine. "So, what's changed?"

I frown at him. "What do you mean, what's changed?" My voice is rising.

And he's getting annoyed.

I can see from the telltale line between his brow and the darkening of his eyes.

"I mean, you were happy to be my fuck buddy for the tour and up to last night, but now, suddenly, you're not. So, I'm wondering, what's changed between you climbing out of my bed this morning to now?"

"About sixty seconds ago, I realized I'm in love with you. That's what's changed."

And there it is. My absolute fucking inability to filter anything that comes out of my mouth.

I watch his face reverberate with shock. That shock quickly transforms to absolute horror.

My hope for anything beyond sex with Tom burns away into ashes and blows away in the gentle breeze.

He shakes his head. "You don't love me."

My eyes fill with tears. I can't stop them any more than I can stop the fact that I love him.

Pride hurting like a bitch, I bite out, "So, you're telling me what I feel now? I thought your commands stayed in the bedroom."

His eyes snap up to mine. He's angry, the angriest I have ever seen him.

"You have no fucking right telling me you love me!" he roars.

His voice is so harsh that it startles me, forcing me back a step.

"We were just fucking! Fuck buddies. Nothing more. You agreed. Love was never supposed to come into it." He drags his hands through his hair.

His features are tight. My heart is breaking.

"I-I...this wasn't something I planned on." My voice is small. "I didn't mean to...fall..." I grip the helmet tight to my chest like it's a life raft. I desperately need something to cling on to.

Tom lets out a careless laugh that strikes me like a hand across the face.

"What did you think was gonna happen when you told me you love me? Did you think I'd tell you I felt the same? That we'd ride off into the sunset and live happily ever after? I'm not that guy, and you fucking know it. I don't do love. Never have, and I'm not about to start now. I am interested though—at what point did I give you the impression that I might?" His voice is getting harsher with each passing word. "Was it when I was fucking you up the ass? Or maybe when I fucked you under that stage? Or was it when I had you down on your knees while I fucked your mouth—"

"Stop it," I gasp, each of his words feeling like a blow to the chest.

It's painful enough to know he doesn't feel the same about me. But to know the thought of me loving him makes him this angry...hurts beyond words.

Tears are running down my face. I press the leather sleeve against my cheek, trying to dry them, but all that happens is I get a lungful of Tom. It ignites my pain further.

"You never gave me any indication that you felt the same," I whisper, my voice broken. "It was all me. My mistake."

I turn to leave, but Tom grabs my arm, keeping me there. He's clearly not done with inflicting his rage on me.

"This whole thing was a mistake." He runs his free hand through his hair, tugging on the strands. "*Fuck!* I never should have started this with you."

*A mistake.* If he'd hit me, it would have hurt less.

"Get off me!" I cry, trying to pull my arm free.

Having Tom touch me right now is like pouring salt in my bleeding wound.

But he doesn't let go. It's like he doesn't even feel me right now.

"I never should have let this happen." His eyes are on the pavement, his head shaking. It's almost as if he's not even talking to me in this moment. "I should have known this would happen...especially with a girl like you."

*A girl like me.*

If I needed anything to bring me back, it was that.

I force strength into my weak body. There might still be tears on my face, but I make sure my expression is one of total anger.

"You've made your point." I hold my voice steady. "I get it. You don't care about me. I'm hearing that loud and clear. Now, let me go."

I see what I think is a flicker of emotion in his eyes. Or maybe it's that stupid shred of hope I'm desperately holding on to that sees it. The hope that's willing him to tell me he doesn't mean any of this. That he feels the same for me as I do for him.

He drops my arm, his eyes scarily hard. "The sooner I'm out of here, the fucking better." He pulls his helmet off the handlebar. "You and me, we end here. Are we clear?"

And that hope gets trampled under his words.

I armor myself against him. "Crystal. Don't worry. After today, you won't ever have to see me again." I start to walk away.

But I'm not done. Not just yet.

I turn and stare at Tom, not recognizing the person before me. The Tom I got to know these past six weeks never would have been this cruel or hurt me this badly. The Tom I spent time with, falling in love with...

Or maybe that's just it—I never really knew Tom at all.

And that possibility hurts more than everything else.

Curling my fingers into my palm, I take a deep breath. "I wish you'd never stepped foot on that tour bus. I wish I'd never let you anywhere near me—let alone, in my heart." A tear falls down my cheek. I wipe it away. "You never deserved any part of me that I gave to you. You're a *mut* of the worst kind, Tom Carter."

His eyes lift to mine. I see what I think is a trace of hurt in them, but it's gone so quick that I could have imagined it.

"That's exactly what I am. It's good you finally remembered. Now, you can take your declaration of love and tell it to someone who wants it."

I suck in a painful breath.

My soul and whatever was left of my heart shatters to pieces.

He lifts his helmet to his head but pauses. His eyes move to mine, his gaze pinning me there.

My heart might be breaking, but I can't look away from Tom. I never have been able to. Once he catches me with his eyes, I'm bound to him.

I don't know what he sees on my face or what happens in this moment, but true pain fills his eyes and an agonized breath escapes him.

"You deserve better," he says, low and rough. "You deserve better than me."

His helmet is on, his motorcycle roars to life, and then he's gone, disappearing into the thick of the LA traffic.

And I'm left standing here. The only things to show my time with Tom are his words echoing in my mind, my shredded heart, and the tears staining my cheeks.

# TOM 27

## An Hour Later—A Bar, Downtown LA

Lyla loves me.

She can't love me. She can't because…well, because I'm Tom Carter. I don't do love.

I can't love her. I can't love anyone.

Never have, and I'm not about to start now for a tight pussy and awesome rack…and a beautiful smile.

Sure, I care about Lyla, but love…it never factored in.

Lyla's a good girl who's been dealt some shit hands in life. If she were with me, all I would do is continue to hurt her because that's the kind of man I am.

She deserves better than me. She's deserves a man who can—

A wave of anger has my jaw clenching, and my hand tightening around the glass of Jack at the thought of Lyla with another man.

I take a hard drink of the whiskey, trying to settle the rattled emotions inside me.

This is ridiculous. I don't get jealous. I'm not that guy. I'm the one who doesn't give a shit. The guy who fucks a woman and walks away, clean.

I don't care. Ever.

And I need to stop caring about Lyla and who or what she does. Right fucking now.

It has to stop.

I need to get my life back on track.

This sleeping with only one woman has messed with my head. I just need to bang some chick, and I'll be back to normal. And that normal needs to start now.

I let my eyes drift across the bar to the brunette who's been staring at me since I arrived.

My eyes meet hers, and I see the look instantly.

She wants to fuck.

*Perfect.*

I let my eyes give her the once-over. Checking her out like I should have done the moment I arrived here.

I don't usually lapse like this. I've been doing too much lapsing as of late, and that's the problem.

This will get me back on track.

The brunette is tall, curvy. Definite hips and ass. Small tits, but I can live with it. I'm not looking to marry this chick. Just bang the hell out of her.

Sure, she's no Lyla, but that's the point.

Being with a blonde right now would be way too close. I need to be as far away as possible from anything remotely resembling Lyla.

The point of this is to get my mind off Lyla and my cock buried in someone else. And this brunette chick, who is clearly up for it and is the complete opposite of Lyla in every way, is perfect for what I need right now.

Tossing my drink back, I climb off my stool and make my way over to the brunette.

## Fifteen Minutes Later—A Restroom Stall, A Bar, Downtown LA

"Fuck yeah. That's it, sugar. Get down on your knees, and suck my cock." I close my eyes to the feel of—*shit, what's her name? Macy, Lacy? Seriously, who gives a fuck as long as she gets me off?*

I just need to get her mouth around my cock. Then, I'll be back to the old me, and Lyla will get the fuck out of my head.

The image of Lyla standing on the sidewalk, telling me she's in love with me is stuck in my brain.

The things I said to her. She was crying.

*Fuck.*

I didn't mean to hurt her. I just panicked. She'll never forgive me after what I said.

*Whatever. Like it matters. I don't need her to forgive me. Because Lyla and me are done.*

I just did what needed to be done. Like ripping off a Band-Aid. Hurting her now and ending it saves any unpleasant shit in the future.

I might feel bad now, but the second this chick sucks on my cock, it will all just disappear.

Music suddenly comes on loud in the bar. Someone must have fed the jukebox. The heavy guitar line of "Boulevard of Broken Dreams" by Green Day starts to hum through the wall.

I feel a tightening in my chest. An ache…like my heart is…

*No.*

Focusing my mind on the events occurring, I look down at the brunette fumbling with my jeans. For someone so eager to get on her knees, she's taking her sweet time getting them open.

Impatient to get her mouth around me, I take over. Yanking the buttons open, I get my cock out.

I'm barely semi.

*What the fuck?*

Whatever. It doesn't matter. It's just because of this stupid not sleeping around that I've been doing. Only having sex with Lyla has just confused things. Confused my cock, but he'll get back in the game once I get going with this chick. He'll come to life when he gets in her mouth.

I need to be the Tom I used to be. The Tom who fucks and walks away. The Tom who doesn't care. Because that's the Tom I can work with.

Palming my cock, I stare down at her. "Open up, sugar, and make sure to suck me good and hard."

She smiles up at me. Her smile is nowhere even close to being as beautiful as Lyla's.

"I'm gonna suck you so good that you'll never want me to stop."

*I highly doubt that.*

But I roll with it. I watch her open up her mouth and slide my cock between her lips.

"Shit. Yeah, that's it," I hiss, palming the back of her head urging her to take more of my cock. "Take him all."

With my cock in her mouth, she starts bobbing her head up and down, sucking me hard.

I close my eyes, trying to relax, as I focus on the feel of what she's doing.

But nothing is happening.

*What the fuck?*

Needing this, feeling desperate, I grab a handful of her hair and start to pump my cock in and out of her mouth.

I just need to get hard, then I can fuck her, and everything will be back as it was.

I'll be back to my old self.

I keep at it for a few minutes, fucking her mouth, but still nothing is happening. He's not even grown another centimeter.

*What the hell is going on?*

This never happens to me. Ever.

The brunette lets my cock out of her mouth with a pop, and she starts to run her tongue all over him, making this moaning sound as she does.

It's nothing like the sweet sounds Lyla makes when she sucks me.

It's actually getting kind of annoying. I'm tempted to just shove my cock back in there to shut the girl up.

"I love your dick," she murmurs, taking me in her hand, she starts jacking me off. "So fucking big. I can't wait to have it inside me. I love your band. I have for years. I've seen you in concert twice. I can't believe I'm here with you. That I have your dick in my hand, and real soon, we're gonna be fucking." Her eyes lift to mine. "You've got a condom on you, right? Because I don't have any."

Of course I have—

No, I don't.

I don't have one single condom on me because I stopped buying them when Lyla and I started going clean.

When she let me have more of her.

And last night…she let me have all of her.

My head starts to spin.

I press my hand to the wall for support. The bass pumps through the bricks, echoing the mournful tune into my body. Billie Joe Armstrong's somber voice feeds the bleak lyrics into my mind.

I close my eyes, trying to shut it all out…but all I can see is Lyla.

The way she looked lying in my bed. My belt tied around her wrists. Washing her in the shower. Her washing me. Kissing her. How breathtaking she was down on her knees in front of me, her beautiful blues gazing back up at me. Moving inside her…having deep, slow sex. Staying inside her until she fell asleep. Holding her in my arms because I couldn't bring myself to let her go. Unable to sleep because I didn't want to miss a moment of the time I had left with her, knowing I would eventually have to let her go.

*I let her go.*

A pain lances across my chest. I can't fucking breathe.

*I need…I need to leave.*

*No, I can do this. I can fuck this chick.*

*This is what I do. This is what I'm good at.*

We're in a public restroom. They should have a condom machine in here. I'll just buy a pack, fuck her, and then go home.

The blow job clearly isn't working. It isn't getting Lyla out of my head. But covering the memory of the last time Lyla and I were together by being inside someone else will.

It has to.

I open my eyes and look down…but instead of seeing the brunette, all I see is Lyla staring back up at me.

*What the fuck?*

Lyla's big blues blinking up at me. Her gorgeous mouth smiling at me in that sweet way she does.

Panic hits me. A panic I haven't felt since that day when I was thirteen years old, and my life changed forever.

The day I lost everything. The day I stood by powerless to stop what was happening.

*I can't do this. I need to get the fuck out of here. Now.*

"I can't do this."

I try to move, but the brunette doesn't hear me, and she tries to put my cock back in her mouth.

"No." Hands firm on her shoulders, I push her away. "We have to stop."

She stares up at me, confusion on her face. "Did I…did I do something wrong?"

"No." Sidestepping her, I tuck my cock back in my jeans and quickly fasten them up. "You didn't do anything wrong." I suck in a breath, the feeling of guilt and a whole shit load of other emotions I can't even begin to contend with hitting me. "I did."

I yank open the door and practically run out of there, leaving behind the confused brunette still on her knees.

I can barely see straight as I try to make my way out of the bar.

Finally, I make it to the door. Pushing it open, air hits my lungs with force, leaving me gasping. The pressure on my chest is so intense I feel like I'm going to explode.

Lyla's broken me.

*She fucking broke me!*

She got inside my head and screwed everything up.

*I care about her. More than care about her. I lo—*

*No.*

*I can't do this. I can't feel like this.*

*I need to…Christ! What do I need?*

*Time.*

*I need time. That's all.*

I tried to jump back into my old life too soon.

I'll just take a few days to sort my head out.

Get out of the pussy state of mind I've let myself fall into with Lyla.

I liked the life I had before—no, I fucking loved it. Before I started making promises, trying to think I could change to help Jake. But that was bullshit. And Tru and Jake are fine now.

I kept my promise. I did what I said.

But things need to go back to the way they were.

Easy. No complications. No expectations.

Nobody telling me they love me.

And me…I go back to not lo—

Caring about anyone but myself.

I go back to the life I had before. It worked. It kept all my crap at bay.

But since Lyla, all I've done is feel every day.

Feel her.

I've become the man I never wanted to be.

Weak.

I can't be weak. I can't care about her. I can't risk turning into him.

I can't ever risk becoming my father.

And to not become him means I have to go back to being the man I was before, no matter how much it might hurt to let Lyla go.

## Two Weeks Later—A Shoe Store, Robertson Boulevard, LA

It's funny how time stands still when your heart is broken. Like somehow, your heart has control of the ticking clock called life.

Time stilled when Dex broke my heart.

And now…after Tom…well, time and everything in between has ceased to move. I'm just drifting through the days. Nothing matters.

There's just a gaping hole in my life where Tom was.

He came barreling into my world and knocked away every defensive wall I'd built up. I was stupid to think it wouldn't affect me…*he* wouldn't affect me. That he wouldn't work into my affections. I know the kind of girl I am. I attach feelings to sex. I was naïve to think I could do the whole fuck-buddy thing with Tom and walk away clean.

And now, I'm in love with Tom and he's out of my life. I'm broken, defenseless, and weak, and I don't know how to fix it. I can't seem to fix the void he's left in my life. No matter how much I throw myself into band stuff and try to keep busy, nothing is helping.

His absence is always here. Every minute of every goddamn day.

I miss talking to him. Laughing with him. Fighting with him. Loving him.

I have this constant ache, like I've lost a limb. I'm just trying to figure out how he embedded himself so deeply within me in such a short space of time. Wondering if I will ever feel whole again.

"Have you called him yet?"

My eyes move from the spot on the wall of the shoe store to look down at Shannon, who's crouched before me while fitting a pair of shoes to my feet. They have about a hundred tiny fastenings on them. If you ask me, I think they look like hooker shoes, but

Shannon seems to think they'll go with the dress we just bought for a magazine photo shoot I have to attend with the guys in a few days.

Shannon has been hired as our permanent stylist, which I'm happy about. The only downside is I have to put up with Ashlee as well, but she focuses more on the guys while Shannon looks after me, which I'm sure Ashlee is happy about.

"Have I called who?"

Shannon gives me a look while tugging hard on another strap and fastening it. "You know who—Tom."

"No. Why would I?" I shift in my seat, averting my eyes.

"You know why. There." She fastens the last buckle, sounding out of breath. "I thought I was never gonna get those fuckers fastened. Stand up," she tells me.

I get to my feet, wobbling on the ridiculous heels.

"Walk for me. Let's see how you look in them."

"I thought I was a singer, not a catwalk model?"

"You're not tall enough to be a catwalk model, so shut up your moaning and start walking, sista." She grins.

I stick my tongue out at her and then start to make my way up the aisle, heading toward the mirror in front of me. I look like a complete tool. The shoes actually do look hot. I just can't walk in them.

They even look good with my cutoffs and the Angry Birds T-shirt I'm wearing, the one Tom bought for me.

Okay, I like to torture myself by wearing the gift he bought me. And I also might keep his leather jacket in my bedroom, so I can wrap myself up in it at night. I hate myself for holding on to him when he hurt me so much.

"I look like an idiot," I complain.

Shannon comes up from behind, looking at me in the mirror. "No, you don't. You look hot. We're getting them. Now, sit your ass back down, so I can take them off."

I take a seat. As she works on getting one shoe off, I work on unfastening the other. With my leg hitched up on my thigh, I start unbuckling.

"So, remind me why you haven't called Tom."

I let out a sigh, trying to put on a pretense of being bored by her question, when really, all I'm attempting to do is stop my pain from bleeding out all over the floor of this store.

"I have no reason to call him."

*You and me…we end here.*

"Bullshit. You miss him."

"I really don't."

*I do.* I miss him so badly that I feel like I can't breathe most days. And at the mere mention of his name, I want to scream out the pain tearing at my insides.

Aside from torturing myself with his leather jacket, I also go to bed every night listening to "Thought I'd Died and Gone to Heaven" on loop because he told me that's his song for me. Analyzing those lyrics, wishing that he had meant those words in the way I wanted him to and not just to serve as a reminder of a time when he once screwed me under a stage.

Steeling myself, I say, "Even if I did, what does it matter? Tom doesn't miss me."

*He can't stand the sight of me.*

"Yeah, he does."

My head snaps up, my mouth instantly dry. "He does? Has he said something to you?"

"No. But it's that right there." She lets go of the shoe to point at my face. "That look on your face when you thought he missed you—it's relief. And now, crushing disappointment because you know he hasn't said that to me." She grabs my foot again and starts yanking at the buckles. "The two of you need to sort your shit out." She stops pulling at the shoe and stares me in the face. "Tom might not have said that he misses you to me, but I saw him yesterday, and he looked like shit. I've *never* seen Tom look like shit. And he looked fucking awful. So, I made a point of mentioning your name, and when I did, he looked like I'd just shot his puppy, and then he was out of there a minute later."

I can't hide my care anymore. "He looked like shit?" *Is it wrong that the thought of Tom looking like shit makes me feel a little better?*

"Yep, he was unshaven and well on his way to growing that fucking beard back. Unlike last time though, it doesn't look hot. It looks gross, like he hasn't washed for a week. Same with his clothes. And he stank of whiskey. He had dark circles under his eyes that even I wouldn't be able to cover. He looks like total shit, and I'm guessing it's because he misses you."

"He doesn't miss me."

*The sooner I'm out of here, the fucking better.*

My lips turn down at the corners.

Shannon sits up on her haunches and grabs my hands, holding them together on my thighs. "I don't know what happened between the two of you. I only know the tidbits you've given me over these last two weeks, but it's clear you care about him, and he cares about you. Just call him. What have you got to lose?"

I slide my hands free and move my eyes down. I start on those damn buckles again.

"Pride. I'm not calling Tom. The last time I spoke to him, he made it abundantly clear that he doesn't want anything to do with me. Anyway, even if he has changed his mind, it's too late. I've moved on."

"Bullshit," she mutters. "Stubborn, the both of you." She grabs my foot, yanks it over to her, and finishes removing that damn shoe.

# Thirty Minutes Later—Robertson Boulevard, LA

"You wanna grab a coffee?" Shannon asks as we walk toward my car.

"Sure, let's just dump these bags in the trunk first."

I unlock my car and pop the trunk. I throw the shopping bags in and shut down the lid.

"Shit," Shannon utters.

Lifting my gaze to her, I follow her stare across the street, and my eyes land straight on Tom. He's standing by a black town car parked outside a swanky restaurant.

I can see from here that he looks tired, not his usual pulled-together self, and the beard is definitely making a comeback.

But that's not the reason I feel like someone is standing on my chest.

No, what's causing that is the sight of the willowy and very gorgeous brunette who is with him.

They're standing close together. They look friendly, like they know each other really well.

Intimately well.

She puts her hands on his arms while speaking to him. Tom smiles at whatever she's saying. He says something back to her, and she laughs.

I hate her instantly.

She lifts her hand to his face and leans in and kisses his cheek.

I stop breathing.

It's like a car crash. I want to look away but I can't.

I want to scream too.

But I do neither.

I just stand here, like a fucking statue, watching them.

Tom opens the door of the town car for her. She climbs in the backseat.

*Don't get in the car with her. Don't get in the car with her.*

He starts to climb in.

My heart sinks. I close my eyes, breathing through the hurt.

When I open them, Tom has a foot in the town car with a hand on the roof, and he's staring across the street at me.

I can see the shock of seeing me here evident on his face.

He's not happy to see me.

*Why would he be?* He made it clear how things stood the last time I saw him.

His cruel words come back to taunt me, echoing in my mind.

I'm frozen to the spot, held hostage by his stare, as pain runs through my veins like poison. It's absolute agony.

A moment ago I was praying he wouldn't get in that car, now I'm willing him to do just that.

He mouths my name and starts to back away from the car.

*He's coming over here.*

*Shit.* My heart starts to pound a painful beat against my ribcage.

I can't take another heartbreaking confrontation with him. I need to get out of here. *Now.*

Adrenaline fires my body into action. I bolt around the car and yank open the driver's door. I yell at Shannon, "Get in the fucking car!"

Her face jolts in shock. But I don't care. I just need to get out of here, and I'll do whatever is necessary to make that happen.

I've already got the engine on, and I'm clicking in my seatbelt when Shannon gets in the car.

I glance out the side window, and I see that Tom is trying to cross the busy street, eyes fixed with purpose on my car.

Heart climbing out of my chest and running down the street and away from him, I put the car into drive. With one quick check in my side mirror, I slam my foot down, getting us out of there.

We drive in silence for a long moment.

"You okay?" Shannon asks softly.

I nod, afraid to speak, in case I burst into tears.

"That might not have been what it looked like."

I take a fortifying breath. "It doesn't matter."

"Clearly, it does. You're in love with him." It's not a question.

I could argue or lie, but there's no point.

"He knows." I let out a shallow breath. "I told him the morning after our last night together. He gave me a ride home, and before he left, I told him that I'm in love with him." I feel my bottom lip tremble. I take another strengthening breath before I speak again. "The short version is, he doesn't feel the same."

"I find that hard to believe. I saw the way he was with you."

I shake my head. "Trust me, he doesn't. He said to me, and I quote, 'Take your declaration of love, and tell it to someone who wants it.'"

"Oh, honey. Well, if that's the truth, that he doesn't love you—which I highly doubt—then Tom Carter is a bigger goddamn fool than I thought he was. He's always been a player, but when I saw him with you, I thought it was different. I saw the way he would look at you when he thought no one was watching, and I thought that was it for him, that *you* were it."

I know she doesn't mean to, but her words are hurting me. A stray tear escapes, trickling down into the corner of my mouth.

"Can we…just not talk about this right now?"

"Anything you want, honey." She reaches over and turns on the radio.

Bananarama's "Cruel Summer" starts to beat out into the car. I start to sing along, channeling my pain in the way I know best.

The song is just coming to an end when it's cut off by my cell ringing through the Bluetooth set in my car.

A glance at my phone screen tells me it's Aunt Steph calling. I don't feel up to talking, but I haven't called her in a while, so she won't give up until I answer. My Aunt Steph is persistent like that if I go too long without talking to her.

"Hi, I'm just in the car with a friend. Can I call you back?"

"Ly…" she says, her voice breaking.

The sound comes like a hand around my throat.

"It's Dex. He's in the hospital. He-he—" She starts to sob.

My pulse hits adrenaline. Panicked, I swerve out of traffic. I vaguely register a horn blaring and then the sound of Shannon cursing low, but none of that matters. I can't be driving this car right now.

Skidding into an open spot on the side of the road, I hit the brakes. "Dex? Is he okay? Oh God, what happened?"

Aunt Steph takes in a deep breath. "Dex…he took a lot of pills…alcohol. They're saying…the doctor said he overdosed…but he wouldn't do that. He wouldn't try to…not on purpose—" She breaks down again.

*He overdosed?*

*Dex. Overdose.*

No, that can't be right. He wouldn't hurt himself like that.

Then, I remember how he sounded that night in San Diego.

Desperate. In pain.

How my mom used to sound.

The last thing he said to me was…*I'm sorry.*

*Oh no.*

He tried to kill himself.

It's my fault. I wouldn't listen to him. I wouldn't forgive him.

Guilt overwhelming me, I bury my face in my hands and begin to sob.

## Forty Minutes Later—Waiting Area, Cedars-Sinai Medical Center, LA

"You want anything to drink, honey?"

I look up into Shannon's perfectly made-up face. I imagine that I look like a total mess. Not that looking good is really high on my list of priorities right now. I still rub my fingers under my eyes, trying to clean away the mascara I know is there, not wanting to scare people with my panda eyes.

"Hold on. I've got some wipes." Shannon rummages in her bag and pulls out a pack of makeup wipes.

She's always prepared. She takes one out and tilts my face up toward her. She starts to clear the makeup from underneath my eyes.

"You'll give me a tic, rubbing at your eyes like that. I'm not having my superstar looking old before her time." She gives me a gentle smile. "There. All done." She throws the wipe in the trash.

"Thank you," I say.

"Not needed. It's my job to care about your appearance."

"I didn't mean just the face clean. I meant, you being here...I really appreciate it."

She sits beside me and pats my hand. "The face clean is me doing my job. Me waiting here with you...this is me being your friend."

"I'm glad you're my friend," I say, resting my head against her shoulder.

I really need a friend right now. I try not to think about the one person I wish were here.

At that thought, my best friends come bursting through the door.

I called Cale the moment I got off the phone with Aunt Steph. I knew he would want to be here. Sonny was going to be my next call, but after Cale got over the initial shock, he said he would call Sonny. To be honest, I was glad I didn't have to make the call. The only other call I wanted to make was to Tom. I wanted to speak to him so badly that it hurt me not to.

"How is he?" Cale crouches down before me.

Sonny takes the seat on my right.

I shake my head. "I don't know. The doctor came out when we got here. They're treating him right now. He said he'd come back when he had more to tell us."

Cale takes my hand in his and squeezes it.

I can't stop the tears from starting again, them spilling down over my cheeks.

"Don't, Ly…don't you blame yourself for this," Cale says.

I bite my lip, trying to stop the tears. "Cale…that night in the club, he was begging me to talk to him, and I wouldn't listen."

He cradles my face in his hands. "Listen to me. You had every good reason not to listen. You haven't done anything wrong. Nothing. Do you hear me?"

"Cale's right," Sonny says in a gentle voice.

I meet Sonny's eyes.

"Don't put this on yourself," he adds.

Nodding, I rub the tears from my cheeks.

"Let me get us some drinks since it looks like we're gonna be here a while," Shannon says, getting to her feet.

## Two Hours Later—Waiting Area, Cedars-Sinai Medical Center, LA

It's been an incredibly long two hours.

The doctor finally appears. He's a different doctor than the one who came to talk to me when I first arrived. This one is younger. He looks tired, harried.

Rubbing a hand through his curly brown hair, he says, "Dexter Henley's family?"

Already on my feet, I say, "I'm Dex's sister. How is he?"

"Miss Henley—"

I don't bother to correct him. It would only confuse an already confusing situation even more.

"I'm Dr. Lowe. I've been treating Dexter. He's going to be fine."

I exhale in relief. Feeling Cale's hand on my back, I smile at him.

"Dexter had taken a significant amount of pills. We were lucky that he'd been found when he had, as his body hadn't had time to absorb the drug. I administered an activated charcoal, which binds the drug so that the body can't absorb it, and he's responding well to the treatment, which means he'll make a full recovery and there will be no damage to any of his organs."

"Can we see him?" I ask.

The doctor looks over the four of us. "Only family is allowed to see Dexter at this time."

"We'll wait here." Cale squeezes my shoulder.

"Just tell him we're here," Sonny says.

I give Cale and Sonny a soft smile. "I'll tell him."

I fall into step beside Dr. Lowe. "Doctor, when my Au—" I falter and correct myself to avoid confusing the doctor. "When our mother called, she said that Dex had…tried to commit suicide. Is that true?"

He stops walking and turns to me. "The pills Dexter overdosed on were a prescribed anti-depressant. He took a lot of those pills and combined them with alcohol. He might not have meant to attempt suicide…but in my professional experience, when a patient combines the amount of pills Dexter had with alcohol then one would assume an attempt on life, yes."

I close my eyes on the pain crushing my insides.

Exactly how my mother died.

A tear runs down my cheek, and I brush it away.

"Dexter is going to need a lot of help and support. Because of the nature of what's happened, I had to contact the psychiatric department. A counselor will be here in a few hours to evaluate Dexter and see if he is a danger to himself. Even though Dexter seems to be doing okay at the moment, it's standard protocol."

"I understand." I give a brisk nod.

We start walking again until Dr. Lowe stops outside a door.

"This will have to be a quick visit," Dr. Lowe tells me.

"Okay."

Heart pumping, I press down on the handle. I step inside the low-lit room. Immediately, I see Dex laying on the bed, his face turned away from me. A machine attached to him is beeping. A drip is running in his arm.

Unsure if he's sleeping, I take a quiet step closer.

"Dex," I speak softly.

Slowly, his head turns, eyes meeting mine.

His eyes are dark, sunken. His skin sallow. He looks a shadow of his former self.

Seeing him like this—*my big brother*—my eyes fill with tears. I bite my lip to stop it from trembling.

"You're here," he says, his voice rough.

"I'm here." I take a small step closer. Part of me wants to be close to him, and the other part of me holds back.

He looks away from me. "I'm sorry you had to come here," he rasps out, his tone emotionless.

"Stop it." My voice is sharp, but I can't help it. So many emotions are roiling inside of me, and it's hard to control them.

Dex's eyes slowly come back to mine.

I walk up to the end of the bed, curling my fingers around the metal frame. "Why?" It feels like the hardest question in the world to ask, but the most important.

I need to understand why he did this.

He lets out a sigh, scrubbing his hand over his face. "I don't know."

"Yes, you do."

His stops rubbing at his face, and he brings his eyes to mine. I see it all in there—the pain, the loss.

"I just wanted it all to stop," he says in a whisper.

"You wanted what to stop?"

He exhales softly. "The regret. The guilt. The loneliness. The silence eating me alive. I made the biggest mistake of my life. I hurt and lost the most important person to me, all for someone who didn't matter when it came down to it."

"What happened...with you and Chad?" I've never asked him this question. Truth be told, I never wanted to know because him being with Chad, or not, wouldn't have changed anything for me.

"It didn't continue past that night."

I take a deep breath, processing that information. "Why?"

"How could it?" He shakes his head, regret swimming in his eyes. "The fact is, I love you more than I would ever love him."

"But that didn't stop you from screwing him—" I cut off, knowing this isn't the time. My breath is coming in heavy. I can feel myself starting to panic.

My fingers slip from the bed frame. I'm ready to leave, and Dex knows it.

"Ly, don't go, *please.*"

The panic in his eyes and voice makes me stay. I hold on to the metal frame again, needing it for balance.

"I wish I could give you a reason why I did what I did," he says in a low voice. "The only one I have is...I was weak. Chad pursued me, and I couldn't seem to say no. Every time it happened, I would tell myself that time was the last, and I wasn't going to let it happen again. Then, I would find myself right back in that same situation with him." His eyes meet mine. "I was in love with him...or I thought I was. I want you to know that I didn't have an affair with him as some sort of challenge." He lets out a defeated sigh. "Whatever it was I felt for Chad though...in the end, it didn't matter."

"Why did you move to LA?"

"To be closer to you. I thought if I was closer to you, I might stand a chance at repairing what I'd done. I couldn't do that when you were on the other side of the country. Then, I got here and found out that you were going on tour for six weeks. I have the worst timing ever." He lets out a self-deprecating laugh. "But I stayed, knowing you'd be back. I thought if I could just get to see you, talk to you, then it'd be okay...we'd be okay. I just needed to get you to listen to me. If that happened, then, I thought everything would be okay.

"Then, I finally got my chance in San Diego, and after what happened that night...it truly hit me that I'd lost you for good. There was no going back. In that moment, it was worse than thinking you were dead. You were still living your life, but I just couldn't be a part of it, and it was my own doing. The best part of my life was *us*. You and me. And Cale and Sonny. The band." He runs a hand through his hair. "I guess...things just spiraled after that night. The depression got worse. I wasn't turning up for practice. I was drinking more, getting high. The guys in my band were getting pissed off with me. Then, I missed an important gig because I'd was out partying, and the next day they pulled me in and told me I was out.

"So, I didn't have you, and then I had no band. I just felt lost…angry at myself, and I wanted to stop hurting. I took some of my pills, knowing they'd dull the pain. I washed them down with vodka. I guess I took too many."

Anger bursts inside me like an erupting volcano.

"You took too many? Are you fucking kidding me right now? You could have died. If your roommate hadn't found you, I'd be standing over your dead body right now!" My chest is pounding, head hurting. "How the hell do you think your mom and dad would feel if they lost you? If you'd died exactly the same way my mom had, how do you think your mom would feel from losing her son the same way she had her sister? How the hell do you think I would feel?" I beat my fist against my chest.

Sad eyes meet mine. "Relieved…I thought you would feel relieved, Ly."

His words me like a wrecking ball.

"Screw you!" I yell at him. I head for the door, my body shaking hard with every emotion I'm feeling right now.

"Lyla, wait!" he cries.

I spin on the spot. My hands are clenched into fists at my sides. I feel like I could punch a hole through the wall.

He's sitting up in bed, his face anxious. "I'm sorry. I didn't mean that. I just thought your life would be easier without me around."

My nails dig into my palms. "I would rather have a hard life than you be dead. Don't you get that? I might be angry and hurt, but you're still my family. My flesh and blood. I don't get to stop loving you, Dex, just because you hurt me."

His head lowers. "I'm sorry. I wasn't thinking when I took those pills. I just wanted to stop feeling. And I know you have every right to be angry with me, but please, not right now." He slumps back, rubbing at his eyes. "Not right now."

I take a few deep breaths. "I shouldn't have yelled." I move back to the bed. Grabbing the chair near the bed, I sit in it. "We can't keep doing this," I say quietly, "hurting each other like this."

His eyes lift to mine. "I know."

I blow out a breath, flexing my hands on my thighs. "You did an unforgiveable thing. You hurt me badly. Worse than Rally ever did." My lip quivers. "All the shit with him, I expected. I expected

Rally to let me down. But not you. You were the one person I trusted above everyone, and you betrayed me."

"God, I'm so sorry." His voice breaks on a sob. He wraps his arm over his stomach like he's in pain. "If I could take it back, I would. I'd give anything to go back and do it differently. I wouldn't go near Chad. I would tell you upfront how I was feeling about him before anything could happen. I wouldn't do what I did." Tears are streaming down his face.

"The betrayal wrecked me so badly—not because it was Chad—but, because it was *you*. You were my fucking hero, Dex. I adored you. I never thought you would hurt me like that."

"Neither did I," he says sadly. Using the sleeve of the hospital gown he's wearing, he wipes his tears from his face.

He lowers his hand to the bed, and tentatively, he reaches for mine. I let him take it.

"Ly, I know I don't deserve your forgiveness or to have you back in my life...but will you to consider trying..."

My eyes lift to his and I see them shining with fresh tears. I let out a breath. "When I got that call from your mom, for a split second...I feared the worst." I rub my eye with the heel of my hand. "It made me realize that no matter how mad or hurt or betrayed I feel by you...nothing would be worse than not having you here, alive and well. I knew if you were gone, and we hadn't fixed the broken between us, then, regret would eat me alive. I'm not saying we can go back to how we were because we can't. But I'm saying, I'll try and work toward something...forgiveness. But you need to promise me that you'll go to counseling, and get real help."

A soft smile touches his lips. "I will. I promise." He squeezes my hand.

"You get help, and then you and I can start talking...with someone's assistance. Knowing you and me, I think we're gonna need a mediator in this." My lips lift at the corner, attempting a smile.

"Anything. As long as I get to have my sister back in my life, I'll do whatever it takes."

I see a shadow by the door, and I lift my eyes to see Dr. Lowe there. He lifts his wrist and taps his watch, letting me know that it's time to go.

"I have to go." I nod in the direction of the door.

Dex looks at the doctor and then back to me. He gives me a joyless smile.

"You'll see me again." I squeeze his hand before letting go. I get up from the chair and start to leave. I stop when I remember something. "Sonny asked me to tell you that he's here, him and Cale."

Surprise touches Dex's face.

"Sonny and…Cale? They're here?"

"Yeah." I smile lightly. "Came as soon as I called. They wanted to come in and see you, but the doctor said family only."

He nods in understanding. "Will you tell them I said thanks…for coming?"

"I will."

I'm at the door when his voice pulls me back.

"Ly…I know you said I have to get help first before you and me can start to work on things…but I was wondering…if I can maybe…call you tomorrow? Just to say hi."

I pause for a moment. I turn to him and shake my head. "You don't need to call. I'll come back in the morning. Your mom and dad will be here. I'll pick them up from the airport and come in with them. I've got a feeling that you might need the support."

He smiles. "Tomorrow, then."

"Tomorrow."

I close the door to his room behind me, and I let out the breath I've been holding all night before making my way back down the hall.

Cale, Sonny, and Shannon are all sitting where I left them, sipping on machine coffee.

Sonny gets to his feet. "How's he doing?"

I lift my shoulders. "He's doing okay, considering what happened. We talked. He's real happy that you guys came to the hospital."

"And how are you doing?" Cale asks, coming over to me.

"I'm okay," I sigh, feeling mentally and physically exhausted. "I said I'd come back in the morning…that we can try to fix things."

"Sonny and I will come back with you."

"Aunt Steph and Uncle Paul will be here then."

"I know," Cale says. "But I need to talk to Dex, too. Figure some stuff out with him."

I meet his eyes, understanding.

I think we all have a lot to figure out.

"We gonna get out of here?" Sonny asks. "I fucking hate hospitals."

"Let's go," I say.

We all start walking toward the elevators. I get my cell from my bag.

I missed two calls and a text from Tom.

I check the time on the first call. He called while I was here, about thirty minutes after I saw him on the street with that woman. *Does he know about Dex? But then, who would have told him? Why did he call?* He told me he doesn't care about me.

Fingers trembling, I open up the text.

*We need to talk. Call me.*

*That's it?*

I'm assuming he doesn't know about Dex then. Well, I'd like to think that if he did, his text would say something more than that. I know he's a bastard, but I don't think he'd be that callous.

*And really, what do we need to talk about? How he doesn't give a shit about me? How he has clearly moved on from me?*

*Thanks, but no thanks.*

I haven't heard from or seen him in two weeks, and after I see him with some woman, he calls and texts.

*Probably feeling guilty or even worse sorry for me.*

*Yeah, well, I don't need his goddamn pity.*

I delete his text and clear my screen of his calls. I speed dial Aunt Steph. She and Uncle Paul should be in the air now on their way here, but I wanted to let her know that I've seen Dex.

I listen through her voice mail greeting. "Hey, it's me. I just saw Dex. He's doing okay. The doctor said he's gonna be fine. I mean, obviously, he's not fine, but he will be…with some help. I just wanted you to know that I've seen him, and he's doing okay. I'm gonna head home because they won't let us stay any longer with it being so late here. Call me when you land, and I'll come get you at the airport."

I'm going to have to borrow Cale's car to pick them up since mine is only a two-seater.

Just as I'm thinking that, Cale puts his arm around me.

We come to a standstill at the elevators. Sonny presses the button, and I rest my head against Cale's chest while we wait. I'm thankful to have them. I might not have Tom, but I have the best friends a girl could wish for. The elevator arrives, and we all get in. When we reach the ground floor, I walk out with Cale's arm still around my shoulder.

We approach the electronic doors. They slide open, and the night air brings a chill in with it. I shiver. I'm still in my cutoffs and T-shirt.

Cale rubs my arm. "You cold?"

I smile up at him. "I'm okay." Then, I look ahead.

That's when my heart falls out of my chest.

Tom is standing across the road, leaning up against his Range Rover, his eyes fixed on me.

## A Breath Later—Outside of Cedars-Sinai Medical Center, LA

Tom pushes off the car and starts to walk toward me. His eyes don't waver from mine as his long legs eat up the distance between us. He's still wearing the same clothes he was in earlier. The thick stubble graces his chin.

He looks as hot as ever. I hate that.

My feet are glued to the spot, my legs shaking. I feel Cale's grip tighten on my shoulder.

To say Cale is not happy with Tom is putting it mildly. Cale is my best friend. I tell him everything, and I told him what happened between me and Tom—well, barring the sex details, of course. I also left out some of the crueler things that Tom said to me. I knew if I told Cale those, he would have gone to Tom's house to have words with him, and the last thing I want is those two fighting.

Cale is pissed at the way Tom left things with me. I've tried to make Cale understand that Tom hasn't really done anything wrong—apart from being a mean bastard when he ended things. He never led me on, never gave me false promises. If anything, he was always honest with me.

It's my fault that I fell in love with him.

The fact that Tom doesn't feel the same is not on him. No matter how much I want to be angry with Tom, feelings just aren't something that can be controlled.

From the start, I knew that Tom wasn't a feelings kind of guy. It just took him telling me the way he did for it to hammer home.

Although…him being here right now is doing nothing for my heart.

Tom comes to a stop a foot away from me. Up close, I can see how tired he truly looks. He has dark circles around his eyes, like he hasn't slept in a really long time.

My heart starts to pound in my chest.

"Lyla." His voice is raspy, but it still feels like a balm over the open wound on my heart. I realize that I miss him more in this moment than I have in the last two weeks. It hurts to have him so near and not be mine.

"Hi." My voice sounds small. I hate that. I need to woman up. I take a fortifying breath. All I managed to do is breathe Tom in. His familiar scent. It reminds me of times lost.

Pain lances across my chest.

Tom's eyes flicker to Cale's hand on my shoulder, and they harden. Then, his eyes come back to me, and they soften in my gaze.

"Are you…" He scratches the stubble on his chin before his fingers work up to the hair on his head. He tugs on the strands. "Can we, um…talk?"

I don't know why, but I look at Shannon. Maybe it's because I know she'll encourage me to talk to him, and encouragement is what I need right now because my head is saying to tell him to fuck off. Even though my heart is reaching her grubby little fingers out in desperation for him.

Shannon does encourage me. *Talk to him*, she mouths.

I look back to Tom. I can see the unease lining his face, his body tense, as he waits for my answer.

It hurts to look at him.

I look over his shoulder and say, "I don't know."

"*Please*, Lyla."

The angst in his voice has my eyes coming straight back to him.

He looks afraid.

I take a deep breath. "Okay…"

That one word from me has him visibly relaxing. It has me wondering what's so important that he needs to talk to me urgently.

I turn to Cale, causing his hand to slip from my shoulder. "Head on home without me. I'll see you there." Then, I remember that I'm Shannon's ride. "Could you give Shannon a ride home? If that's okay with you, Shannon?"

"Sure it is." She smiles big. She's happy that Tom's here to see me. I think beneath her cool exterior, is a closet romantic.

Cale hasn't even looked at me yet. His eyes are angry and on Tom. I don't know if Cale is going to be difficult about this or not.

Then, he drags his stare from Tom to me. "Ly, I'm not gonna try to talk you out of speaking to him. You do what you gotta do. But you need me, you call me, and I'll come straight away."

"I know. Thank you." I smile, touching his arm.

He turns his eyes back to Tom, jaw clenched. "I don't care who the fuck you are. You hurt her again, and I'll come after you—"

"*We'll* come after you." Sonny steps up.

My heart plummets. Tom's not exactly a pacifist, and I really don't need a confrontation between them all right now.

Tom looks between the both of them, then, he sighs. "I fucked up. Hugely. I know. I'm not planning on hurting Lyla again, if I can help it. But if I do, then I deserve whatever I have coming."

*Well, holy shit.* My heart flutters back to my chest, and begins to beat double time.

Cale looks at Tom with a renewed sense of respect. He gives Tom a sharp nod and turns to walk away. Sonny gives Tom a hard stare and follows Cale.

Shannon lingers a moment, giving me a big smile and a mini thumbs-up, before she trails after Cale and Sonny.

Listening to her heels clack against concrete, I ease my eyes back to Tom to find his eyes on my chest with an unnamed emotion on his face.

"You're wearing"—he gulps down—"the shirt I bought you." There's something resembling hope in his eyes.

Shrugging, I toss my hair over my shoulder. "Don't read anything into it. I just happen to like the shirt. How did you know I was here?"

He pushes his hands in his back pockets, rocking on his heels. "Shannon. She called me when you first arrived here. You were talking with the doctor."

I frown at her retreating back. *That sneaky little biatch. We'll be having words later.*

"Don't be angry with her," Tom says softly. "She thought that you might, um…need me. Well, she said that after she chewed my ass out for hurting you." His jades meet with my blues. "I'm so sorry, Ly."

I want to tell him that I don't need his apologies, and I don't need him here, but it would be a lie.

I look away. "When did you get here?"

SAMANTHA TOWLE

He shifts on his feet. "I came as soon as I got the call. I've been here a few hours or so."

My heart squeezes. I hate that he can make me feel this way. "You waited out here all that time...for me?"

His shoulders lift, his eyes pinned to the ground. "I wanted to make sure you were okay."

"Why didn't you come inside?"

The doors whoosh open behind me, and some people walk out.

Tom and I move away from the doors, giving us a little privacy.

Standing before me, closer now, he says, "I wanted to come in and see you, but I didn't know...how things stood with you, whether you would want to see me. I know what Shannon said, but when you saw me earlier, you bolted...so I wasn't sure." His eyes dim.

A chill attacks my body as I remember exactly how I felt when I saw him on the street with that woman. "You were with someone."

"I can explain that. I called you before Shannon called me because I saw your face. I knew what you were thinking." He takes a step nearer. "We need to talk."

I look up into his face. "About?"

"Us."

"There isn't an *us.*"

He shakes his head. "No, but there should be."

His words shake me to my core. I can't find any of my own to attempt speech.

"But before us..." He lifts his hand like he wants to touch me, but then he lowers it. "Are you okay? Your brother...is he okay? Shannon didn't know anything when she called."

I wrap my arms around myself. "Dex is gonna be okay...physically...but he tried to, um...he tried to...he overdosed."

Tom nods. "Shannon said."

I swallow down. "Luckily, the pills didn't make it into his system, so there's no permanent damage or anything."

"That's good." He moves a little closer. "Most importantly, how are you?"

I shrug, looking past him. "Dealing. There's a lot to figure out, but I'll get there. I always do."

"You will. You're the strongest person I've ever known."

He reaches out again to touch me, and this time, he doesn't stop. His fingertips graze the skin on my arm. Heat sears into me.

I want and need him, but I don't know what he wants from me. I don't know what I saw earlier or what he's been doing during the time we've been apart, and I can't forget how badly his words hurt me.

Confused, I step back, away from his touch. "Don't…"

Disappointment fills his eyes, frustration lining his brow. "Ly, the woman you saw with me earlier—"

"I don't want to talk about this right now." Fear hits me, quickly turning to panic. I might want the truth but not right now. My heart can't take another beating tonight.

"I know this is the worst timing ever, but it's not what you think. The woman you saw earlier is my sister."

That gets my attention.

"You have a sister?" I'm relieved but surprised.

He glances around, like he's checking for people. "Yes," he answers, bringing his stare back to me.

"How did I not know—" I cut myself off. "Of course I didn't know. You never told me anything about yourself, but then again, we were only fucking, like you said. So, why would you share? Now that we're not *fucking*, am I allowed to ask if you have just the one sister or more? Any brothers? Pets? Do you have any kids I don't know about? A girlfriend?"

I'm stepping into the crazy zone, but I can't help it around him. He brings out the crazy in me.

"Just the one sister. No brothers. No pets. Definitely no kids." He gives me a grim smile with his hands locked behind his neck, showing off the taut muscles in his arms.

Even in this difficult, fraught-with-emotion moment, my attraction for him flares.

"And no girlfriend." He gives me a pointed look. "You're right. I haven't shared anything with you about my life…but I want that to change. I need to tell you some things about me…things I need you to understand."

"Why?"

"Lyla…"

"No, Tom. Why do you need me to understand you?"

He shifts, his arms wrapping around his chest. "Because I care about you."

"Oh, you care about me now. Funny, because only two weeks ago, you couldn't give a shit about me. What's changed?"

"Everything…everything's changed." He thrusts his hand through his hair, his eyes skirting our surroundings. "Can we just not do this here?"

"Here is as good as any place. You wanna talk? Talk to me here." I'm digging my heels in. I'm being difficult. I know that, but I don't feel like giving him easy right now.

"Lyla, the things I need to say to you are not things I want to air in public."

Remembering who Tom is and how his life would be fodder for the press, as would be my own, I huff out a sigh. "Fine. Where do you want to talk?"

"My house." He gives me a hopeful smile.

"Your house?" My first and only time there was our last night together. "I don't know." I retreat back a step.

"Just to talk." He holds his hands up. "Nothing more."

I run a hand through my hair, my fingers getting stuck in the tangled ends. "Okay…I guess. But my car is here, so I'll have to follow you there."

"Or you can leave it here, and I can bring you back to it later."

I tilt my head, eyeing him with suspicion. "What would be the point of that?"

His eyes turn serious. "I'd get more time with you."

My heart bursts out of my chest and wraps herself around him.

But my angry head tells me that he could have had the last two weeks with me, if he'd pulled his head out of his ass before now.

"Okay," I acquiesce, handling my feelings. "Your car it is."

I follow Tom over to the Range Rover, feeling a little surprised when he opens the door for me. Hand on my back, he helps me in. His touch burns through my clothes.

He doesn't even try for an ass grab.

I don't know whether that's a good thing or not.

Feeling rattled, I try to calm myself while Tom rounds the car to the driver's side.

He climbs in and shuts his door with an expensive clunk.

Then, it's just him and me in his car in the dark.

Suddenly, everything seems so much more pronounced.

The sound of my breathing, the thumping of my heart.

Tom's breaths, his aftershave, the strength and size of him in this small space.

It's all overwhelming me.

He starts the car, and the middle of *that* song by Bryan Adams starts to play.

The song that he said reminded him of me. The one I've tortured myself with for the last two weeks.

Heart in my throat, I glance across at him. I'm pretty sure my feelings are scrawled all over my face.

He reaches his hand over and gently touches my cheek with his fingertips. "I've been listening to it a lot these last couple of weeks."

Speechless and on the verge of tears, I look away from him and out the window.

## Twenty Minutes Later—Tom's House, LA

The drive to Tom's house was quiet. I spent the whole drive trapped inside my head, wondering what he wants to talk to me about and also trying to figure out what I want to say to him.

He pulls up outside the gates to his house. Using a remote, he opens them.

Watching them part slowly, my heart goes into overtime.

By the time he's pulled up outside his house, my heart is attempting a cage break through my ribs.

Without a word, Tom gets out of the car. I unbuckle my seat belt and open my door.

Tom's here, and he takes my hand, helping me out. My body jolts at the feel of his big hand touching mine, electricity snaking through my body, desire pooling between my legs.

No matter what's happening between Tom and me, my body will always want him.

As I climb down, I see his eyes skim my legs, a flare of desire igniting in them.

I feel a shot of relief. It's good to know I still have that effect on him. I was beginning to worry that it had gone. He didn't once look at me in a sexual way since seeing him tonight at the hospital.

His fingers thread through mine, clutching my hand.

I freeze, my heart warring with my head.

"Don't pull away. I just need to hold you…even if it's a small part of you." His voice is thick with meaning.

His chest is pressed against my shoulder, reminding me how good it feels to have Tom's body touching mine.

My head starts to spin.

Lifting my head, I stare up into his eyes and nod.

With his grip tight on my hand, he leads me into the house and straight to the living room.

It's the first time I'm seeing it. It's much like his bedroom—manly, dark wood, white walls, a comfy-looking black L-shaped sofa, a huge flat screen on the wall.

"Can I get you anything to drink?" he asks, leading me toward the sofa.

"No, thanks."

Tom sits and tugs my hand, pulling me to sit down beside him.

We're at the corner, so I shuffle over, letting go of his hand, I put a good bit of distance between us.

I can see from the look on his face that he's not happy about the distance, but I need to talk to him with a clear head, and Tom touching any part of me leaves my mind fuzzy and my judgment clouded.

Determination in his eyes, Tom shifts over to me, leaving little room between us. Then, he turns his body toward mine, which presses his jean-covered knee up against my bare outer thigh.

The contact is like a live wire on my skin.

I sigh, and look at him. His eyes are dark, and telling me that if I move, there will be trouble.

I stay put.

He leans forward—forearms on his thighs, hands linked together—bringing him even closer to me. He exhales, and I feel the warmth of his breath on my skin.

"Why am I here, Tom?"

His eyes study me silently for a moment. "I need you to know how sorry I am for the way I behaved. The things I said to you the last time we saw each other were unforgiveable. I'm so sorry."

I clench my jaw. "Oh, you mean when I bared my soul to you, and you told me—and I quote—'Take your declaration of love, and tell it to someone who wants it.' Then, you rode away from me without a second thought."

"There was a second thought." His expression turns to granite. "I've regretted what I said every moment since."

"So, why? Why hurt me like that if you didn't mean it?" The pain from that day is still so raw inside me.

"I don't know…fear." He shrugs.

"Fear?" I'm confused and pissed off, and it's telling in my tone.

Guilt sharpens his expression. "What I'm trying to say is…maybe deep down, I thought if I hurt you, then it would make walking away from you easy. If you hated me, then there would be no going back. I just didn't factor in how much I would miss you. How empty things—*I*...would feel without you." His smile is crooked, heartfelt...rueful.

"I don't understand. If you wanted me, then why did you push me away?"

Maybe I'm just being dumb here, but I can't understand his logic.

He drops his gaze. "Because I'm fucked up."

"No, you're not." I shake my head. "You're emotionally detached but not fucked up."

His eyes come back to mine. "I'm fucked up, Ly. If you knew everything about me—things I've done, the way I've behaved— you wouldn't be saying that."

"Even after the way you behaved toward me that day, Tom, it didn't change how I view you. And it's not about to change with whatever you need to tell me now."

"I just hope to God you're still saying that when I'm done telling you everything." His hand rubs over his hair. He seems nervous, uncomfortable. "The things I have to tell you...my timing really sucks, but to make you understand...well, *me*...I have to tell you this."

"So, tell me. I'm listening." I stare at him, encouraging him with my eyes.

"Okay." He takes a deep breath. "What happened with Dex today...I understand what you're going through."

His eyes move down. After a moment, he lifts them to look at me. I see a vulnerability I never thought I'd see in Tom.

"I know how you feel because when I was thirteen years old, my father committed suicide."

"Oh God, Tom, I'm so sorry." I grab his hand, squeezing it.

With what's happened with Dex, it's still so raw. And knowing what it felt like to lose my mother, my heart aches for Tom.

His fingers curl around my hand. "With Dex and how you lost your mom...how the press portrayed it...you and I have a lot more in common than you realize."

"Not a great thing to have in common though," I say, fingers tugging on my lip.

He takes my hand from my mouth. Holding both my hands, he laces our fingers together. I turn my body into his, his leg positioned between mine, putting us face-to-face.

He shakes his head. "No, it's not. But there is more to you and me than just that. I just need you to know that I understand how you felt when you were younger after you lost your mom. The press attention…" His gaze digs into the carpet beneath my feet. "My dad wasn't famous in the sense like your mom, but my family's name is…recognizable. And the way he died made the press very interested in us."

*His family name?*

"Your family name? Carter?" I say, confused, trying to think of recognizable Carters. I don't get past President Carter, but there's no way Tom's related to him. I think.

He gives me a regretful smile. "No, Ly…Carter isn't actually my surname. It's my middle name. My surname is Segal."

I give him a look of confusion. "Segal? You mean, like the whiskey you hate?"

"Yeah, Firecracker, like the whiskey I hate. Thing is…that whiskey I hate technically belongs to me. Well, the company does. My full name is Thomas Carter Segal, the Fourth."

*Hold the fucking phone.*

*He's Thomas Segal? Isn't Thomas Segal dead? Didn't he die, like, a few hundred years ago?*

*Don't be so fucking stupid, Lyla. Of course he's not that Thomas Segal. He must be his great-great grandson or something.*

*Holy shit.*

*Okay. We need to pause for a moment.*

To put this into perspective, Tom telling me that he's Thomas Segal IV is pretty much like him telling me that he's Jack Daniels's great-great grandkid.

Jack, Jim, Johnnie, and Thomas—four of the biggest names in whiskey.

And I've been sleeping with Thomas.

*Well, fuck a duck.*

"Okay," I squeak. "How did I not know this? How does everyone not know this? Because you are famous for being in TMS. Come to think of it, why are you in TMS when you own Segal whiskey? And why do you hate the whiskey you own? And-and…" I'm running out of steam.

He lets out a soft laugh. "That's a lot of questions, Firecracker."

"I know. I'm sorry. I'm just confused." Taking a hand back, I rub my head.

"I know. It's confusing, and I'm sorry I wasn't upfront with you from the beginning."

"You don't have to be sorry. You didn't owe me your family history because you were sleeping with me."

"Yes, I did."

Lifting his head, he stares at me, and the force of his gaze hits me straight in the heart.

"There was more to us than just sex from the start. We both knew it. I just chose to ignore it for a long time, whereas you were brave and faced up to it."

He rests against the sofa, his head tipped back on the rest.

His words have me riveted and following him. Kicking off my shoes, I climb up on the sofa, sitting close to his side with my legs tucked under my bum, my thighs pressed against his. My eyes are on his face, desperate to learn all about him.

He tilts his head my way, sorry eyes on mine. "You deserved to know everything about me from the start, what you were getting into, and I'm sorry I held back like I did." He drags a hand through his hair. "My past isn't a warm and fuzzy story, and it's not one I share. The only people who know my past are Jake and Den. And Jonny, who took it to the grave with him. I only told them once TMS started getting big because they had a right to know the baggage I carry. My past is the kind of news the tabloids love. Fortunately, no one's ever dug far enough into me to discover it, and I've made sure it stays that way. Being the womanizing, bass-playing member of the band keeps people's interest in me to that level. Who I'm screwing that day gets old after a while. People lose interest."

He reaches over and brushes my bangs off my forehead. "Do you remember what I said to you when we were at the piano that day?"

*The frontline isn't somewhere I want to be. I like things easy, simple. I get to play, do what I love, get the rewards from it with marginal cost to myself.*

"Yes." I nod.

"I did like things simple. I didn't want to be on the frontline...but I do with you." He takes my hand again. "I don't want easy if it means I can't have you. You're important to me. More important than anyone ever has been. I want you to know me…the real me. I want you to understand me, my life up to this point."

My eyes close on his words. I feel him move nearer, then, his hand cups my jaw.

I open my eyes. "You're important to me, too, Tom. I want to understand you. That's why I'm here, why I'm listening."

His fingers draw a path across my jaw and down my neck. "As you've probably guessed, my great-great grandfather was the patriarch of Segal whiskey. His name was Jean-Pierre Segal. He came over to the U.S. from France in the mid-eighteen hundreds."

*Tom's French…kind of…*

*Holy wow.*

He just went even higher on the hotness scale.

"Jean-Pierre settled in Danville, Kentucky where he met my great-great grandmother, Sarah Thomas."

*Kentucky.* I remember how on edge Tom was while we were at that festival in Kentucky.

"Sarah's father, John Carter Thomas, had died that previous year and left her the farm she grew up on. She and Jean-Pierre married, and he took over running the farm. They farmed corn, and he decided to start producing a whiskey from it called bourbon that had become popular. Some farmers were making good money off it, and my grandfather needed to make money as Sarah was pregnant with my great-grandfather. He was born a week before they successfully distilled the first batch of Segal whiskey. They decided to name my great-grandfather, Thomas, after Sarah's family name, and, Carter, for his middle like her fathers. Jean-Pierre named the whiskey after his son. And that's how Thomas Segal whiskey was born." He lets out a self-deprecating laugh. "I don't even know why I told you all that. It's not really relevant to the details of my shitty life."

Leaning close, I press my forehead to his. "Everything about you is relevant. It all matters. I want to know everything about you."

His fingers skim my cheeks. "Have I ever told you how amazing you are?"

"Not lately." I smile.

He traces his finger over my lips. "Well, you are amazing. You're the best person I've ever known."

I settle back, resting my shoulder against the sofa, ready to hear the rest of his story.

"So, you know my dad was Thomas, the Third." He's referring to his tattoo. "Dad took over running the company when my grandpa no longer could. My dad was the head of the company, the exec chairman, and his younger brother, my Uncle Joe, was CEO. I was primed for taking over one day. My whole life was spent in Danville, Kentucky"—I hear the Southern in his accent at that moment—"being groomed for the day I would take over the company. I was to graduate high school, go to an Ivy League school, and then take on a job at Segal's and learn the business. My life was mapped out. Then, everything changed when I was thirteen."

I'm just about to ask about his Southern accent, what happened to it, when his eyes meet mine. The pain I see in them feels like it's my own. It's that strong.

"When I was thirteen, my dad discovered that my mom was having an affair. She had been for quite some time with…my Uncle Joe. My dad caught them together."

Seeing the direction this story is going, I move closer, sensing that Tom needs me near right now.

"Everything fell apart. Mom moved out of our home and in with Joe. She wanted to take us with her, but I wouldn't leave my dad. Heather, my younger sister by five years, didn't really grasp what was happening, and she wanted to be with Mom. So, Heather went with Mom, and I stayed with Dad. I was always closer to him." He sighs. "It hit him bad. He'd not only lost his wife, but he lost his brother, and he was being forced to continue running a company with him. He was drinking more and more. Everything was a fucking mess. I was a kid, trying to hold everything together. At that point, I thought that things couldn't get worse, but I was wrong.

"I was out at a friend's house, and I called Dad to check in, but he wasn't answering. I don't know, but something just felt off. I had this weird feeling in my gut, so I left my friend's house and rode my bike home. When I got near the house, I saw Uncle Joe's car in the driveway. I knew him being here wasn't good, so I dropped my bike and ran into the house. I called out for Dad, but I didn't get a response. There was music playing—'Ordinary World'—so I figured he couldn't hear me over that."

The pain in his expression is crippling. And I remember him telling me that is his dad's song, how he hasn't listened to it for sixteen years.

My stomach tightens into knots.

He scrubs his hands over his face. "Christ, this is hard." He gets to his feet. "I need a fucking drink. You want a drink?"

I shake my head.

"Gimme a minute." He leaves the room and comes back minutes later with a glass of amber liquid in his hand.

"Jack." He lifts the glass, tipping it from side to side, as he lets out a weak laugh.

Taking the seat beside me, Tom sits for a moment, just swirling the whiskey around the glass. Then, he throws the contents back and dumps the glass on the floor beside the sofa.

"The music was coming from our living room, so I went in there. The TV was on, and the music video was playing on it. I turned the TV off, and that was when I heard voices coming from my dad's office. I knew that he was in there with Joe, so I started to run for his office. I don't know what I intended to do. I just knew I had to be there. I just made it to the hall when I heard Joe yell out. He sounded panicked. Not even a second passed when I heard it. The gunshot.

"Stupid as it was, I ran in the direction of the gunshot, not away like most normal people would. I burst through the door to the office. That was when I saw Joe on the floor, bleeding out from the chest, and my dad was standing there with his gun in his hand. I ran to Joe and pressed my hand to his chest to try to stop the bleeding, but there was just so much fucking blood. It was all over my hands, my clothes…everywhere."

He holds his hands out in front of him, like he can still see Joe's blood on them.

I touch his arm. He blinks back at me.

"I could hear Joe choking on his own blood. I was screaming at my dad to help, but he just stood there, gun still in his hand, eyes vacant. Then, Joe"—Tom rubs his eyes—"died…right there with me kneeling beside him. My hands pressed to his chest."

A tear runs from his eye, but he quickly wipes it away. Then, all I can see is a thirteen-year-old Tom dealing with something as horrific as that would have been. For everything I've suffered, finding my mom, I still can't imagine what that did to him. My heart is hurting badly for him.

"Joe was dead," he says in a broken voice. "And I was scared. I jumped to my feet, yelling at my dad, yelling that Joe was dead and that he'd killed his brother. But he wasn't there. He was just empty. And I was fucking terrified. I knew he would never hurt me, but he was just standing with the gun in his hand. Then, suddenly he seemed to come to. He put the gun down on his desk. He looked at me and said, 'Tommy, go get the phone from the kitchen. Dial nine-one-one. Tell them what's happened.' Then, he"—Tom takes a painful-sounding breath—"told me he was sorry."

Tom's face is agonized. Another tear runs down his cheek. He doesn't bother to wipe it away. I watch it run a path to his top lip.

"I was just a kid, Ly, and he was my dad, so I did what he told me. It wasn't until I was at the kitchen door that I realized something. Why would he send me to the kitchen for the phone when he had one in his office? And I knew, I just fucking knew. The whole way, running back to his office, my heart was beating so hard." He presses the heels of his hands to his eyes, like he's trying to block out whatever he's seeing right now. "I was steps away from his office when the second shot rang out." He blows out a ragged breath. "My dad shot himself in the head…and I saw him there, face down on his desk. Blood…there was just so much fucking blood."

"Jesus, Tom." Tears are running down my face.

I wrap my arms around him, pulling him to me. I feel his chest shudder, and then he buries his face into my neck.

We sit like that for a long time. And I let him get out the pain that he's kept buried for so long.

I go to the kitchen and get him another whiskey. I pour myself one even though I don't like the stuff. After what I just heard, a drink is needed.

I bring the drinks back. Handing him his, I sit down beside him and take a sip of the disgusting whiskey.

He rests his glass on his thigh.

"So, what happened…with you and your family's company?" I ask him, not sure what to ask.

He takes a sip of his drink. "With dad and Uncle Joe gone, the board took control of the company. I was to take over when I turned eighteen. But I couldn't do it." He shakes his head.

"Everything had changed for me. My life, as I knew it, was over. I blamed my mother for what happened, and she was no use to anyone. She was a basket case. Heather and I were left to fend for ourselves. I didn't want anything to do with the company that was trying to tie me to it. I was grilled by the cops about what happened over and over. I was getting hassle at school from the kids. I was the rich kid who saw his dad murder his uncle and then kill himself. I was a pariah. Constantly getting into fights. People who were once my friends suddenly weren't. The press was having a fucking field day. They were camped outside our house. I felt trapped.

"I'd lost my dad. I'd seen him murder my uncle and then kill himself. I just wanted to bury the pain, bury that night…forget it ever happened. But I couldn't get away from it. Reminders were everywhere. So, I started drinking, smoking weed…having sex to block it out." He meets my eyes.

"I was fourteen when I lost my virginity with some junior at a party. I was drunk and high, and I just wanted to feel normal. I couldn't even remember her name afterward, and I'm pretty sure she never got mine. But what I did remember was that while it was happening, while I was having sex with her, I didn't feel like shit. I didn't have to think about everything that was wrong with me. In that moment, I wasn't Tommy Segal, the heir to the whiskey fortune, and son of the man who shot his brother before committing suicide. I was nothing. Nobody but a warm body for her to fuck. She didn't care about me, and I didn't care about her. I liked the way it felt, and I wanted to keep on feeling that way. I guess that was when sex became a coping mechanism for me. I could just switch off and lose myself in another person, forget everything. It worked for a long time until it just became the norm. Having disconnected sex was just what I did…until you.

"And as for the company…" He laughs harshly. "I barely managed to graduate high school. I was partying hard, screwing around. I wouldn't come home most nights. My mother couldn't control me, and after a while, she stopped trying. I turned eighteen, and it was supposed to be all mine, the company—Segal fucking whiskey."

He looks at me. "Even with the scandal of what happened, it didn't affect the business. I was the hoping the disgrace would burn the company to the ground, but it didn't. It made it bigger, popular.

Sales increased. That first year after their deaths, sales went up by fifty percent. Apparently, people like a shot of scandal with their whiskey. Fucked up, right?"

He rubs his face, looking frustrated. "I was eighteen years old, and they were trying to get me to run Segal's under the guidance of the board. I could barely tie my own fucking shoelaces most days. I was a mess. I just wanted out." He lets out a heavy breath. "I was just a kid. A screwed-up kid. So, I took some money from my trust, enough to see me through. I packed a bag, got in my car, and drove to New York."

He lets out a miserable sounding sigh. "I ran away. When I arrived in New York, I dropped my surname and became Tom Carter. For the first year, I just bummed around, partied, got high…slept around. Then, one night, I met Denny at a mutual friend's party. We got to talking about music. He was into it in a big way. I liked him. He was a cool guy. We just clicked, and it had been so long since I'd had a real friend. The friends I'd made in New York were just people to party and get high with. But Den, he was different. We started hanging out, and he made it his mission to get me on the straight.

"Den was in college, so I decided to go, too. I had no clue what I wanted to do, but I'd always loved music. Den was doing a BA in music, but the thick shit was having to repeat the year as he'd flunked out." He smiles with fondness at the memory.

"I took the same major as Den, but we took a few different classes. I was interested in musical history, whereas Den was interested in composition. He met Jake and Jonny in that composition class. Introduced us, and the rest is history." He takes a drink of his whiskey. Leaning forward, he puts the glass on the coffee table in front of us.

He comes back to me and takes my hand in his. "I never thought we'd get famous. We were good. I knew that. But how many bands get signed, right? I was having fun with them, and they felt like family. Steady. Something I hadn't had for a long time. So, when we started to take off, I couldn't leave. And I thought, correctly, that no one would give a shit about the bassist who likes to screw lots of chicks. No one would be interested in me or where I came from. And if anyone did ever ask about my family in interviews, I would just downplay it. They were interested in Jake and Jonny, and that worked well for me. I got to be with the guys, doing something that I'm good at, and that I love." He looks at me with tenderness.

"I was happy, Ly. I hadn't been happy for a long time. Then, things went to shit when Jonny died. I just couldn't fucking believe it. I thought that was gonna push me over the edge. I couldn't see straight. Jake and Den weren't coping. I thought we were gonna fall apart.

"Then, out of the blue, a month after Jonny died, I got a call from Heather. In all my selfishness, I'd just left her behind. I never even said good-bye. I thought about her every day, but I just couldn't go back. When she called, it was like old times, when we were kids, before everything happened. She asked to see me, and of course, I said yes. I was living in LA by this point, so she flew in the next day. We met up, and after that, she became my lifeline…that was, until you.

"Heather had taken on running the company as CEO. She'd graduated early, gotten her business degree. She was always smart, way smarter than I ever was. To this day, she's still running Segal's. And I make sure to see her regularly. She usually comes here to see me 'cause I don't like to go out to Kentucky if I don't have to. Every time I see her, I try to sign the company over to her, and every time, she refuses and asks me to come run it with her." He lets out a soft chuckle. "I let Heather down all those years ago when I left. But I won't make that mistake with her again."

"She sounds really great, Tom."

His eyes meet mine with warmth. "She is. You're alike in a lot of ways…spunky, argumentative."

"I'm not argumentative." I grin.

"Firecracker." He presses his finger to the tip of my nose.

"And what about…your mother?"

His eyes darken. "Heather sees her. I haven't seen her or spoken to her since I was eighteen. I can't forgive her for what she did. If she never had an affair with Joe, then…"

He stops there, and I don't push it. I, better than anyone, know how hard it is to forgive and forget.

He puffs out a breath. "Ly, what I said to you that day…when I pushed you away, reacted like I did…after you told me you were in love with me…" He shakes his head, regret in his eyes. "Sure, there's a reason why I've lived my life the way I have, using sex to get by, but I also liked my life. It was straightforward. I didn't have to care about anyone but me. And after my dad, after what happened, why it happened…I promised myself that I would never put myself in that position. I swore to myself that I would never fall in love. I would never give a woman the opportunity to shred me like my mother did to my father.

"I was afraid that if I fell in love, and she broke me the way my mother did with my dad…that I wouldn't be able to cope, the way he couldn't…"

He meets my eyes, and I see it there in his. His fear. He doesn't have to say it out loud.

"So, I kept an emotional distance from women, taking what I wanted, and then walking away. It was easy…until you." He touches my face, running his fingertips over my cheek, into my hair. "I couldn't get you out of my head."

"Still, you pushed me away."

"I panicked. What you were telling me…deep down, I knew that I felt the same, but I was fighting it. Fear had me fighting it." He lets out a soft laugh. "You scare the motherfucking shit out of me, Lyla Summers."

"You scare the motherfucking shit out of me, too, Tom Carter." I give him an uneasy smile, baring myself to him again. "What I feel for you…I've never felt anything like it for anyone ever."

A light turns off in his eyes, and he removes his hands from my face, leaving me with a cold sense of foreboding.

He sits forward. I follow him.

I let my feet fall to the floor, the hardwood cold against my skin.

"Ly…I want to be with you, and I hope…*really* hope"—he gives me a nervous look—"that you want to be with me, too—"

"I do," I say quickly, cutting him off, afraid of where this might be going.

He tips his head to the side. His eyes meeting mine, he stares deep into them. The look in his greens makes my stomach sink.

"I've always been straight with you. Apart from the stuff about my family, I've never lied to you, and that won't change now."

My heart starts to beat hard in my chest.

"I can't ask you to start something with me if you don't know all the facts."

My hands are shaking.

"After I left you that day...I made a mistake."

## A Heartbeat Later—Tom's House, LA

*No. No. No.*

The room starts spinning. Shakily, I get to my feet. I edge around the coffee table, putting it between us.

"You've been with someone else," I choke the words out.

He gets to his feet. "No. Yes."

"Oh God." I cover my face with my hands.

Suddenly, he's here, his hands on mine, pulling them from my face. "This isn't what you think. I didn't—"

"It never fucking is with you!" I stagger back, shoving him away. "I'm sorry for you. Sorry for what happened to you, how you lost your family, but I can't take this." I'm edging away from him. "I can't do this. I'm not stupid. I know who you are. I knew there was a big possibility that you slept with other women these last two weeks, but to know that you were with someone straight after you left me there on the sidewalk in front of my apartment..." I clutch a hand to the pain tearing open my stomach. "After what we'd done hours before...I let you have sex with me *there*...I let you—" I cut off, the memory of him moving inside that intimate, private place, now sullied by his confession.

My gaze slices to his, my eyes swimming with tears. I can see the fear and remorse on his face.

"That was important to me." My whispered voice breaks. "What we did...I gave that to you because I trusted you, and to now know that hours later you went out and had sex with someone else..." A sob breaks from me. Tears are carelessly dripping down my cheeks. I move toward the door. "We might not have been together at the time, but it feels like a betrayal." I swipe at my face angrily.

Tom strides over to me, taking me by the shoulders, and I don't have the energy to fight him off.

"I didn't have sex with her. I haven't had sex with anyone since you." He's breathing heavily. "No one since you, I swear. I went to that bar, thinking if I had sex with someone, it would fix me, put my life back the way it was before you. I was feeling too much for you. I was scared. I panicked, so I reacted in the only way I knew how. I thought going back to my old ways would fix it."

I wrap my arms around myself. "Who was she?"

He shakes his head slowly. "I don't know. Just some woman in a bar."

"You didn't have sex with her. So, what did you do?"

*Why am I asking this? Do I really want to know? Will it make any of this better?*

*No.*

But the sadistic part of me needs to hear this.

Tom stares at me, indecision in his eyes. I can see pain tearing at his features.

"Lyla…you don't want to hear this."

But that doesn't stop me. Any rational in me is gone. I'm pain, blinding pain, and it's in the driving seat.

"You didn't fuck her," I say bitterly. "So, what? Did she get down on her knees and—" I don't get any further than that. My own words hit me hard, like a blow to the stomach, winding me.

Tom grabs my face, forcing me to look at him. He winces at whatever he sees there. "No one is better than you. Do you hear me? *No one.* I made a dumb fucking mistake, out of fear, but I couldn't go through with it because of you."

His words should soothe, but instead, they ignite my anger like the striking of a match.

"Well, I'm so fucking sorry that I'm getting in the way of you and your whores!" I scream in his face, hitting at his chest.

He doesn't let me go. "Stop it. I want you in my way all the fucking time." His voice, like his face, is determined. "I want you here with me every minute of every day. I want you more than I have ever wanted anything in my life. I know I fucked up, and I'm so sorry for that. I wish I could take it back, but I can't. And you're right. We weren't together, but in here, we were."

He taps chest. "I was trying to get you out by reverting to my old ways. I wasn't thinking straight. But I'm thinking straight now. Thinking is all I've been doing for the past two weeks. Thinking about you and the time we had together. God, I've missed you like crazy. These last two weeks without you have been hell. I know it's been my own doing, but I stayed away because I needed time to figure things out. I needed to be sure that I can be the guy you deserve. A guy who can give all of himself to you. Then, I saw you today, and I realized something."

My mind has suddenly cleared. My anger is dissipating as I hang on his every word, needing to know what he's going to say next more than I need my next breath. "What did you realize?"

"I realized that you already have me. You're it for me." Taking my face in his hands, he wipes my tears away. "I'm in love with you, Ly. I have been for a long time. It just took me a while to realize it. And when I did, I realized that my fears don't mean shit anymore. In that moment, staring at you across the street, seeing you standing there, I knew...you kicked me on my ass. In that moment, I knew I would do *anything* to take away the hurt I caused you. I would give up everything, including myself, for you...because I would rather have a moment of everything with you than a lifetime of nothing."

*Oh my God.*

*He's in love with me?*

I'm choked with tears, stunned at his confession. "You love me?" I whisper.

He presses his forehead to mine, a smile touching the edges of his lips. "I love you."

The words whisper over my skin, seeping into my heart, filling it...completing it.

"Ly..." He takes a deep breath. "I know I have no right to ask...but I need to know if you still feel the same. Or have I screwed things up? Have I lost you?"

I close my eyes on a blink. My mind is running at the speed of light. I'm trying to grab on to something, anything...

Anger. Pain. Want. Need.

I could argue and fight this, fight how I feel for him. I could walk away because of a mistake he made when we weren't together.

Or I can forgive him. Put it behind us and let us start from now.

I'm working toward forgiving Dex for what he did to me. The least I can do is try the same for Tom.

I open my eyes. "I'm in love you, Tom. That doesn't stop just because you act like a dick."

He moves his forehead down, his nose moving over my skin, as he breathes me in. "I am a dick."

"Yeah, you are. The biggest dick ever. And I don't mean that in a flattering way."

He lets out a soft chuckle. "So…I haven't lost you?"

"No, you haven't lost me."

"Thank God." His arms come around me, his face buried in my neck. I feel the relief in his body. I hear it in his breaths. And that's when I realize just how much I mean to Tom. The knowledge soaks into every part of me, warming me.

Lifting his head, he slides his fingers around the nape of my neck and up into my hair. "I'll make it up to you, I swear," he whispers the promise over my lips.

"I know." I press my hand to his face.

"I'm nothing without you, Ly. I just don't work without you. You've broken me." He smiles. "You are everything to me, and I will spend the rest of my life showing you that you didn't make the worst mistake of your life by falling in love with a mut like me."

"You're not a mut. You're an ex-mut."

"An ex-mut. I like it. Makes me sound badass."

"You're an idiot." I laugh, slapping his chest.

"And you're beautiful."

Then, his hands are on my ass, and he picks me up off the floor, causing me to squeal in surprise. I wrap my legs around his waist.

"I seriously fucking love you, Lyla Summers."

"Good, because I seriously fucking love you, Thomas Carter." I trace my fingers over the stubble on his jaw. "But the beard has gotta go."

He grins. "Whatever you want, darlin'."

Then, he kisses me. A breath-stealing, toe-curling kiss. I can feel Tom pouring everything into this kiss…all of himself into this one kiss…showing me with his body how much he really does love me.

"So, it's been two weeks," he says, coming up for air. "That's twenty-eight orgasms I owe you on top of the rest still outstanding."

I bite my lip in thought. "We don't have that long. I have to pick up Aunt Steph and Uncle Paul from the airport in a few hours and take them to see Dex."

"So, we'd better get started." He carries me over to the sofa, taking us both down to it. He slips his hand up my top. "And I'll come with you to pick them up. Meet your family."

*He wants to meet my family?* This will be a big thing, especially for someone like Tom.

"Are you sure you want to meet my family? It's not too soon?"

His hand stops on its path to my boob. "I already met your brother."

"And you punched him."

He gives a slip of a grin. "In my defense, he did deserve to be punched."

"Yes…he did," I agree.

"So, can I meet your family if I promise not to punch your uncle?"

"I'm happy for you to meet my family." I giggle as his fingers whisper over my ribcage, tickling me. "I just don't want you to feel pressured. Meeting the family is a big thing."

"Nothing is too big when it comes to you." His mouth drops to mine, his lips brushing gently over mine. "Don't you get it yet?"

I slide my arms around his neck, winding my fingers into his hair. My heart is so full of everything…full of him.

"Get what?" I whisper.

His eyes stare deep into mine. "That this is it…you and me…we're forever. You're my heaven, Firecracker."

## One Week Later—A Huge House, Littleborough, England

"…the luckiest man in the world to have her here with me right now. I'm even luckier that she agreed to marry my sorry ass."

I watch on from my seat next to Tom as Jake leans down and kisses his bride.

We're at Jake and Tru's house in Littleborough for their wedding reception.

Jake surprised Tru with a wedding at their special place called Lumb Falls here in the UK. It was so romantic and a really beautiful wedding.

When Jake had called Tom to let him know about his upcoming nuptials, I had been with Tom. Tom had told Jake that we were together. I'd heard Jake say to Tom that it was about fucking time.

That had made me smile.

When Tom had gotten off the phone, he'd told me that both Jake and Denny had been on him during the two weeks we were apart. Apparently, they had gotten sick of his mopey, unshowered, and moody ass, and they'd told him to get his fucking act together, and apologize to me, and then beg me to take his sorry ass back.

With me now being Tom's girlfriend, Jake had invited me to the wedding.

So, we had flown over to England, and I just got to see the most romantic wedding ever.

Now, we're just finishing up listening to the speeches after eating an amazing dinner.

Jake takes his seat after finishing off his speech, and now, we're all clapping and cheering, raising our glasses to toast the happy couple.

Tom has his arm slung around the back of my chair, his fingers playing with my hair, while he catcalls Jake for being sappy. Although he is teasing, I can see Tom's eyes are shining.

I lean over and whisper in his ear, "Tom Carter, are you about to cry?"

He stares at me in horror. "Of course I'm not gonna fucking cry. Um...all *male* here." He emphasizes by thumping his hand against his chest. "I don't cry."

I know that's not true. A week ago, I'd held Tom while he cried in my arms after he told me about his dad. But I won't remind him of that. I'll leave him with his man pride intact.

"He cried at *Forrest Gump*," Denny says, leaning across the table from his seat next to Tom. "We watched it one night back when we were in college, and he cried like a fucking baby at that part when Lieutenant Dan turns up at Forrest's wedding. Magic Legs," Denny says in a Forrest Gump voice. "I called Tom Magic Legs for about a year after that." He chuckles.

"What the fuck, dude?" Tom hisses. "I can't believe you just told her that." He turns to me. "Ly, I was drunk, and it was a really fucking sad part in the movie. I didn't cry like a baby, like fucknut here is saying. I might have shed, maybe, one minuscule tear. But that was it. Asshole here called me Magic Legs 'cause I'm an awesome dancer."

"You keep telling yourself that, Magic Legs." Den looks at me again. "Cried like a baby," he reiterates, grinning. He runs his fingers under his eyes, catching pretend tears.

I start laughing, but I clamp my hand over my mouth when Tom gives me a death stare.

"Can't believe you cried at *Forrest Gump*, man," Smith says, shaking his head at Tom.

Smith is TMS's lead guitarist. He took Jonny's place in the band when they started recording again. And seriously, I'd never tell Tom this, but holy wow, he's seriously hot. He's wife, Carly, is really gorgeous too.

Tom flips Smith off before taking a swig of his beer. "Whatever," Tom says, turning to Denny. "You're no better. Hey, Simone, did Den tell you that he cried like a little bitch when we were watching Beyoncé sing 'The Star-Spangled Banner' at Obama's inauguration?"

Simone is Denny's fiancée, and Tru's best friend. She's really pretty and so sweet. She's really made an effort to make me feel welcome and part of the group.

Denny gives him the middle finger. "Thanks for that, assface."

"You're welcome." Standing up, Tom gives a half-bow. Then, he sits back down.

Simone laughs. "Don't worry, babe. I still love you even if you are a dork." She leans over and gives Denny a peck on the lips.

"Smith cried when we got married," Carly, shares.

"Jesus, babe." Smith gives her a look.

She just shrugs, smiling.

"I think crying on your wedding day is sweet," Simone says.

Denny stares at her. "Don't expect me to cry on our wedding day."

Tom leans forward. "Simone, the second you say I do, he'll be The Star-Spangled Banner all over again, trust me."

He winks, and Simone giggles.

Denny lifts his hands in defeat. "Fine, whatever. I'm man enough to admit that I cried while hearing Beyoncé kill our national anthem. It was a bad experience for me. Fucking horrible. I still have nightmares about it now." He fake shudders.

"True," Tom agrees, nodding. "Seriously, what was up with that? But then, she did totally make up for it when she sang it again live for the press."

Simone and I look at each other and bust out laughing.

"Jay-Z is one lucky bastard," Tom muses. "Really, who cares how she sounded? She's seriously hot. I pretty much spent the whole time looking at her—"

"Um…hello?" I stare at him, returning the death stare I received moments earlier. "Lyla Summers. Your girlfriend. You remember me?"

"Like I could ever forget you." He grins down at me, and he presses a kiss to my pursed lips. "Don't worry. Just an observation, babe. Window-shopping is not a crime. As long as no purchase is made, it's all good."

"Right…" I graze my teeth over my bottom lip. "So, you won't mind if I do some window-shopping then?" I cast a glance around. "Because I'm seeing some seriously hot British men here that I could spend hours window-shopping over."

"Okay. Enough." He takes hold of my chin, turning my head back to his. "Let's not get carried away here. Rules have changed. As of now, we only window-shop each other. Deal?"

"Dealio." I smirk, knowing I won that round.

He leans in and presses another soft kiss to my lips.

"Ugh, can't you leave the poor girl alone, Tom Cat?" I turn to see Stuart pulling up a chair beside me.

"Jealous?" Tom smirks at him.

"You wish," Stuart bites.

"What?" Tom cups his ear. "You're saying, you wish you could have my meat? Sorry, dude, but I'm off the market now, and sausage never was my thing anyway."

"Yeah, how did that happen exactly? And I don't mean the meat, but you off the market?" Stuart looks at me. "Seriously, I need to hear this story. How did a great girl like you end up with our Tom 'Cat' 'Rub the Lamp' Carter?" He gives me a look of total bewilderment.

"Stuart's just jealous 'cause he never got to rub the lamp," Tom says, putting his arm back around my chair.

"You've seen the tattoo, right?" Stuart asks me. He winks, letting me know he's teasing Tom.

"I've seen the tattoo." I nod before sipping my wine.

"And you still want him?"

I cast a glance at Tom and then look back to Stuart. "Yeah, I do." I smile.

"And that's because my girl is the smartest girl in the world." Tom's arm comes around my neck, pulling me close, and then he presses his lips to my temple.

I love it when he calls me *my girl*.

"Oh God, now, he's doing random acts of PDA. I feel vomit rising. Seriously, Tom, if you get down on one knee, I'm outta here."

"Um, no proposing today. I've got Tom down for being with Lyla for a year before he pulls out the ring. Tom proposes to Lyla within the year, and I'm down five thousand bucks."

My head whips around to Denny.

"Jake and I made a bet," Denny tells me at my questioning stare.

*Um…what the hell?*

"Yeah, I bet up to a year…but now, I'm thinking six months max, and Tom Cat will be getting down on one knee." I hear Jake's voice, and look up to see him and Tru standing at our table.

They look ridiculously beautiful together. *Perfect.*

"Why aren't I in on this bet?" Stuart asks Jake.

"You want in?" Den asks.

"You know I do." Stuart laughs.

"Yeah, count me in," Smith says.

"Seriously, what the fuck? What is it with people betting on me recently?" Tom exclaims.

He gives me a look, reminding me of the bet I made with Sonny. The bet I made as an excuse because I was jealous over seeing Tom with another woman.

It takes me a minute to realize that Tom's not freaking out over the mention of marriage with me. It's surprising, but nice to know that marriage could be a possibility down the line for us.

Way, way off in the future.

"Tru, you remember Lyla?" Jake says, gesturing to me.

"Of course I do." She smiles. She moves around the table and walks with an effortless grace, considering she's in heels on grass. She leans down and kisses my cheek. "Thanks so much for coming out to our wedding."

"Thanks for having me here." I smile. "It was a beautiful service."

"All on Jake. I can't take any credit for it." She gazes at him lovingly.

Tom's arm comes around my shoulder while he continues to talk to the guys.

I see Tru's eyes follow his movement. Then, she looks at Tom. Catching his eye, she gives him a playful grin.

"Not a fucking word, Bennett." He points at her.

Still smiling, she corrects him, "Wethers now."

"Damn fucking right you're a Wethers," Jake says, pulling up two chairs for them.

He lets her sit first. She sits by Simone, and Jake sits next to her.

"And I wasn't going to say a word," Tru continues to Tom. "I was just going to say that it's good to see you happy."

"Should I be worried that she's not giving me shit?" Tom asks Jake.

"Nah." He puts his arm around Tru, bringing her close to his side. "She's feeling sentimental today. Right, baby?"

"Right." She smiles up into his face.

I can see the love between them, like it's a living, breathing thing.

It's wonderful to see.

Tru looks over at Tom, a smile edging her lips. "Give me until tomorrow, Tom, and we'll be back to our bickering selves."

"Thank fuck for that." Tom laughs, running a hand through his hair. "You were starting to scare me for a moment there. But as we're being nice today, I want to say that you look really beautiful, Tru."

"Thank you, Tom."

"Okay, enough!" Stuart's hand goes up. "Tom, you're freaking me the fuck out. Acts of PDA, telling Tru she looks beautiful? Seriously I'm not used to all this niceness. It's too much, too soon. Can someone just hurl some abuse at me or Tom just so I can feel normal again?"

"Calm the fuck down, Powder Puff. You know I'll never be nice to you." Tom smirks at him.

"And the world is right again." Stuarts places his hand dramatically against his chest, setting us all off laughing.

Calvin Harris's "I Need Your Love" starts to play. I love this song. It's such an infectious tune.

Turning my head, I see the makeshift dance floor start to fill. Tru's mom, Eva, and her dad, Billy, are on there. Eva has Tru and Jake's son, JJ, in her arms. As Eva gently sways with JJ, Billy throws out some interesting dance moves. Eva throws her head back, laughing at him. I smile at them both.

"I need your love," I whisper-sing along with the lyrics.

Tom leans close and says in my ear, "You wanna ditch these losers and dance with me?"

"Sure I do."

He takes me by the hand, and I let him lead me onto the makeshift dance floor.

When we move past Billy, who's still going at it, he pats Tom on the back. Tom smiles at him and then pulls me close, wrapping his arms around me. He starts to move us to the music. He's a surprisingly good dancer.

"So, you really are Magic Legs." I grin up at him.

"I told you. I dance as well as I fuck."

"Can't argue with that." Inching onto my toes, I brush my lips against his.

"Ly," he murmurs. "I've been thinking about something…something I wanted to ask you."

"Okay. Just checking here, but you're not gonna get down on one knee and have Jake win his bet, are you? Because I love you and all, but we've only been together for a week," I tease.

"Technically, nine weeks, if you include the tour and my fuck-up fortnight." He smiles at me. "And don't worry, Firecracker. The only reason I'll be getting down on my knees in front of you tonight is to bury my face between your hot thighs." His fingers dance over my ass.

I shudder against him, my panties instantly soaking. I love it when he's so direct about sex.

"You're wet," he whispers in my ear, knowing full well that I am.

He knows what his words do to me.

"Yes," I breathe.

I'm wet and so ready to have him inside me that it's not even funny.

"You wanna find a dark corner and have a quickie?" I bite my lip suggestively.

His eyes darken. "Like I would ever turn you down for sex…but before we disappear to that dark corner, there's that something I need to ask you…"

"Oh, yeah, sure…go ahead." I stare up into his eyes.

He suddenly looks unsure, nervous. It makes me a little nervous as to what he needs to ask me.

"Well, I've been thinking…seeing you this past week, working toward forgiving Dex after what he did to you and the way you forgave me when I fucked up. You're an amazing person, Lyla. And it's got me thinking. Maybe I need some closure in my past. I'm not saying I can ever forgive my mother…but it's been eleven years. I was thinking maybe it's time I go see her. Talk to her."

I put my arms around his neck. "I think that's a really good idea."

"Okay. And I wanted to ask if you'd come with me?"

"Of course I'll come with you."

He exhales. "Okay, good. While we're on the fix-it road, do you want to go see Rally at all? I'm guessing he knows we're together…and he'll be having a shit fit," Tom muses, his face turning into a grin.

"He'll definitely be having a shit fit, but"—I shake my head—"I don't care. And I don't need to see him or talk to him. There's nothing to fix with Rally. We didn't fall out. We just didn't communicate, and that was his doing. He was never there. He let me down my whole life. I'm not gonna chase after a man who doesn't want me in his life."

Tom's expression changes, and he holds me closer, pressing his lips to mine. "I want you in my life all the time. I love you," he murmurs over my mouth. "And all this…" He gestures around at the wedding party going on around us. "I know the guys were joking before about us getting married, and it's definitely too soon…"

He emphasizes with his eyes. And I nod, agreeing.

"But I do know that the day I decide I want to get married…you'll be the girl I'll be asking."

The emotion I feel at his words momentarily overwhelms me. My eyes glittering, I say, "I guess we have a lot of amazing things to look forward to together."

"We do." He smiles. "There are a *lot* of things I want to do with you, Firecracker." His smile transforms into a mischievously sexy grin. "Starting with that quickie in the dark corner." He grabs me by the hand.

Laughing, I let Tom drag me away, quickly looking around to make sure nobody witnesses us sneaking off.

I stare at him as he leads me into Tru and Jake's house.

My heart is so full of love for Tom.

A love I never thought I'd be able to feel—let alone, feel it for Tom Carter.

It's funny how the one person I thought I would never be with in a million years turned out to be the one I was looking for all along.

Who would have thought it? The untamable Tom Carter, and me, Lyla Summers, the one who tamed him.

Or what I should probably say is, the untamable Tom Carter who tamed his ways for me.

# ACKNOWLEDGMENTS

Ending The Storm Series has been a real toughie for me. The TMS family has been a big part of my life for a long time now, so letting them go has been difficult. A lot of tears have been shed, a lot of wine drank, and countless tubs of Ben & Jerry's devoured to get me through it.

As always, there are people to thank for putting up with my crazy, but the first always has to be my husband, Craig. He's the one who listens to me when I talk about the characters in my head, and he doesn't look at me like I'm crazy when I speak of them as if they're real. He listens to my 3 a.m. meltdowns because I can't figure out the next scene in my book. He's a total gem. He's my very own BBF.

My children, who let Mummy spend time with her books—I love you beyond time and space, to infinity and beyond.

My girl, Sali Benbow-Powers—I could ramble on about how much I adore and appreciate you. Instead, I just have two words for you—Bom Sex!

Trish Brinkley—You brighten my days. I can't wait to squeeze you in July! I heart you a million.

A big thank you to Christine Estevez—Girl, you are a one-woman dynamo!

My amazingly supportive agent, Kimberly Whalen—As always, thank you for everything you do.

I want to thank my editor, Jovana Shirley (Unforeseen Editing), for doing an amazing job. With your help, TTS became everything I wanted it to be and more. Also, sending a big thank you to Najla Qamber Designs for creating TTS's beautiful cover.

To all the bloggers who work tirelessly to help our books reach new readers—My appreciation to you is never-ending.

And to you, my readers—the ones I converse with online, the ones I've met, the ones I haven't—I'm sending you the biggest thank you of all.

**SAMANTHA TOWLE** is a New York Times, USA Today, and Wall Street Journal bestselling author. She began her first novel in 2008 while on maternity leave. She completed the manuscript five months later and hasn't stopped writing since.

She is the author of contemporary romances, *The Mighty Storm*, *Wethering the Storm*, and *Trouble*. She has also written paranormal romances, *The Bringer* and The Alexandra Jones Series, all penned to tunes of The Killers, Kings of Leon, Adele, The Doors, Oasis, Fleetwood Mac, Lana Del Rey, and more of her favorite musicians.

A native of Hull and a graduate of Salford University, she lives with her husband, Craig, in East Yorkshire with their son and daughter.

34007346R00189

Made in the USA
Lexington, KY
19 July 2014